Trinity of Man Book 2

The End Of Sorrows

Duane Wooters

iUniverse, Inc.
New York Bloomington

iUniverse books may be ordered through booksellers or by contacting:

iUniverse
1663 Liberty Drive
Bloomington, IN 47403
www.iuniverse.com
1-800-Authors (1-800-288-4677)

ISBN: 978-1-4401-6299-2 (sc)
ISBN: 978-1-4401-6300-5 (ebook)

Printed in the United States of America

iUniverse rev. date: 07/20/09

Matthew 24:4-8

And Jesus answered and said unto them *"Take heed that no man deceive you. 5: For many shall come in my name, saying I am Christ; and shall deceive many. 6: And ye shall hear of wars and rumors of wars; see that ye be not troubled; for all these things must come to pass, but the end is not yet. 7: For nation shall rise against nation, and kingdom against kingdom; and there shall be famines, and pestilence, and earthquakes in divers places. 8: All these are the beginning of sorrows.* KJV

Prologue

Sometime during the history of mankind, the world fell into chaos. Israel became a Nation on May 14, 1948, and great hope sprang from that event. Word spread throughout Christendom that the world had now entered into the final days. Israel is the time clock for Biblical prophecy. Those prophecies were now coming to fulfillment. Christ would soon return to redeem the saints.

A Christian must get his house in order, and become a good and faithful servant—a servant who could be found doing the Lord's work at all times. He must be ever watchful, lest he be caught asleep and unprepared for the Lord's return. A great air of expectancy swept around the world.

But time dragged from days to months to years, and the attention of man turned to other things. The hope that rose from the new era slowly diminished. Man continued to marry and give in marriage, taken up with the daily search for wealth and pleasure.

In the years following 1948 mankind experienced wars, and heard rumors of many more. Nuclear holocaust loomed just around the corner. Earthquakes devastated many cities killing thousands. Volcanoes erupted claiming the lives of thousands more. Floods and famine swept over many lands and millions more died. Toxic waste and toxic spills fouled the water, and the air.

Mankind groped for answers in the wasteland of society, bewildered by the confusion. Man's love for God waned as the faith of many dwindled into lukewarm embers. The world had fallen into a moral dilemma that left it without a conscience—or any guidelines for re-establishing one.

The global economy collapsed sometime during all the commotion.

The production, distribution, exchange, and consumption of goods and services throughout the world had lost its' balance. No one noticed as little things, one upon the other, brought about the slow demise.

Economists everywhere grappled with the problem, but to no avail. There were no quick and easy answers. The failure of agriculture, of banks, the steady rise of unemployment, the falling value of currency on the world money market, strikes, inflation, deflation, trade deficits—these and many more less noticeable factors brought the economy of the world to a halt.

Some time into the twenty-first century the desperate situation worsened, as welfare programs designed to help failed under the strain of thirty-percent unemployment. The fabric of society unraveled and anarchy ruled the day.

Despair, fear, and hatred replaced love and compassion as the world reeled under the greatest crisis it had ever known.

This headline in a well-known newspaper in the United States was the headline that heralded a possible shred of hope. PROMINENT ISRAELI PROFESSOR ASKED TO SAVE THE WORLD.

The content of the story read:

Jerusalem—Prime Minister Ari of Israel announced today that Jehosea Cahmael, a well-known Philosopher Economist and Mathematician at the University of Tel Aviv, has been asked by the United Nations to help solve the world economic crisis. Professor Cahmael is the originator of the Trinity of Man Philosophy, and has many followers throughout the world. The Prime Minister said Cahmael had reluctantly accepted the request. No further details are known at this time, but the announcement brings a glimmer of hope to our despairing world.

His reluctance turned out to be short-lived. He gathered his followers and began a massive census taking effort that they completed within a few months. Six months later the changes had started and the world retreated slowly from the precipice of total destruction. Within two years Cahmael rejuvenated the worldwide economy and redistributed goods, and food. He eradicated hunger. Life became better then it had ever been. People rejoiced. Celebrations marking the three-year anniversary were held in every country in the world. The world had something to celebrate now.

Despair and hopelessness disappeared. The world owed their salvation to Jehosea Cahmael. He didn't stop there. He made peace happen in a place where it was thought to be impossible, the Middle East. Then the world looked on him in awe.

Although it may never be known publicly exactly what transpired among Cahmael, the Israelis, the Palestinians, and the other Arab countries that day, this much is known; they struck an agreement—an agreement that changed the face of the Middle East. It brought about the lasting peace so sought after by all parties. It gave the Palestinians a homeland, and allowed the Israelis to rebuild Solomon's Temple—Jehosea Cahmael truly became the Savior of the world.

Not everybody agreed. Pastor Tom Horn and Father Vince Nalone didn't. They claimed that Cahmael was the Antichrist, doing good only to deceive the world. No one listened to the warnings that claimed Cahmael was killing anyone who spoke out against him.

They were driven into hiding when Tom Horn's church was bombed. Sheriff's Detective Tony Arzetti helped them escape by spiriting them away to Arizona, and then had to join them himself or be arrested.

Wanted for murder in the wrongful death of a Sheriff and five of his deputies in a helicopter crash, the three friends and three others were pursued to Northern California where they found protection at Camp Armageddon. The camp was run by Panguitch Hewey, a self-proclaimed prophet of God, who claimed his mission was to destroy the Antichrist.

When Jehosea Cahmael came to San Francisco, Hewey claimed it was God delivering the Antichrist to him. He made plans to go there and in the midst of a bloody attack, kill Cahmael, whom he claimed is the Antichrist. The six friends got themselves included so they could go and, hopefully, warn the police.

Hewey allowed them to go for reasons of his own. They were held captive by Hewey in San Francisco and thus unable to warn police of the impending disaster. Hewey then turned them in to the police as being the terrorists that were planning a bloody attack. This was a ploy to distract the police from his own attack—an attack that never happened.

Tom and Vince managed to escape only to stumble into a trap set by Cahmael. In an ill-fated attempt to shoot Hewey they were tricked into shooting the Pope instead, and were arrested for his assassination. The two men were tried and executed in the first worldwide public execution in history. The End of Sorrows continues the story during the first year after the execution.

Chapter 1

The Hyatt Hotel in San Francisco sets at the foot of Market Street, across from the Ferry building. It is Shires Lampton's favorite place to stay in San Francisco, but never above the fifth floor. He hates high places, especially in San Francisco where an earthquake might shake a building apart—anywhere above the fifth floor is too far to fall.

He sat in his suite on the fourth floor, before a window overlooking the Bay and the Ferry docks, studying his research notes when the phone rang.

"Mr. Lampton, this is the front desk. A package was just delivered here for you. You may pick it up at your convenience, or I can send it up with room service."

"Send it up please," he said. His brow wrinkled. He wasn't expecting anything. He returned to his notes at the desk, and worked on them until room service tapped on the door. He handed the uniformed bellman five dollars and retrieved the manila envelope; the lump inside felt like a very thin book.

It wasn't. It was a DVD with a 'stick-it' note attached. The penmanship was almost illegible—*thought you might be interested, especially the very end*—it read.

He inserted the disc and pushed the play button. It showed the headless bodies of Vince Nalone and Tom Horn lying on the pavement on Howard Street by Moscone Center. "Poor misguided bastards," he thought, remembering his interview at the hideout north of Flagstaff. He watched it for a few moments before he skipped it forward. He went too far, and the street was now empty. He moved it backward to the bodies, and then ran it forward again. The bodies began to evaporate. *That's what it looked like to him—evaporation.* He replayed it, and paused it with the bodies partially gone. *Beam me up Scotty* ran through his mind. It looked exactly like teleportation from the old Star Trek series of the twentieth century.

The public execution of the two men five months earlier had been headline news for a couple weeks, but it had receded into background noise like old news does.

He wanted his cameraman, Felix, to see this. Shires was happy when Felix answered his phone immediately.

"I have something I want you to look at, and, if you can, bring that friend of yours from the film lab. Have him bring his kit along."

Important stuff? Felix asked.

"Don't know what to think of it."

I can probably drag Mark with me and be there in an hour, give or take, Felix said.

"See you then," Shires said, and closed his phone. He walked back to the screen to stare at the disappearing bodies, then skipped the DVD backward to review the event. As he went forward again, he paused the picture every few seconds to watch the changes.

The picture had to have been altered, but why? A good animation and editing expert could do wonders with videos. He would soon find out the truth.

Felix Gunther and Mark Kellum arrived about an hour later. Shires showed the video immediately. Neither man spoke during or after the evaporation of the bodies.

"Play it again," Felix said

"How about the rest of the video? Is it more of the same?" Mark asked.

"Yes. Just the dead bodies and then the evaporation," Shires answered.

"Well, it looks authentic to me," Felix said.

"Let me show you something I noticed earlier," Shires said. He skipped backward on the disk and replayed it in short bursts.

At the first stop he said, "Notice the contrast between the background here and where I stop next; I saw this earlier."

At the second stop he pointed to the lighter background, "Notice the difference?" he asked.

"It's lighter for one thing," Felix observed.

"Why?" Shires asked.

"Light, from somewhere, I suppose," Mark guessed.

"Could it be from the editing process?" Shires asked.

"Definitely could be. I can't rule that out," Mark said.

"Why would somebody do that?" Shires asked.

"Makes it a story," Felix suggested.

Mark opened his kit and sat down in front of the screen. "Let me run a couple quick tests. Let's see what might be going on here."

Mark busied himself studying the video and after a few minutes he said, "I can tell you right now that there is nothing to indicate that this has been touched up in any way."

"You're saying it looks authentic?" Shires asked. He was surprised.

"I'm saying with this rudimentary test it looks that way."

"Could you prove that beyond the shadow of a doubt?" Shires asked.

"Well, there are more tests I have to do before I can make a statement either way, but, in the end the answer will be definitive."

"Well, I think, with further tests, you'll find that it has been altered. Even here in the twenty-first century we still can't transport solid matter through space," Shires said confidently. "Could you take it with you and check it out?"

"Sure, I'll get back to you as soon as I have an answer."

When Shires was alone the question of *why* bothered him. Why was he sent the picture? Why had it been altered? What did somebody hope to gain from all this? And, most especially, what did they want him to believe had happened to these bodies?

Chapter 2

Kinzi Tern paced the dayroom of the San Francisco County Jail, watching the clock. Her appointment with Shires Lampton would be at three. *What did he want?* She had never met the man. She had seen him on TV a couple of times. The last time she had heard anything about him was for the interview he held with Tom and Vince. *What was he looking for at this late date?*

"Kinzi Tern report to the visiting area," the loudspeaker blared. It was exactly three. *Well, the man is prompt.*

Lampton's gray hair was windblown and mussed—not the usual nattily dressed fellow from TV. He wore jeans with a long sleeved red and black checkered cotton shirt. His clothes fit his slender body well. Kinzi guessed he was about six feet tall.

A glass partition separated them. Kinzi picked up the phone, and Shires did the same with the one on his side.

Shires had never seen Kinzi Tern before today. Her face was covered with freckles, giving her an innocent, girl-next-door appearance. He had come to her as kind of a last resort.

He supposed he could find the twisted tree trunk on his own, but wanted the exact location pinned down a little better. He didn't relish the thought of searching through the Coconino National Forest in search of a briefcase buried under the twisted trunk of some tree. That's what Vince Nalone's father had told him five months ago—just after the execution. He had said, "Vince wants me to tell you that his briefcase with all the names is buried under the tree with the twisted trunk out there by their hiding place. He told me to give it specifically to you, nobody else."

Back then, Shires hadn't been too interested and never bothered with

it. Now, with the new information he had received from Mark Kellum, he had changed his mind. When Mark returned the video he said it had not been tampered with in any way. Everything on it was authentic. That was when Shires decided it was time to familiarize himself with Tom Horn and Vince Nalone.

None of the other three terrorists knew of any such tree. If they did, they weren't telling him. Tony Arzetti, Greg Littlejack, and John Monroe all claimed ignorance. Kinzi Tern was his last chance to make the search easier.

"Miss Tern, my name is Shires Lampton. Thank you for talking to me."

"No problem," she answered.

"How are you doing?"

"All right for someone whose been held forever without a court appearance. I guess they don't give us a day in court under the Cahmael Regime. So, I'm a little angry, otherwise I'm okay."

Shires knew the four were being held as domestic terrorists. Under that heading they could be held indefinitely and never be brought to court. It dated back to the old Patriot Act that passed right after 9/11/2001. That was a long time ago, but it had never been rescinded. Now it fit right into the scheme of things.

"How well did you know Vince Nalone and Tom Horn?"

"I suppose just about as well anyone could under the circumstances."

"Anything different about them?"

"Like what?"

"Like anything. I don't know, just anything that didn't seem right."

"I never noticed anything. Why do you ask?"

"I'm just trying to get a better handle on who these men were, and why they died so willingly for their belief," Shires said.

"They were two men who had suffered a lot for what they believed. Otherwise, they weren't any different from you or me."

"Are you sure about that?" Shires asked.

"Positive," Kinzi affirmed.

"How had they suffered?"

"Tom lost his wife and daughters and Vince blamed himself for their deaths. He was the one that sent Susan into the church to tell the group that Tom and he were going to be late. They were still there when the explosion happened. So yes, I think the two men suffered grievously."

"Nothing different about them otherwise?"

"Nope."

Shires wrote something on the page of a small notebook and held it to the glass down low where it couldn't be seen by observers. It read: *The walls have ears. I need some answers without speech. Can we do that?*

Kinzi nodded.

Shires made small talk and asked general questions for the benefit of the recorders while they conversed silently.

"*How about a twisted tree trunk?*" Shires wrote.

Kinzi shrugged and mouthed "Where?"

Shires wrote "*Flagstaff.*"

Kinzi frowned, still not understanding.

"*Hideout,*" Shires wrote.

"How long were you with the survivalists?" Shires asked as a general question for the benefit of the eavesdroppers.

"About a year and a half," Kinzi answered while she tried to remember a twisted tree trunk, and then she remembered the location. "While I was with them I worked in the hangar with the choppers. We ate our lunches just north from there," she added cryptically.

Shires got the message, nodded and smiled. Now he knew where to look, but he didn't know how to get there. The police had handled the transportation to the scene the night of the interview. That had been over a year ago.

"*Know anyone who can help me find the hideout, now?*" he wrote.

Kinzi started to shake her head, and then remembered Alan Noble, and nodded her head. He had been left behind that night.

"Did you ever attend any of the meetings at the church?" Shires asked aloud.

"One meeting," she lied, "With a man I met at a sporting goods store in San Bernardino."

It was Shires turn to frown, and then he realized she was answering his written question as well. He got the point about the store, but San Bernardino threw him.

"San Bernardino?" he asked.

"Yes," she answered while shaking her head 'no', and then she mouthed *Kingman.*

"*Man at sport gds store in Kingman?*" he wrote.

She nodded.

"*How contact?*" he wrote.

"Was there ever a time when you considered leaving the survivalists?" he asked aloud.

"Mr. Lampton, you have five minutes," the guard said.

"Once, when I saw a notice on a bulletin board. It had the fish sign of the early Christians. It intrigued me. I guess they quit using the sign now, half of it anyway."

Shires was frowning again. She had answered his question in a cryptic manner again. Now, could he figure it out. He looked back at the door where the guard was stationed, then quickly wrote, "*I shld lve a msg on the bullet bd at sport gds store in Kingman with a semi-circle on it?*"

Kinzi nodded her head and smiled. "By the way," she said, "You gonna help us get out of here sometime soon?"

Shires ignored her question and hung up the phone.

Kinzi knew Lampton would never help them. He was too tied to the system, helping them might put his job in jeopardy. He was, after all, a big important reporter. She hoped she hadn't divulged too much information to him. He did seem sincere. She hoped he was for Alan's sake. That is if he even contacts Alan. She didn't know whether they still used the bulletin board to communicate or not.

CHAPTER 3

Shires drove to Kingman, Arizona. It would take a day, but the drive would give him time to wrap his mind around the skimpy amount of information he had accumulated. Unfortunately, none of it was about evaporating bodies. All he knew for sure was that two men had been beheaded; two men who were like any other men, according to those that knew them. So, what is the explanation for the sudden disappearance of their bodies? The official version remained the same. The bodies had been cremated and the ashes strewn on the surface of a sewer treatment facility. Evidently, the video had been stolen from wherever they stored such information. It was definitely not for general distribution.

What, if anything, did the disappearance have to do with Cahmael? It was after their execution that he had eased into power without the slightest effort. There had been no election. He was never declared leader, president, or most exalted ruler. One day he was there and everybody seemed to be happy about it.

The most obvious turning point came with the resurrection of the Pope. That one act solidified Cahmael's position in the world. Personally, Shires didn't buy it. He had watched the video over and over, and, even with all the blood and brains, it still seemed staged to him.

Would the Pope be a willing participant in such deception? Shires didn't think so and therein lay the weakness of the argument. Still, there was something strange about Cahmael's sudden rise to power, and Shires couldn't quite put his finger on it.

Then again, maybe Cahmael wasn't in control, but everyone did his bidding, including governments from every country around the world. Peace had settled over the earth, and that was the main point. Nobody cared much about anything else. A headline in one New York paper dubbed him the Prince of Peace.

Even the temple in Jerusalem was being rebuilt. It would set majestically beside the Dome of the Rock—after Medina and Mecca the Dome was the third most holy place in all of Islam. Such a thing would have been impossible to imagine a couple of years earlier. Cahmael had been directly responsible for that.

The story told by the press said that Cahmael had convinced the Muslim hierarchy, all the Mullahs and the Ayatollahs, that they needed a new public image. After half a century of purportedly sponsoring terrorism they were hated by the non-Muslim world. The unanswered question was what had Cahmael done to move them to that point.

Perhaps the scariest part of the Cahmael Regime was the kangaroo court with him being both judge and jury. These televised events started with Tom Horn and Vince Nalone and were now watched in every country around the world. The trial ended badly for the accused if he/she didn't repent and ask for Cahmael's forgiveness; this was always granted if they swore allegiance to him, and called him 'Lord'. There was little resistance after witnessing the misadventures of Horn and Nalone.

Shires took a side trip to Pasadena to visit the Southern California administrative offices of the Resurrection Church of Christ. He didn't call for an appointment because he wanted an unvarnished opinion, not some canned speech with a lot of spin.

The receptionist informed him that the director was away, but he could talk to the assistant director, a man named Malcolm Tubbs. Tubbs was an older black man with gray hair, neatly dressed in a light blue business suit, with a white shirt and red tie. Shires figured he was six foot four, maybe taller.

"Come in Mr. Lampton, have a seat. I've seen you on TV. What can I do for you?"

They shook hands and Shires thanked him for taking the time for an interview.

"I'm looking for background information on one of your pastors, Tom Horn. I'd greatly appreciate any information you could give me about him."

The man's face clouded instantly. "Exactly what kind of information are you seeking?"

"Well, for instance, what kind of man was he?"

"He was fired from his Pastorship for preaching blasphemy. However, before that he was a fine pastor."

"Blasphemy?" Shires asked

"Yes! He believed that Jehosea Cahmael was the Antichrist."

"And you don't?"

"Church doctrine holds that the Church will be raptured before the Antichrist comes to power."

"So you don't believe that Cahmael is the Antichrist?"

"Church doctrine wouldn't allow us to believe it."

Shires was getting the feeling that the man was being evasive so he asked him outright, "Do you personally believe that Cahmael is the Antichrist?"

"No, I do not."

"So you're not convinced by Cahmael's behavior that he's the Antichrist?"

"Not in the least. We live in perilous times. After all, he has done nothing but good in the world. Even the goal of the Trinity of Man is only to will the good for others. It's so very simple. So, no, I neither doubt the man nor question his methods."

"You're very comfortable with that belief?"

"Yes I am."

"I have a video I'd like to show you? I'd like your opinion on it."

"Sure. There's a monitor right here," Malcolm said. He stood and walked to a table at the back wall and held out his hand. "I'll put it in."

Shires had never shown the video of the evaporating bodies to anyone, but he wanted Malcolm Tubbs' opinion. "Run it for a minute or so, that'll show you what it is, and then skip to the end; I gotta warn you, it shows Tom and Vince's headless bodies. It's not a pretty sight," Shires said.

Malcolm nodded slightly and started the tape. The gruesome sight played out before them. After he skipped it forward, they watched the bodies evaporate, and then it was done. Shires said nothing, waiting for Malcolm to react.

"This video has been edited, hasn't it?" Malcolm said.

"That's exactly what I thought, so I had a friend test it in the lab. The video has not been touched. What you see is exactly what happened."

"You're kidding me, right?" Malcolm asked. He looked like a man who had seen a ghost.

"No. I'm serious. It hasn't been touched," Shires assured him again.

The man, who had been so positive, so sure of himself, seemed shaken by what he saw. He retrieved a Bible from a small shelf on the wall and thumbed through it. "Let me read something to you. This is from Revelations, the eleventh chapter. I'll read it just the way it is written and then I'll paraphrase it the way some may interpret it." He read

"Then a measuring rod like a staff was given to me, and I was told, "Get up and measure the temple of God, and the altar, and the ones who worship there. But do not measure the outer courtyard of the temple; leave it out, because it has been given to the Gentiles, and they will trample on the holy city for forty-two months. And I will grant my two witnesses authority to prophesy for 1,260 days, dressed in sackcloth. (These are the two olive trees and the two lampstands that stand before the Lord of the earth.) If anyone wants to harm them, fire comes out of their mouths and completely consumes their enemies. If anyone wants to harm them, they must be killed this way. These two have the power to close up the sky so that it does not rain during the time they are prophesying. They have power to turn the waters to blood and to strike the earth with every kind of plague whenever they want. When they have completed their testimony, the beast that comes up from the abyss will make war on them and conquer them and kill them. Their corpses will lie in the street of the great city that is symbolically called Sodom and Egypt, where their Lord was also crucified. For three and a half days those from every people, tribe, nation, and language will look at their corpses, because they will not permit them to be placed in a tomb. And those who live on the earth will rejoice over them and celebrate, even sending gifts to each other, because these two prophets had tormented those who live on the earth. But after three and a half days a breath of life from God entered them, and they stood on their feet, and tremendous fear seized those who were watching them. Then they heard a loud voice from heaven saying to them: "Come up here!" So the two prophets went up to heaven in a cloud while their enemies stared at them. Just then a major earthquake took place and a tenth of the city collapsed;

seven thousand people were killed in the earthquake, and the rest were terrified and gave glory to the God of heaven."

"Now that's the way it reads right out of the Bible and this is the way it'll be paraphrased by those who might believe that Tom and Vince were those angels."

He read again

"And I will grant my two witnesses authority to prophesy for 1,260 days, When they have completed their testimony, the beast that comes up from the abyss will make war on them and conquer them and kill them. Their corpses will lie in the street. For three and a half days those from every people, tribe, nation, and language will look at their corpses, because they will not permit them to be placed in a tomb. And those who live on the earth will rejoice over them and celebrate, even sending gifts to each other, because these two prophets had tormented those who live on the earth. But after three and a half days a breath of life from God entered them, and they stood on their feet, and tremendous fear seized those who were watching them. Then they heard a loud voice from heaven saying to them: "Come up here!" So the two prophets went up to heaven in a cloud while their enemies stared at them."

It was Shires turn to be speechless. "It says that in the Bible?" he asked. He was taken by the descriptiveness of the passage.

"Well, I paraphrased it somewhat, but that's the gist of the text, yes," Malcolm said.

"There was no loud voice and they didn't rise up and go into the sky. They simply evaporated into thin air. I'm sure there's a simple explanation for it—no angels, nothing supernatural. When I get the answer I'll let you know," Shires said.

"Was there audio on the tape?"

"Not that I heard."

"Then you don't know if there was a voice, do you?"

"Of course not. In my opinion, this tape is not a picture of a supernatural event. It's simply a record of something that has yet to be explained. That's all it is."

"There are a lot of religious people who will disagree with you my friend."

"What do you mean?"

"Many Christians, when they see that, will believe that Tom and Vince were taken directly to heaven, just like the angels in the Bible. It will convince them that Cahmael really is the Antichrist, since it was the Devil who killed the angels."

"My God," Shires exclaimed, "They're that easily convinced?"

"It fits the scripture. If it fits the scripture, they'll believe it."

"What about you? You said earlier that Cahmael wasn't the Antichrist. Have you changed your mind?"

"I'm not so sure now, but I won't speak of this to anybody until I hear a plausible scientific explanation from you. How long do you think it will take?"

"I don't have the slightest idea."

CHAPTER 4

Malcolm Tubbs sat for a long time after Shires Lampton's visit, staring at the picture of Christ hanging on the wall at the front of his office.

What's the meaning of all of this? Cahmael can't be the Antichrist. Tom Horn and Vince Nalone weren't angels. It did look like their bodies disappeared into the air though—is that possible? What other meaning could there be?

Uneasiness crept through him. *If this were true would he be able to denounce the teachings he had believed all his life? It must have been a terrible decision for Tom Horn.* Malcolm had two daughters and a son, and two grandkids. *All their lives would be at stake. God forbid that he might ever have to make such a grim decision. There has to be a scientific explanation for the disappearance. Cahmael cannot be the Antichrist.*

He knew he had to wait for Shires to get back to him before he reacted in any way. It was going to be a difficult wait. He closed his eyes and asked the Lord to forgive his momentary lack of faith.

CHAPTER 5

A sporting goods store with a bulletin board shouldn't be too difficult to find, but it was. Shires finally found it in Joe's Camping Supplies. His note read: I NEED A GUIDE FOR THE NATIONAL FOREST NORTH OF FLAGSTAFF. He included his cell phone number and signed it with an arc. As a backup, he ran the same ad in the local paper; sans arc, of course.

It was nearly a week later, early morning, when his cell phone vibrated. He had been ready to give up on the idea and go on to Flagstaff and search there.

"You wrote the ad?" a male voice asked.

"Yes."

"Where are you?"

"Motel Six," he answered.

"Go to the restaurant across the street. Ask to sit in a front booth. I'll find you."

The hostess frowned when he asked for a specific booth, but she seated him anyway. He ordered coffee and breakfast. He had finished breakfast when his phone vibrated again.

"You're Shires Lampton, the TV reporter," the voice said. It was more of a statement than a question.

"Yes."

"You doing a story?"

"Yes."

"What kind of story?"

"Well, I'm not going to discuss that over the phone. You'll have to talk to me face to face. I'm here as you requested, so you going to come in?"

A long pause, then the call was disconnected. Shires asked for more coffee and waited another fifteen minutes, and still no visitor; just as he stood to leave a bearded stranger slid into the seat across from him. The man had not seen a shower for some time—his clothing was in need of soap and water as well. Shires detected a smell of fried onions. He hoped his revulsion wasn't apparent. Shires didn't offer his hand and looked around for the waitress, wondering if someone might be coming to usher the man out. The waitress appeared, but the stranger declined food and coffee.

"Let's get our business done and get out of here," he said.

"Well," Shires said, "you know my name, what's yours?"

"My name's not important," he said frowning, "the only reason I answered your ad was the half circle. Who told you to use it? I know you ain't no believer."

"Kinzi Tern."

The man's face lit up immediately, but he quickly masked it. "What you want from me?"

"Take me to John Monroe's campsite."

"Why there?"

"That's none of your business. Can you get me there?"

"That area is still patrolled so we'll have to go in at night. That okay with you?"

"How soon?"

"A week, earliest."

"How will I meet up with you?"

"Just get to Flagstaff and keep your cell phone on," he said and disappeared through a side door. The smell of fried onions lingered.

Shires looked through the door where the man had disappeared and wondered who he was. He had the idea that he might have been Alan Noble, but he didn't know, and doubted it would make a difference one way or the other. The man had been living off the grid for a long time. *Is that how these people survive?*

CHAPTER 6

The week would give Shires time to make two copies of the video (one for himself, the other for Felix with instructions to guard it with his life), and to call a friend in Washington D C. Maybe she could shed some light on disappearing bodies.

Jordan Smith worked as an assistant program manager for DARPA, an anagram for Defense Advanced Research Projects Agency. The agency was started right after Russia surprised the U.S. with Sputnik in 1957. Its stated mission is to prevent such surprises in the future, and to come up with some of its own. They work with advanced research in any area that could have a military application; for example, computers doing machine translation—changing one language into another with the speed and expertise of a human translator, for intelligence gathering purposes.

Shires didn't think that human evaporation was a new weapons application, but Jordan would know if something extraordinary were being developed. She might not be able to tell him outright, but she could say he was on the right track, or maybe heading in the right direction.

His history with Jordan went back ten years. Back then they shared their lives, an apartment, and bed. They withdrew amiably from that relationship two years ago and remained good friends.

Thinking back, he couldn't pinpoint the exact reason they split. He supposed it was lack of time, and the sharing of it with each other. She was often out of town checking on the progress of different research projects, and he was busy globe-trotting in pursuit of the latest story.

She was a bright, beautiful woman with a Master's degree in Business Administration. He sometimes doubted the wisdom of his decision to leave her. Many nights since then he had thought of her. The vision of her raven black hair spread over the pillow stuck in his brain, along with the sight of her smooth skin wrinkled only by the smile that radiated from her lips.

He left a message on her voicemail before he flew to Flagstaff, but didn't get her call back for another two days.

"Boo," she said, using her pet name for him like she always did, "it's so good to hear from you. How are you?"

""Fine babe, just fine."

"Oh I know you are," she said teasingly, "Where is that beautiful body of yours located?"

"Flagstaff."

"What are you doing?"

"Presently, I'm chasing ghosts."

"Ghosts?"

"Sorta, yeah. I need a favor."

"Anything for you, Boo, you know that—within reason of course," she chuckled.

"I have a video for you to see," he said, smiling at her innuendo.

"Okay, send it along and I'll take a gander. You going to tell me about it?"

"No, not over the phone. Just look at it, especially the end, and give me your opinion."

"What kind of an opinion are you looking for?"

"How."

"That's it?"

"Yep. That's it."

"Okay. Send it to my old address. I guess you know what that is."

Shires assured her that he did and they talked on for few minutes, enjoying a conversation that was long overdue for both of them. They ended with promises not to be such strangers and to call each other more. When they finished, Shires sat for a long time before he walked to the post office to send the package. He had felt a tug at his heart. *Maybe he should rekindle that old flame.*

CHAPTER 7

Shires received the call on the evening of his fifth day in Flagstaff.

"Where are you?" the voice asked.

"Best Western."

"Still driving the black Suburban?"

"Yes."

"I'll be waiting by it around ten. Don't come any sooner, and bring everything with you, especially your walking shoes," the caller disconnected.

He had about an hour and a half to get ready. He was already set to go—had been since the day he arrived. He was anxious to get this little trek finished. The thought of walking shoes wasn't appealing, but he wasn't a stranger to it. He and Jordan hiked every time they'd had a chance. It was the *skulking through the night* part that worried him.

Shires wondered how much this guy was going to charge. He never asked the question since the visits were always so abbreviated. Tonight he would get the answer. He brought a thousand bucks in hundred-dollar bills—*should be enough for a down payment, at least.*

Shires left his room at five minutes until 10. That would get him to his vehicle right on the hour as he had been instructed.

He saw no one as he approached and opened the cargo hatch to load his gear.

"Get in, start the engine, and unlock the passenger side," a voice ordered in a barely audible whisper.

Shires complied, but didn't see anyone until the man opened the door and swung himself into the seat.

"Let's go," he said.

Shires drove slowly out of the parking lot, and headed north on Highway 89. The smell of fried onions fouled the air again. Shires ignored it as much as possible and struck up a conversation.

"By the way, I'm willing to pay you for doing this."

"Not necessary. I work on the barter system. There will be a favor we will want from you. That will be the payment for tonight's little episode."

"Why barter?"

"No paper or computer trail. It's clean and neat. It's how we have to work."

"Why?"

"It's the times we live in—the time of the Antichrist. It's against the law not to have a Cahmael chip. You can't buy or sell without it, so we have to live off the grid and steal to survive."

"It's not unlawful to buy without a chip. I do it all the time," Shires said.

"What do you mean?"

"I mean you don't have to have a chip to buy things. You do need a Cahmael card, but that's all. Who told you such a thing?"

"I don't have to be told. It's going on all around us, all the time, like the creeping crud. It came with Cahmael and it's getting worse. You got the chip?"

"Yes, I do."

"Well, the time is coming. They'll make everybody get the chip. They say it's for national security. Within the next year everybody will have it," the man said.

"So why don't you at least have a card so you can eat?" Shires asked.

"They'll track you down if you have a card. Nope, the only way to stay out of the system is not to get in it. Do you remember when Cahmael first started? He took a census. Why'd he do that? He wanted to account for everybody. He wants everybody to have the chip."

"There's nothing bad about the chip? It's just a bar code for identification purposes—keeps your identity from being stolen. Like you said, it's for national security and for our own safety and welfare."

"Man, you're a walking advertisement for Homeland Security, and the FBI's reasoning to get the chip. You know the chip is the Mark of the Beast prophesized in the Bible don't you?"

"Are you kidding? That's just a whole lot of paranoid baloney."

"No, it's not. I wish I could convince you otherwise."

"Save your breath," Shires said. He was tired and they had a long night ahead of them.

"How much farther?" Shires asked.

"Turn off where it says National Forest."

Shires felt better knowing he'd be leaving the highway. But he didn't feel better when he saw the flashing red light in his rearview mirror. A moment of panic seized him. *How he had broken the law?* Nothing came to mind. He pulled over and braked the Suburban to a stop.

"You're my cameraman Felix Gunther. We're heading out to do a story in Colorado Springs. Let me do the talking."

They sat there waiting. The patrol car whizzed by.

"Patrolman late for dinner," the passenger said. He laughed.

It was the first humor Shires had seen in the man. He was laughing at Shires. Shires knew it, but he didn't care. Better to be laughed at, then to explain yourself to the police.

They turned off onto a service road just before Timberline and drove north another thirty minutes into the forest.

"Stop here and turn off you lights."

Although Shires couldn't be sure, the area seemed vaguely familiar.

"This is where the helicopter dropped you off after the interview. You recognize it?"

"I thought it looked familiar."

"Grab your gear. Let's get out of here."

Shires' backpack carried a small shovel and pick he bought in Kingman. Those were tied across the top. The pack was empty except for a flashlight. His load was light, and he was glad, for his new friend set a brisk pace.

They had walked for twenty minutes, Shires figured, when the man suddenly raised his arm and stepped behind a tree. Shires found a tree and did the same.

Voices floated through the forest from somewhere up ahead. His guide moved back to him. "Poachers, I think," he said, "We'll go around them. Come on."

Shires hurried to follow, wondering what poachers hunted out here. He figured it was deer.

An hour later, they reached the compound that Shires remembered as the main camp.

"What is it you're looking for?" the guide asked.

Shires thought it was unlikely anyone could beat them to it now. "I'm looking for a tree with a twisted trunk. Vince's briefcase is buried under it. Kinzi said it was north of the old hanger."

The man nodded in the moonlight as if he knew exactly where it was, and he did. He led Shires right to the tree. Shires untied the shovel and pick from the pack and retrieved the flashlight from inside.

Recent rains had compacted the ground making it impossible to find the burial site.

"Look for an indentation in the ground," he said.

"Like this?" Shires asked, shining the light on what appeared to be a depression in the ground.

"Exactly, dig there."

Two feet down Shires struck something solid. He dusted the dirt away to reveal the briefcase. He pulled it from the hole, and set it on the ground. It showed no sign of wear from its interment. It was locked and Shires had no key. So he slipped it into the backpack with the flashlight and slung it onto his back. He was ready for the return trip.

When they reached the vehicle, his new friend bade him farewell, telling him how to get back to the highway. "Remember, you'll get a phone call about the favor you owe us," he said, stepping into the trees and disappearing from Shires' view.

Shires drove back down the old dirt road. He was tired, but he was happy with the night's work. Now he might be able to get a handle on the Cahmael thing, and maybe learn a little bit about Vince Nalone and Tom Horn.

It was five that morning and he was almost back to Flagstaff when his cell phone vibrated.

"Boo, we have a problem."

CHAPTER 8

Shires' flight to Washington, D.C. was delayed thirty minutes, but he was finally on his way to help Jordan. Evidently she had misread her friendship with her boss, and had shown him the video. He went into orbit, demanding to know where she got it. She wouldn't tell him. He made a big hullabaloo about it, called the director who, after viewing it, immediately accused Jordan of being a threat to National Security. They didn't arrest her, just questioned her most of the night. She hadn't been able to call Shires until the next morning.

Shires felt responsible. He hadn't meant for her to share it with anyone. She was only trying to gather information for him, and thought she could trust her boss. Now she had been suspended from her job pending further investigation. Shires had inadvertently put the woman he loved on a collision course with the FBI and Homeland Security. He had to make it right.

His flight landed at Dulles International a little after noon. He rented a car for the drive to Falls Church.

When Jordan opened her apartment door, she rushed into his arms. Maybe it was lust, or love, or the tension of the moment, whatever it was, they went with it and made love for a long time—reveling in the newness and the oldness of their relationship.

Afterward they lay on the bed and talked of old times, new times, and of Jordan's predicament. Shires did *not* want her to become a target for Homeland Security.

Jordan lay with her head on his chest. Shires kissed the top of it. He took a long breath enjoying the scent of her. It had been a long two years.

"Did they give any indication what was so disturbing to them?" Shires asked.

"It has to be the disappearing part, because Doug didn't react before that."

"Could it be a project of some kind?"

"Well, it's not one of mine. That's why I wanted Doug to see it. I never thought he would do that to me. I sensed it was more than just a project, but I can't say that for sure either. Their reactions were so overboard. They demanded to know where I got it. I wouldn't tell them, and that made them even angrier."

"Would you say they were shook-up?"

"Almost. Yes, that's a good description of everybody who talked to me."

So what could get an Agency all shook up over two bodies evaporating into thin air? Shires wondered.

That evening, Shires sat down at the table to pick the lock on Vince's briefcase. He tried unsuccessfully for thirty frustrating minutes. *If Vince had wanted to share the contents so badly, why didn't he furnish a key?*

"Can I help?" Jordan asked.

"Be my guest," he said, sliding it across the table to her.

She pointed a fingernail file and tweezers at him, one in each hand, emulating a two-gun draw, "Just call me Calamity Jane," she said chuckling at her joke. Shires rolled playfully from his chair to the floor like he'd been shot, grabbed her leg, and tickled her foot. She laughed and tugged her leg from his grip.

"Stop that now. Let me finish the job," she pleaded, still laughing.

He sat back on his chair and watched as she inserted the file into the slot and moved it up and down while jiggling the briefcase. The latches popped loose.

The feat amazed Shires. "Have you learned a second profession since I left? What were the tweezers supposed to do?"

She laughed. "It's something I picked up from my brothers. You just never asked me to do it before. The tweezers are for plucking my eyebrows."

Shires laughed heartily, shaking his head as he did so. "Only you could make me laugh like this," he said, "What was I thinking when I left you?" He leaned across and gave her a lingering kiss.

Jordan pulled away after a few moments. "You better remember that, just in case you ever decide to leave me again. But first things first, buddy. Check the contents of the briefcase, and then we'll work on the other."

He let out a pouting sigh. Jordan patted him on the head. "It'll still be there," she assured him.

Shires skimmed through the contents. Letters, it was all letters. He read one from a man begging his good friend to be careful to whom he spoke about Jehosea Cahmael being the Antichrist. Another friend of theirs had been killed in a freak accident the week before. He handed it to Jordan and picked up a small, wrinkled newspaper article. *Wichita Man Killed In Hunting Accident* it read. Shires started to read it when Jordan interrupted him.

"You think Jehosea Cahmael is the Antichrist?" she asked, "and that's why you're doing this…this…whatever you're doing?"

"Research; I'm doing research for a story, and no, I don't believe Cahmael is the Antichrist. That video that I sent to you started it all. I showed it to one of the church leaders in Tom Horn's denomination, and he said he might believe that the bodies of the two men ascended into heaven, unless I found a scientific answer to the contrary."

"But, where'd you get the video?"

"I don't know. It was delivered to my room with a note attached. The note said *thought you might be interested; pay close attention at the end.*"

"So, you sent it to me?"

"No. First I gave it to a friend to check out in his lab. I thought it was a hoax, or a joke. He said it hadn't been tampered with or edited. Then I sent it to you. It has to be something explainable. I didn't mean for you to share it, though. Sorry, I should have warned you."

"What's the name of your story? JEHOSEA CAHMAEL: THE ANTICHRIST! And you're going to be the first to proclaim it to the world? Well, that should make him so happy he'll want to kill you."

"No, I'm not doing a story on the Antichrist. I'm doing it on the first two men to die at the hands of Cahmael. I wanted to know if there was anything different about them since they sort of evaporated into thin air."

"Why would there be something different about them? I don't understand."

"I didn't either, and after talking to the folks that were with them,

I still didn't. Then I talked to Mr. Tubbs from Horn's denomination. He watched the video and was clearly shaken by what he saw. Then he read the eleventh chapter of Revelations to me, and I understood why religious people might think that Tom Horn and Vince Nalone were angels."

"Angels?" Jordan was aghast. "Are you pulling my leg, Boo?"

"No. Get on your computer and type in Internet Bible, scroll down to the book of Revelation, and click on chapter eleven.

She typed in the information, waited a moment, and began to read. Then she stopped, looked at Shires, and asked. "You want me to read it to you?"

"No. I've already read it."

"This does not resemble our two guys at all. I never heard of Tom Horn or Vince Nalone until they assassinated the Pope," Jordan said.

"My reaction exactly; that's why I sent the video to you. I wanted a logical, earthbound explanation. The church that Horn belonged to says Cahmael can't be the Antichrist because, according to their doctrine, they'll be gone in the Rapture long before he arrives."

"I've heard of the Rapture, but I never really understood it. My friend Virginia believes in it. I don't talk to her much about religion."

"Well, this Mr. Tubbs from Tom's Church believes that the evaporation of those bodies will make a lot of people think they were the two angels raised up in the last days to prophesy, like it says there in Revelations. Then, when they were killed, they were taken to heaven."

"Too bad it didn't have audio. You might have heard the mighty voice calling to them," Jordan chided.

"The only resemblance that Tom and Vince have to that scripture is that they were two men who were publicly executed and whose bodies were left lying unburied in the street for three days. Evidently, that would be enough for a lot of people.

"Mr. Tubbs says, 'it fits the scripture' and that would be enough for him too, especially if I don't find a logical, scientific explanation. I need you and DARPA to give it to me. I'll bet you any amount of money they have one, and that's why they're so upset."

"I'll call my friend, Olivia. She works on some different projects from mine. Maybe I can get an answer from her."

"Would it make a difference if I went to the agency and explained it?" Shires asked.

"Do you think that's a good idea? They might not believe you and arrest you."

"They have no reason to arrest me."

"I don't know, Boo, I'd rather you didn't do that. Let's just leave it alone and see how it works out. Okay? I'll talk to Olivia tomorrow. We'll see what's going on."

It was three in the morning when a white van with a logo that read Murphy's Tire and Wheel Alignment parked by the open garage that housed Jordan's car. Two men dressed in white coveralls climbed out and checked the license plate number. One of them slid under the car, the other stood watch.

When the man finished his task, they climbed back into the van and moved slowly away.

CHAPTER 9

Pope Linus III was unhappy. Although he believed that the power of God fell upon him with the donning of his cap and robe, he felt the powerlessness of the human spirit within. He prayed for grace every day. Being the Pope was an awesome undertaking. He felt the terrible weight of that responsibility; it bore down on him day after day. He didn't have the answers and he knew it. *How did the other Pontiffs fare so well?*

He had an extra burden with the presence of Jehosea Cahmael, who had been his guest for the past few months. The man's presence shouldn't have been so oppressive, after all He was the Son of God, and He had resurrected Linus from the dead. But Cahmael refused to claim he was the Lord; always giving deference to Linus with the utmost humility. "I'm only your humble servant," he would say.

"What's a Pope to do while the Lord Jesus Christ is a guest in his house?" He had asked himself that more than a few times. He longed for a trusted adviser, like he had been to Pope Julian, but he only had his secretary. He wished he could be less inhibited. He could just ask Cahmael and be done with it. But it would be like telling Jesus he was a pain in the behind. He couldn't bring himself to do it.

There would be some distractions coming in the future and Linus was happy for that. The one that most especially excited him was the anniversary of the birth of the state of Israel. That would happen on May 14, next year. The Israelis, at Cahmael's request, had timed the dedication of the newly constructed Temple of Solomon to coincide with the celebration. That was eight months away. Linus was pleased that Cahmael had agreed to attend the ceremony as a member of the Vatican entourage.

Cahmael mentioned to him that it would be the greatest meeting of religious minds the world had ever seen, with even greater implications for the future of mankind.

However, Linus was troubled over more than just the presence of the Lord. Benevolence had always been a foregone conclusion within the church, and willing the good fit right into the doctrine. But it seemed to him that there was a harsh side to the Lord when he sat in judgment. It seemed that *willing the good* may not have been the main objective—it was more about the worship of Cahmael. It was, at the very least, a deadly *either/or* situation—accept Cahmael as your Lord and Savior or die. Linus never expected such vindictiveness from Jesus. Maybe this was the Lord of the Old Testament? He never expected a darkside from Jesus; but then, who was he to question this apparent fallibility? He had spent his life pleasing God, and he had no plans to stop now. But he felt the guilt that comes with doubt. It tore at his heart. He could find no peace. He, Pope Linus III, was the embodiment of God on earth, and he should know these things.

And he wondered about Civil Law and what had happened to it. Under Cahmael it had lost its civility and its love. Cahmael now practiced his own form of law, which appeared to be a dictatorship. He did his law-making from inside the Vatican. That bothered Linus, but he said nothing, figuring that God, after all, should know what He was doing.

And then one day a call came to the Pope's attention. It was a call from the Minister of Defence in England to Cahmael. He was requesting information about the recent order to move some military assets into the Mediterranean Sea. It was the first time Linus had heard of such a thing.

Cardinal Mencini—his acting advisor in the absence of an appointed one, and his secretary—spoke of it as a normal occurrence since Cahmael had taken up residence.

"He's speaking for you when he answers their questions, your Holiness," Mencini said.

"You mean those are my orders?" Linus asked. A frown creased his brow.

"Yes."

Cahmael had spoken to him about the possibility of ruling Europe from the Vatican. Linus had thought it would be as a figurehead only—never hands-on.

"So, do you know why I told them to move their ships to the Mediterranean?"

"Ships and troops, Your Holiness; it was for security during the dedication of the Temple in Jerusalem next May," he explained.

"Already? Are we expecting trouble?"

"Always."

CHAPTER 10

Sergeant Roy Cassidy resented the San Francisco Police Department for overlooking his contribution to the capturing of the terrorists Kinzi Tern and Tony Arzetti. If it hadn't been for him both terrorists would have gone unnoticed. So that was twice the department had snubbed him, just like they had when he took a bullet in the line of duty—the bullet that pulled him out of action and placed him behind a desk for the rest of his career. So there he sat at the front desk answering phones, and any questions some civilian might have about the department, as if nothing at all had happened.

Someday they would realize his value again. But in the meantime, besides his desk job, (his day job as he called it) he made it his full time project to watch Michael Arzetti, there was something going on there. Cassidy couldn't quite put his finger on it, but it was there.

Roy knew every move the kid had made—every arrest, every visit to see his father, even his favorite ice cream. He was a regular at Hardy's gym, just down the street from the apartment he shared with his sister Ann, who attended San Francisco State.

Arzetti visited his mother, Peggy Woodhill, and his younger sister, Martina, who lived with her, once each week, and he never missed a Forty-Niner game unless he had duty that day. The kid was a good, upstanding citizen.

Roy sensed there was more to Arzetti then met the eye, though. He felt the kid had been ready to help his dad back before they arrested him, but the arrest interrupted whatever he was planning to do. So Roy continued his surveillance.

Sometimes Arzetti disappeared right under his nose, and Roy

couldn't find him. That bothered him for he was good at his job, and tailing a subject was almost second nature. The fact that Mike Arzetti could slip away from him was a challenge he couldn't resist. Michael couldn't know that he was being followed, so why the secrecy? That question spurred him on. He had to know why Arzetti disappeared and why he took such precautions.

It was only by accident or fate, he couldn't decide which, that he discovered the truth. Although he wanted it to be, it wasn't from his good detective work either. In fact, he wasn't thinking about Arzetti when he made the discovery. It was a signboard advertising a magic show and one word stood out—misdirection. The importance of the word didn't sink in immediately. It did one night, a few evenings later while he was following Arzetti on foot. The subject took the usual turn into an alley. When Cassidy arrived at the alley there was no one in sight.

He had followed Arzetti down this same alley before and knew where he would go, and he should still be able to see him. Cassidy couldn't run because of his leg, but he hurried as best he could to get to the corner. No Arzetti. He must have eluded him in this alley. So Roy slowly retraced his steps, watching for any escape route. The word *misdirection* repeated itself over and over in his mind. He had never lost Arzetti down this alley before. The kid had set him up.

An old tire leaned against the splintered, weather-beaten door making it look as if it hadn't been used in years. On closer inspection, Roy discovered that the tire was actually attached to the door. The door could be opened and closed while the tire remained unmoved. The door opened upon a narrow walkway.

Roy followed the walkway and found another door—a very heavy fire door without a handle. A notepad and pencil hung on the wall with instructions to slide a note under the door. He figured it was a password system, and didn't want to blow his surveillance after all this time, and went no farther. He looked for an imprint on the page that might give away the password, even used the side of the lead to shade the page, no luck. They were careful, whoever they were, and Michael Arzetti was right in the middle of it.

CHAPTER 11

It had been three days since Shires Lampton's arrival, and DARPA still hadn't contacted Jordan regarding the status of the investigation surrounding the video. It had taken Jordan two days to contact her friend, Olivia, who was surprised to hear about her dilemma.

They had agreed to meet at Hornblowers for lunch at noon today. It was now one o'clock and Olivia hadn't arrived. Jordan called her cell, but didn't get an answer.

"Let's go find her," Shires suggested, "you know the way?"

"Sure, but let me drive. I'm better at driving than I am at giving directions."

"Go right ahead. It's your car anyway."

Jordan drove the route that Olivia was most likely to have followed. Because it was Saturday, she would have been coming from home. They saw nothing unusual until they approached her house and found police cars clogging the street.

"Stop here. Let's walk," Shires said. He had a bad feeling about this, but he didn't want to share it with Jordan.

"What happened?" Shires asked of a bystander.

"Not sure, heard something about the death of the woman that lives there. Don't know what happened."

"Oh my God, Olivia?" Jordan gasped her hand flying to her mouth in disbelief.

It was difficult for Shires to believe as well. "Let's get out of here," he said, grasping Jordan's arm, and pulling her toward the car.

Jordan was crying by the time they reached the vehicle. Shires backed into a driveway, turned around, and sped away. Questions raced through his mind. *How'd she die? When?* Maybe they should have stayed longer, but paranoia had set in. *Did it have anything to do with her talking to Jordan?* He hoped there was no connection, but you never know.

In Jordan's apartment later that evening Shires switched on the TV and built a toasted avocado sandwich. Jordan declined food and rested on the couch. He sat at the table to eat while he watched the local news.

Police are investigating a possible homicide in Arlington, the reporter said, *A woman was found dead with two gunshot wounds to the head. Police here aren't speculating as to a motive in the case. Her body was found by the cleaning lady around seven this morning. It is believed she may have been a victim of an interrupted burglary.*

One thing Shires knew for sure, the story was out of whack with reality, because burglars aren't usually killers. He had done a report on types of crime and the usual modus operandi. Rapists can be killers, but burglars tend to run from confrontation. Shires figured the burglary story was only a cover, and wondered what the truth really was.

That evening, Jordan answered a knock at the door. Two detectives from the Arlington police department wanted to ask some questions about the life and death of Olivia Melton.

Jordan invited them in and seated them at the dining room table.

"Would you like some coffee?"

They both declined. Shires introduced himself and sat down.

"You're the TV guy," said the one who introduced himself as Henry Akers.

Shires confirmed that he was, and nothing else was said about it.

"Ms. Smith, how long have you known Olivia Melton?" asked the other detective, Frank Wise.

"Well, I've worked at the agency for eleven years, so I'd say I've known her for at least ten."

"Did she have any enemies?"

"Not that I know about. She's divorced, but she was on good terms with her ex the last time I talked to her about him. Other than that, I don't know of any other possibilities. I don't think she was dating."

"So you worked with her at DARPA?" Akers asked.

"She was an assistant project manager like me, but we worked on different projects."

"What kind of projects?"

She explained how DARPA came into existence, "…and our mission is never to let another Sputnik happen," she finished.

"So what kinds of projects were you and Olivia working on?" Akers persisted.

"I know what my projects were, but I don't know about Olivia's."

"So what were your projects?"

"I'm sorry I can't tell you. That's classified information."

A long silence ensued. Neither detective said anything. Akers turned to Shires. "What do you know about all this?" he asked.

"I'm completely in the dark."

"The great Shires Lampton completely in the dark. I doubt that." Wise said to nobody in particular.

Akers turned back to Jordan. "Ms. Smith, do you think it's a possibility that Ms. Melton was murdered over something at work; a project or something like that?"

"I don't know. Anything is possible I guess."

"According to her day planner, she had a luncheon appointment with you today at Hornblowers."

"That's correct."

"When did you talk to her to arrange that?"

"About seven last night."

"Did she seem okay at the time?"

"Yes. Everything was fine, at least I thought so. We talked for about thirty minutes."

"You never detected any stress or anxiety in her voice?"

"None that I could tell."

"Like maybe she was being threatened; anything like that?" Wise added.

"No. She was relaxed and laughing when we talked," Jordan insisted.

"The medical examiner placed the time of death to be about eight last evening. It was soon after you talked to her."

"Can you think of any reason at all that she might have been killed?" asked Akers.

"No, I truly can't. She was a sweet person. I can't believe anyone would ever want to kill her."

"Well that about does it for us. Thank you for your candor. If you do happen to think of anything, here's my card," Akers said as he handed it to her.

They stood and walked to the door. Before they departed, Akers turned to add, "Just for your information, due to the sensitive nature of your job, the FBI and Homeland Security will want to question you, so I'd keep myself available for awhile."

CHAPTER 12

Mike we had a visitor last night. Somebody found the notepad by the door. I think they might have tried to pick up the password. I have each page coded for such emergencies and there is a page missing from the pad. Maybe we should consider some changes. Send an answer before next meeting.

Michael Arzetti folded the note and slipped it back in the envelope. It had been placed under his doormat during the night.

He had joined the underground at the urging of his father, Tony Arzetti, who was convinced that there might be some difficult times ahead. He felt that the underground would be a good support system.

It was fast becoming impossible to buy anything without the Cahmael Card, and soon a computer chip implanted in either the hand or the forehead would replace the card. To survive without the card or the chip would require friends in the underground. He knew full well that being caught meant execution—hence the need for extreme precaution.

Michael tried to think of anyone who might be following him, no one came to mind. That would be the only way an unknown person could have found the door. He was the only member who used it that night.

Secrecy must prevail. That was the deal, even if it meant killing to preserve it. He didn't know who was following him, but he had to find out quickly—it was life or death.

What did they know? The question bothered him. He became guarded in his conversations, even with his patrol partner, George Wildes.

"What's wrong with you?" George asked.

"What are you talking about?"

"You. You've hardly said three words all morning. You're way off somewhere. What's going on? You can't have problems at home; you're not married, or did Annie throw you out?" he joked.

"Somebody is following me," he said before he thought. Telling George may not be a good idea, but he needed some help, and he knew he could trust his partner. He just wouldn't tell him the whole truth.

"What? Are you kidding me? Get real man, why would anyone be following you?"

"That's exactly what I asked myself, and I don't have an answer."

"Well, I got your back, Mike, what you want to do?"

"It might just be a case of paranoia, but I'd like you to follow me some night. Take a look at who might be on my tail. Would you mind?"

"I'm free any night. When?"

"How about tonight?"

"Fine with me; what time?"

"I usually leave home about seven. I'll stick to that schedule. If my friend is there I don't want to disappoint him."

Ann had gone to spend the evening with their mother and sister. Michael ate his dinner alone, waited for seven, and thought about what he had done by including George in what might become a murder—murder would be necessary if the pursuer were hostile. Mike didn't want to do it, but he had sworn to protect the secrecy of the underground at all costs. He hoped the incursion had been an accident; kids playing around, something simple like that. He was a cop first and foremost, and he did not want to kill anybody in cold blood.

At first, he had been angry with his father for being involved with the terrorists. It had cast such an ugly shadow over him and his chosen career. Later, he discovered the true nature of Tony Arzetti's involvement. Knowing the truth made him feel better, but the knowledge did little to help him free his dad.

Homeland Security and the FBI clung stubbornly to the false premise that Tony Arzetti, Kinzi Tern, Greg Littlejack, and John Monroe were terrorists. Their rationale was that they were friends with Tom Horn and Vince Nalone so they must have been involved in the plot to assassinate the Pope, and might be a part of any future terrorist acts.

His dad told him that the only way he could prove their innocence was to find Panguitch Hewey. The best way to find him would be by joining the underground.

"You'll be able to find him and you'll be prepared for anything that might come up. I want you to be in the underground for the sake of your sisters and your mom too. Promise me you'll do that."

Mike promised, but it had taken Mike some time to find Henry Maples and the underground. Ann knew Henry from their classes at San Francisco State. Henry had asked her if she might be interested in joining. She wasn't, but she knew someone who was, and introduced her brother. Henry Maples ultimately led Mike to Nathan Conrad.

At seven that evening Mike Arzetti left his apartment on his journey to nowhere with the hope he might discover who was so interested in his life, praying he wouldn't have to kill him.

CHAPTER 13

Roy Cassidy was excited about finding the door, and decided to keep on watching it as often as he could. But he would have to observe from a distance, as there was no cover nearby.

He found a small niche in a wall a block away and hid there the first evening. His binoculars would bridge the gap for him. At seven-thirty he saw Mike Arzetti approaching. He was hurrying, and, as far as Roy could tell, didn't give the door so much as a glance. Roy wouldn't be fooled a second time. He would wait here until Arzetti returned.

He saw the second figure out of the corner of his eye and ducked before he could be observed. It was Arzetti's partner. What was George doing? This was getting interesting indeed.

Roy waited another two hours, but Arzetti didn't return. Why was someone else following Arzetti? If it were Internal Affairs they wouldn't use his partner. There was no reason to investigate Mike Arzetti. He had done nothing wrong.

Mike and George met at the Gordy's around ten that evening. Mike was surprised that there had been no one following him, but decided to try another evening anyway—one more time before he abandoned the idea.

George was inquisitive, wondering what it was all about. Mike didn't tell him about the underground, but did give him a plausible answer.

"All I can figure," Mike said, "is that it has something to do with my dad and that terrorist thing he was supposedly involved in. I visit my dad every week, so maybe they think I'm connected to it."

"What gave you the idea that someone might be following you?"

I don't know exactly," he lied, not mentioning the door, "I guess it was little things, furtiveness of people around me, and a good case of paranoia."

George Wildes listened to his friend and wondered if he was being told the full story. He wanted to believe his friend. He really did.

CHAPTER 14

The next evening, Mike Arzetti repeated his walk, but he changed his instructions to George Wildes. Without telling his friend why, he instructed him not to enter the alley where the door was located. George knew nothing about the door, and Mike wasn't going to tell him.

"I think that is where the guy most likely would pick up my trail if he's following me," is all he said about it. Mike had given some thought to it and had decided that if he were the guy he would watch the door to see who uses it.

So the trap was set. George followed but didn't enter the alley. Instead, he hid behind a dumpster. It was almost dark, an hour later, when George saw the figure emerge from the small niche in the wall, and follow Mike.

George wondered why the guy had waited so long. He could tell it was a large man in the darkness, but his features were indistinguishable. At the end of the alley, a lonely light bulb struggled to hold back the night. When the figure walked under it, George received the shock of his life. It was Sergeant Roy Cassidy.

Later, Mike Arzetti was just as shocked when George told him.

"So what are you going to do about it?" George asked.

"I don't know," Mike answered, knowing full well that he couldn't let it continue. Cassidy had something to do with getting his dad and Kinzi arrested. Mike was positive that he was up to no good. He was looking for something—a fishing expedition evidently, since he didn't know anything.

The thought of killing Roy Cassidy was repugnant; yet, he had sworn to do that to protect the underground if it became necessary. He knew he couldn't do it. Desperation would have to seize him, but he wasn't there yet.

Maybe he could talk to the man, find out what he wanted.

Mike visited his dad the following Saturday. Tony Arzetti was concerned, and warned against talking to Cassidy.

"He's doing it for personal reasons, has to be. He's the desk sergeant, and, the last I heard, they don't do investigations. He's fishing like you said. I would suggest that you continue like you know nothing about him."

"I'd like to, Dad, but the underground is going to insist that I do something, and if I don't, they will."

CHAPTER 15

Jordan received a call from DARPA on Monday morning telling her she could return to work. The problem had been resolved. They never said what the discrepancy had been, and she didn't ask.

Shires was relieved. His producer was screaming for him to come back to California, but he hated to leave Jordan so soon after renewing their relationship. They discussed it and Shires decided to divide his time between California and Washington D. C—two weeks in each place, unless he was otherwise involved.

One question bothered Shires. It `stuck in his mind as if it had been scrawled on a sticky note. *Why had DARPA settled so easily?* One moment they were ready to fire Jordan, and the next, all was forgiven. *Come on back to work.* He didn't want to mention his concern, figuring it wasn't necessary to worry her needlessly.

He returned to San Francisco on Monday, frustrated because his investigation into the video was at a standstill. Maria Sanger, his producer, called him early Tuesday morning.

You need to get started on the Harrigan probe. It's been hanging fire for months. I have done some background on it and Felix has done some camera work.

Shires promised he would attend to it immediately. William H (Hap) Harrigan was a real estate broker with large holdings throughout the state. The investigation was looking into his fraudulent claims about some of his properties. It mostly had to do with zoning—selling some property as commercial when it wasn't; that sort of thing. His cell phone interrupted his thoughts.

When he answered an unknown, insistent voice said, *Lampton, we need to talk.*

"What makes you think that?"

I'll tell you when we meet.

"Why would I meet with you?"

Are you interested in finding out what really happened when the Pope was assassinated?

"You mean that charade they put on for the public?"

...Yeah...whatever.

"Maybe; Who is this?"

I'll tell you when we meet, not before.

"Where and when?"

Board the ferry to Vallejo tomorrow at noon. I'll see you there.

"How will I know you?"

You won't. I'll know you. The line went dead.

Shires could only speculate as to what this guy might know, so he watched the video of the assassination of Pope Linus again. It was called assassination but the Pope was still alive. Cahmael had resurrected him from the dead. Technically he had been dead—pronounced so by three different doctors at the scene—hence the death penalty applied.

During their trial, Tom Horn and Vince Nalone claimed that they had been compelled by some force outside themselves to shoot the Pope. He studied each frame carefully, looking for any indication that they weren't operating under their own power.

He pictured marionettes being dragged along with their loose legs flopping behind them. He saw nothing of the sort. At one point, Tom Horn appeared to stumble, but righted himself immediately. That looked a little odd, but it was nothing to hang your hat on. It appeared that Tom's feet pointed to the ground for a split second, like he might be attempting to stand on his toes. It was only a momentary thing, and just might have been the camera angle for all Shires knew. Still, he noted it for further viewing.

The next day, Shires donned his sweats for the ferry ride. It would be chilly on the water in October. He snapped the fanny pack strap around his waist and headed for the elevator. He always carried a necessity bag when he had no pockets. Today, it also carried a tape recorder.

Shires jogged slowly to the ferry dock. The air was crisp with a bit of a chill. He paid the fare, round trip, walked to the observation deck, and sat down. He studied the faces of the other passengers, trying to memorize each one. Who was it? Which one had called him?

The ferry reached the middle of the Bay and still no contact. It docked on the Vallejo side without a word from the mysterious caller. *This would be the last time he would fall for a wild goose chase. What had he been thinking?* He waited an hour and caught the ferry home.

"Don't turn around," said a voice from behind him. "You seem upset. Sorry about that, but I had to be sure that you weren't followed."

"Why the cloak and dagger stuff?"

"To maintain our little secret. I'm going to tell you who I am, but I don't want you to see my face. I want you to know me by name only. Is that understood?"

"Any good reason for that?"

"I feel safer that way. I will contact you. You must never call me. Do you understand?"

"Yes."

My name is Mike Arzetti. I'm a San Francisco cop, my dad is Tony Arzetti, so you can see my interest in having you investigate the assassination and maybe proving his innocence. I can't do it alone."

"And you think I can help?"

"I know you can. With the information I'll give you, I think you'll be able to prove lots of things. I can't do it because of where I work. You can. Are you interested?"

Shires' skepticism kept him at bay, but he was intrigued by the prospect. "Okay, for the sake of argument, give me an interesting tidbit and let me be the judge."

"Ever hear of Panguitch Hewey?"

"No."

"My dad says he's the real terrorist. He had planned to assassinate Cahmael. He set up my dad and his friends as decoys. Something must have happened though, because his attack didn't take place. It's like he just disappeared."

"So how would my finding this man prove your dad's innocence?"

"According to Dad, Hewey had a camp out by Grass Valley called Armageddon. If you can find it, you might be able to find Hewey and maybe get some answers."

Their conversation ended abruptly when a stranger sat down nearby. Shires stood, walked to the side of the ferry, studied the water for a few moments, and then moved to a different seat. He glanced over. The stranger was there, but anyone who might have been Mike Arzetti had disappeared.

CHAPTER 16

Jehosea Cahmael is speaking for you when he answers the questions asked by the media, your Holiness, Cardinal Mencini had told Pope Linus

You mean those are my orders? Linus had asked.

Yes.

Cahmael had spoken to Linus about the possibility of ruling Europe from the Vatican. Linus had thought it would be as a figurehead only—never hands-on.

So, do you know why he ordered them, or rather why I ordered them, to move their ships to the Mediterranean?

Ships and troops, Your Holiness. It was for security during the dedication of the Temple in Jerusalem next May, Mencini had explained.

Already? Are we expecting trouble?

Always.

That conversation had haunted Linus ever since the day he had talked to the Cardinal about it. It was only October and the Mediterranean was overrun with troops from all over Europe. Ostensibly they were helping to keep the peace. But there was an ominous undercurrent about it. Distrust reared its ugly head.

In the United Nations the U S A, Britain, and China were expressing their concern over the amount of personnel and armament the European Union and Russia now had in the Middle East.

The United Nations Security Council is made up of fifteen members. There are five permanent members: the United States, Britain, France, Russia, and China—non-permanent members who serve a two-year term hold the other ten seats.

The United States Ambassador, Henry Genoe, said the troop buildup was disconcerting at the very least. He asked the Security Council to condemn the European Union for its aggressive behavior. The vote was ten to five against condemnation.

The United States, Britain, and China were the only permanent members who voted for the resolution. France and Russia voted against it, as did eight non-permanent members.

The news pleased Cahmael.

"Linus, my dear friend, we've won a battle and didn't have to fight for it," he said when they were alone in the Pope's study.

"Was winning the battle important?"

"Of course. We have the support of the majority of the world to do as we like in the Middle East."

"As we like? I thought the build-up was for the security of the temple dedication. That is what it's for…right?" asked the Pontiff. The implications of the whole affair upset him now, just as it had after his conversation with Cardinal Mencini.

"Of course it is. It's also a peacekeeping mission. There are many uses for it. Don't worry my friend it is all for the good and everything is about willing the good, but there is another matter I need to discuss with you."

"Yes?"

"It's about the underground church."

"Underground church? What are you talking about?"

"Remember the underground church from back in the days of the Roman Empire?"

"Yes. It's the foundation of the church. It's how we started."

"Well, how would you feel about another one?"

"There can't be another one. There is only one church."

"Not according to these people."

"Who are they?"

"Disgruntled misfits who claim that I'm the Antichrist. I am accused of heading a conspiracy to silence all those who oppose me—like the two men who assassinated you."

"That's terrible. I thought those two were isolated cases."

"I wish that were so."

"What can we do to stop them?" the Pontiff asked. He walked to the window and stared into the courtyard below.

"Make it difficult for them to exist." Cahmael answered as he walked to his side.

The mere thought that Cahmael was the Lord sometimes took Linus's breath away. He was breathless now with Cahmael standing beside him.

"How can we do that?" It was almost a whisper, but all that Linus could muster under the present circumstance.

"By requiring everyone to have the chip implanted. They couldn't buy or sell anything without it. With the technology we have we would also know the location of every implanted person. We have the program in place now, but only on a voluntary basis. We could change that and make it a requirement for the sake of security, and the prevention of identity theft.

"I would like for you to make a plea for the opposition to cease and desist or dire consequences will befall them. You know how to say it tactfully, and say it during one of your weekday sermons. Then we'll start with the new program in Europe and let it spread around the world."

Pope Linus was silent for a long time before he finally nodded his head.

CHAPTER 17

Roy Cassidy had taken a month's leave of absence. He claimed he needed a rest. His real reason was to watch Mike Arzetti more closely. He was about to discover something. He just knew it. His gut told him so.

On Wednesday morning, he followed Mike to the ferry and watched him board. He didn't follow because of the limited space aboard the boat—too easy to be discovered.

He waited for him to return instead. Almost three hours later he did, alone. Roy waited a while longer to see who else might have been aboard, but saw no one until, at the very end, he noticed the TV reporter, Shires Lampton. *Could Mike have been talking to him?*

He racked his brain for an answer to that question and found none. Mike's partner, George, had been following him, and now maybe he's meeting with Shires Lampton—curiouser and curiouser.

Here's a San Francisco cop whose father's in jail for being a terrorist, sneaking around, slipping through secret doors, talking to a TV reporter. What does all that add up to?

It was late in the afternoon when Roy stopped at a sports bar for a hamburger. The TV blared, making it difficult to hold a conversation, which was all right with him. He had no need to talk to anyone. He wanted to think.

His contemplation was interrupted by an argument that broke out three tables over.

"Man, shut up about the underground!" shouted a heavy-set man.

"Look, I have a friend that belongs to it. It's all about church and stuff. He's a religious guy. Says Cahmael is the devil, and that's how he raised the Pope from the dead—stuff like that. He says they're going to require a computer chip to be implanted in everybody and that will be the Mark of the Beast like it says in the Bible," said a slender man.

Roy listened intently.

"That's a crock. They can't do that. It's an invasion of privacy," said another

"Well, I'm not gettin' the chip," said another.

"What chip? What are you talking about?" asked a fourth.

"The chip he's talking about is supposed to be the Mark of the Beast, but they'll say it's for security, and that it will protect you from identity theft," said a man who had just joined the conversation.

"I heard that they've made it mandatory in Europe, and Homeland Security wants it to be the same here. Congress is working on a bill right now," the newcomer added.

"Well, I'm not going to have anything to do with it," said the heavy-set man who had started the argument.

Roy chuckled at their conversation. The fools didn't know when they were well off. The chip was only for their protection, nothing more. The Mark of the Beast was all a bunch of crap. Cahmael raising the Pope from the dead was a set up. Cahmael had no more supernatural power then he did. All these religious nuts were way out of step with the rest of the world. They couldn't accept new technology no matter how much it might improve their lives. They have to demonize it and make it bad like they did with Cahmael.

Roy couldn't wait for the chip to be mandatory. It would make his job a whole lot easier. All you'd have to do is log on to the national ID database at the Office of Screening Coordination and Operations at Homeland Security—this office oversees databases of digital fingerprints and photographs, eye scans and personal information from millions of American citizens. Then all you have to do is type in the name of the person you want. It would instantly tell you the person's location, as well as where he had been since the day he received the chip. What a way to fight crime.

Roy injected himself into the conversation. "I've been listening to you and did I hear you say that the underground thinks that the chip is the mark of the beast?" he asked as innocently as possible, while seating himself next to the group.

"Not the underground, the underground church."

"Is there a difference?" Roy asked.

"I don't know. Do any of you guys?" the fellow asked looking around the group.

They all shook their heads.

"I thought they were the same," one said.

"So the underground church believes that the chip is the Mark of the Beast. What do you think?" Roy asked.

"You tell us. If you can't buy or sell anything without it what would you call it?" asked the heavy-set man.

"I'd say it's a computer chip injected under the skin and not a mark at all. It's something like taxes, a necessary evil that you'll need to buy and sell things—like a sales number. There's nothing heebee-jeebee about it. It's just like they say. It's protection for you, and that's all it is," Roy answered.

"I happen to think it's the Mark of the Beast," said the heavy-set man. "After all, Cahmael did raise the Pope from the dead."

"It was all smoke and mirrors, staged to fool the world into believing that, but it wasn't true," Roy said.

"And how do you know that?" asked the heavy-set man.

"You actually believe that somebody can come back from the dead?" Roy asked.

"Sure, can't you?"

"No I can't."

"I saw it on TV that day. I'm convinced."

"I saw it too and I'm not."

"So you're going to get the chip?"

"Of course," Roy said. "I'm a cop. I don't have a choice."

CHAPTER 18

Grass Valley is set in the mountains of Northern California. It's a picturesque mountain community The hills and forest that encompass it are a part of the Sierra Nevada Range that forms a rib-like barrier on the eastern side of the state .

Two days had passed since Shires had the ferry conversation with Mike Arzetti. By coming to Grass Valley, he was accomplishing two goals: investigating the real estate holdings of one Hap Harrigan, and checking out a man named Panguitch Hewey at his Camp named Armageddon.

Harrigan liked to buy in mountain communities where the separation between private and commercial property was somewhat blurred due to the vagueness of the zoning laws. In some communities there were no zoning laws and property was whatever the owner said it was. Shires had a list of ten questionable properties.

His first stop was at the Harrigan Real Estate office located in an old house set between two residences—an odd location for an office since it seemed to be on residential property, not commercial.

Shires knew he could be recognized, so his cover story was that he was looking for commercial property for a friend who wanted to start a business in the area. He was also looking for the location of Camp Armageddon, and needed directions.

A large map covered most of one wall, showing the town and the surrounding area. The lone saleswoman running the office introduced herself as Shirley Golden. If she knew who he was she made no mention of it. She gave Shires a list of ten locations he could look at for his friend. Then she pointed to a location on the map halfway between Hills Flat and Glenbrook.

"Camp Armageddon is right around there—give or take a mile or so. You get close, you'll find it, or they'll find you—one way or the other. You sure you want to go there? Those people aren't very friendly."

"Why do you say that?"

"Because they aren't. Ever since about a year ago, maybe a little longer. You remember they had all that trouble in San Francisco with the assassination of the Pope?"

"Yes."

"It seems like everything at the camp changed then. They used to be friendly," she said and paused for a moment. "Well, friendlier than they are now anyway. They've become suspicious of everybody. I don't know that suspicion is the right word either, but they're definitely stand-offish."

"Do you think they'll talk to me?"

"I wouldn't bet on it. I guess you could try though. One of the properties on the list I gave you is out in that direction."

Shires thanked her, climbed in his Jeep, and drove east on Highway 174 toward Hills Flat. Three questionable properties lay in that direction. Shires couldn't say that the property might be illegally represented as commercial, as was the location of the real estate office he'd just left, but he could note it as property to be checked further in the County Recorder's office. He felt there was a definite problem with the real estate office since it appeared to be nestled in a residential area.

The three other properties looked to be somewhat questionable, so he marked them for further investigation, and went looking for the turnoff to Camp Armageddon.

He tried four different side roads, but found nothing. He was ready to give up when he saw recent vehicle tracks. He followed them, driving slowly, and came to a gate that blocked his path.

The gate was a one-pole affair laid horizontally across the road about three feet off the ground, and cradled in the crotch of a tree on each side. The pole was a heavy tree trunk that had been skinned of its bark and trimmed down to a more slender size. Still it took all his strength to lift it out and lay it aside. He supposed it would have been a two-man job on a usual day.

Shires had driven another quarter of a mile when he came to a dry creek bed. The tire tracks disappeared. He was searching among the rocks for a sign when a shot rang out and a bullet sprayed him with rock chips from a nearby boulder.

He ducked behind a large boulder yelling, "Hey! Don't shoot! I'm Shires Lampton. I've come to talk to the people of Camp Armageddon."

CHAPTER 19

Shires crouched behind the boulder for what seemed to be an eternity before a tall man dressed in camouflage fatigues stepped out of the trees. He leveled an automatic weapon at Shires.

"Who are you?" he asked.

"Shires Lampton. I'm a TV reporter."

"What are you doin' here?"

"I came to talk to Panguitch Hewey."

"Why?"

"I have some questions I'd like to ask him."

A cell phone chimed. The man pulled it from his pocket, flipped it open and said "Yeah."

He listened for a moment then said, "Some guy. He claims he's Shires Lampton; wants to talk to the boss. I was just sending him away." He listened again and then said, "Okay."

He lowered his weapon a little and motioned for Shires to follow him. Shires breathed easier, knowing he wouldn't be shot. He followed the man through the trees, away from the dry creek bed, and up a path only noticeable if you knew where to look.

The guide stopped suddenly, turned, and handed Shires a black hood.

"Slip this over your head," he said.

Shires followed instructions and then stood unmoving not knowing what to do next. He felt helpless and wondered if coming here had been such a good idea.

"Put your right arm out in front of you!"

Again, Shires did as he was told. His hand touched the man's shoulder.

"Now keep your hand there while we walk!"

They walked slowly for what Shires figured was an hour, give or take a few minutes.

"You can remove the hood now."

The brightness of the sunlight made Shires squint until his eyes adjusted. They were standing in an empty clearing. Shires saw nothing that he could identify as a camp. Two men dressed similarly to his guide were waiting with their weapons slung over their shoulders. They could just as well have been members of a military unit. Shires didn't think either man was Hewey—both were too young.

"Exactly why do you want to see Mr. Hewey?" asked the man who seemed to be in charge.

"Some friends of mine were accused of being terrorists and are being held in jail. I'd like Mr. Hewey to clarify their involvement."

"What makes you think he'd know?"

"My friends claim they were brought to San Francisco by Mr. Hewey as part of a scheme to kill the Antichrist. Hewey then told the police the six of them were the terrorists who planned to kill the Pope and cause a lot of bloodshed. They would like Mr. Hewey to contact the authorities and tell them the truth. Now, I understand that won't do much good since nobody will believe him, but it is a start."

"Toward what?"

"Proving their innocence. Also, they wanted to know what happened and why the attack never happened?"

"We'll let you speak with Mr. Hewey. That might answer all your questions," the man said. Then he turned away and motioned for Shires to follow.

They walked through the door of a cavern that appeared to have been dug out of the side of the mountain. The room they entered was an assembly area with tables and benches. It looked like a large dining hall. A kitchen was off to one side. Food was being prepared as they passed.

The hallway was dark and led to a room dimly lit by one candle. A man lay on the bed. A woman stood beside him holding a cloth in her hand.

"Mr. Hewey, this is the man we found wandering around by the gate."

There was a grunt of affirmation from the man on the bed. He mumbled something Shires didn't understand. The guard seemed to understand for he answered. "He wants to know why you stopped the attack on the Antichrist."

More mumbling emanated from the prone figure.

"You want me to tell him?"

"Uh huh," was the reply. Even Shires understood the affirmation.

"The day that was supposed to be a glorious day," the guard explained. "The day that we would do God's work and destroy the Antichrist. The very day our great leader was felled by a stroke that completely incapacitated him. This happened moments before the attack was to begin. We were not prepared for that contingency so we were forced to abandon our plan."

The woman wiped the man's mouth. That's when Shires realized Panguitch Hewey was paralyzed.

CHAPTER 20

Michael Arzetti knew Roy Cassidy had followed him to the ferry. He watched to see if he boarded. When he was sure he hadn't, he kept his rendezvous with Shires Lampton.

Cassidy's presence was becoming a nuisance for Mike. Other members of the underground were concerned as well—they urged Mike to put an end to it immediately.

Mike couldn't bring himself to kill the police sergeant and decided, against his dad's advice, to talk to him. What would be the harm in telling him he knew what he was doing and would he please stop? His friends in the underground didn't like the idea, but they humored Mike and told him to try, but do it quickly.

Mike chose to confront Roy in the alley where the door was located. It would be deserted and they could be alone.

He started from his apartment around seven that evening, taking his time so he would be easy to follow. Halloween decorations were everywhere announcing the upcoming arrival of ghosts and goblins. Jack-o-lanterns smiled from every porch. The homes looked cheery and bright, awaiting the trick-or-treaters who would arrive in a week or so.

He hated to enter the alley and leave the cheerfulness he found in the Halloween decorations behind. It was dull and dreary between the buildings, like the mission he sought to accomplish.

He exited at the far end and immediately dodged behind a dumpster to await Roy's arrival. He heard footsteps approaching.

Roy Cassidy wasn't expecting Mike Arzetti to be waiting for him anywhere. He believed he had the upper hand when it came to surveillance, so the sight of Mike waiting for him was a stunning turn of events.

"Roy," Mike said as if greeting an old friend, but instead of asking, "How are you?" he asked, "What the hell are you doing following me?"

It was unexpected and Roy had no answer. He mumbled something before he blurted, "I'm looking out for you."

"Really? Why would you be looking out for me?"

"Somebody has to, hell, your own partner is following you. What do you think that's all about?"

"I don't know what that's all about," he lied, "but you need to explain your own behavior. Leave my partner out of it. And don't tell me you're looking out for me! That's a lie. You know it and I know it."

A long silence ensued while Roy thought over what he should say next. Not knowing his life depended on it, or that Mike was trying to save him, Roy continued the antagonistic attitude. He had been a policeman too long to be intimidated by circumstance, or a rookie cop.

"What I do on my own time is strictly my business," he said. "If you want to know the truth I think you're up to something that involves your dad, and I'm planning to prove it. I'll catch you when your guard is down."

"Roy, I'm warning you to stop following me."

"What? What? You're threatening me?"

"I'm not threatening you. I'm telling you that it would be in your best interest to stop—that's all."

The words no more than left his mouth when a shot rang out. Roy fell dead at Mike's feet. Mike drew his weapon as a reflex and scanned the area for a sniper. His cell phone rang. He was sure he knew who was calling. He answered it.

Get out of there! Turn around and walk away! Go right now!

CHAPTER 21

The thing about information is how little of it you have, compared to how much is readily available. The important thing is to gather and understand it.

Rumors surrounding the shooting of Officer Roy Cassidy flew like a gathering of flies on dead meat. The main story was that a sniper was shooting policemen. They were all told to be aware of where they were when they answered a call. "Assess the area as you drive up to the scene," warned the shift supervisor.

Warning after warning led to paranoia. Incidents between police and the public increased as tempers flared. Michael Arzetti knew the truth, but couldn't tell it, not without incriminating himself.

His partner, George Wildes, knew part of it. He knew the part about Roy Cassidy following Mike. Being a good partner, he had never asked why. That was Mike's perspective about what his partner might know. It remained so until the morning, two days after the shooting, when George tossed the notebook into his lap. They were in the locker room getting dressed for patrol.

"What's this?"

"Read it."

Inside the cover it read—PROPERTY OF ROY CASSIDY—and somehow, without reading any farther, Mike knew he was in trouble. But he read on.

May 4th—Today I have taken on the burden of investigating Michael Arzetti. I think I see things about him that no one else does. It's a gut feeling so I'm going to go with it. I'm good at gut feelings.

May 10th—I can't write here every day. I'll do what I can—nothing so far. I don't think I'm wrong.

Mike skimmed quickly through the pages reading only the sentences highlighted by a yellow marker.

August 19th—Discovered a door tonight in the alley off of Maple Street where Arzetti always seems to disappear.

And the other one highlighted was *October 9th—George Wildes is following Mike—curiouser and curiouser.*

He tossed the notebook in his locker as nonchalantly as possible. The cat was out of the bag with his partner and now he needed to put it back.

Neither man said anything until they started to leave.

"I think it would be a good idea to bring the notebook along in case we find a good place to ditch it," George suggested.

Mike stared at him for a moment and then, as if finally understanding what his partner had said, retrieved the notebook from his locker. Later in the car, Mike asked how he came to have it in his possession.

"It was lying on the desk out front. I was being nosey and paged through it. I realized it was something you should see. I don't know who laid it there, or if anybody else read it. I do know one thing, if you get rid of it, it'll be your word against theirs."

"How'd you know it wasn't a setup?"

"They were cleaning out his desk. It didn't seem to me that anyone was paying attention to what they were putting out there. Like they didn't really care and just wanted to get it cleared out.

"One thing's for sure, if anybody read it and put two and two together, you might be in more than a little trouble."

Mike laughed an empty laugh. "That's the understatement of the year," he said.

"You've gotta be honest with me Mike, did you kill him?"

"No! No! No! A thousand times no. I swear I did not kill him. You've gotta believe that."

"It is connected with you though…right?"

Mike thought for a long time before answering. He debated about telling George the truth. In the midst of his thoughts, the radio broke the silence with a public disturbance call. Mike hit the gas, turned on the flashing lights, and raced to the scene only three blocks away.

An hour later, with both parties satisfied—two neighbors had disagreed over their property line and how far the other's dog was allowed to roam—Mike and George were back on the road.

"I don't know whether you know this or not, Mike, but Roy was killed in the same alley where I spotted him following you—the very same alley. What a coincidence!"

Mike couldn't tell whether his friend was joking or not. He smiled wryly and agreed that it was a great coincidence. If Mike told George the truth and he agreed not to tell, that would make George an accomplice to murder. If George didn't go along, he could turn Mike in for the same thing. Mike decided on the truth, figuring that if George were going to give him up he would have done it long before now.

"Okay, George, here it is—the complete unvarnished truth."

Mike left out nothing, covering from the time he joined the underground all the way to the killing of Cassidy.

George listened and remained quiet long after Mike had finished. The silence bothered Mike. Finally, after an hour or so, George spoke.

"I suppose you have to kill me now that I know the truth," he said then chuckled and went on. "A comfortable answer to our dilemma would be it I join you in the underground. Otherwise we might end up being at odds with one another. What do you think, partner?"

For the first time since they had climbed in the car some four hours earlier, Mike Arzetti relaxed a little.

"Sounds good to me, partner; by the way, were you the one who highlighted those entries?" Mike asked almost as an afterthought.

"No. If it wasn't Roy, it had to be somebody else."

Mike didn't want to hear that. Now he had to worry that a third person knew his secret.

CHAPTER 22

Shires returned from Grass Valley the night before Halloween. He busied himself with compiling a report for his producer about Hap Harrigan's holdings. The report didn't satisfy him. He could have done better, but his attempt at investigating the holdings of the man had been only half-hearted. The story belonged to his producer. He felt no commitment to it.

An unexpected call came from Jordan. Her excited voice filled his ear. The information about the evaporation of the bodies in the video had been released. The effect had been caused by new battlefield technology, which was designed to clear enemy bodies from the battlefield by disintegrating them, saving the time consuming work of mass burials. They never used it. The bodies of Vince and Tom were utilized as one of their many tests. All the video should have been confiscated, but somehow they had missed the one that Shires received.

It pleased Shires that his own theory had been vindicated. His theory claimed Cahmael was not the Devil, only a mere mortal like the rest of us. The assassination of the Pope had been staged. The Pope never died—thus never resurrected. Poor Tom Horn and Vince Nalone had been victimized by what appeared to be a much larger conspiracy.

Jordan also had new information about a list of millions of names under the purview of DARPA and their Total Information Awareness Program—a supposedly defunct program that never went defunct. Personal information about each and every person named would be transferred onto microchips to be injected into the rightful owner.

It's not a secret program anymore. It'll soon be put into effect on a nation-wide basis; the rationale being identity theft prevention. But Boo, the scary part is the chip will also be a locator. They'll know where you are all the time. Isn't that an invasion of privacy?

Shires considered the whole microchip idea to be an invasion of privacy. The government didn't need to know everything about its' citizens and, as far as identity theft, he felt the problem had been greatly exaggerated.

They talked for a bit longer and with Shires promising he would visit next week, they bid each other farewell.

Shires sat for a moment staring at nothing in particular, thinking of the disappointment some religious folks might feel when they heard the evaporation of the bodies had been a man-made process—nothing angelic about it.

He thought of Malcolm Tubbs at the Administrative Offices of the Resurrection Church of Christ, found his name on his cell, and punched it. He had promised Mr. Tubbs an answer. He now had a definitive, scientific one.

This is Malcolm Tubbs, the voice said.

"Malcolm, this is Shires Lampton the man with the video showing evaporating bodies."

Yes Mr. Lampton.

"This is straight from the horse's mouth. It's man-made technology that clears the battlefield of the bodies of dead enemy soldiers by disintegrating them."

Thank God you've found a logical explanation. I can't thank you enough for letting me know. If this had really been something unexplainable I would have had to reassess my religious beliefs. Thanks again.

"No problem," Shires said, closing his phone.

A few hours later Shires was busy finishing the real estate story of Hap Harrigan when his cell phone vibrated.

It was a strange voice, almost a whisper. *Was the video interesting?* it asked.

"What a coincidence you called today. I just received word about it. I don't know if you thought it might be a spiritual happening, or what you thought. It's simply a man-made technology that disintegrates the bodies of dead enemy soldiers left on the battlefield. They were testing it. Those two bodies happened to be one of their many tests."

A long silence followed. *Who told you that?*

"DARPA declassified the information this week."

I'm disappointed in you. I thought you would do a thorough investigation. Instead you take the word of a government entity. The government isn't going to tell you the truth. They're lying. I don't know why, but they are. My friend, I was there that day. I saw the looks on their faces when it happened. I'm telling you right now, you'd better dig deeper because it wasn't a test.

CHAPTER 23

Shires awoke the next morning with the mysterious caller's words ringing in his ears. *I was there it was not a test.* The attitude of the mysterious caller had angered him, but he didn't get a chance for rebuttal. After the tirade the phone went dead. Shires didn't believe him. The idea was outlandish and unscientific. The guy was pushing hard for the event to be called a miracle from God—the usual stuff of myths and fables. All it takes is one claiming to be an eyewitness, and whoosh, off it goes—spreading like wildfire.

The claim would be the Lord took Tom Horn and Vince Nalone directly to Heaven. The Bible says He took the angels killed by the Antichrist the same way. Thus, by simple deduction, Tom and Vince were angels, so Cahmael must be the Prince of Darkness. The video had been left for the world to behold.

Shires would have none of it. He had to speak out against it. That was when the germ of a story called The Antichrist Myth dropped into his mind.

The phone interrupted him.

Can you meet me today, same time same place? I need to see you again, it said.

Shires recognized Michael Arzetti's voice, but said nothing.

"I'm right in the middle of a project. How long will it take?"

About the same as last time…Three hours…tops.

Shires reluctantly agreed and left immediately for the ferry landing. They met on the observation platform with Shires sitting in front and Mike behind. Shires knew Arzetti only from the one clandestine meeting they had earlier—the one that sent him looking for Panguitch

Hewey. Shires figured that was the reason for this meeting, but didn't understand the urgency.

"Thanks for coming so quickly."

"No problem. I'm not that far away. I talked to Panguitch Hewey about his failure to attack. That very day he had a stroke and he never attacked. He's completely paralyzed. He can talk, but not plainly. He has to have an interpreter. I doubt if he'll ever tell anybody anything."

"Well, that might have become a moot point. The underground is hearing rumors that there is a program to be started after the first of the year that will release prisoners. Have you heard of such a thing?"

"No."

"How about a video showing Tom Horn and Vince Nalone being taken directly to heaven? I saw their bodies just disappear into thin air."

"It's a hoax perpetrated by somebody. I don't know by whom, but it's definitely a hoax. The Department of Defense says it's new battlefield technology to get rid of dead bodies. That's what I believe it is. There is some guy claiming he was there and saw it happen. I don't know who he is, but I don't believe him."

"A fella named Nathan Conrad came to our underground meeting the other night. He showed us a video. He claimed he gave you a copy of the same video and you showed it to the government. He claimed he was there and saw the bodies disappear—said it wasn't a hoax. He said you said it was new battlefield technology."

"It is. A friend of mine works for DARPA and that's the official word from them."

"Conrad says the government is lying."

"Of course he would say that. He wants you to believe that Cahmael is the Antichrist. If those two bodies were taken into heaven it's a strong case for that, but don't be fooled. Are you in the underground because of religion?"

"No, but most people are. Those at the meeting the other night believed Conrad's story."

"Don't let yourself get sucked in. That's all I can tell you. I'll check out that other rumor about a prisoner release. Anything else?"

There was no answer. Mike Arzetti had gone.

CHAPTER 24

Pope Linus III stood on the balcony above the courtyard waving to the crowd below. It was his favorite way to pass an afternoon, especially one this close to the holidays. He believed in being a visible Pope, trying mightily to emulate his idol, Pope John Paul II.

"Pardon me for disturbing you, Your Holiness, but Lord Cahmael has a question that must be dealt with immediately," Cardinal Mencini said.

Pope Linus quickly blessed the gathering and hurried to follow the Cardinal. Jehosea Cahmael was waiting in the conference room.

Cardinal Mencini excused himself and left.

Cahmael wasted no time. "The United States is dragging its feet on the prison reform you suggested."

"How's that?"

"It has instituted a time frame in conjunction with the injection of the chip for everybody. The injections and the prison reform in the United States both begin on the first of March of next year. That's not soon enough."

"My Lord, your powers of persuasion are formidable. I refer you to what you did in the Middle East. I suggest you do the same."

Cahmael smiled. He'd been itching to treat the first-term President to some serious persuasion. He had refrained because he was a good ally.

President Butcher had a mind of his own. To Cahmael's knowledge he asked for counsel from no one. He wasn't about to take orders from the United Nations or from Cahmael.

"Dear Linus I would ask for your help on this. It must look to the world as if we are putting no pressure whatsoever on the man. He will reject our suggestions otherwise."

"How can I help, my Lord?"

"Call him. Ask him to meet here with us regarding some subject that is benign, but important…"

"Such as…?"

"His appearance and speech at the dedication of the Temple of Solomon."

"I didn't know he was speaking."

"I'm not saying he is either, but that will be the advertised topic of our conversation with him. You call him and then put out a press release that he has been invited to the Vatican for that discussion. Do it as quickly as possible."

When President Butcher received the call he accepted the invitation from His Holiness, saying he would come immediately.

After he hung up he sat for a moment wondering what might be the real reason for the invitation. This was the first he had heard he might be speaking at the dedication. An invitation from the Pope was also an invitation from Cahmael. He didn't trust Cahmael even if he was close to the Pope.

He shrugged off the doubt and called his head of security to arrange the trip.

CHAPTER 25

Mike Arzetti was excited about the possibility of a prisoner release. Even if his dad had to be injected with the chip, it would be better than rotting in prison. According to Nathan Conrad, the chip implantation could be undone. Mike hadn't mentioned that to Shires Lampton. Shires had never said whether he agreed with the underground or not, so Mike was wary about any disclosures he made to the man.

Mike hadn't known until after he joined, that the underground existed to protect and hide the members from the Antichrist. He had joined at his father's suggestion as a precaution against future emergencies such as being unable to buy food—things like that. Now, with the possibility of his dad being released, he was glad he had followed that advice.

The underground was a very loose-knit web of people—some lived on the fringe of society, others lived normal lives. They were invisible. The only way you could say they were organized was that they had a secret sign of recognition—a half arc. Two half-arcs placed together would make a picture of a fish. They used only the half-arc and never completed the fish. The fish was a sign used by the early Christians of the Roman Empire days. It was not the sign for the present-day underground, but they let outsiders believe that it was. Thus they could weed-out any spies who might try to infiltrate.

They all, with some exceptions, believed Cahmael to be the Antichrist, and to swear allegiance to him meant eternal damnation. This view would cause problems when it came time to lie about swearing allegiance to Cahmael when getting the chip injection.

The question was simple; could you swear false allegiance—not really mean it in your heart and not be eternally damned? Mike thought so, but he didn't have anything riding on the outcome like the religious folks. They believed any capitulation to the Antichrist was a denial of Christ. They couldn't do it and would have to suffer the consequences, just like Tom Horn and Vince Nalone. For them there were no shades of gray—no middle ground; no compromise, and no excuses.

Mike knew his dad felt the same as he did. Tony Arzetti would jump at the chance to get out of jail, and said so the day Mike told him of the impending release.

"Can you get a message to Kinzi through the underground? Tell her to take the deal and I'll see her soon," Tony said.

Mike had been unable to visit Kinzi because of the terrorist charges against his dad and her. He could only visit one. He chose his dad, of course. He assured Tony that he would get the message to her.

"The problem with your dad and his girlfriend joining the underground is twofold," Nathan Conrad told Mike later. "First, they're accused terrorists so they'll be watched extra close after their release. Second, they will have already been chipped so they'll be easy to follow."

Mike assured him that all the details would be worked out and the secrecy of the underground wouldn't be compromised.

But Nathan Conrad gave him a dire warning. "I believe," he said, "that this prisoner release is nothing more than a trap to track down the underground on a worldwide basis. Cahmael knows contact will be made with the underground. He's counting on it. Therein lies the danger to all of us."

CHAPTER 26

President Richard R. Butcher stared from the window of Air Force One as it landed at Leonardo Da Vinci Airport 32 kilometers west of Rome. They left Dulles International at 4pm yesterday and, after 8 hrs 44 minutes of flight time, arrived at 9 44 this Thursday morning.

President Butcher liked to sleep while he flew. Flying was boring; however, he hadn't slept much on this flight. His mind worked overtime on what he considered to be one of the best speeches he had ever written, and he had written many, and was proud of that. If history were going to remember him as a great President, it would also be as a literate one. He especially liked his reference to the Dome of the Rock and the Temple of Solomon as being the *bookends to peace on earth—a monument to the efforts of Jehosea Cahmael—the peacemaker of all peacemakers.* He knew Cahmael would like that.

The plane taxied to the far side of the airport away from the main terminal. A line of black SUV's snaked its way toward them like a six-sectioned centipede. The President watched the proceedings in an aloof manner, slightly disinterested. He wished his wife Lydia had come, but she had other commitments that she couldn't cancel on such short notice. He was disappointed about that, but he was ready for Jehosea Cahmael.

The reception was grand. Pope Linus III received him while sitting on his throne. He wore his soft crown for the occasion. In fact he never wore the heavier gold one. He supposed there might be a time when he would, but he didn't know what that event might be. The soft crown was no more than a cap—nothing regal about it, but it was comfortable.

President Butcher dutifully knelt and properly kissed the ring on the

Pontiff's hand—a distasteful chore he observed for ceremonial purposes only. He bowed his knee to no man, nor God, his representative, or any other deity. This was a fact about himself that he never disclosed to anyone. In fact, Lydia didn't know. He had always attended church with her, but she was completely unaware he was an atheist. Even the fundamentalists who loved him so dearly were unaware. They believed God had sent him—a belief he never discouraged. He was a politician above all else. Lies didn't bother him.

Pope Linus III talked with the President for a few moments and then they were guided to the conference room where Cahmael awaited their arrival.

"President Butcher, I've heard so much about you. I'm honored to make your acquaintance," Cahmael said graciously.

"It is I who am honored, my Lord," Butcher answered just as graciously.

Butcher watched Cahmael warily as they shook hands. He had never seen the man before and was surprised by his height—well over six feet. The man was handsomely dark with his Middle Eastern heredity. His infectious smile flashed with pearly white teeth. He was in his early thirties, and immaculately dressed in a blue suit, white shirt with no tie. To Richard Butcher he didn't look formidable at all—on the contrary, he looked absolutely friendly, almost compliant and ready to please. Butcher had handled many political foes. Jehosea Cahmael would be no different.

Cahmael read the confidence exhibited by his guest's body language and smiled inwardly. Butcher was a man who expected to get his way. In his sixties with a full head of gray hair, he looked Presidential standing there with his gray Armani suit covering his six-foot frame. A blue shirt and a red, white and blue striped tie completed his ensemble. Here stood the President of the United States presiding over the greatest superpower in the history of mankind. At his fingertips lay more destructive power than could ever be imagined. He was an adversary to be reckoned with.

"Have you given some thought to our request that you speak at the dedication of the Temple?" Cahmael asked.

"Yes I have. It would be a great honor, my Lord. But why would you want me to speak?"

"The United States was the first country in the United Nations to recognize Israel as an independent country. It would be fitting for you to speak. After all, it will be another momentous occasion in the history of Israel."

"Then I accept your invitation on behalf of my country. I will have the Secretary of State draw up the letter of acceptance when I return."

"There is another matter I'd like to discuss with you. It has to do with the chip injection and the prisoner release, which you have scheduled for next year."

"Yes. They are coordinated to start the first of March. We can inject the prisoners as we release them."

"Why then? Why not sooner?" Cahmael asked rather abruptly.

The President liked neither Cahmael's tone nor his attitude. No one challenged him. He made the decisions and other people complied.

"I beg your pardon. What difference could that possibly make to you?" Butcher retorted.

"A difference of four months. I want it started now," Cahmael said matter-of-factly.

Butcher didn't believe he was hearing this. Who did this man think he was, telling him how to run his own country. He didn't answer. Cahmael spoke again.

"You say your reason for delaying is to coordinate, but I know your true reason is to allow your friends to maximize their profits on the stock market. First the bad news that Saravan Drugs is seeking protection under Chapter Eleven of the bankruptcy act, so the stock price will drop. Then your friends buy it and voila, wonder of wonders, Saravan Drugs is awarded the contract to supply all the syringes and paraphernalia for the injection program. Then the stock rises to be sold at a tidy profit. Isn't that how it works?"

Again Butcher didn't answer. That Cahmael knew his plan surprised him.

"You know, Mr. President, it was greedy men like you that brought the world to its knees. All of you were given a great responsibility, but none of you could get past your greed. What amazes me is that you're still doing it. This time you'll have to forego the profit and do something for the good of the people. I insist that you start the injection program immediately. Forget about the stock market ploy".

"My plans have been made. I'll likely not change," he replied. Richard

Butcher didn't like to be told what to do. He wasn't going to change his plans. That was final.

Cahmael's countenance never changed. He knew the man would refuse. Very quietly he said, "Call your wife."

"Why would I want to do that?"

"Get her opinion."

"I never confer with my wife on any decision."

"You should on this one."

"I don't think so."

"Please. Consult your wife."

Cardinal Mencini entered. "Pardon me for interrupting. There is an urgent phone call for the President," he said pointing to the phone that sat atop the desk. The President picked it up.

"Hello."

Mr. President. The First Lady has been rushed to the hospital. We don't know at the moment, but it appears she may have had a heart attack.

CHAPTER 27

The murder of Roy Cassidy wasn't going away any time soon. The department had sworn to get the killer of one of its own. Mike Arzetti tried to ignore the turmoil of the investigation going on around him. He concentrated on his job of policing the streets, and preparing for his dad's release from jail sometime in the future.

But that changed one November morning. He was passing through the squad room and overheard Ron Alvarez, the lead detective in the Cassidy murder case, say to another investigator. "We've traced the bullet to a rifle belonging to a Marine sniper, Alan Noble. He was one of the deputies who helped free Tom Horn and Vince Nalone from custody over in Arizona. He dropped off the grid right after that. We think he's with the underground now."

Mike didn't linger, and hurried to the locker room where he found his partner, George Wildes, dressing for his shift. Mike changed quickly.

George had joined the underground a few days after the death of Roy Cassidy. Later that morning, he told George what he had heard. George listened intently, saying nothing.

"How well do you know this Alan Noble?" George asked finally.

"Don't. I've never seen the man, but if he helped those guys escape, I'll bet my dad knew him."

The following Saturday Mike asked his dad about Alan Noble.

"We left him behind when we escaped from Flagstaff. Time was short, couldn't wait," Tony Arzetti told his son.

"Do you think we should warn him?" Mike asked.

"Don't know if we can. I don't know where he is. Your friend, Shires

Lampton, ask him. He interviewed Tom and Vince at our camp. He might have a contact or two."

Mike didn't know whether he could call Shires a friend or not. Shires had found Panguitch Hewey for him and that definitely took some effort, so he asked for a third meeting.

Shires hadn't had time to check on the prisoner release when he received the call from Mike, and wondered what could be so urgent. He had been putting his affairs in order so he could spend a couple weeks with Jordan, but he always had time for Mike Arzetti.

Shires had never heard of Alan Noble. Mike was disappointed.

"So, are you out to arrest him?" Shires asked.

Mike didn't want to tell his real reason, which was to warn Alan that the police knew his identity. He was wanted for murder of a cop. Instead he said, "Just need to ask him some questions."

Shires thought about the man that had been his guide in Flagstaff and wondered. "Describe him to me," he said.

The only description Mike knew was what he overheard that day. "Well, I guess he would be good at outdoor stuff. He was a Marine sniper. My dad knew him. Said he'd been left behind when they escaped from Arizona. Does that help any?"

"Not much. That's a really vague description."

"I know. Sorry about that."

The more Mike talked the more Shires realized that his guide probably had been Alan Noble. "What if I were able to get a message to the man, what should I tell him?"

"Tell him to contact Tony Arzetti's son Mike in San Francisco."

"That's all?"

"Yep! That's it."

"Anything else?"

There was no answer. Mike Arzetti had disappeared. Shires supposed he could look for him on the boat, but he respected his need to remain incognito. He was going to see Jordan anyway, so he'd make a stop in Flagstaff and attempt to give Alan Noble the message.

CHAPTER 28

The sudden announcement of the first of December start date of the National Chip Identification Program, and the National Prisoner Release Program caught Gregory Chamus off guard. The President had appointed him the leader of the stock market maneuver.

"Changing the date kills the project," he complained to Hal Skidmore, the President's Chief-of-Staff.

"I don't know what to tell you, Greg," Hal said. "We had no warning of the President's change of mind. He came back from the Vatican Conference, and went immediately to Lydia's bedside. He had a burr under his saddle about something. After he talked to her doctors, he told us to start the programs immediately. He didn't tell me why, and I haven't asked."

Lydia Butcher improved and was released from the hospital a week later. Doctors were at a loss to explain her sudden illness, or her just-as-sudden improvement. What they thought had been a stroke had been nothing more than a seizure of some kind—'idiopathic' the doctors said, which meant they didn't have the slightest idea what was wrong with her.

The President needed no explanation—he got the message and advanced the start date for both programs to December 1st. His Cabinet was aghast. He didn't care. He perceived a threat to Lydia. Many things could be said about him, and probably would be, but nobody could doubt his love for her. He didn't realize this same love could be a chink in his armor. Cahmael knew it, and used it to blackmail him.

He didn't believe the rumors about Cahmael being the Antichrist, but the coincidence spooked him—something he would never admit to anyone.

Dick, what do you think you're doing? It was his Chief Economic Adviser, Earl Price, on the phone. Richard Butcher squelched the anger that sprang up within him. Earl had been his friend since they were kids, and was the only person in the world, other than Lydia, who could question his judgment, although it usually angered him.

Keeping his voice mellow, and though he knew the answer, he asked the question anyway, "What are you talking about, Earl?"

A long silence ensued. *Are you with someone?*

"No…why?"

You're being evasive. You know why I'm calling. Our friends are not going to be happy about this early start. What in God's name were you thinking?

"Earl, I don't want to talk about this on the phone. Come to my office around three. I need to talk to you anyway."

He also needed time to think about what he might tell his friend. How do you say you capitulated out of fear? Cahmael had been so adamant about getting Lydia's input. The mere fact he called attention to her underlined the threat.

That afternoon, while awaiting his friend's arrival, Dick Butcher sat staring through the window of the Oval Office at the snow as it fell on the White House lawn. The snowfall soothed him. It muffled sounds and accentuated the silence. The world under the snow settled into peaceful tranquility. He wished he could reach into that tranquility and calm the turmoil that raged within him. He would be lighting the White House Christmas Tree next week. To all appearances, everything was as it should be. It was him. He felt odd, almost powerless, under the threat of Cahmael's manipulation. He hated it.

Earl Price was agitated when he arrived. Obesity caused him to breathe heavily after the exertion of walking, but he didn't sit down. Instead, he paced the floor while he listened to the story of Lydia's illness.

That agitated him even more. "You gave in to this guy. I can't believe it—you of all people. Are you sure Cahmael had something to do with Lydia's illness?" Earl Price exclaimed. His chubby face grew red as his blood pressure rose.

"Earl, calm down and sit down before you have a heart attack. I'm not sure about anything. Nothing has been lost. We can make up the money another way."

"It's not the money. It's the power. If you give in now, you'll have to do it again and again. There will be no end to it. We are the greatest superpower in the world. We can't be ruled by blackmail. You have to get rid of the...problem." Earl sank into a chair as he finished the sentence. His heavy body rested nervously. He was a bald man with bulging eyes.

Butcher thought his friend resembled a potato bug. Mexican field workers in his hometown of Porterville, California called them Los Ninos de la Tierra (children of the earth)—bug-eyed little creatures with fat, round babyfaces. He never called Earl that name, but at this moment he was ready to call him every name in the book, and Potato Bug would be one of the least offensive.

What he was suggesting defied the bounds of human decency. Lydia was the woman he loved, not some enemy to be disposed of with the swipe of a hand. *She's inconvenient—so dispose of her?* Absolutely not!

Earl sat for some time staring quietly at his friend.

"I'm sorry," he said at last, "that statement was too abrupt, too cold. I know you love Lydia. I love Lydia. But you are in charge of the greatest superpower in the world. You have at your fingertips the most destructive weapons in the history of warfare. You must be your own man. You cannot be ordered around by anybody."

The words rang in Dick's ears. What Earl told him, he already knew. Lydia was the light of his life. She completed him, and she had to disappear or die because his love for her was his Achilles heel. Her being alive allowed him to be controlled.

He had to do something about Lydia before somebody else did it for him. Earl was only the tip of the iceberg. Any one of those involved in the market maneuver might consider the same solution. Of course, they hadn't heard the news in detail. At this point, they knew only that the plans had been changed.

Hal Skidmore told him how upset Greg Chamus had been. He had some explaining to do to Greg, but then he had to explain to a lot of people; most of all though, he had to save Lydia's life.

CHAPTER 29

Shires phoned-in an ad to the Kingman, Arizona papers. It was similar to the one he placed earlier in the year. It read: *Looking for help again. Need to talk to the man who led me into the National Forest a couple months ago.* He gave his cell phone number for contact; however, this time he flew to Flagstaff. He would give Alan Noble two days to answer, and then he'd go on to Maryland. He hadn't seen Jordan for much too long. His original promise to alternate every two weeks had fallen through. This time he promised he'd see her immediately after Flagstaff.

The call came early the second morning. A male voice asked for his location. The caller was upset when he discovered Shires was in Flagstaff, and wouldn't allow him to pass on his message over the phone. "Stay where you are. I'll call you later today." Then the line went dead.

Shires planned to fly out at three that afternoon. He'd arrive in Maryland at seven thirty-five. Now he had to wait. He called the airlines to change his flight time. The next available flight was at 9. He reserved a seat, and then called Jordan to say he'd be late. She was disappointed, but understanding.

The second call came at 5P.M.

Where are you?

"Best Western by the airport."

Go to the restaurant. Sit in the booth at the back. The line went dead.

Shires did as he was instructed and ordered a sandwich while he waited. Thirty minutes later his cell chimed.

Do not react to my question, just answer it. Do you know you're being followed? the voice asked.

"How can that be? I just got here yesterday."

Modern technology; you can't escape it. Have you talked to anybody?

"My girlfriend Jordan back in Maryland."

What did you tell her?

"Just that I'd missed my interview, and I'd be late. That's it."

Well, you've picked up a friend from either Homeland Security or the FBI. He's that young fella in jeans and a parka sitting at the counter. We can't meet, sorry. The line went dead.

Shires ignored the younger man as he passed. He scanned the restaurant for the caller, but to no avail. He paid his bill and went to his room to await flight time, somewhat disappointed that he had failed to pass along the message.

A knock on the door surprised him. He opened it to be confronted by the young man from the restaurant, and another man.

"Mr. Lampton, I'm Ted Johnson, an officer with Homeland Security, and this is my partner, Howard Skinner. Do you know the man who has been calling your cell?"

The question was unexpected. He knew it was possible to intercept cell phone conversations, but it surprised him that anybody listened to his. "No I don't," he answered.

"Sir, what do you know about the underground?"

They were standing in the hallway. It felt awkward to Shires. "Would you gentlemen like to come in?"

"Certainly, thank you," Ted Johnson said, stepping inside the room. He was followed closely by the second man who repeated the same question in a rather testy voice.

"So, what did you say you knew about the underground?"

"All I know is they're a bunch of religious nuts who think Jehosea Cahmael is the Antichrist."

There were only two chairs in the room. The officers seated themselves, and Shires sat on the bed. It was a windy November day. The windowpanes vibrated from the gusts. The sound of the wind made it feel cold to Shires.

"How do you know Alan Noble?" Johnson asked, writing something in a small notebook

"I don't know any Alan Noble."

"That was the name of the man who called you. You know…the same man who identified me in the restaurant," Johnson said.

"How do you know it was him?" Shires asked, forcing himself to stay seated on the bed. He wanted to pace, but that would make him appear as nervous as he felt.

"Voice imaging; you've had conversations with Mr. Noble before."

"So, you must monitor my cell. How long you been doing that?"

"Since you interviewed Horn and Nalone at the terrorist camp a couple years ago. You seem to have a special connection to the underground," Johnson said.

"Why do you say that?"

"You get all these calls from a wanted man who is hiding in the underground. He's wanted for questioning in San Francisco for the murder of a police officer."

That information took Shires by surprise. *That must be why Mike Arzetti wanted to talk to him, or was there more to it than that? It didn't seem like Mike wanted to make an arrest. He wouldn't have sent a message through Shires if that were the case. What did Mike Arzetti know? And why hadn't he told him someone had been killed?*

"I didn't know an officer had been killed."

"So, does Alan Noble know to call you by the newspaper ad?" Johnson asked.

"I didn't know who would call me. I have no control over it. The ad is a way to contact a source," he lied.

"Right, and you have a message for the source—not the other way round," Skinner said.

Shires knew he might be in trouble. It wouldn't be difficult to tell them the content of the message, but he didn't want to reveal Mike Arzetti's role in sending it.

"What was the message you were supposed to deliver?" Skinner asked again.

Shires slowly realized they were asking questions about which they should already know the answer. *They said his phone had been monitored for two years. If that were true, they would know about the message and his meetings with Arzetti on the ferry.*

So they know about Mike. But Mike hadn't contacted him about anything other than finding Hewey, and this present situation. Mike had said nothing about Noble other than he wanted to talk to the man. So they must think Shires Lampton is the one with the contact to the underground.

"I don't know why you're asking me that question. You already know the answer. You said yourself you've been monitoring my cell phone."

"We want to know the content of the message you were supposed to deliver for Arzetti," Skinner spat this out like he had a bad taste in his mouth.

The content…there was no content. They had to know what Mike asked him to do.

"Look," Shires said at last, "all Arzetti wanted me to tell Noble was come to San Francisco and see him."

"That's all? That's it? No hidden meaning?" Johnson said, frowning in disbelief.

"That's the size of it," Shires said, and chuckled to himself when he realized they thought he might be using a code.

"Mr. Lampton, you're under arrest for aiding and abetting a murderer. You have the right to remain silent. Anything you say, can and will be used against you in a court of law. You have the right to an attorney. If you cannot afford an attorney, one will be appointed for you. Do you understand these rights?"

Shires didn't argue. It would have done no good. His answer was a quiet, "Yes, I do."

CHAPTER 30

Opponents of the proposed prisoner release program were adamant. *It is risky and dangerous* claimed an editorial in a San Francisco paper.

Proponents countered with, "*Not so. We're not talking about serial killers and rapists, only those convicted of less violent crimes, and they will be monitored by the chip. It will be implanted before their release. They will actually have closer supervision than they had in prison, and we will have slashed the cost of their imprisonment.*" The plan would definitely save taxpayer money.

It was simple. To receive the chip, and be released from jail or prison, one must swear allegiance to Cahmael. The chip would then be implanted in the palm of the right hand with the understanding that the chip's tracking system would monitor each individual. They would be placed in halfway houses in the Bay area so they could integrate back into society. This would happen on Monday, December 1. If any one of them committed a crime, or even happened to be near a crime scene, he or she would be hunted down and summarily executed. No excuses accepted. It was also a death-penalty offense to remove the chip, as well as death for the party who removed it.

Even with those dire consequences, Mike Arzetti was excited about the early release date for his dad and Kinzi Tern. John Monroe and Greg Littlejack would be released the same day. All four had to be swallowed up by the underground in an untraceable fashion—not an easy task with 24/7 chip monitoring.

Mike Arzetti, his partner, George Wildes, Nathan Conrad and four other members of the underground held a conference the Thursday night before the Monday release date. The underground safe house was located at a winery in the Napa Valley owned by Harold and Beverly Goodin. Paul and Caroline Royce were also in attendance. The purpose was to formulate a plan for removing and destroying the chips without alerting law enforcement.

According to Nathan Conrad, removal would be a simple procedure. Complications might arise afterwards. An alarm could be triggered by the removal. It might be sensitive to DNA, or warmth, or movement. Any plan for removing the chips had to assume that to be true. If it were, law enforcement would immediately know the location of the removal, and that the chip was not with its rightful owner. The old *toss the cell phone into a passing vehicle* scenario wouldn't work.

The next question was response time. How quickly could law enforcement get to the location? This, Nathan Conrad figured, was the one weakness of the program—the weakness they could exploit. Millions of people to monitor, even with the help of computers, would be a daunting task. It would be next to impossible to respond quickly to every infraction. Nathan suggested that they work on the concept of a minimal response time—three to five minutes.

So, how could they accomplish all this? Mike suggested they remove the chip while inside a moving vehicle, and smash it immediately to avoid being tracked. Nathan thought that was a great suggestion.

"Should it be public or private transportation?" Beverly Goodin asked.

"How about inside BART while passing under the bay?" George Wildes asked.

"Too many people to explain it to," Nathan said. "I think private transportation is going to serve us best. There are just too many questions to be answered with public transportation."

"We could use our motor home," Caroline Royce suggested.

"No we can't," Nathan said. "Anytime we break the law we can't use anything that's connected to any one of us. We'll have to steal a vehicle, preferably one that won't be missed for about eight hours. That'll give us time to use it and get it back to the rightful owner. Is everybody clear about that?"

"Returning the vehicle would get the owner in trouble. We need to steal the vehicle and then abandon or wreck it. That will get the owner completely off the hook," Mike said

"You're right, Mike. Good observation," Nathan said as he picked up the papers spread around him on the table, and slipped them into his briefcase.

"I know somebody who can get the vehicle. He'll get it, drive it, and abandon it after he wipes it clean of prints. There's one drawback with using him. He'll have to be paid," George said.

"Could he get a motor home like Beverly suggested?" Nathan asked.

"I'm sure he can."

"I think it would be worth the money, but can he be trusted?" Harold Royce asked.

"He's already a criminal. I don't think he'll go running to the law. For the right price, I'm sure he can. He's not going to know all the details. He won't even know he's working for the underground. In fact, he doesn't have to know what were doing. All he has to do is drive and let us off at a certain point, and then get rid of the vehicle," George said.

"You're not going to tell him the details?" Beverly Goodin asked.

"All he needs to know is where to pick us up, and where to drop us. That's it."

"Wow! I didn't know you knew all these criminals," Mike said jokingly.

They all laughed.

" Okay then, let's meet next Tuesday night. We'll know exactly where the four of them will be living. George can talk to his friend… get an estimate. Then we'll set the plans in concrete. So, to sum it up, we've decided to use a stolen private vehicle. We will pick up the four, on a certain day, at a central pickup point. We'll get their chips removed and integrate them into the underground that day. Is that everybody's understanding of the discussion we had here tonight?" Nathan asked as he stood.

They all affirmed it was, and the meeting ended.

CHAPTER 31

Jordan Smith lay in bed and worried. It wasn't like Shires to miss calling her after he promised. His flight was at 9 PM Mountain Standard Time—11 PM her time. He was supposed to call her just before he boarded. It was now midnight and no call. She dialed his cell. The message recorder came on immediately. Evidently he had shut it off.

It was almost one when the phone rang. Jordan was apprehensive as she picked it up. "Shires?" she asked.

You always call me Boo, he said cheerily.

"What's wrong?"

I got arrested.

"For what?"

Consorting with terrorists…I guess. That's what they claim anyway. I'll tell you all about it when I get there. I don't have long to talk, but wanted to let you know.

"Where are you, Boo?"

County jail in Flagstaff.

"Oh Boo…I'm sorry, honey."

They don't have anything on me. They're trying to pressure me into giving up a source. I'm sure I'll be released after seventy-two hours. That's all they can hold me without pressing charges. So, I'll see you sometime Sunday night. I'll call you from the airport. Gotta go…I love you.

"I love you too, Boo," Jordan said, then listened to the line go dead.

She felt lonely. She never felt that way usually, but now, right after Shires' call from jail, she felt the loneliness from her younger years creeping in. She remembered it…hated the feeling. It had gone away after she met Shires fifteen years ago.

She settled into bed again and was drifting off to sleep when a knock on the front door woke her. She jerked to a sitting position, startled by the noise. *Who could that be?* Her alarm clock showed two-thirty. Her first reaction was to ignore it, but the second knock was louder, more persistent. She thought of calling the police, then decided to check who it might be.

She pulled on her robe, walked down the hallway past the kitchen to the front door, and peered through the peephole. A man and woman stood there.

"Who is it?" She asked.

"Police, Ms. Smith. We need to talk to you," said a female voice.

"At this time of the morning? Couldn't it have waited for a decent hour?"

"No, it couldn't. We need to talk to you now," said an insistent male voice.

Still wary of her visitors, Jordan unlocked the door but left the chain lock attached. She opened the door to the end of the chain. "May I see some ID please?"

Two badges, with pictures, and marked Homeland Security appeared in the opening. "Okay," she said, and undid the chain.

"I'm Martha Weldin, a Homeland Security Officer, and this is my partner, Hugh Michaels. Sorry to disturb your sleep."

"You didn't. Haven't been there yet," Jordan said sarcastically. They declined the seat she offered on the couch.

"We don't have time to get comfortable," Martha Weldin said, "I need you to get dressed. We want you to come with us to our office."

"What's this all about?"

"About your friendship with Shires Lampton."

"Shires Lampton?"

"Yeah the man who called you about an hour ago."

"But what's he got to do with anything?"

"We'll talk about all that later. Now, please, get dressed we need to go."

"Am I under arrest?"

"Not at the moment. We just want to talk to you," Martha Weldin assured her.

CHAPTER 32

President Butcher didn't tell the truth about changing the date. He just couldn't do it. Lydia would be in too much danger. The only man who knew the full truth was Earl Price, and he would never tell.

Instead, he made up a lie. He said Cahmael had convinced him to start early for two reasons. First: The United States, being the greatest superpower, should be in the lead on all these matters, plus it would help grow the economy. Second: The excuse for waiting was weak, and, after thinking about it, too obvious.

Mr. President, those are two of the lamest excuses I've ever heard, Earl Price proclaimed on the phone, the morning after their conversation.

Earl was livid. Dick Butcher could tell by the tone of his voice. That wasn't a good thing for him, given his obesity and his high blood pressure.

"Earl, settle down. You'll have a heart attack," he warned, then added, "Anyway, that's how I'm going to spin it."

You can't leave the country open to manipulation. I thought you were worried about that. I guess I was wrong... His voice trailed off and the connection was lost.

The President received other phone calls that morning. One from Jehosea Cahmael commending him for his quick response time in the matter of the injection program.

I can see that I will be able to depend on your support in the future. I like that. We can have a long-lasting partnership. I'd like to start it right now by having you move some of your military assets to the Mediterranean—a couple of Carrier Groups.

"What would be the purpose of such a deployment?" Butcher asked.

He purposely left off the Sir or Lord to show his contempt, but Cahmael ignored the sleight.

"Security before and after the dedication ceremony at the Temple of Solomon in May. I'll give you two months to complete the movement. I'd like one of the groups moved immediately. That will show your good intentions."

Cahmael was not asking, he was ordering. Butcher knew it. "I'll see what I can do," he said, refusing to jump at Cahmael's command.

He cradled the receiver of the red phone, the *Hotline*, as it was so aptly named, and wondered about other presidents who had held it. What historic words had passed through the mouthpiece...what secrets? He bet none of them had ever been subject to such blatant extortion.

A light knock on the door interrupted his thoughts.

"Yes," he said.

Brad Thomas, the Secret Service agent assigned to guard his door, leaned into the room and said, "Mr. President, you need to come with me right now. The First Lady has been shot."

CHAPTER 33

Five other agents joined Thomas, their guns drawn. They encircled the President and moved him cautiously down the hallway.

"Mr. President, your wife has been taken to Walter Reed. I don't know her condition. We'll get you there as quickly as possible," one of the six said.

Dick Butcher didn't know who said it. He was numb and floating in a sea of unreality, disconnected from the world. He wanted to ask what happened, but the words wouldn't come out. Was Lydia badly wounded? Was she dead? That thought made him cringe, and a lump formed in his throat. Tears stung his eyes. *I have to pull myself together. After all, I am the President of the United States.* He remembered thinking that, but it didn't help. Someone had kicked the wind out of him.

How had a anyone been able to get so close to his wife? Security was tight. Shooting Lydia should have been next to impossible. He had a number of questions, but he was sure none of the men surrounding him were ready to answer any of them. They escorted him to a side entry and on out to the helicopter waiting on the lawn.

Walter Reed Medical Center is 6.4 miles north of 1600 Pennsylvania Avenue. The President's helicopter landed there about seven minutes after takeoff.

The same six men escorted him in through a side entrance where a hospital briefing team awaited their arrival.

"Mr. President, I'm Doctor Gregory Zanoff. Your wife is in surgery as we speak. I must be frank with you sir; it doesn't look good. She has massive trauma to the head. We're working to relieve the pressure on her brain. Only time will tell, but we will keep you posted every fifteen minutes. Do you have any questions for us?"

"Not at the moment, doctor, unless you can tell me what happened?"

"Sorry sir, I'm not privy to that information. We will keep you posted on her medical condition, though."

"Okay, good. Thank you Doctor Zanoff," he said, reaching to shake the doctor's hand.

The briefing team left the room, and Dick Butcher began pacing. He had to. He couldn't sit down. Lydia lay dying in a room down the hall. He wanted to be with her. He still didn't know what happened. *Who shot her? It must have been a terrorist—that's why the agents were being so cautious.*

A few minutes later, Bill Smiley, head of the Secret Service, and Henry Bishop, head of the CIA, arrived to brief him. Their faces were grim.

"Our news is not good Mr. President, Sir," Bill Smiley said, and handed him a folded note. "Here read this," he said.

Dread raced through him as he unfolded the paper. It read:

Dick,

There is no good way to tell you I'm sorry. Please believe me, I am. I did what you could never have done. I am so sorry to cause you such pain. I love you and I love Lydia. I don't expect your forgiveness, but I did it for you and for the country.

Earl

He sat staring at the note for a long time. Tears streamed down his face. He made no attempt to wipe them away.

Minutes passed before he could ask, "What about Earl?"

"He shot himself, right after he shot the First Lady. He died at the scene," the Secret Service Director said.

Dick Butcher gathered himself together, and, forcing a presidential smile, shook hands with each man and thanked them for coming. Then they were gone. He was alone again except, for his ever-present, ever-watchful Secret Service Agents.

Doctors came and went over the next few hours, each assuring him that everything was going as well as could be expected—nothing new had developed.

The lead surgeon finally arrived. He had been in surgery for a long time, and looked as haggard and exhausted as Dick Butcher felt.

"Mr. President, I'm Doctor Hugo James, the neurosurgeon who's been attending the First Lady," he said. "There is massive swelling in her brain. I have a drain in it. I'm sorry to tell you the prognosis isn't good. She's in a profound coma, and I don't think she'll survive…I'm sorry."

Tears came again to his swollen eyes. He didn't try to wipe them away; he had no strength to move his arms anyway.

"May I see her?" he asked weakly.

"Yes, of course. I'll take you to her."

He stood slowly and followed the doctor to Lydia's room. Lydia was pale. Her beautiful face was drawn, almost set like plaster, Dick thought. Her beautiful black and gray streaked hair had been shaved from her head and replaced by a bandage resembling a helmet. Tubes protruded from her skull, her nose, and her mouth. Dick couldn't cry anymore. His eyes burned and smarted, but no tears came.

Doctor James excused himself and left the room. Lydia's hand was cool and soft to his touch; those beautiful hands, so soft and reassuring, so pleasurable at other times. He raised her limp hand to his mouth and kissed it.

In his pocket, he felt the vibration of his cell phone. Who would be calling? He rarely received calls on it anymore. Other than Lydia, Earl, and the Secret Service, no one else had the number.

"Hello." he said quietly.

"Do not despair, my friend, all is not lost. Kiss her hand, then bend down to her face and whisper that you love her. Remember, Mr. President, I am always with you." The phone went dead.

Dick frowned, not quite believing what he just heard. Nevertheless he did as he was told. After he whispered he loved her, he kissed her face too. She flinched away from the kiss and moaned. Dick's heart leaped.

The moan startled those attending her. Lydia was in a profound coma. Usually, the next step was death. There was no way she should flinch from a kiss, or even feel it. The monitor showed that her heart rate was increasing. Her blood pressure was rising as well.

"What's going on?" asked a female voice.

"I don't know," said another.

"She appears to be coming out of the coma," a male voice said.

"That's impossible," said a nurse.

"Quick, take the tube out of her throat," Doctor James ordered, "Mr. President, you'll have to move for a moment, Sir," he added.

Dick complied, laying Lydia's hand gently on the sheet, and stepping away from the bed. He was afraid to hope that what was happening meant that Lydia would live. The comments made by the attending staff made it seem so. His spirits climbed.

The tube had just been taken from her throat when Lydia's lashes fluttered. Her eyes opened, swept the room, and stopped on Dick. A slight smile formed on her lips.

"Honey, I love you," she whispered in a hoarse voice.

CHAPTER 34

Mike Arzetti was tired and decided to go to bed early Friday. He had volunteered to work an extra shift Saturday morning, and had just turned off the light when the apartment phone rang. He figured it must be for his sister, Ann, because he always received his calls on his cell. She had gone to spend the night with a friend, so he let the answering machine pick it up.

Leave a message after the beep, Ann's voice said cheerily.

I need to talk to Mike Arzetti, a male voice said.

Mike jumped from the bed, ran to the living room and snatched the phone from its cradle.

"This is Mike," he said.

When we hang up, erase my message from your machine.

"Okay," Mike said.

Don't say anything just listen to me. We have a problem. It seems your friend's cell phone is bugged; has been for a couple years. I hope you haven't said anything to him that might compromise the underground. I don't think you have or they would be visiting you, and they might anyway, so be prepared for a visit from Homeland Security. Now, in the future, it is imperative that you find another way to contact him. Your voice must disappear from his cell phone. Understood?

"Yes."

Okay…good; one more thing. The man has an implanted chip in the palm of his right hand. Remember they know his exact location at all times. Just thought you'd like to know. Have a nice night. And then the voice was gone.

Mike cradled the phone and stared out of the window into the night.

In the distance, he could see the light from the windows of the high-rises in the San Francisco business district. He wondered if there were people inside the lighted rooms; who were they and what were they doing?

It had been Nathan Conrad on the phone. He wondered where the guy received his information. It seemed he knew everything. Mike pressed the button to erase the message. Conrad's voice disappeared from the answering machine.

Mike searched his memory for anything he had said to Shires Lampton over the phone that might be construed as connected to the underground. Nothing jumped out at him. He had burned Roy Cassidy's notebook. Roy had been after him, not Shires.

Mike had wondered just how much Cassidy might have known. He was sure Cassidy suspected him of having a connection to the underground, but lacked the proof. If he'd had it, he would have arrested Mike. Roy wasn't one to sit on that kind of information.

Mike's dad had told him that Lampton already had the chip implant. Lampton had told Tom and Vince during the interview at the camp outside Flagstaff. So was Lampton a spy of some kind? He didn't think so, but it might be prudent for him to be careful in the future. He knew Lampton had probably been tracked to the ferry, but the chip couldn't tell them who he met there. Did it really make any difference? He wondered.

Mike arrived at the station around 6 A.M. on Saturday. He noticed a paper stuck to the bulletin board. The word *attention* had been stamped across it in red. The notice read:

Monday, December 1ˢᵗ is the first day of the National Chip Identification Program. All officers are required to receive the chip injection. Be here at 9 A.M. with proper photographic identification, preferably your California Driver's License. If you are on duty at that time, you may come in at 3P.M.

Loring Thomas—Chief of Police.

CHAPTER 35

If Shires Lampton had seriously thought about it, he would have known how he had been traced. It wasn't all by cell phone. It took another inmate at the Flagstaff jail to remind him.

"That chip ain't only for identification. They can track you with it too."

Shires remembered the chip injection nearly two years ago. It had been so simple. You appear, show some ID and swear allegiance to Cahmael. They give you a blood test and swab your mouth for DNA and you're done. He didn't figure swearing allegiance to Cahmael was any different from swearing to anything else, and it certainly made his life better. He didn't have to worry about identity theft anymore. It made plane travel a whole lot easier. With the chip, he traversed airports without the delay of security checks

The chip was in his right hand. It had been reported that some thieves had gone to the extreme of severing a victim's hand to steal the chip. He didn't worry about it, and never had it changed to his forehead. He had joked with Jordan that if they were going to sever something—better his hand than his head.

Sunday morning arrived. Shires had been questioned about his underground contacts. They had mentioned his meetings with Mike Arzetti a number of times. He maintained that Mike was only a source in the police department. As far as Shires was concerned, that was a true statement.

Shires was unaware of any other contacts he might have who were connected to the underground. His guide to the survivalist camp out in the National Forest might belong to the underground. Shires didn't know his name. All he knew was how to contact him through the paper.

They even asked him about this trip to see Panguitch Hewey. That had been at Mike Arzetti's request. It was an attempt to help his father, Tony Arzetti, get out of jail. He had only known how to find Hewey from Tony Arzetti's directions—and those were only general, not specific; no underground connection there.

They released Shires about noon on Sunday. They said nothing to him. He figured they couldn't find anything, either that or it was a warning—*We're watching you*. He didn't care much either way just as long as they let him go.

He caught a cab to the airport, and called Jordan from the cab. There was no answer at her home. He tried her cell. His call went immediately to her voicemail. It was shut off. That was strange for a Sunday.

At the airport, Shires booked a four o'clock flight straight to Dulles International then went to a restaurant. He ordered soup and a sandwich with coffee.

He tried Jordan's home phone and cell again to no avail. It was not like Jordan to be gone on Sunday. Shires couldn't call her friend Amelia. A burglar had murdered Amelia—a story Shires never believed. As far as he knew, the murder was unsolved. What did Amelia have to do with anything? Why would somebody want to kill her?

The more he thought about Amelia, the more he worried about Jordan.

"Here's your order, sir," the waitress said, interrupting his thoughts.

He moved his elbows to allow the waitress to set the food on the table, looked up at her and smiled.

"You look worried," she said, making conversation.

"Does it show that much?"

"'Fraid so…anything anybody else can do?"

He smiled at the concern, and said in jest, "'Fraid not."

She laughed. "We have some good pie for dessert. You really ought to try it."

"I'll think about it," he called to her back as she walked away. She waved her arm signaling she heard.

Even talking with the waitress while he ate apple pie a la mode didn't shorten the afternoon. Time dragged. He tried Jordan's phones again and again.

He arrived at Jordan's apartment in Falls Church, Virginia at 9 that evening, and let himself in with the extra key from the planter by the door. The apartment looked undisturbed, but there was no Jordan. He searched all four rooms. In the bedroom, beside her jewelry box he found a hastily scrawled note. It read:

Boo, it's H S, they're taking me.

CHAPTER 36

On Monday morning, Jordan Smith was taken from her cell, given her street clothes, and told to get dressed. She had been asked a lot of questions regarding her relationship with Shires, and about the underground. Did she know anybody who belonged? Did she know if Shires knew anybody who was a member? What were their names?

"We need to make a stop at the infirmary to get your chip injection before we release you," Officer Helen Goodlow said.

"Why me?"

"Today is the first day of the National Chip Identification Program. Everyone being released from jail must get one."

Jordan knew that Shires had the chip in his right hand. He said it expedited going through the security checks at airports. "What do I have to do?" she asked.

"It a fairly simple process; you swear allegiance to Cahmael and the nurse gives you the injection. That's about it."

"So how does my specific information get on the chip?"

"A computer scans it on," Goodlow said, and pushed open the door to the infirmary. "Here we are," she added.

The smell of disinfectant greeted Jordan. The room was white with green borders. The whirring of a small motor could be heard. It was like most other infirmaries Jordan had visited—clean, sterile, and quiet. A female deputy sat at a computer.

Jordan was directed to sit in the chair next to her desk, and then the inquisition began. Jordan divulged a large amount of personal information about herself and her family. She gave her blood type, and they swabbed her mouth for a DNA sample. It surprised her they needed so much information. An hour later, they seemed satisfied.

"Does it take this long for everybody?" Jordan asked.

"No. Evidently you missed the census the Trinity of Man followers took about three years ago, when Cahmael was first asked to help," Goodlow said.

Jordan didn't remember. "They asked for that much information, and people gave it to them?" Jordan asked.

"In those days, if you remember, we were in dire straits. I think folks were happy to divulge personal information just to get the help."

"Why didn't the census people talk to me? I was right here in D.C."

Before Goodlow could answer, a man burst through the clinic door, "Stop this immediately!" he ordered. "Ms. Smith, come with me. Goodlow, you and Jamie make sure all the information you just took on Ms. Smith is erased from the hard drive. Is that understood?"

"Yessir," the two answered in unison.

CHAPTER 37

Shires Lampton hadn't slept. He called the police, but they had no record of a Jordan Smith ever being arrested. Of course, they wouldn't. Homeland Security didn't tell them. Shires knew that, but he was desperate, and worried—grasping at straws.

Jordan called around ten Monday morning. "Boo, come and get me at the Federal Building in DC," she said.

An hour later, he was hugging a tearful Jordan, who told him the story of being ripped from her bed in the middle of the night then taken to a detention facility in DC where they kept her in isolation for the next three days. Nobody talked to her. Even the officer who brought her meals didn't say a word.

On the second day, she was taken to an interrogation room and asked about her relationship with Shires. *Did she know anything about his contacts? Where did he spend most of his time? Who was his favorite author?* Questions like that. Otherwise, she never saw the light of day.

"And then the strangest thing of all happened. I had been taken to the infirmary to get the chip injection. I sat there for an hour giving all this personal information. Then some guy walked in and told them to stop and erase all my information, then he escorted me out of the building. That was it. Nobody explained anything. I never received the chip injection. They just released me."

Shires listened and wondered what was happening. Had everyone gone crazy? You could live a whole lifetime and never be arrested, or interrogated, or even questioned for that matter. Now, in the space of four days, Homeland Security had talked to him and Jordan. Evidently, they hadn't been arrested, just detained.

Shires had no explanation for why Jordan hadn't received the chip; although he suspected it might have something to do with her work at DARPA, he couldn't be sure.

"Are you doing anything new at work?" Shires asked. He nosed the rental car into the parking lot of a Chinese restaurant. The restaurant had a mural of the Great Wall of China on the front. The entryway was painted black and red, and shaped like a wide door with a curved top. It looked like a Chinese ideograph. Shires always wondered what it meant, but had never taken the time to research it.

"You hungry?" he asked.

"Starved," she answered without answering his first question.

"You think my work might have something to do with not getting the chip?" Jordan asked as she climbed out of the car.

Shires came around and took her hand. "I don't know," he said. "It would be logical if it did. What did they say when you called in this morning?"

She thought for a moment. "That was weird, Boo, I talked to my supervisor, Greg Fields. He didn't seem particularly surprised that I had been…detained, quote unquote, and told me to take off a couple days. Then he added, "We have some new stuff to work on when you get back.""

Shires gave his name to the hostess, who seated them immediately.

"Were you working on anything special before?" he asked as they followed the Cheongsam-clad woman.

"No, nothing at all. Just the usual stuff."

"Honey, there ain't anything usual at DARPA. You know that. You work there."

"I meant nothing different from the usual, unusual stuff," she said, and chuckled as they sat down.

The hostess handed them menus, and, in slightly Mandarin accented English, told them their waitress would be there momentarily.

Shires ordered sweet and sour chicken with rice and white wine. Jordan, ever the weight watcher, had egg-drop soup and tea—then proceeded to eat sweet and sour chicken from Shires plate. She loved to do that. Shires expected it and loved her for it. She said it showed how much she cared for him. Mostly, he accused her of being a closet eater, hiding behind his gluttony.

They were mostly finished with lunch when an explosion in the parking lot rattled the windows and shook the building. Fortunately no restaurant windows shattered.

Shires jumped up to look. It was closeby their car. They finished quickly and hurried outside. The police and the fire department were already on the scene. The fire department sprayed foam over the flames, while the police cordoned off the area to keep the public away.

Shires could see the car next to his rental had blown up. A rumor circulated among the spectators saying the police found an incinerated body in it. The owner of the car was there, very upset, but glad he hadn't been the one in the car.

"You're the owner?" a detective asked the man standing next to Shires.

"Yes, I am."

"Did you have anybody with you?"

"No sir."

"We found a dead body in your car. You don't have any idea who that might be?"

"I don't know."

"Sir, come with me please," the detective directed.

"What kind of car was it?" Shires asked the owner as he was taken away.

"A white Dodge four-door," the owner replied.

The car was just like Shires' rental, even the same color. He overheard a detective say to another, "It looks like the poor fool who made the bomb burned himself up in the process."

Shires' car had the windows blown out, so it became part of the investigation. When he called the rental company and explained his problem, they immediately delivered another.

Shires never mentioned his suspicions to Jordan, but he feared the bomb had been meant for them, with Jordan being the main target. It was just too close, too coincidental to be coincidental. He didn't know why he felt so scared for her, but he did.

CHAPTER 38

President Richard Butcher hadn't left his wife's room except to shower, and to take care of some State business over the phone. He felt relief and gratitude to Cahmael for saving Lydia; although the doctors said they had seen recoveries just as miraculous with brain-damaged people, there was little doubt in his mind that this had been the work of Cahmael. He didn't want to believe it, but he did. The relief of his grief had been so great it was difficult for him to believe anything else.

Admiral Lemuel Perkins, Chairman of the Joint Chiefs, was against the deployment of two Carrier Groups in such close proximity in the Middle East.

"It's still a dangerous world out there. We don't know who might have a secret weapon that could do some serious damage to our ships. I'm against such a deployment. There doesn't need to be so much security for the Temple Dedication. One Carrier Group in the Mediterranean is good enough," he said.

It wasn't what the President wanted. This was what Cahmael wanted. As far as Dick Butcher was concerned what Cahmael wanted, he got. But he couldn't argue over the phone. Monday morning he had to leave Lydia's bedside and go to a meeting with the Joint Chiefs. Perkins' resistance had forced him to leave Lydia. It stuck in his craw. Dick was gunning for the Admiral when he reached the meeting.

Perkins opened the meeting with a greeting to the President, whom he said was there to place a request before them.

Dick was doing a slow burn. His burn increased with the mention of the word *request*.

"I'm here," Dick said, rudely interrupting, "to give an order to my

Joint Chiefs. It's not a request. If any of you disagree with this order, and don't want to comply with it, you may place your resignation on my desk. Now, I want that second Carrier Group deployed immediately. This order is not up for discussion. I trust you gentlemen will keep me posted on its progress. Thank you for your time," he finished, and abruptly left the room.

That would give them food for thought. They all valued their careers. He knew his order would be followed; he had made it perfectly clear what he wanted. Every once in a while it's necessary to remind the Military who is in charge.

As he walked back, he thought of Earl—poor Earl—poor misguided Earl. He sacrificed himself for nothing. Dick had tried many times after Lydia's condition improved to forgive the man, and grieve for him, but it never happened.

It should have. Earl had been a friend since second grade. They played sports together—neither was terrifically good. What they lacked in ability they made up in heart and courage. They did excel in brainpower and both won scholarships to Berkeley where they graduated Magna cum Laude. They competed with each other, even through Yale law school. Dick met Lydia at Yale. She was studying Literature. The three became inseparable friends. Dick married Lydia after Yale, and Earl was best man.

Both men won jobs in prestigious corporate law firms—Earl in New York and Dick in San Francisco. Their paths separated for a number of years after that. Lydia taught English Literature at San Francisco State.

Earl went into economics and law, specializing in anti-trust cases that had economic implications, i.e. wage disputes; price-fixing; illegal monopolies etc.

When Dick Butcher became President, he called on his old friend to be his Chief Economic Advisor. Earl gladly accepted. They were together again.

Dick and Lydia Butcher never had children. Earl Price had never married, so the three became a family of sorts.

CHAPTER 39

Monday December 1, was the start date of the National Chip Identification Program in the United States.

If Mike Arzetti wanted to remain on the force, he had to get the chip. Both he and his partner, George Wildes, received theirs at the end of shift at 3 Monday afternoon.

His religious friends in the underground counseled against it, saying no job was worth going to Hell for. They couldn't get the chip because they felt swearing allegiance to Cahmael would be denying Christ— they'd go to Hell for sure. He didn't believe that religious stuff. Besides he wanted to get the chip to be in a position to help family and friends if the need ever arose. He knew some of them wouldn't have the chip, like his Dad, and his Dad's friends.

He took George with him to the underground meeting at four. There they would set the date and time for his Dad's chip removal. On the way, they had to pick up George's friend, Sly Norman, the car thief. He lived in Berkeley—in student housing, no less. Thievery paid his tuition.

They were to meet at the home of Paul and Caroline Royce in Vallejo. Harold and Beverly Goodin would be there along with Nathan Conrad. This time however, they didn't go to their house. On the way, Mike stopped at a pay phone to call and let them know about the chip—he never used his cell for underground business. Mr. and Mrs. Royce moved their motor home to the parking lot of Wal-Mart a mile away. To the surveillance people it would appear as if Mike and George did nothing more than go shopping.

Their information regarding the placement of the four target individuals was incomplete. Tony Arzetti, Kinzi Tern, John Monroe, and

Greg Littlejack were somewhere in the Bay Area, but they didn't have exact locations yet.

Sly Norman said he could have a motor home ready anytime they asked, but he needed twenty-four hours notice, and an address so he could pick them up. He wanted ten thousand dollars—half up front and the rest on delivery.

Nathan Conrad argued about the price, but capitulated in the end. Sly said his days of thievery were numbered with the advent of the chip. He figured he had a month before he would have to get it—maybe he could stretch it out for two months, but no more. He had to make enough for next year's tuition in that time. He won the argument.

After some discussion, it was decided that the extraction would be on Thursday night. Mike would visit his dad and tell him to bring the others to the BART station in Berkeley and take the train to the El Cerrito station, get off there, and find the motor home in the parking lot.

Mike wanted to go with them, but that had become impossible since he now carried the chip in his hand. He and George wouldn't be as free to meet with the underground. They'd have to work around it, though, for there was much to be done, both now, and in the future—plus he was looking forward to spending more time with his dad.

CHAPTER 40

Melissa Hardin was excited. Her new job with Homeland Security included enhancing the functionality of the government's information-gathering program. She had the chip in the palm of her right hand already. Homeland Security required it. They told her the palm was used so fingerprints could be scanned simultaneously.

Homeland Security was law enforcement. She had never thought about having a career in that field, but the job was perfect for her. She guessed she could make a career of catching criminals. *The bad guys better watch out Melissa Hardin is here.*

By her own assessment, Melissa was drop-dead gorgeous. She was twenty-three years old with blonde-brown hair and brown eyes. She stood five-foot-four and weighed a hundred and fifteen pounds—a great build by anybody's standards. She had a college degree, a job making more money than she ever dreamed of. Plus, she was in the thrilling position of serving her country amid the most trying of times. She was sitting on top of the world.

Melissa graduated Summa cum Laude from San Jose State with a degree in Computer Science. She was hired immediately after graduation by Homeland Security especially for the National Chip Identification Program to be initiated in the near future.

The government had developed the chip-tracking infrastructure, which only included receiving the chip's signals and storing the information in a database. Her task would be to enhance the program's functionality by inventing creative ways to use the basic tracking data that was stored in a central database for her region of interest—the San Francisco Bay Area.

It was her job to write data mining programs that would extract useful information such as movement patterns and interactions between people, etc. Her real love was writing programs. She couldn't believe she had stepped right into the perfect job.

They hired her in June, and she immediately buried herself in the work. It amazed Melissa when she realized the amount of control she would have over the people within her area. The enormity of it was awesome and breathtaking.

She wrote a program to track each and every individual over a period of time to build a history of movements. That movement history would refine the search for anomalies. She included surnames and how those names interacted with each other. She then went beyond that, and began implementing 'pattern recognition algorithms' to detect other anomalies in the movements and interactions between people, i.e. suspicious or criminal behavior, etc.

She could enter a name and the computer would show other surnames with which that person had interacted, as well as where that same individual had traveled over the past day, week, month, or year.

Her superiors were ecstatic. They instituted her program nationwide, gave her a substantial raise, and promoted her to Team Leader over five other people. The promotion was no big deal to her, but the raise and recognition were. She knew they'd have her writing more programs in the future.

A month ago, she thought she had to wait until March, but the President had changed it to the first of December. Now, Monday the first was here. The day for which she had been waiting had finally arrived. There was data in the computers already, but it was nothing compared to what would be coming in shortly.

Melissa Hardin was ready to rule the world.

So let the fun begin.

CHAPTER 41

Jordan Smith slept soundly on Shires Lampton's arm. Her breathing was soft and steady. Shires studied that beautiful face—not a care in the world. How could he tell her somebody was trying to kill her?

He couldn't sleep. He hadn't been tired since Monday afternoon. It was early Tuesday morning now, and he was no closer to solving the question than he had been yesterday when it presented itself. The more he thought about it, the less sense it made. Why would anyone want to kill Jordan Smith?

He knew she had been skipped when the original census was taken three years ago, but yesterday they had the perfect opportunity to include her, but they chose not to. They purposely didn't inject her, and then, just hours later, a bomb exploded near their car.

Shires wasn't prone to overreact, nor did he believe in conspiracy theories, but the near miss by the bomb had him looking over his shoulder.

If, for some reason or another, Jordan were a target, it was very unlikely he could find out who was behind it in time to save her life. His only hope was to make her disappear as quickly as possible. *How could he do that? Even if he were able to do it, would Jordan consent to such a thing?*

He hadn't discussed it with her. Someone trying to kill you is a frightening prospect, and he didn't want to scare her, but her friend Olivia had just been murdered. She had worked with Jordan. He knew it might be his overactive imagination, but he wanted to prepare for the worst while expecting the best. He wondered if that were possible.

Did he know anyone who could help him? He wished he knew how to contact Alan Noble by some means other than the newspaper ad. That was when the thought struck him...*maybe he could.*

He had to get Jordan to Arizona. He could be tracked, but they wouldn't know Jordan was with him, since she didn't have the chip—that is if they traveled during a time when she wouldn't be missed. It was a long shot, but one he had to take. Leaving her at the mercy of some unknown killer was unthinkable. She couldn't even go back to work on Wednesday.

The thought galvanized him. He had to act quickly. There could be no more thinking about it. Shires wasn't accustomed to emergency situations. He liked the adventure that went with reporting, but the stories he reported were without peril for him. He always joked that it was for that reason he never became a spy.

The glowing hands of Jordan's alarm clock showed four-thirty. Shires hated to do it, but he had to wake her and tell her the terrible truth. They had to get out of town.

He kissed her forehead. She smiled and let out a long, luxurious sigh. "I love you, Boo," she whispered.

"I love you too, sweetheart. Could you wake up for a bit? We need to talk," Shires whispered back.

"Okay," she answered sleepily, yawned as she raised up in bed, leaned against the headboard, settled herself, crossed her hands in her lap like a little girl, smiled and said, "Okay Boo, shoot."

She was so beautiful. The pink satin nightdress unleashed her sexiness. He'd rather be making love, but this had to be done. He had rehearsed what to say a few times in his mind. Now that the time had come, he was speechless.

"Sweetheart...I can't sleep..."

"You poor baby. You woke me up to tell me that?"

"No! No, it's the reason I can't sleep that we need to talk about."

"Okay. What is it?"

"I think somebody is trying to kill you." That wasn't how he meant to say it, but that's what came out.

A long silence followed. Neither spoke.

"I wondered about that," she said at last, "but you didn't seem bothered, so I just figured it was my imagination."

"I think I need to get you away from here. I need to make you disappear, so they can't get to you."

"Do you really think it's true?"

"Sweetheart, I'm not going to take any chances. I might be wrong… maybe I'm just paranoid. This has been hanging around in the back of my mind ever since Olivia was murdered. I don't know why, but I had the same feeling then as I do now."

"You think Olivia's murder had something to do with me?"

"I think everything ties together…some way…yes, I do."

"You want me to disappear?"

"Yes. I think that's the only way we can keep you safe."

"What if I don't want to disappear. That would mean giving up my whole life, my identity…everything."

"I don't have a way to test my suspicions, sweetheart. I wish I did. We have to leave right away this morning. You're due back at work tomorrow. If we start right now, we'll have a twenty-four hour head start before anybody knows you're missing."

"You mean we're going to pack right this moment and leave?"

"Yes."

"Boo, I don't want to do that."

"Oh baby…please…please do it. I could never live with myself if anything happened to you. Please, do this for me."

"What if you're wrong?"

"I hope I am. I just hope I am."

Shires checked the trip on Mapquest and discovered they had twenty-two hundred miles to go and it would take them thirty-three hours to get there if they averaged sixty-five miles an hour.

They left for Arizona by rental car just before sunrise on Tuesday the second of December.

CHAPTER 42

Lydia Butcher continued her miraculous recovery. By Wednesday the third of December, President Dick Butcher felt confident enough to leave her bedside to attend the funeral of Earl Price. She was receiving the best care in the world. He had no reason to stay with her constantly except for an irrational fear she might die if he left her.

He had to attend Earl's funeral. Earl Price had been his best friend—everybody knew it. The story they had circulated about the shooting was spin—a complete fabrication. The spin said a lone gunman entered the White House posing as a Journalist who had an interview with the First Lady. Earl was killed when he jumped between the gunman and the First Lady. She was wounded by a second shot before Secret Service Agents were able to kill the gunman. As much as he might hate Earl at the moment, he had to attend his funeral for appearances.

Cahmael phoned that morning wishing him well, and inquiring into Lydia's health.

"She's doing very well, Lord Cahmael, thanks to you," Dick said. He still had problems with addressing him as Lord, but he thought of the Dukes and Lords he had met in Great Britain and utilized the 'Lord' name on that basis. *Above all, he did not want to disrespect the man who had saved Lydia's life.* He knew that was an irrational thought, but he couldn't pry his mind away from it.

Thank you for the timely movement of your naval assets. I appreciate your cooperation, kind Sir, Cahmael said.

The man had good intelligence. The order had only gone out on Monday the first, and Cahmael already knew. That was quick, almost too quick. How did he know?

"Anytime, Sir. Your wish is my command," Dick answered. Having said it, he had immediate second thoughts, and wished he could take it back. Earl's warning, *We cannot be blackmailed*, raced through his mind. Dick shrugged off the thought. Cahmael completely ignored the statement.

My thoughts and prayers will be with you today, and so will the Pope's. I'll see you later my dear friend. The call ended.

It had been Earl's wish to be buried at Arlington National Cemetery. In fact, it had been promised to Earl as part of the agreement to become Economic Advisor. Dick thought about ignoring the promise and burying him elsewhere (in an unmarked grave in Potter's Field for instance), but it wouldn't have looked good. He had to keep up appearances and go with the spin. A State funeral with burial in Arlington was the order of the day.

It was a cold day in the Capital. A breeze made it colder. The grayness of the cloudy day made the occasion more somber than Dick thought it should have been. Earl had no family to pander to and that was good. The President wasn't in the mood for it.

He would be lighting the White House Christmas tree tomorrow evening. It was a few days late, but he thought it was a likely possibility that Lydia might be able to be wheeled where she could see it. She had made remarkable progress. She was walking again, with assistance, but walking all the same.

The caravan reached the cemetery and wove its way to the gravesite. A tent had been set up for the family and dignitaries. Since there was no family, Dick was seated in the first row with his Cabinet Members seated to his right. The wind whipped the corners of the tent, reminding everybody it was winter. Snow crunched under the feet of the coffin bearers.

The Chairman of the Joint Chiefs, Admiral Lemuel Perkins, had sent his Assistant, Captain John Ramsey, to represent him at the funeral. That made the President very unhappy.

The White House Chaplain, Reverend Harry Traynor, started the service with a prayer. He preached the usual graveside sermon extolling the virtues of the departed. It droned on in the President's ears, but he hardly heard. Thinking of Lydia wiped out any interest he might have in the service.

They fired the twenty-one gun salute, played Taps and then folded the flag. They presented the triangular folded flag to the best friend of the deceased, the President. The gesture took him by surprise. He never thought about receiving it. Tears stung his eyes. His shoulders shook from sobs long overdue. Grief from the loss of his friend swept over him.

CHAPTER 43

If you asked Mike Arzetti, he might say the investigation into the death of Officer Roy Cassidy had pretty much hit a brick wall; but, even then, it still hung over his head like an apparition from hell. There were no leads other than the bullet they traced to a rifle owned by Alan Noble, and Alan Noble had disappeared.

Mike wasn't involved with the investigation, but he had a lot riding on it. He suspected Alan Noble shot Roy Cassidy to keep him from identifying Mike as a member of the underground. Mike had sent Shires to tell Alan to call him so he could warn him that the police knew his identity.

Shires tried to make contact with the man, but the meeting had gone awry when Homeland Security arrived on the scene. They chased Alan away before Lampton could pass the message.

Most of the time, Mike could put all that out of his head, but he had been reminded this morning when he received a call from Shires at the precinct before he and George left on patrol.

"I'm using a land-line because they listen to my cell," Shires said. "I need to make contact with someone in the underground. My fiancée's life is in danger. I have to make her disappear, and you have connections. Can you help me?"

"Where are you?" Mike asked.

"Somewhere between Virginia and California. I stopped to call you at the Precinct before you left for patrol."

Mike thought quickly. *Today was Wednesday. He knew they were set to get his Dad tomorrow and wondered if this might gum up the works.* What he decided to do was against his better judgment.

"Look, you need to get to San Francisco. Start driving and call me on my home phone tonight around 9. The number is listed. By the way, does she have a chip?"

"Sure, and no she doesn't have a chip," Shires answered and hung up.

Mike figured he would talk to Harold Goodin. If anybody could help, it would be him. Making her disappear would be easier without a chip. He knew Shires had one. Nathan Conrad's phone call had confirmed it.

At 6:00 that evening, Mike called Harold Goodin. He wasn't home and didn't get back to Mike until 10:00 that evening. Mike explained the circumstances. Harold thought for a few moments. *I hate to have two things going on at the same time,* he said, *but maybe we can work it out. Does Shires have the chip?*

"Yes."

But she doesn't. Is that right?

"Yes. That's correct."

Tomorrow we have to deal with your Dad and his friends. We pick them up in El Cerrito around noon. Is that what you told your Dad?

"Yes. I told them to catch BART from wherever they are and get to the El Cerrito station, then go to the parking lot and find the motor home like we discussed. They're due to arrive about noon."

Okay, then I think we can work Shires' problem in later that day. He'll have to bring the woman to Napa. He must get off Highway 29 at Trancas. Turn right on Trancas and get immediately into the left lane for a left turn at the first light. That will take him into the Bel Aire Plaza. Trader Joe's will be on his right.

"*Leave the woman on the sidewalk in front of Trader Joe's around seven and drive away. We'll pick her up there. She should set any luggage she has on the sidewalk, stand beside it, and wait. You can assure him she won't have to wait very long.*

"*He must drive away immediately, and continue on up Hwy 29 past Calistoga to Hwy 53. Follow that to Hwy 20 and turn right for about 37 miles and merge on to Interstate 5 toward Redding. At Redding, he will turn Northeast on HWY 299 and go to Burney.*

"*From there he will turn South on HWY 44 toward Susanville and then on to Reno. At Reno, he will hit Interstate-80 and go back to Sacramento, and then on back to San Francisco. They'll be tracing his chip, so he must not deviate from these directions. He must remember to make pauses every now and then at any small town along the way to do something other than get gas or spend the night. We don't want the stop in Napa to be anything different from any of the other stops he will make.*

Mike had written down the directions, so he didn't repeat word-for-word everything Harold told him, just enough to let the man know he understood.

Shires had called Mike at home about 9:00 that evening. It was before he had received the information. Mike explained that he didn't know anything as yet. Shires would have to call the next day to find out what to do. Shires agreed quickly and hung up. Mike almost wished he hadn't for he wanted a reason to reject Shires for he didn't trust the man. But Mike knew the rules, and he had to abide by them. If people were serious about getting into the underground they wouldn't ask questions, and they'd be willing to accept things as they came. Someone who asks a lot of questions, and needs to be reassured probably doesn't want to join. Those people are rejected immediately. Mike had wanted an excuse to reject Shires Lampton. Harold had no reservations with Lampton, so Mike let it go.

CHAPTER 44

Shires Lampton and Jordan Smith had taken turns driving. They had driven all day Tuesday—Tuesday night and most of Wednesday to get to Flagstaff. They had to average sixty-five miles an hour to make good time. They used a trick Shires had learned from a friend. It was called truck tagging—just fall in behind a truck and let him take you along at speeds in excess of seventy-five miles an hour—truckers know the location of the highway patrol. He had called Mike Arzetti from a public phone that evening, and was told he would have to drive on to California—still without knowing anything—and call again when he got there.

They were exhausted but they drove again, taking turns—one slept while the other drove, just as they had done the entire trip. They drove through Arizona and into California going North on Hwy 99. They stopped along the way for Shires to call Mike about 7:00 Thursday morning. He wrote down everything Mike told him. It was good news to Shires, but Jordan didn't agree.

"Boo, you're going to leave me in the middle of nowhere. I'll never see you again."

"It's not the middle of nowhere, it's the Napa Valley—beautiful wine country, you'll see."

"But I'll never see you again, will I. Say it! Say, 'Jordan I won't be able to see you!' Say it Shires!"

He couldn't bring himself to say it. It might be true, but he held out hope it wasn't. He wanted to see Jordan as much as she wanted to see him. He hadn't discussed that part with Mike. He just wanted to get Jordan to safety—the sooner the better.

"I'm not gonna say it sweetheart, because it's not true. There will be times when we can see each other, but they'll be few and far between.

"Boo…honey…you and I both know that few and far really means mostly never and never," she said. Jordan picked up the paper on which he had written the instructions, studied it for a moment and said, "Look at these directions. You're going to do some serious driving to cover up the fact that you dropped me in Napa. These people aren't kidding they know what it takes to hide in plain sight.

"They won't be worried about us seeing each other. They'll only be concerned about not being discovered. If that means we don't see each other, well then, so be it." She had been waving the paper at him as he drove

She was having second thoughts. Shires could tell by her posture and said, "Sweetheart, we've come a long way. You're tired and worried…"

"Shires!" she interrupted sharply. "Of course I'm tired and worried. You're tired and worried. We're both tired and worried. We're exhausted for God's sake, but we're talking about the rest of our lives here. I can't pass this off as just another little speed bump in the parking lot of life. This is a major obstacle and we're going to crash right into it. Don't you see?"

"Sweetheart, I know this is not a bump in the road. I know that, baby. It's a serious step we've taken to protect you. If you go back to your normal life there's a possibility you'll be killed. I don't know why they targeted you and Olivia. All I can think is the two of you must have been involved in something that was so sensitive they don't want you to live, with or without the chip. It seems to me if they kill you without the chip there'll be less explaining to do—maybe that's why they didn't give you the injection. Do you know if Olivia was included in the first census?"

"No, she wasn't. We used to wonder about that, but we figured they just missed us, and would come back later—they never did. She didn't have the chip either."

"Can you remember working on any projects with her?"

"Well, if you want to call it working together, we did once, but just for a moment. It was a UFO project of some kind. It had to do with alien technology, but we were taken off of it almost as soon as we started.

"In fact, Boo, we never started. They announced we were going to be involved, they told us what it was, and then, just as suddenly, we were jerked away. They never explained why. That was the only time the two of us ever came together at DARPA for work purposes."

"I don't think they'd want to kill you over UFO stuff or for the video I gave you, but you just don't know how the minds that make up the government work. Some of them are really scary. Baby, please do this for me. I promise I'll see you as much as possible. I can't lose you. I love you too much."

"Do you love me enough to have the chip removed from your hand and come hide with me?"

The question caught Shires off guard, but he didn't have to think about it. He knew the answer. "If the situation calls for it, I'd do it in a heartbeat, Sweetheart."

CHAPTER 45

Melissa Hardin watched the computer screen. Everything had appeared normal since Monday when the program began. She guessed it was normal. There had been no reports of anomalies happening anywhere in her area—nothing that drew her attention, anyway. She couldn't tell if people were in or out of their areas of normal travel. She didn't yet have enough information to apply anomaly checks, but it was pouring in.

Melissa was the leader of five people. She could access any of their screens and see what they were seeing at any given time. Besides searching for anomalies herself, she also answered any question a team member might have. There had been many this first week of the program.

The one that had surprised her most occurred on Thursday about 1:30 in the afternoon. She knew the exact time because they had to catalogue each and every anomaly, and state its nature.

"Melissa, I have the mother of all anomalies on my screen," Ron Hartwell, a programmer three cubicles down from Melissa, called excitedly.

Melissa clicked to his screen and saw nothing unusual.

"What am I supposed to be seeing, Ron?"

"Back up the program about five minutes," he said.

She did that and noticed a grouping of four chips together in the same area. She checked location and found they were at the BART station in El Cerrito.

Suddenly one of the chips disappeared from the screen, then another and another until all four were gone. She grabbed the red phone, spoke her name into the mouthpiece and heard the ringing on the other end.

Central, answered the female voice.

"Possible violators at BART station in El Cerrito," she said.

What is the violation?

"Destruction of chip; They've disappeared from the screen."

The system was working. The computer notifies the programmers when it recognizes an anomaly, and alerts the programmers who notify Central Control of its nature and location. Melissa knew the operators at Central Control would be focusing the spy camera in on the BART station as she spoke. They would want to know exactly where those people were when their chips disappeared, and where did they go afterwards?

She typed on her screen. *Ron, get the names and history of those who disappeared. We need to send the info to Central Control right away.*

"I'm already on it," he answered in a loud voice.

This was definitely the one anomaly that didn't need history. Actually, Melissa hadn't expected it—especially so soon after the beginning of the program.

It surprised her that someone might not want to be involved in the National Program. It was such a convenient way to prevent identity theft. How could they possibly not want it?

As far as being tracked and swearing allegiance to Cahmael, those were minor things. She pledged allegiance to the flag almost every day in school, swearing allegiance to a man was no more than that. She couldn't see anything wrong with being tracked either, especially if you have nothing to hide.

She had heard there were people hiding in the underground who thought that Cahmael was the Antichrist, and they were hiding from him. It was such an outlandish belief she couldn't imagine anyone falling for it.

Here are the names, appeared on Melissa's screen.

And then the screen showed the following: *Anthony Arzetti, Greg Littlejack, John Monroe and Kinzi Tern are the four missing. They have a common history. They were part of the group who claimed that a person named Panguitch Hewey was going to start trouble in San Francisco and kill Jehosea Cahmael. They were arrested and charged with terrorism and second-degree murder in the deaths of a Sheriff and five of his deputies in Arizona, but they were never brought up on those charges. It doesn't say why.*

They were friends of the two men who were publicly executed, Tom Horn and Vince Nalone. They were released this past Monday as part of the prisoner release program. I have their complete history all the way back to High School. Do you want that?

Melissa typed in *No, but send that info to Central. They will want to know it.*

The name "Arzetti" rang a bell. She searched her database and discovered a Mike Arzetti. He was a San Francisco cop. She brought up his info. His father, Anthony Arzetti, was one of those arrested for terrorism and ultimately released last Monday. *Hello guys, small world isn't it.*

CHAPTER 46

Officers from Homeland Security confronted Mike Arzetti and his partner, George Wildes, after their shift Thursday afternoon.

They identified themselves as John Blake and Amanda Roberts, and asked Mike if they could talk to him. He agreed and followed them into an interrogation room.

Mike knew it had to be about his dad, but he was actually surprised at how quickly they had responded. His dad could only have been missing a short time, yet here they were. He was impressed and a little worried. He thought it would take them at least a couple days to get to him. *Did his dad and his friends have enough time to get away?*

"You and your dad are very close, isn't that true?" asked the female officer. She was a tall, slender, black woman in her late twenties, Mike guessed.

"Yes. Yes, of course it is. Why? Is something wrong?" he asked with mock concern.

"You don't know?" John Blake asked. Mike could hear the sarcasm in his voice, indicating he thought Mike already knew all about his dad's escape. Blake was a short, balding, powerfully built white man in his late thirties.

"No. What are you talking about?"

"Your dad, and three of his friends, jumped the chip program this afternoon, and you're telling us you don't know anything about it?" Blake asked.

"That's correct. I'm telling you I don't know anything about it."

"And you expect us to believe that?" The woman asked.

"Actually, I really don't care what you believe," Mike said, and started for the door.

"Where do you think you're going?" Blake asked.

"You forget? I'm a cop. I know my rights. I'm not under arrest, and as far as I'm concerned this conversation is over."

"I just want to warn you that what your dad has done is a death penalty offense. If you're involved, it's the same for you."

Mike wanted to lay some choice words on these two, but held his tongue and walked out the door. He knew what the guy told him was true. He was angry to be reminded of it so soon after the fact. He also knew that fear lay just below the surface of the anger.

He hadn't thought about it much until now. But to be confronted so quickly had brought out the stark reality of the enormous seriousness of the step his father, and his father's friends, had taken.

This was not a situation to be taken lightly. He could feel the paranoia creeping into his bones—what about George? Would he stick with him now that he too would face the death penalty? George had known when he joined the underground that deadly contingencies could arise, but would he keep the faith? Mike figured his worry was unwarranted since George was also implicated in covering up for whoever killed Roy Cassidy. But still, the death penalty hanging over your head is a sharp turn from the everydayness of other concerns.

"What did they want?" George asked when Mike arrived in the locker room.

"They were fishing. They wondered what I might know about my dad running from the chip program today."

"Your dad did what?" George asked in a shocked voice as if he were amazed at the news.

Mike applauded him inwardly, for he had reacted as anyone who had been surprised. If somebody were listening they would be hard put to believe George Wildes had any knowledge of the escape of Anthony Arzetti and his friends.

But could they keep up the charade for an indefinite period of time without slipping up along the way? Mike wondered.

CHAPTER 47

It was 7 P.M. President Richard Butcher stood poised to throw the switch that would light the Christmas tree in the Blue Room of the White House. He squeezed Lydia's hand. She loved the Christmas season. They had delivered the tree the last week of November. It had been decorated that day, but they had postponed the lighting until tonight so Lydia could be present. They brought her back to the White House just for the lighting.

"Five…four…three…two…one…time," the Secret Service Agent said. The President flipped the switch. The lights were spectacular. Dick heard Lydia gasp and say, "Oh honey, it's beautiful." Those few words made his evening.

He had to mingle with the kids and others who had gathered to watch the lighting. He did his duty halfheartedly, wanting to get back to Lydia. An hour or so later the crowd dispersed at the urging of the Secret Service and he was left alone again with Lydia. He sat beside her and took her hand. Lydia squeezed, and he squeezed back as they shared the beauty of the lights in silence. He wanted the moment to last forever—it wouldn't.

Tomorrow he had to meet with the five men who had been disappointed by the early start date of the National Chip Identification Program. Four of them were CEO's of large companies, and the fifth was CIO of a large bank. They were angry. He would tell them he got cold feet at the last moment and called it off. He knew he'd have to do some fast-talking to keep their support. They were the underpinnings of his whole government. They helped him get elected. He owed them, and they didn't appreciate what he had done.

Not many people appreciated him. All he wanted to do was lead the country in the right direction, and not let it fall into the hands of the degenerates who would destroy it—degenerates who would allow all sorts of excesses, and to Dick Butcher that was unacceptable.

He didn't attempt to make his own beliefs into government policy, preferring to work through the backdoor by using the bureaucracy that actually ran the government.

It was so simple to let the bureaucrats follow the guidelines. Let them take the heat for the ineptness of government. Dick had promised the large corporations many things and he had kept his promises. They'd just have to give him a pass on this chip injection thing.

Most promises were easy since the work had already been done for him by other well-meaning administrations. It's surprising what can be done in the name of freedom and equality.

This thing with Cahmael's blackmailing would blow over. He knew it would. If only he'd had time to convince Earl of that. Cahmael was a fraud. He couldn't withstand the heat that could be brought to bear. Dick Butcher wasn't sure Jehosea Cahmael understood whom he was taking on when he decided to blackmail America.

He felt Lydia's hand relax. She had fallen asleep. He stared at her soft face. She looked so peaceful. God, he loved her.

CHAPTER 48

Although Shires was close to exhaustion, he drove most of the day on Thursday. He had to time it to arrive in Napa at 7 that evening. He didn't want Jordan waiting any longer than necessary. He hated dropping her off and dreaded all the miles ahead of him, but he had to do it because it disguised the actual drop-off point. He feared his failure could lead to her death.

He didn't know how the underground could hide so many people. There must be thousands, and they all had to hide in plain sight.

At four that afternoon, Shires stopped for gas, and Jordan wanted a bottle of water. He pumped the gas then entered the convenience store to get the water. The TV was reporting national news. It showed the President lighting the White House Christmas tree. Shires paid scant attention to it. His mind was intent on getting Jordan to Napa and into hiding. He seemed like he was being watched, now that he knew the full capability of the chip in his hand.

He felt pushed by circumstance to get Jordan to safety, while at the same time he dreaded the moment he would have to relinquish her to the care of others. They didn't talk about the moment of parting. They had an agreement—neither of them would discuss it.

They ate at Applebee's Restaurant alongside the I-80 Freeway in Fairfield.

"Where do you think I'll be taken?" Jordan asked. They had delivered the food and Jordan was cutting her steak. Shires noticed she was having a full meal, including mashed potatoes, instead of her usual water and crackers diet, but he didn't mention it. Jordan liked to do symbolic things.

This would be her last meal with him for a long time. She was making it memorable.

"I don't know," Shires answered.

"I think they'll keep me on the West Coast."

"What makes you say that?"

"'Cause I'm from the East Coast. I'm known there. I'm too familiar, so it seems logical to me. You've already done the hard work by bringing me here. I think they'll go with that."

"You're probably right. Man, it's gonna be difficult..." Shires said and stopped himself. He was thinking out loud about missing her. They had promised they wouldn't speak of it. He had to remind himself constantly that doing it this way meant she would be alive. He'd just have to figure out a way to see her.

"Look, Sweetheart, I think I know a way we will be able to see each other."

Jordan looked at him but said nothing. He knew she was trying not to get her hopes up, but he wanted her to have some hope of seeing him.

"I will talk to them and see if you'll be able to visit me. If we were to sneak you in, you could stay there for a long time and no one would be the wiser. When I'm home, I always eat my meals in anyway. We'll try that anyway. I can't see a problem with it...can you?"

"Of course, there's a problem with it. There has to be. It sounds too simple. The biggest problem will be surveillance. They will be watching you, Boo. As soon as they realize I'm gone, they'll be at your door. Then they'll watch you night and day."

They finished their meal in silence. What Jordan had said was true. Homeland Security would be relentless in their pursuit of her. He just wished he knew why.

At 6:55 that evening, Shires Lampton pulled into the Bel Aire Plaza in Napa. Remembering that in all probability the spy camera could be watching his movement, he parked where Jordan could get out and move quickly under the canopy fronting the stores.

He told Jordan to stay in the car while he retrieved her suitcase from the trunk. With that done, Jordan climbed out and jumped quickly under the canopy. They kissed a long goodbye kiss. Then she took the handle of the rolling suitcase, turned her back on him, and walked down the sidewalk to Trader Joe's. They didn't speak.

Shires didn't look back, and returned to HWY 29. The lump in his throat made it difficult to swallow. He felt the tears stinging his eyes, and still he drove on. He had to get distance between them before he changed his mind.

CHAPTER 49

The Control Center of the National Chip Identification Program for the West Coast is located in San Francisco. It is housed in an enormous warehouse near the waterfront. An innocent-looking old-brick building, bristling with multitudes of communications hardware spread over its roof, yet concealed from vision—only an airplane flying over could see it. The basement is filled with computers and software. They were ready for all imaginable contingencies.

Matthew Stoneham, a thirty-nine year old computer whiz with waist length black hair and a full gray beard, manned the controls of the spy chip camera like a jet pilot. He had done work like this for years, but now it had become a thousand times more interesting. *Before, it had been find the bad guy lurking around a corner or behind a wall. Now, it was watch everybody…what a concept!*

His first taste of real action under the new program had come on Thursday afternoon with the disappearance of four people. When the call came in he was playing a computer game he had designed, but against which he had never won—that bugged him; for as hard as he tried he couldn't beat it.

He put the game away and sprang into action, typing in the coordinates of the El Cerrito BART station, causing the eye in the sky to focus in for a closer look.

He typed in the time twenty minutes prior to the disappearance of the chips, noting, in real time, the almost empty parking lot before he did so. The photos came in at the rate of one every fifteen seconds and afforded an almost moving picture of the scene below. He froze that twenty-minute photo for comparison later, then miniaturized it and moved it to the upper right hand corner.

The maneuver that Matt had just performed with the computer and the spy camera was unknown to the general public. They might know they are being spied on, but they didn't know the degree. Seeing back in time is only possible if there is a picture of the past available. That would only be possible if there were enough cameras, and storage space for the cyber videos.

There were many cameras. Matt Stoneham had seen to that. He helped in the placement of a camera to cover every quadrant of the earth—forty of them, four over each pole, eight at forty-five degree angles from each pole, and sixteen as a belt around the equator. There was some overlapping coverage, but it was felt that would be better than leaving unobserved areas. The cost had been enormous—billions of dollars Matt figured, but the money was always there. It had never been mentioned in any appropriations bill. It was as if the program didn't exist. The two companies that built the equipment were never identified.

Matt knew their identities because in his early career he had worked for DARPA and helped develop the spy camera program under the guise of alien technology. The word 'alien' was an anagram for Aerial Lens Insect Eye Nomenclature. In other words the lens for the camera was a copy of the eye of a fly. As each camera took wide angle pictures it also took close-ups with the small cameras imbedded over the surface of the larger lens—hence the nomenclature of a fly's eye.

All these digital videos were compressed using an advanced algorithm not generally available to the public. This compression helped with the crowding problem of so much information over such a long period of time in cyber space. The compression was accomplished with a forgetting algorithm that would begin taking place after the first six months. In the first six months one picture would be taken every fifteen seconds—a total of 5760 pictures per camera per day. With forty cameras that is a total of 230,400 pictures per day.

In the compression algorithm this total is saved for a six-month period. The age of the saved memory is the most important part of the forgetting mode of the compression algorithm. At the age of six months the amount saved is cut in half by the forgetting mode of the algorithm. At the end of another six months another half of the saved memory would be forgotten—at the end of another six months the memory is halved again, on and on. The cameras would continue to take the 230,400 pictures. It's just that the farther back in time you go the fewer photos you would keep—hence less detail. As for now, the program was new and nothing would be forgotten for a long time.

One feature allowed the government to create "protected" time regions, allowing them to say this time period on this day should not undergo the data-loss algorithm. This gave them full-resolution for any interesting "events".

Now, Matt Stoneham ran the West Coast Area of Operations for the National Chip Identification Program. He was a hands-on person who loved a challenge. So, naturally, he manned the spy camera controls for the first few days of the new program, just to get the feel of it.

Nothing struck him as unusual at the first twenty-minute check. He froze that photo and moved the picture to the upper right hand corner just below the other snapshot. He continued this segmentation back in time for an hour and a half before his search was rewarded.

Four different people left the train dressed similarly. They all wore dark sweatshirts with hoods drawn over their heads. They didn't walk together, but, as he watched, they all went to a motor home parked in the lot. He immediately alerted Homeland Security to look for the motor home. He fast forwarded the video looking for their return and found it about forty-five minutes later. They left alone in five-minute intervals until all four had returned to the BART. And then, to his surprise, a fifth person, and a sixth, and then a seventh, also exited, and headed for the train. *Who were they?* Then the chips disappeared, one at a time, from the computer screen. The motor home drove away. It parked out-of-sight under a freeway overpass a short distance away and never moved again. He couldn't see the driver leaving.

Homeland Security's unmarked car arrived about ten minutes after the motor home left the area. He directed them to the overpass that hid the motor home. The car approached with its lights flashing. The vehicle was empty. The perpetrators were gone, but they couldn't have gotten far.

Matthew Stoneham was elated. He knew they'd catch these guys quickly. The system had worked perfectly.

CHAPTER 50

The Lear Jet crashed about 7:30 Friday morning as it came in for a landing at Dulles International. Dick Butcher watched the coverage from Lydia's bedside, but he was thinking more of the upcoming meeting than he was of the news. The phone rang. He picked it up. "Yes," he said.

Mr. President, the voice said, *This is Bill Smiley. I have some bad news, Sir.* There was an expectant pause as if he were waiting for the President to say something. Finally, Dick obliged and said, "Go ahead."

The gentlemen you were scheduled to meet with this morning have been killed in a plane crash at Dulles.

"All of them?"

All five, Sir. All five CEO's perished.

The news stunned him. He glanced back at the TV before he said, "Thanks Bill. I want a briefing as soon as possible. Can you work that out?"

Yessir, right away.

Thanks again," Dick said and hung up.

He didn't know what to make of the news. It was a turn of events he never expected. He clicked off the TV and settled back in his chair to ponder what he would do now. He wasn't close to any of them, but they were tied to him through politics and, as much as he hated to admit it, greed. He had never thought about his relationship with them before today. There was no sadness in him for the loss, only a deep sense of dread over the people that would replace them. Would they be as willing to support his Presidency?

He no longer had to explain his behavior, or give his reason for changing the start date of the chip program. He had dreaded that because he would have had to tell about the threat on Lydia's life, and his capitulation. He didn't want to, but it would have been necessary to tell these men—now that had become a moot point.

The phone rang interrupting his thoughts. He figured it was Bill Smiley.

"Yes," he answered expectantly.

Mr. President, how are you and your lovely wife today? Cahmael asked.

For some reason the phone call didn't surprise him even if it had been unexpected. Five men who might have been a potential threat to himself and to Cahmael had just died, and there was Cahmael. The coincidence was eerie. Dick was beginning to think it wasn't coincidence.

"Fine sir, just fine. Lydia is recuperating well. She's walking again with assistance, but walking for sure. She was able to watch the festivities last night."

Saw them myself. I must say the tree was beautiful.

"Thank you, I think the staff did an outstanding job."

I will agree with you about that. How is the chip program progressing?

"It seems to be perking right along. No big problems as yet anyway, but it's only been a few days."

I hear you've had some problems with people choosing to go elsewhere; four people, to be exact. This is not good. I trust you will throw all your resources into finding them.

"You know I will, sir."

You must do it quickly. We'll make an example of them. Say hello to your lovely wife for me, The line went dead.

How had Cahmael found out about the escape so fast? Dick had only been briefed on it at bedtime last night. Cahmael would never say how he might know, he was a man of few words. Dick Butcher couldn't remember ever having a long conversation with him. Any that he'd had were filled with implication and innuendo, never an outright statement of fact.

Now, Gregory Chamus and Hal Skidmore were the only others who knew of the stock maneuver. He liked the thought, and he wondered if he truly had Jehosea Cahmael to thank for it, or had it been a stroke of fate that Cahmael used to his advantage?

CHAPTER 51

Friday morning, Tony Arzetti sat on the couch of a small travel trailer where he and Kinzi would be living for a few days. They had been told they would not stay long at any one place.

He wondered if they had done the wise thing. Now they would spend their lives as fugitives, unable to work and have a normal life. Of course, a normal life nowadays was difficult to define.

He was sure Cahmael would have them killed the first chance that presented itself—especially if he could make it appear to be an accident.

Yesterday, he and Kinzi along with John Monroe, Greg Littlejack, Nathan Conrad, Elma Watson the nurse who assisted, and Grant Holden the doctor who removed the chips, had pulled off what they thought was the coup of the century.

They had escaped from chip surveillance when, after having the chips removed, they made it appear as if they had reentered BART and boarded the train. Instead, they had removed and discarded the hooded sweatshirts they wore, and mingled with the crowd at the El Cerrito station.

Their getaway car, a stolen SUV, arrived quickly. Beverly Goodin drove it. Her passenger was Sly Norman. He was the thief who had not only stolen and driven the motor home, but also smashed the chips.

She had picked him up under the overpass where he abandoned the stolen motor home—a spot where it was impossible for the spy camera to see him. Sly had also stolen the SUV she was driving. It had been an add-on, and he had increased his price by a thousand dollars to do it.

They had covered themselves in every way possible. Even to the double back; a risky maneuver, but clever if they could pull it off. It's a criminal's natural instinct to get away, and a cop's mindset to work on that premise. So they didn't run, they waited at the scene mingling with the small crowd, while sending the police on a wild goose chase. At least they hoped that's what they had done.

Their instructions were simple. When the car arrives only one person can get in. Another must walk to the end of the block. The car will drive away and come back in a little while to pick up the one at the end of the block. Each person would be picked up in a different place, and no two would be picked up at the same time. This was done to divert attention away from a group of people getting into one vehicle. It took a while. After they had been loaded in, they spied the unmarked car approaching the motor home with its lights flashing. It had driven right past them.

They didn't stick around to gloat. Beverly nosed the car into the street toward I-80. It would take them to Hwy 37, which in turn would take them to Hwy 29 and north to Napa.

Tony and Kinzi had been dropped at this site, the others were dropped elsewhere. Tony didn't know where. They were told this would be their home for two weeks. It had been stocked with enough food and drinking water to last two people for a month. They would be moved every two weeks for the first year, and leaving the place was not permitted.

"It's like being in jail, Tony," Kinzi complained while they were eating breakfast.

"Oh no, it's not. In jail I slept by myself. I love your warm little body next to mine, sweetheart. I'll take this life anytime."

She smiled her sweet, freckle-faced smile he loved so much. He wondered how long they could keep ahead of the law. They had committed a crime punishable by death. It would be the same gruesome death suffered by Tom and Vince. He pushed the ugly thought from his mind.

CHAPTER 52

Mike Arzetti and George Wildes went to Gordy's Bar on Friday night for burgers and beer. Mike hadn't been there since before Roy Cassidy's murder. He had no rational reason other than it felt strange.

Friday nights were usually busy because Gordy held a wet T-shirt contest. Mike and George attended whenever possible. It drew some great-looking chicks. Mike had met a few and had taken a couple home on nights he knew his sister would be gone, but he'd never had a serious relationship.

Tonight would have been no different except for one contestant—the winner, Melissa. Mike and George had never seen her before. She was "out-of-this-world" beautiful.

Mike found his way to her booth carrying an extra beer, which he handed to her.

"A present for your win. Congratulations."

"Well, thank you very much," she said, giving him one of the greatest smiles he'd ever seen. "Care to join us?" she asked. She was sitting with two other women.

"Great, but it'll have to be me and my friend George over there." He pointed to George who raised his hand.

"Sure," they agreed in unison.

Mike motioned for George to come over.

When George arrived. Melissa introduced herself and her friends.

"I'm Melissa. The redhead is Terri, and the other blonde is Carmen Roadend. You're right, I said *Roadend* and we don't know the nationality of it. Neither does she, but she claims to be Dutch. We just take her word for it." They laughed.

"Well, I'm Mike Arzetti and this is George Wildes. I'm Italian and he isn't." They laughed again.

Mike sat beside Melissa. George sat at the other end of the curved booth beside Carmen Roadend. None of the girls in the contest had been required to give their last name. Carmen did because nobody believed her anyway. They never gave their true last name in any bar. It kept unwanted male attention away from their door. They worried about stalkers.

"We were told this is a cop bar. Is that true?" asked Terri the redhead. They all looked at her. She spread her arms in a questioning gesture and said. "What? I'm the only one here without a guy sitting next to her, so I figure I get to ask the questions."

"Oh you poor woman," George said, and climbed over Carmen to sit between her and Terri. George put his arm around her and gave her a big hug. "Is that better?" he asked.

"It's a start," Terri said.

"Since I'm sitting next to you, I'll answer your question. Yes, this is a cop bar. I confess. I'm a cop. Mike's a criminal, but he likes to hang around with us."

"So, you guys are partners?" Melissa asked.

"Yes we are…have been for nigh on to a year," Mike said using his best southern drawl. "And what may I ask do y'all do?"

"Well Suh, if you really must know, we ah govmint hoes," Carmen matched his drawl with one of her own.

"Ah begs to differ madam, we ah prostitutes and we ah working undercover," Terri added.

"We ah cheap too," Melissa interjected amidst the laughter.

"Does this mean you won't tell us where you work, because if you did you'd have to kill us?" George asked.

"We use torture. Killing is against our religion," Terri answered.

"We can give you a hint. We work for Homeland Security. We're computer operators. Melissa is our supervisor," Carmen said.

"Well, there you go. Now you've told them everything," Melissa protested indignantly. "Now we'll have to torture them," she said, laughing as she did so.

"You're their supervisor and you brought them here to this den of iniquity to display their breasts?" George asked, feigning distaste.

"Wonderful job, Melissa…wonderful job. You did good," Mike said.

The five new friends talked on into the night. Melissa felt drawn to Mike and it worried her. She remembered his name from yesterday. His dad was Tony Arzetti, the man who, along with three others, jumped the chip program and disappeared. She should stop this right now, before it progressed any farther. She knew she should just get up and walk out, but she didn't.

The bar closed at 2 AM, so they went to Mike's apartment to continue. The girls followed in their car. Mike stopped at a 24-hour grocery and bought bacon and eggs. He served breakfast about four in the morning.

"I've never done this before," Melissa said to Mike as they stood by the sink washing dishes.

"My first time too," Mike admitted. "I was having fun and didn't want it to end."

"Me neither," Melissa concurred.

Mike leaned over and kissed her. She turned toward him. He encircled her body with his wet hands and kissed her again. It was a long, lingering kiss.

"Sorry…didn't mean to get you all wet," he apologized sheepishly.

"Oh don't worry about it. You can get me wet like that any time you want," Melissa said and kissed him again.

Terri and Carmen were in the living room taking turns dancing with George—the music played quietly on the stereo. Ann, Mike's sister, was gone for the night, but they didn't want to wake the neighbors. At one point, while George and Carmen were dancing, Terri went to the kitchen to fetch Mike and Melissa and saw them kissing. She smiled, backed away and sat on the couch. *What a night this had been!*

CHAPTER 53

Shires Lampton spent Thursday night in Reno. Even in his fatigued condition he couldn't get his mind off Jordan. He purposefully didn't look back when he dropped her, thus avoiding any last image of a forlorn woman being abandoned in the middle of nowhere. But the image seared his heavy heart. It stuck in his brain. He didn't sleep much. Every time he closed his eyes he saw her.

He was exhausted when he arrived home Friday evening—way too tired to argue with his boss, Clyde Johnson, who called at nine that evening.

Where have you been? Clyde's angry voice demanded.

The sleeping pill had just kicked in when Shires answered. It took a moment to gather his thoughts.

"What are you talking about?"

You. You have two projects hanging fire, and you're absent from the firing line. Where have you been? I've bugged your producer to the point she's avoiding me. I'm always leaving messages, but she never returns my calls. I'm just about ready to cancel both projects. You better come up with some good answers, or your career might be in the toilet. Kapeesh?

Shires managed to mumble "um huh" or something that resembled an affirmative answer.

Saturday morning, Shires ordered breakfast from room service and waited for it to arrive. He ate slowly, feeling rested after the good night of sleep—drugged though it was, it still felt good. He poured a cup of coffee to sip before he called his producer, Maria Sanger.

Shires, where have you been? Clyde's been after me about our lack of progress on Hap Harrigan.

"I had just taken a sleeping pill when he called. Did I hear him right? He said we're behind on two stories…what's that all about?"

When we finish Harrigan, he wants an interview with Jehosea Cahmael.

"He what?"

You heard me, Shires. I said Jehosea Cahmael.

"Cahmael doesn't give interviews."

That's why he wants it, silly. We would be the first.

"That's all he wants, just an interview?"

Well, you know Clyde, he'll take more if he can get it.

Shires thought for a moment, sipped his coffee, and said, "I might have the beginnings of a story from my earlier trip to Grass Valley. It's something that goes back to the assassination attempt on the Pope. It might be an angle. I'll talk to you about it later. Did Felix get up there to get the extra video we needed?"

He did and he's ready to do the voiceovers whenever you're ready.

"I know it's the weekend, but would you call him and ask him if he could make it this afternoon?"

Well, like you say it is the weekend, but I'll call him and get back to you, okay?

"That would be great," Shires said and hung up. He took the coffee to the window as he stared at the Ferry Building across the street.

Leave it to Clyde to come up with such an asinine, yet challenging, assignment. How could you contact Cahmael? It's said he spends time at the Vatican. Maybe he could just ask for an interview—just call the Vatican and ask; they could only tell him 'No', and what if the answer were 'Yes', what then?

First question for Cahmael: "Are you the Antichrist?" Answer to first question: "Are you an idiot?" Not a good line of questioning—might lead to short interview. He knew he had to ask that question, so he'd do the old trick of putting the onus on somebody else and ask, "How do you respond to people who say you are the Antichrist?

Above all, he knew he would have to go without a hidden agenda. Straightforward would be his mantra for that interview—if it ever happened.

Shires walked to his computer and called up the narration he had prepared for the Harrigan story, looked it over, and printed it. He would read it from hardcopy. The thought of an interview with Cahmael was still in the back of his mind when Maria called to say that Felix would come. Shires thanked her for all her efforts, and added, "Why don't you put through a call to the Vatican. Ask what our network might do to get an interview with Cahmael; that is, if you don't have anything to do," Shires said and chuckled.

Okay. If I'm successful what do I get?

"A trip to Rome for one thing...and a dinner at the best restaurant there."

You're on Mr. Lampton. See ya in Rome, she said gleefully and hung up.

Maria never ducked a challenge. She would get the interview if she had to pull some of her own teeth.

"Hey, Felix, are you ready to film an interview with Cahmael?" Shires asked when he arrived later in the afternoon.

Felix Gunther stared at his boss. "You are kidding...right?"

"I don't know...Clyde gave me the assignment. I guess we will if I can get an appointment with him."

"I don't like the idea."

"Why not?"

"I don't trust him."

"Why?"

"He's the Antichrist, isn't he?"

"You believe that baloney?"

"I'm not sure, but I didn't really want to get close enough to find out either."

"So, if I get a date to go, you going with me?"

"Of course. I wouldn't miss it for the world."

They both laughed as they finished setting up Felix's equipment. Shires had noted his cameraman's reticence and knew he wasn't joking. He wondered if getting close to Cahmael might change his own opinion of the man.

Shires had tried desperately all that day to fill his brain with other things, but the image of Jordan Smith was there to greet him every time he closed his eyes.

CHAPTER 54

Every morning Melissa Hardin read her e-mail immediately after arriving at work. Monday morning was no different, except she was a little more tired than usual. She had spent the complete weekend, from start to finish, with Mike Arzetti. She couldn't believe she'd done that, but it was just how things had worked out.

The weekend had started as a dare. They had heard about the wet T-shirt contest at Gordy's Bar from Carmen's neighbor, a cop named John Ito. He said the bar was a 'cop bar', meaning it was a favorite hang out for off-duty police. They talked and laughed about it, then Carmen said, "Let's do it."

At first Melissa refused to go. Any woman exposing her breasts to cold water and leering men was probably a slut. It was not something she would ever do—especially in front of a bunch of low-lifes in a bar—cops or not.

"You girls are chickens," Carmen said, "I dare you to come with me."

They finally gave in. Terri caved first, then Melissa. So, like sheep to the slaughter, they were led down the primrose path to self-destruction, they joked later. It turned out to be the standing joke of the night after Melissa won. She hadn't even planned to enter. However, that reluctance didn't last. The cajoling of Terri and Carmen got the better of her—along with the help of a couple beers to lower her inhibitions. Ultimately, she found herself in the ladies bathroom with Carmen and Terri slipping out of her blouse and bra and into a white T-shirt with GORDY'S stenciled on the back.

She shook her head when she thought about it. They were standing on stage, all fifteen contestants, waiting for the inevitable splash of cold water, and still the coldness shocked her. It almost took her breath away.

The clapping started. It rose and fell as each contestant was named and pointed to. The girls who received the loudest applause stayed on stage while the others exited. The final five included Carmen, Terri, Melissa and two others. Melissa felt the warmth rising in her cheeks when the applause acclaimed her the winner. Even thinking about it now made her blush.

It was embarrassing sitting there in the crowded bar having just won a wet T-shirt contest, even after she removed the wet shirt and dressed in her street clothes. Men leered at her as they walked by raising their eyebrows and giving her the high sign with a thumb in the air. Why did she ever let them talk her into it?

And then Mike Arzetti walked into her life—all six foot-two of him, with his curly black hair, dark complexion, and pearly-whites flashing when he smiled. He just walked up, handed her a beer, smiled, and said "Congratulations". And that had made everything okay again. Just like magic it happened—a really crappy moment turned into a most wondrous thing. They began a conversation that continued the whole weekend and was still going on this morning when she climbed out of his bed to come to work.

It hadn't been all sex. It had been conversation and discovery. Carmen and Terri had given George a ride home Saturday morning, leaving her alone with Mike. The tender kissing that started in the kitchen continued into the bedroom and on it went.

An email dragged her out of her thoughts. It read: *Attention West Coast—television investigative reporter Shires Lampton, according to chip tracking, was visiting his girlfriend, Jordan Smith in Falls Church, Virginia. He returned to California last Tuesday, but Jordan Smith has disappeared. She should have returned to work last Wednesday but she didn't show up. It is not known if foul play is suspected. Be on the look out for any suspicious behavior by Mr. Lampton.*

Melissa typed in Lampton's name and called up his tracking information to see what others he might be talking with.

Most recently he had talked to Maria Sanger and Clyde Johnson. Before that, the list included many other names she didn't recognize, and two that she did—Jordan Smith and Mike Arzetti. Mike's name being there shocked her. Why would he have called Shires' cell? She called up a copy of the conversation.

Lampton, we need to talk.

What makes you think that?

I'll tell you when we meet.

Why would I meet with you?

Are you interested in finding out what really happened when the Pope was assassinated?

You mean that charade they put on for the public?

…Yeah…whatever.

Maybe. Who is this?

I'll tell you when we meet, not before.

Where and when?

Board the ferry to Vallejo tomorrow at noon. I'll see you there.

How will I know you?

You won't. I'll know you. The recording ended.

Melissa wondered why Mike was being so cryptic in the conversation, but didn't go any farther with it—after all this was only one conversation. She couldn't ask him without giving away her access to his movements, but made a mental note to check it out later.

She traced Lampton as he drove from Virginia to Flagstaff last Tuesday—then on Wednesday, when he drove from Flagstaff to Modesto. Thursday, he drove from Modesto all the way to Reno before he stopped for the night. Friday, he drove back to San Francisco.

Now why did he do that? Why did he go around in a big loop? Why didn't he just go straight from Modesto to San Francisco? That was curious behavior.

She knew he probably had a good reason. In all likelihood he had been working on a story. Still, it was an anomaly. She had to report it to Central Control and let Matthew Stoneham do his camera thing. He would find the truth.

CHAPTER 55

Nathan Conrad was not pleased with Mike and George over their little escapade with the girls. He told them so during a BART ride they shared from San Francisco to the Berkley station. It was the Monday evening after Mike's weekend with Melissa. The meeting had been prearranged, since it had to be public because of Mike and George's ID chips.

The underground's public meeting places were few and each was numbered. The ferry was number one; BART from San Francisco to Berkley was number two; Fisherman's Wharf number three. The safe house in the Napa Valley was number four. The only information a member of the underground needed about a meeting in the San Francisco area was date, time and number.

"The problem is this. These girls work for Homeland Security. In all likelihood they know a lot about you."

"I don't think so," George said.

"You guys are members of the underground and you have implanted chips. You're traceable. Any one of them could find out and expose you and the underground cell to which you belong. We would rather kill them then let that happen. So remember, even the lives of these girls are in your hands if you continue a relationship with them. Do I make myself clear?"

Mike Arzetti flashed back to the night of Roy Cassidy's murder. He knew Nathan was serious. Yet he wanted to continue his relationship with Melissa. She certainly didn't pose the same kind of threat as Roy. She was only a computer operator, nothing more. Roy had been actively seeking to connect him to the underground. Melissa wasn't.

Nathan Conrad's chubby face glowed a reddish hue. Mike wondered about his blood pressure. The stress was showing on his face.

"I have a serious problem with the underground. You guys can't go around killing people. I know you're doing it to protect everybody, but it's ridiculous and stupid."

"Look. I'll only say this once to you," Conrad said. His eyes flashed as he said it. "We're not playing a game here. There are many lives at stake. Either you guys take it seriously or get out before you do any harm."

"The idea that we can't have girlfriends sticks in my craw," George said.

"I'm not saying that. I'm saying you must be aware of whom you are dating, that's all."

"And women who work at Homeland are on the 'no list'. Is that what you're saying?" George asked sarcastically.

"No, I'm not saying anything of the sort. I'm just warning you in general that's all."

"Do you think it's necessary to warn us about every little thing?" Mike asked.

The chubby man stared hard at the two as the train pulled into the Berkeley station. "Nothing of the sort," he said. "You gentlemen understand the seriousness of the situation. I'll leave it at that."

"Understand this," Mike said as they all walked through the station, "I will continue to see Melissa Hardin. If anyone so much as lays a finger on her, I'll give all the information about the underground here in the Bay area to the authorities. Mark my words. Stay away from Melissa Hardin."

"You better be right about her," Nathan Conrad warned before he disappeared down Shattuck Street.

CHAPTER 56

Matt Stoneham worked tirelessly to unravel the mystery of the disappearing 'chip jumpers' as he called them. He had studied the photos over and over. The only train through the station at that time had been headed for Berkeley. Homeland had reached the Berkeley Bart stop within minutes, but they found nothing. Nobody remembered hooded sweatshirts and they didn't recognize photos. The 'chip jumpers' had pulled off a vanishing act right before his eyes. That was impossible. There had to be a trace of them somewhere. He just had to find it.

The call from Melissa Hardin changed his focus to Shires Lampton's cross-country drive. He hated to give up his chase of the 'chip jumpers' for something that seemed to him to be small potatoes compared to criminal activity. But thanks to modern technology the photos would be on record for the next three and a half years minimum. He could hunt them down at his leisure.

The first thing he noticed was the speed with which Lampton did it—that, in and of itself, suggested urgency. According to the photo history time-line, Jordan Smith was with him when they stopped in Flagstaff, so she wasn't a missing person, just missing from work. That was until Matt viewed Shires' arrival in Reno and discovered he was alone. Somewhere between Flagstaff and Reno she left his company, but where and why?

Matt couldn't understand why Jordan Smith was on anybody's list. She wasn't a fugitive, and now he knew she wasn't missing. Why waste his time by continuing the search?

Melissa Hardin didn't have an answer, so he made the decision on his own to stop the Lampton surveillance and get back to the 'chip jumpers.' It was much more interesting to chase real criminals.

He returned the cameras to the moment when the motor home drove away from the parking lot, moving to the overpass out of the cameras' line of sight. He waited then to view the vehicles that emerged from the overpass. He was determined to follow each and every one to its final destination. The driver of the motor home had to go somewhere. Matt Stoneham wanted to know where.

A Volkswagen Bug appeared from the opposite side. He followed it to the shopping mall where it parked. The driver walked into Starbucks. There was no one else in the car. Satisfied it wasn't the right person, he backed up the photos and allowed the Volkswagen to pass while he waited for another vehicle.

A motorcycle came through going the same direction as the motor home. It emerged momentarily with no passenger.

A black SUV moved into view on the other side of the street from the motor home. Matt backed up the photos again looking for the SUV's entry under the overpass. It had arrived just a moment before the motor home, and exited some five minutes later—plenty of time to pick up a passenger.

He watched the vehicle go into the BART parking lot. It drove to the end of a platform that served as an approach to the cashier's office. A woman waited there and climbed into the passenger side. The SUV turned and moved out of the lot and down the street toward the shopping center. Matt couldn't discern the number of people in the vehicle. And that was the flaw in the system. The pictures were from directly overhead—never a side view. He had to follow the SUV until it disgorged all the passengers. If he were correct this vehicle now held two passengers—the driver of the motor home and the woman from the BART parking lot.

He kept his eyes open for any store that might have a security camera near where the vehicle had to pass. Homeland agents could go there, view the tapes and possibly discover the license number. Unfortunately, there were none in that particular shopping center. He wished this were London where they had a camera on every corner. That's a project he'd definitely like to suggest to the powers that be—anything to enhance the system.

The phone interrupted his thoughts.

Matt this is Henry Vandye.

General Henry Vandye the director of Homeland Security doesn't usually make phone calls to the hired help. What did he want?

"Yessir."

How are you doing with the Jordan Smith thing?

"I'm tracking her. She's okay, but I still don't have a definite location on her." he lied.

Keep on it. We want a definite location within the next twenty-four. You understand?

"Yessir! You shall have it!"

The line went dead. Matt stared at the phone for a moment. At least he now knew whose list she was on, but that didn't answer the question, why?

CHAPTER 57

President Dick Butcher had known the stock maneuver might come back to haunt him. Gregory Chamus and Hal Skidmore were the only others who knew about it now that the CEO's had died. It was Monday morning two weeks after the Lear Jet crash that killed them, when the call came.

What's going on? Hal Skidmore's raspy voice demanded over the phone that morning.

"Forgetting protocol and manners are we? What are you talking about?" Dick asked. He was sure he knew, but he asked anyway. It was a habit of his.

Sorry, Mr. President, but this has us somewhat confused.

"Us?"

Greg and I.

"Exactly what's confusing you?"

Mr. President, it's been two weeks. Everybody's dead. We need to talk.

"Come to the conference room at three. I'll see you then," Dick told him and hung up.

"What's happening?" Lydia asked.

"Gotta talk to Hal and Greg for a moment this afternoon…nothing to worry about."

"You know Christmas is just a few days away and I'd like to do some shopping, but I don't have the chip implant. When are we going to get that done?"

Dick looked at his wife. This was a discussion he had avoided. He had some serious misgivings about swearing allegiance to Cahmael. He already felt like he owed him, and that act would only add to it.

Should a head-of-state swear allegiance to a foreigner? Evidently the European leaders had no such reservations for most of them had done it a year ago. Even Prime Minister Ari of Israel had complied.

He figured it was all a part of The New World Order that had been coming on for the past few years. Earl Price had talked about it a few months before he died. He was concerned about a one-world government, and said it was probably not a good thing—too much power in the hands of one man.

Dick Butcher didn't mind doing some of Cahmael's bidding, like moving a carrier group here and there, but he didn't know whether he liked the allegiance part.

He saw two sides to Cahmael. On the one side there was the helpful part, using the chip program to protect identities and divide the goods of the world among the people. The second side was the power grabbing going on under the guise of the New World Order. All of that power grabbing added up to the possibility of a huge dictatorship led by Jehosea Cahmael.

"Honey, when can we get the chip injection so I can go Christmas shopping? Christmas is only a week away." Lydia asked interrupting his thoughts.

"Sweetheart, I can arrange for your shopping trip without you getting the injection. We'll get it later."

"No. I want to get it and be done with it. So call whoever and let's get on with it."

Dick Butcher wasn't expecting that from his wife. He had never discussed it with her, and had assumed she would go with whatever he said, but he had never told her of his concern with the allegiance problem.

"Lydia, there's a part of the injection program that I don't agree with. That's why I'm reluctant to get it."

"What's that?"

"Allegiance."

"What about it?"

"There's a part of the injection process during which you must swear allegiance to Cahmael."

"Why is that necessary?"

"I'm not really sure that I know. The rationale used by Cahmael is simple. He says that he did a worldwide census when he agreed to help in the crisis. He says the census helped insure everybody would get a fair share. What he is asking in return is simply that you kneel and swear allegiance to him, making him the Lord of your life when you do so. Then you must promise to follow the example of the Good Samaritan by willing the good for yourself and others from moment-to-moment every day for the rest of your life. That is the way of life within the Trinity of Man."

"What's wrong with that?" Lydia asked and moved to a chair across the desk from her husband.

Dick watched his wife move easily to the chair. Not one remnant remained of her horrible wound. She had recovered completely. He thought of Cahmael's phone calls. Maybe Lydia had asked the right question. "What really is wrong with willing the good?" After all the man has done nothing but good for the world, and, if Dick wanted to admit it, he might even believe Cahmael had something to do with his wife's good health. After his meeting this afternoon he would take her and they'd both get the injection.

CHAPTER 58

To say the members of the underground suffered from paranoia would be an understatement. Every new member was given a rigorous screening before being allowed to know any secrets. The security was overwhelming. It was to Jordan Smith. She had reached the point at which she decided to contact Shires and call a halt to the hiding-out thing. The loneliness wasn't worth it.

For three weeks after her arrival she had lived in a cramped trailer house with just enough room for a bed, a small refrigerator, a small gas stove, a TV, and a flimsy table. Her choice of food was limited to what they delivered to her door—mostly soup and cold sandwiches. The toilet slash shower was an uninviting combination that added Italics to the word *cramped*. A tiny washer/dryer finished the amenities. Everything about being here fed her loneliness and depression. She guessed it must have been a test—if so, she had failed.

The notice of the meeting was a relief. It would be her first chance to get away from the trailer. She sat among other members of the underground during the meeting at a safe house somewhere near her small trailer. She had been blindfolded and escorted to the meeting, and supposed the others had been as well.

"My name is Brother Nathan Conrad," the chubby, bespectacled, balding man with the ruddy complexion said as he moved to stand behind the podium at the front of the room. He wore a gray suit with a red tie and gave the impression he might be important.

"You have been brought here today for some information sharing. Sorry for the isolation, but we don't trust anybody. Unless we have known you previously, you are put through what you all have experienced for the past few weeks.

"Some of you are here for religious reasons and others for other reasons. Whatever your reason, we must have your cooperation at all times. Are you all agreeable to that?"

Jordan reluctantly answered in the affirmative, hoping this meeting might help change her mind. Shires was so positive about her life being in danger. She didn't want to worry him, but she wasn't sure she could take much more of the isolation.

"Now this is my stand on Jehosea Cahmael. I believe him to be the Antichrist, and this is my reason. I have a video to show you." He stepped toward the TV monitor and pushed a button.

"This is a copy of an original video. The original is now in the hands of the government," he said.

The video was familiar to Jordan. She shuddered at the thought of the two dead bodies lying on the street. The thought *scare tactic* raced through her mind.

"I gave the original to the TV Journalist Shires Lampton. His reaction was a disappointment. I thought he might give it some play, maybe do a story about it. I knew he would authenticate it, that is make sure it was real, and he did that; however, a government agency said the disappearance of the bodies was the result of an experiment with new battlefield technology. Lampton dropped the story, and that's the last I ever heard of it."

Jordan couldn't believe her ears. She wanted to scream "Just a minute, sir!" but held her tongue.

"Mr. Lampton was duped by the government. I think they don't want people to believe there might be anything otherworldly about it. You see the bodies evaporating here." He paused until the evaporation was complete.

"That is exactly what happened. I know. I was there. I saw it. There was no experiment. The evaporating bodies came as a surprise to everybody. The Network didn't know what happened. The producers were scratching their heads. Then came the order to shut down the cameras and destroy the videos. That's when I confiscated a copy. I made a number of copies of that video. I didn't want the event to get lost in the maze of bureaucratic baloney like so much other stuff does."

The video had stopped. "Here, let me show that again," he said. He punched a button and the video began replaying.

The man was convincing, Jordan would give him that. It was Shires contention that someone claiming to be an eyewitness to an event usually perpetrated most myths, religions and other hoaxes. Nathan Conrad fit that description perfectly. The underground supplied him with a captive audience.

Jordan had to ask. "Sir, how do bodies evaporating into thin air make Jehosea Cahmael the Antichrist? I don't get the connection."

The room fell silent. You could hear a faucet drip. Either she had asked the right question, or the wrong one. She wasn't sure which.

Nathan Conrad cleared his throat. "I'm sorry," he said, "I thought everybody knew. Excuse me for assuming." He reached for his Bible. "I want to read the eleventh chapter of Revelations to you."

At the mention of the Book of Revelations, Jordan remembered her conversation with Shires back in Maryland when he first brought the video. This man was going to say exactly the same thing. She waited politely for him to explain. He began reading.

"'Then a measuring rod like a staff was given to me, and I was told, "Get up and measure the temple of God, and the altar, and the ones who worship there. But do not measure the outer courtyard of the temple; leave it out, because it has been given to the Gentiles, and they will trample on the holy city for forty-two months. And I will grant my two witnesses authority to prophesy for 1,260 days, dressed in sackcloth. (These are the two olive trees and the two lampstands that stand before the Lord of the earth.) If anyone wants to harm them, fire comes out of their mouths and completely consumes their enemies. If anyone wants to harm them, they must be killed this way. These two have the power to close up the sky so that it does not rain during the time they are prophesying. They have power to turn the waters to blood and to strike the earth with every kind of plague whenever they want. When they have completed their testimony, the beast that comes up from the abyss will make war on them and conquer them and kill them. Their corpses will lie in the street of the great city that is symbolically called Sodom and Egypt, where their Lord was also crucified. For three and a half days those from every people, tribe, nation, and language will look at their corpses, because

they will not permit them to be placed in a tomb. And those who live on the earth will rejoice over them and celebrate, even sending gifts to each other, because these two prophets had tormented those who live on the earth. But after three and a half days a breath of life from God entered them, and they stood on their feet, and tremendous fear seized those who were watching them. Then they heard a loud voice from heaven saying to them: "Come up here!" So the two prophets went up to heaven in a cloud while their enemies stared at them. Just then a major earthquake took place and a tenth of the city collapsed; seven thousand people were killed in the earthquake, and the rest were terrified and gave glory to the God of heaven."

"That's how it reads from the King James version of the Bible," Nathan said, "and now I'll paraphrase it to make it understandable to all of you, and show how it describes Tom Horn and Vince Nalone." He read again.

"*And I will grant my two witnesses authority to prophesy for 1,260 days, When they have completed their testimony, the beast that comes up from the abyss will make war on them and conquer them and kill them. Their corpses will lie in the street for three and a half days. Those from every people, tribe, nation, and language will look at their corpses, because they will not permit them to be placed in a tomb. And those who live on the earth will rejoice over them and celebrate, even sending gifts to each other, because these two prophets had tormented those who live on the earth. But after three and a half days a breath of life from God entered them, and they stood on their feet, and tremendous fear seized those who were watching them. Then they heard a loud voice from heaven saying to them: "Come up here!" So the two prophets went up to heaven in a cloud while their enemies stared at them.*"

"Things are not quite the same from the Bible to reality, but the essence is there. The whole world watched their execution and their ascension into heaven when their bodies disappeared—for me that's good enough. There wasn't a shout of 'come up here!' and the bodies didn't stand up, but the sense of awe is there when I show the video to an audience. The whole scene is awe inspiring when you think of the bodies ascending into heaven.

When he finished his explanation he asked for questions.

Jordan's hand shot up. He pointed to her. "The two men who died in this video do not resemble the two angels in the scriptures you read. They weren't angels. They were just men. How did you get to your conclusion?"

"I prefer to say they were emissaries who gave up their lives to warn the world. In the end God rewarded them. He took them directly to heaven to be with him. If you will notice the number of days God gave them, one thousand two hundred and sixty, that is about equal to forty-two months or three and a half years, which is just about the length of time they had."

"But you're relating them to the two angels who traveled the world to pass out the warning. They are definitely not the same. Tom Horn and Vince Nalone did not travel the world." She surprised herself when she remembered their names.

"In our day and age you don't have to physically travel the world. Their worldwide appearances on TV gave them credence in that department—most especially their execution. That to me was the greatest statement of all."

"So, you're saying the world watched the disappearance of the bodies for some time before the cameras were turned off, but you're the only eyewitness to have been physically on the scene to witness the disappearance of their bodies. That makes the whole story suspect."

"There were others who are not speaking out, but yes I was there. Are you calling me a liar?" Nathan Conrad's ruddy complexion reddened with anger. He couldn't stand to have his veracity questioned.

Jordan didn't back down. "I have a friend who insists that religion, myths and hoaxes are perpetrated by one person who claims to have been an eyewitness."

Someone in the audience asked, "Did he ever name the person?"

Laughter broke out. Even Jordan and Brother Conrad laughed. The moment of humor drained away the tension that had been building.

"I'm not asking you to believe. You don't have to believe to belong to the underground, but in the spirit of the two men who gave up their lives for their belief that Jehosea Cahmael is the Antichrist, I'm asking you to at least consider the possibility. You cannot bend a knee or swear allegiance to him. That is what is required when you get the chip implanted. If you don't do it, you'll be condemning yourself to hell just as sure as we're standing here."

Jordan shook her head, wanting to ask more questions, but stopped herself when Brother Conrad asked who believed that Cahmael was the Antichrist and everyone raised their hand. Her feeling of loneliness rushed back. She was the only one here who didn't believe. She felt smothered—stifled. An irrational panic seized her. She couldn't breathe. She needed to talk to Shires.

CHAPTER 59

Construction of the Temple in Jerusalem had started in June almost a year ahead of the deadline. It was slow at first, but with the constant encouragement of Jehosea Cahmael the work was going well. Windelsohn Construction Company located in Tel Aviv guaranteed completion by April in plenty of time for the dedication on May 14.

Pope Linus was having his doubts about Lord Cahmael. It seemed that the man who had saved his life was pushing hard to get things in order. He didn't understand why, and prayed about his flagging faith many times.

He was surprised when his secretary informed him of the call from WWN asking for an interview with Jehosea Cahmael. Usually the calls were for interviews with the Pope. He didn't mind. There were many things happening in the world at the moment, and he didn't want to talk about any of them. He would gladly allow Lord Cahmael to do the talking.

"I'll talk to the Master about it Brother Jeremy," he said to his secretary. "Did they say who would do the interviewing?" he asked as the priest turned to leave.

"Shires Lampton, Your Holiness."

Linus couldn't remember Shires Lampton. "Send me a bio of the man!" he called after his secretary. Father Jeremy turned at the door and acknowledged His Holiness' command.

The Pope pressed a button. Cahmael's voice answered the intercom. "Yes Your Holiness."

"Master, there has been a request I need to discuss with you."

"I'll be right there Your Holiness."

The considerable respect with which Cahmael treated him made Linus uncomfortable. The man was the Master, the Lord, and for the Lord to treat him as an equal was disconcerting.

Cahmael knocked softly on the door.

"Come in," Linus directed.

Cahmael was an imposing figure standing in the doorway. Linus figured he was at least six foot four—a handsome figure with his olive complexion and white flashing teeth. Early thirties most likely, but Linus had never asked.

Cahmael knelt before the Pope and kissed his ring.

"Master, it is I who should be kissing your feet," the Pope said.

"Not so, dear Linus. You are the most Holy Father."

"But Master you saved my life."

"Never mind my friend. What did you wish to see me about?"

"There is a request from the World Wide News Network for an interview with you. A Shires Lampton would be the interviewer. I don't know much about him, but I've asked Brother Jeremy to furnish a bio."

"I've been remiss. I should have allowed an interview before now. Why don't you tell Brother Jeremy to set up the interview for the middle of January, maybe the fifteenth. What do you think?"

"You don't want to read a biography of Shires Lampton?"

"I'll read it when you get it, but we can OK the interview before."

"I think giving an interview is a good idea. People will get a chance to know you on a more personal level. Maybe win over some of the doubters."

Cahmael chuckled and sat down in the easy chair with wine colored upholstery across from the Pope. "You think there are some doubters out there?" he asked jokingly.

Pope Linus smiled, stood and walked to the window overlooking Vatican Square where people gathered to see him. He waved to the smattering of people gathered below. They waved back and crossed themselves. The faith of the masses never ceased to amaze him. It was a necessity for them to believe. Their life depended on it. There would be few doubters among the faithful.

"Yes Master there are many who refuse to see you in the proper light, but they are not among the faithful such as those folks gathered down there in the square."

Cahmael stood and walked to the window to share the view. Together they watched the people wave again when they saw Cahmael. He waved back. They crossed themselves again.

"Master, I wish they were more actively pursuing the nonbelievers. I think it's terrible so many are hiding in the underground. You have given the world so much. Why don't you request that every country expedite the capture of the nonbelievers."

"Dear Linus, time will run its course. That day of judgement will come, and all will be brought into the open. Mark my words there are movements afoot—examples will be set that should strike fear into the hearts of the nonbelievers. These are perilous times dear friend, especially so for the nonbelievers. Have patience their day is coming"

Pope Linus had never heard Cahmael speak so cryptically—almost Biblical. He knew there was more that Lord Cahmael was not telling.

CHAPTER 60

Melissa Hardin tried to forget her doubts about Mike Arzetti. He called her often. They had become friends and then lovers. She spent Christmas with him and his sister, Ann, at his mom's house in Albany. It was a wonderful day meeting Peg, his mother, and Martina, his younger sister. Melissa was flying to Southern California the next day to have Christmas with her family in Riverside.

She tried during the weeks before Christmas, while their relationship was forming, to find out anything she could about him, but nothing other than the phone call to Shires Lampton surfaced. She didn't want to find anything negative. In fact, she couldn't imagine finding something bad—he just wasn't the type. He was a straight arrow all the way, and so was his friend George.

In all the time she had known him he had never mentioned his father, and she didn't bring up the subject. So when the order came in from her director to monitor Mike Arzetti it came as a shock. They were looking hard for the escapees. Mike Arzetti's dad was one of them. They wanted Melissa and her crew to look closely for any anomalies in Mike's behavior that might be in some way connected to his father.

The phone rang on Melissa's desk. It was Carmen.

What do you think? Carmen asked.

"About what?"

Our orders about Mike, Silly.

"We have to do as we're told," Melissa answered.

And, if we find something?

"We'll cross that bridge when we get there."

Melissa honestly didn't know what she might do. She was duty-bound to report any findings. A negative report would not be good for Michael. Execution was the ultimate result of being charged by Homeland—the indiscretion didn't matter since it could always be linked to terrorism and, finally, to treason, hence the death penalty.

There had been no executions since the death of Horn and Nalone. But Melissa knew it was only a matter of time before some unfortunate soul found his way to the chopping block.

To Melissa it seemed that people willingly received the chip injection. There had been no public outcry about it. She didn't know anybody who refused it. Her family lived in Riverside. They had no problem with it and willingly acquired it for protection against identity theft, which is what most people were doing. It was slowly becoming a part of life. Scant attention was paid to the swearing allegiance part—Americans felt connected to the man anyway. Many churches were endorsing him. The acceptance of Cahmael was everywhere, and growing worldwide.

The phone ringing brought her back to the moment. It was Mike.

What time for dinner tonight? he asked.

"How about I meet you at Berkeley Bart about six thirty?"

Great. George and Carmen are coming with us.

"I know. Carmen told me this morning."

Okay, little Missy. I'll see you then. Love you.

"Love you too, Babe," she said then put the phone slowly and thoughtfully back on its base. Their relationship was getting serious. That was okay with her, she loved Mike, but this order to keep him under surveillance bothered her.

The phone rang again. It was Ron Hartwell. *Here's some additional information on Michael Arzetti. I have a friend in the San Francisco Police. He says an Officer who helped capture Arzetti's dad was murdered a couple months ago.*

"What's that got to do with anything?" Melissa asked rather curtly. She checked herself lest her anger show.

There was a long pause at Ron's end. Then he said, *Well, I thought since we've been told to monitor for any contact with his dad, it might be pertinent to this murder as well.*

"Are you saying he might have had something to do with the murder?"

I don't know. Maybe we should check with the police department. What do you think?

She didn't want to do that, but then Ron said, *I can have my friend run a discreet check.*

She figured she had to give the OK. It might look funny if she didn't. Ron knew nothing about her dating Michael. She wanted to keep it that way.

"That's a good idea Ron. Yes, have him do it."

She felt traitorous. Mike would be hurt if he knew. She had to make sure he would never know.

Later that day, Melissa found the conversation by accident. She had been searching for information on Shires Lampton for Matt Stoneham when up popped a conversation with a stranger about whom they had no information.

She informed Matt who listened to the conversation. He said the only conclusion he could draw from it was that the man was talking about a pirated video of the disappearance of the bodies of Tom Horn and Vince Nalone. *That is always interesting since the underground, according to some sources, views that as proof of a heavenly happening.*

"Heavenly happening?" Melissa asked.

Yeah. They believe the two men ascended into heaven the day their bodies disappeared, he explained.

"Are you kidding me?"

No. We have to find a way to identify this guy. He called Shires on his cell, evidently from a landline somewhere in San Francisco. This is the first solid information we have that Lampton is connected with the underground, Matt finished.

"I don't agree with that," she said. "It sounds more like he called Lampton out of anger. I don't think Shires Lampton knows anything about the underground other than it exists."

I don't know; however, I do think this Mike Arzetti does. Lampton talked to him and zip his girlfriend disappears. The last trace I can find of Jordan Smith is in Napa. After that she's gone. Lampton's back in San Francisco doing whatever he does as if nothing had changed. Now we have two people, Mike Arzetti and this stranger, that Lampton knows who may be connected to the underground.

Here was another reference connecting Mike to the underground.

She had heard it before, and the constancy of facts was building. Mike never mentioned the underground during their times together. Melissa didn't pry, but her curiosity was working overtime. She wanted to know and she didn't want to know.

She would have to turn him in. *Could she do that? No. Never!*

Sometimes Melissa felt like kicking herself for getting involved with Mike.

They all met that evening at the Berkeley Bart Station; Mike and Melissa and George and Carmen. They walked to a Thai Restaurant nearby for dinner.

"You're quiet this evening," Mike said.

"I'm sorry, long day at work. Had a lot going on."

"What do you do in those hallowed halls?"

"We spend the whole day looking for people we can't find," Carmen said jokingly and then she laughed.

Carmen meant for it to be funny, Melissa knew that, but she didn't laugh. She caught Melissa's eye and scowled at her. The scowl wasn't lost on Mike. He saw it and wondered, remembering their conversation with Nathan Conrad. He inwardly shook his head. No, he wasn't going there. He was not going to doubt the woman he loved.

CHAPTER 61

It was a few days after the New Year began when the phone call came to Shires Lampton.

Mr. Lampton this is Harold Grange with Homeland Security and I want you to take me to Panguitch Hewey at his Camp named Armageddon in Grass Valley."

"Why?"

Those people have never submitted to the census for one thing. Now we want them to come in to receive the chip injections like everybody else. It is for the purpose of equal distribution, nothing more.

"What makes you think I can get in there?"

Our records show you made a visit there a few weeks ago.

"Your records?"

"Sir, you have the RFID chip implanted in the palm of your hand. We can monitor wherever you go. We know the exact location of the camp and how to get there from your visit, but we want to go in without bloodshed. So, we want you to introduce us. Do you understand?*

"Who are you talking about when you say us?"

It will be a task force made up of Homeland Security, Federal Bureau of Investigation, and Alcohol Tobacco and Firearms.

"If you go in with all those people, why take me? There's going to be bloodshed. I can promise you that."

We don't want bloodshed. We're taking a calculated risk that we can avoid it. We'll pick you up in the morning. Be ready about five.

"Look, I'm getting ready to fly to Italy. I have a very important interview coming up with Cahmael. I have to get ready for that."

We'll have you back in plenty of time. Remember be ready to go by five.

The dial tone buzzed in his ear for a moment before he placed the receiver back on the cradle. He walked to the window and stared at the ferry landing. It was loading for the trip to Vallejo.

His thoughts slipped over to Jordan. Where was she? What was she doing? He needed to talk to her. He missed her—more now than when she lived on the East Coast. She was so near and yet so far away. He knew there would be trouble at Camp Armageddon. Those people would not go quietly into that dark night. He worried about the confrontation.

He realized it would be a chance for a good story, but doubted they would allow Felix to accompany him. Maybe he'd just bring him and not bother to ask.

He punched Felix's recognition number and waited for an answer. Voicemail answered so he left a message.

He wished he could call Jordan. She had been hiding for over a month now. He didn't have the slightest idea how to reach her. Loneliness swept over him. Jordan must be terribly lonely too. He felt guilty, but the worse guilt in the world is better than grief, he knew that—he consoled himself with the thought.

He spent the rest of the day editing his notes on the questions that he planned to ask Cahmael. He had been surprised when Cahmael had agreed to an interview. Maria Sanger called him crowing about her success and claiming he owed her a dinner in Rome. Interviewing Jehosea Cahmael would be worth ten dinners—and for his career it would be priceless.

Felix called about three in the afternoon. He agreed to go immediately. He liked the idea of the adventure. He loved action, but this little venture may be more action than he, or any government task force, might be looking for.

Shires invited him to spend the night—they would be a united front when Grange and his crew arrived in the morning. Grange would not be happy with the presence of the cameraman. Shires didn't care. He wasn't happy about being drafted into the service of law enforcement—most especially into something that might get him wounded or killed just days before an interview with Jehosea Cahmael.

CHAPTER 62

The assault on Camp Armageddon was a bad outing for law enforcement. One misstep after another compounded the errors that began at daybreak on the ninth of January and ended with the slaughter of many of the camp inhabitants.

The grand total was eleven law enforcement officers dead. Four ATF officers died and seven from the FBI, four of them were in the helicopter. Seventy-seven camp residents were wounded and fifty four died.

Shires Lampton figured it might not have been that way if the task force had followed its original plan—the one that included using him to gain a peaceful entry. But, alas, as is usually the case of law enforcement at the Federal level, jealousy, rivalry, lack of communication and feelings of entitlement jumped in the way of good sense.

The shooting hadn't started when Shires and Felix arrived but the confrontation had. The impatient ATF team failed to wait for the FBI or Homeland. The demand for the immediate surrender of all those in Camp Armageddon went out over a loudspeaker about two minutes after Homeland Security arrived with Shires and Felix in tow. The shot that followed sent everybody diving for cover.

"Cease fire! Cease fire!" Someone shouted.

"It wasn't us Captain. It was them," someone else shouted.

Another shot rang out.

"Cease fire I said," crackled over the bullhorn.

"It was them!" another shouted.

Again over the bullhorn, "Is anybody hit?"

Silence followed the question.

"You in the camp stop shooting. This is Captain Wiggins from Alcohol, Tobacco and Firearms. We want to talk."

There was no answer.

"Shires Lampton is here. He wants to talk to you."

"Who is he? We don't know any Shires whoever he is," a voice yelled.

"The television journalist. He has an offer for you."

What offer? Shires didn't know of any offer. That was when Shires realized he had been setup, and so had the poor folks at Camp Armageddon. Again there was a long pause.

"Okay! Send him in."

Shires didn't like the situation. "Stay here," he whispered to Felix, "let me check it out."

Felix protested, but Shires would have none of it, and walked out alone. Shires didn't know what happened next. He heard someone yelling "Watch out!"

The man standing just inside waiting for him jumped at him grabbing his arm, yanking him through the opening. "Get down!" he yelled as his body slammed into Shires and then fell protectively on top of him—effectively shielding Shires' body from the oncoming bullets, and the devastating effects of the concussion grenade that fell almost at their feet.

Shires went deaf. The silent tableau of flashes and the trail of tracers slicing the air before his eyes told the story. The tracers were coming from unfriendly machine gun emplacements some distance away. The explosions were grenades falling in the midst of law enforcement. It was at that moment the taskforce commander realized just how unprepared they were. They had gravely underestimated the residents at Camp Armageddon.

The helicopter gun ships arrived and slammed their rockets into the strongholds that supported machine gun fire.

Rocket propelled grenades reached out for the choppers. One exploded in a fiery red ball. Chaos danced to flashes as the silent story of death and destruction unfolded before him.

The body that shielded him was limp and heavy. He couldn't move until he rolled the weight away. The man was dead.

The flashes had moved away from Shire' location. A running gun battle had drawn the main assault force up the valley.

Shires looked for Felix. He strained to hear something—anything. The smoke had cleared and the scene of death planted itself in his mind's eye. Bodies lay strewn about like some forgotten battlefield from the Civil War. They weren't all dead. He could see Felix moving and ran to him.

Blood oozed from his chest with every breath. Shires placed the heel of his hand over the wound and pressed. That seemed to ease Felix's pain. Felix's lips moved. Shires pointed to his ears with his free hand and shook his head. Felix seemed to understand and smiled at him then relaxed, closed his eyes and died.

Shires knew he was screaming Felix' name, he could feel it in his throat, but he still couldn't hear it.

CHAPTER 63

President Richard Butcher didn't like answering questions about the debacle at Camp Armageddon. It had happened on the heels of his meeting with Hal Skidmore and Gregory Chamus. They were threatening to go public with the stock manipulation plan. All this just as the calendar moved into the election year cycle—his first since taking office. He would have a clean slate if he could keep the lid on. With a clean slate going in, his re-election was almost assured.

Reporters were pushing for a press conference and the President was ignoring them. He had to say something about Camp Armageddon. His options on what he might say were limited. It was a crackdown pure and simple on those who would ignore the law. It sent a message to others to come into compliance. He let his Press Secretary Colton Armatage answer the questions at the weekly press briefing.

"How does the President feel about the tremendous loss of life at Camp Armageddon?" asked Hal Baird of the Miami Times.

Colton Armatage took a deep breath before he answered. This was the first press briefing since the event of the ninth. Some were calling it a massacre—an ugly term, which he avoided, referring to it only as the 'event'. He knew the questions would all be regarding that. He had prepared himself for the onslaught.

"The President is deeply saddened by this terrible event and sends his sincerest condolences to all the families, both of law enforcement and of the members at Camp Armageddon.

"The President has convened a panel to investigate. The results from that should be known in about a month."

Colton Armatage had learned the art of under-speaking. Stop

talking! Say just enough and shut up. If they want to know more they'll ask the question.

Colton adjusted his red tie and unbuttoned the jacket of his blue suit. He was an impeccable dresser. He had a pinstripe blue suit and a plain blue suit. He alternated between the two, always with a red tie and white shirt with a flag pin on the lapel. His patriotic uniforms, as he liked to call them. Today he was wearing the pinstripe blue. He was thirty-five, slender, with a receding hairline, and wire rimmed glasses.

"Colt, can you tell us what agency was in charge of the Camp Armageddon assault?" asked the next questioner.

"ATF had the lead on this one."

"Who goofed?" was the next question by the same journalist.

Colton ignored the question and pointed to another journalist.

"Come on Colt, answer that last question. Who goofed?" the next one said.

"Who said anyone goofed?" Colt asked.

"Are we supposed to believe the operation was planned just to kill all those people? Isn't it right they only went there to make arrests?"

This line of questioning was getting out of hand. He had to put a stop to it. "Look, there are a lot of questions that need to be answered. I can't answer them for you at this time. Yes the task force went out to make arrests, but nobody knows for sure just exactly what happened. I can't tell you something I don't know. You'll have to wait until the investigation is completed and I get a report. Now let's move on to other questions." He pointed to another journalist."

"My sources tell me there were three agencies involved; ATF, the FBI and Homeland Security. Would you care to comment on that?"

"No I won't comment any further on the subject. Wait for the report." He pointed to another journalist.

"Okay! You won't comment on those involved. Can you tell us why they decided to arrest these people at this time? Was it a crackdown or were they sending a message?"

"At some point in time everybody will have to come into compliance with the law. The law of the land now requires an RFID chip injection to protect your identity. Those folks who refuse to get it are just being obstinate. They had to start somewhere. These folks were well known to law enforcement for their noncompliance."

"So did they plan the massacre?" a voice asked without being called on.

Colton thought for a moment. "You know there was never a plan for bloodshed. That's all I'll say about it."

The same voice still insistent. "You must have known these were violent people. Why would you go in there not expecting gunfire? That's what these people are about isn't it?"

"I can't answer that with any degree of certainty, so why don't we wait until the report comes out, now that's all the questions I will answer about that today," Colton countered. "I'll take the next question not related to the event at Camp Armageddon."

Colton Armatage never doubted the words of President Richard Butcher, not even for a moment. He knew the massacre was the fault of the leaders on the ground, and the lack of intelligence they had about the residents of Camp Armageddon. Still the incident hung in the back of his mind like a Fourth of July banner in the month of December. His own questions were as many and varied as those of the Press.

CHAPTER 64

Mike Arzetti could tell Melissa Hardin was upset about something. She wasn't her same old bubbly self on their two block walk from the Berkeley BART station to his favorite Thai restaurant that evening. Finally, just as they arrived at the restaurant he found out what was bugging her.

"We watched the Press Conference about Camp Armageddon this morning. Did you see it?" Melissa asked.

"I heard about the assault on the camp that's all. I guess it was a little ugly," he answered.

"Ugly? It was terrible. I can't believe Homeland Security took part in such a thing,: she said as they entered.

They found a seat in the back.and waited for the waitress.

"I heard a little about it. I don't think it was Homeland's fault," Mike said as the waitress approached the table. They placed their orders for the special before the conversation continued.

"I can't believe the very agency that I work for was involved in such carnage," Melissa complained.

"I'd blame those people at the camp. My dad told me about them. He said their leader was a lunatic named Panguitch Hewey who swore he was a Prophet; claimed to be the sword of God sent to kill the Antichrist. Hewey had a plot to assassinate Cahmael in San Francisco. That was how they all got there. Somehow Hewey's plot never happened. Dad didn't know why."

He didn't bother to tell her about Shires Lampton's trip to Camp Armageddon to talk to Hewey. He hoped he hadn't said too much. Mike made it a habit never to talk about his dad. He knew Melissa must know something about the case, but he didn't want to discuss it with her. He hadn't seen his dad since he was released from prison, and didn't have the slightest idea where he might have been taken. He kept himself out of that picture completely because of his job. Melissa had never asked him about his dad. He was glad of that.

"It seems to me that somebody in one of those agencies would know of Hewey's violent past. Wouldn't you think?" Melissa asked.

Mike moved aside while the waitress set the food on the table then turned back to face Melissa. She began serving herself with chopsticks.

"I don't know. Dad said that Hewey's group never did anything violent. So it could be that the violence was an unknown quantity. For being the Sword of God, they were as quiet and docile as lambs. Dad thinks there might have been a mole who sabotaged their plans."

Mike knew he was talking too much about his dad. He had to stop. He couldn't tell Melissa what he had just told her was old news. Shires Lampton had discovered that Hewey had a stroke and his incapacitation had prevented the planned attack.

Melissa ate her food thoughtfully as she listened to Michael. He had mentioned his dad more tonight than ever before, but it was all in relationship to what he had said about the members of Camp Armageddon, nothing about the man himself.

Michael and his partner George were the only cops she had ever known personally. She knew that all cops weren't like them. It was difficult for her to believe they might be heartless people ready to shoot others at the drop of a hat. But, just maybe, she might be naïve. The people she worked with at Homeland were definitely not true cops—not in a cop sense of the word anyway.

CHAPTER 65

Shires Lampton's plane landed at 4:00 in the evening Rome time on the 14th of January. His interview with Cahmael was the next day at 1:00 in the afternoon. He had attended Felix's funeral just yesterday. The loss of his friend left a giant hole in his psyche. Felix had been with him for fifteen years and they had shared many adventures, as Felix liked to call them. Felix was excited and looking forward to the Rome trip. Shires blamed himself for his death. Why hadn't he taken him with him that day? Maybe that wouldn't have saved his life, but it might have.

There was agreement among the agencies that the camp members were the first to fire. Whether that was true or not was open for debate. From Shires' point of view he didn't know whose fault it was. Although it seemed to him the police were firing indiscriminately. He didn't know that for sure, so he never made an accusation.

Felix's replacement, Kevin Banks, was fortyish and tall with black hair. He had been a cameraman for eighteen years, but Shires had never worked with him. He was easygoing and friendly—maybe a little pickier about camera angles then Felix had been, but Shires could live with it.

A cab took the three of them the 35 kilometers from Leonardo da Vinci airport to the hotel in Rome. They checked in and then Shires treated his producer Maria Haller, and the new cameraman to the dinner he had promised Maria for getting him the interview with Cahmael.

She was laughing when she told him how easy it had been. "It was a 30 minute phone call. That was it. It was settled, even down to the date and time. I had a more difficult time with our own people. Three hours I spent explaining to them how this might be a good idea. Can you believe that?"

"What was their problem?"

"I think they were waiting for Harvey Wilhite to give the okay. Nobody wanted to stick his neck out. When Harvey came back he jumped all over it. And here we are."

The doorman hailed a cab for their party and Shires told him they wanted to go to the Agata e Romeo restaurant. The cabby nodded and whisked them away for the 10 minute drive through the heavy traffic on Via Carlo Alberto to the restaurant located at number 45.

He had made the reservation a week earlier on the Internet and almost didn't get it. He finally called and begged and they reluctantly agreed to give it to him. Luckily one reservation clerk had heard of him. Shires was keeping his promise in a big way. It wasn't every day you had an interview with the likes of a Jehosea Cahmael. He wanted Maria to remember this dinner.

He wished he could share the moment with Jordan, and wondered how he had spent so many years without her. He knew he could never do that again and vowed to find her immediately after arriving home. The problem with that was simple. He would have to join the underground. He wasn't sure he could give up everything, and leave his life behind.

The older Maitre d' showed them to their table, and in impeccable English orally presented the wine list.

To Shires' surprise his new cameraman, Kevin Banks, spoke to the man in French. The man answered, and the two men spoke for a few minutes.

"He's an interesting old guy," Kevin said later, "He speaks five languages. He learned English in school and the other three Russian, French and German he learned while being a guide for tourists here in Rome. He was a tour guide from the time he was seven years old. That was how he made his money. I really enjoyed talking to him."

"You don't do too badly with Italian yourself," Shires said. "Maybe I should let you do the interview with Cahmael."

"Just between you and me, Shires, Cahmael is one of the scariest people I know. Not because of anything he's done, but because of what he could do if you gave him enough rope. I don't know there's just something about the man. I don't trust him."

Shires didn't say it, but he agreed with Kevin.

CHAPTER 66

President Richard Butcher didn't like the overtones he heard from Cahmael—not overtones so much; more like strong suggestions with Cahmael insisting on public executions for the Camp Armageddon people.

What concerned the President even more was that the man had said it openly in his televised interview with Shires Lampton. His Press Secretary, Colton Armatage, made a video for him to watch. It surprised Dick that Cahmael had even given an interview. Dick Butcher would watch both the video and the interview for the first time. He pressed play on the remote.

The two men were sitting in what appeared to be a conference room. Both men sat on easy chairs with wooden arms that rose up on the sides for arm rests. Cahmael looked relaxed and friendly. Shires sat across from him and appeared tense like a cock ready for a fight. A network announcer introduced Shires and his guest and then Shires began.

I'm here today with Jehosea Cahmael the man who saved the world from economic disaster; thank you Mr. Cahmael for sharing your time.

You're welcome, Shires. The tall dark-haired man shifted easily in his chair. It seemed to Dick Butcher that Cahmael was not only relaxed but he was enjoying himself.

First I'd like to get something cleared up, if you don't mind?

Sure.

How do you answer the people who say you're the Antichrist?

Cahmael smiled, shook his head and said, I was asked by the United Nations to help with a crisis and I did. I don't think that makes me Christ-like in any sense of the word. I have never claimed to be anything or anyone other than myself. The very name suggests that I should be against Christ. I have never said a word about him one way or another. To me he was one of the Prophets and that is it.

It doesn't make you angry?

People can and will think whatever they want. I'd probably be a nervous wreck if I were to allow every little thing to upset me.

Still it must grate at your nerves to have done so much good and have people thinking you're evil?

That's human behavior. I'm an evil person just because I happen to fit into their prophecy in a certain way.

Not just evil. The Antichrist, according to my research, is the devil— Satan himself.

There was silence for a moment and then Cahmael broke into hearty laughter. So I'm Satan. I will admit that's evil, but enough on this subject. Let's talk about the Trinity of Man and willing the good, Shires. For instance, the African countries are no longer rampant with violence and starvation. Until now, no one had done a thing for those people. Is that not one of the greater goods that have come out of this?

I think you could say that. There's been a lot of good come out of what you've done, including the Trinity of Man and willing the good, but they still insist that you're the Antichrist. Why do you think that is?

It seems to me that the lunatic fringe will say what they believe/ They do not want to be confused with the truth. The lunatics don't want you to confuse them with facts because their collective mind is made up. I could say I am not the Antichrist until hell freezes over and still they would insist they're right.

They want it to be the end of the world not realizing what they visualize as the end of the world is really death for everybody, themselves included. These people are refusing to go along with the program that has helped so much and they should be caught and put in prison until they repent, and, if they don't repent, they should be executed.

Dick Butcher pushed the pause button. This was the first time Cahmael had gotten out of character. The tirade seemed a little venomous for such a 'good man'. There was the damning statement. Butcher had allowed Cahmael to publicly execute the pastor and the priest on American soil because the heinous crime had happened so publicly to the Pope on American soil. Out of deference to Cahmael he didn't intervene, but he was not going to allow executions for failure to comply with Cahmael's request. That would be going back to the dark ages as far as Dick was concerned.

Dick Butcher had never been able to dispel from his mind the thought that the assassination of the Pope and his subsequent resurrection had been a staged affair—like any good magician might have done. At the time he hadn't wanted to take on Cahmael publicly by questioning his tactics so he had let it happen. He called it political expediency. He continued the video.

And by repenting you mean what?

I simply mean for them to get the chip injection and swear allegiance to me. That's all there is to it,

What do you mean by 'swear allegiance'?

It is simply a statement of compliance with the program by agreeing to say that I am the Lord of their lives in the sense that they will comply with all my wishes.

When I got the implant I was instructed to kneel when I agreed to comply. Do you apply some significance to the act of kneeling?

It is a position of subservience. It is an act to show that you will serve me.

There are those who say that kneeling is an act of reverence, supplication if you will, to someone holy like the Lord. Do you consider yourself equal to the Lord?

In the fullness of time all will be understood. What I say now will only have meaning in the future. Ask any man what he believes and many will be unsure. I will be here to give certainty back to mankind.

How do you want to be served?

I just want compliance with the chip program. That's all I'm asking. Step up and be counted, have the chip implanted to protect your identity; then join in the buying and selling, participating with the rest of society. It's very simple.

How does all that tie into kneeling and swearing allegiance to you?

My name is synonymous with the program. Swearing allegiance to me is agreeing to go along with the program, which, by the way, everybody must do willingly for it to work.

On the one hand you sound rational, and then you call for public executions and that to me is irrational.

Is there a question in that statement?

No. Here's the question, why public executions?

Fear. Complete and utter fear. It's a Biblical thing. God rules with fear.

Are you trying to be God-like? It appeared that you raised the Pope from the dead and then you began to hang out at the Vatican. What is the significance of that?

The power to heal is within all of us. That is one of the teachings in the Trinity of Man. Faith removes all doubt and all things become possible. There is no significance to my spending time with the Pope. The Pope is my friend, and he's the main connection to God for millions of people around the world. What better person to "hang out" with?"

Richard Butcher stopped the video again. His uneasiness about Cahmael was not going away. In fact, the more he thought about it the more uneasy he felt. He had committed to supporting Cahmael with two carrier groups in the Mediterranean; against the advice of his Military leaders.

But Cahmael had gotten in his head. He knew it. Poor Earl Price had been right. Earl tried to kill Lydia because she was being used for the purpose of blackmail against the President and ultimately the United States. Earl killed Lydia to take away the hold that Cahmael had on Dick, and then he killed himself. Earl Price was sure that once you give in to blackmail there is no end.

Somehow Cahmael had saved Lydia's life or so it seemed to Richard Butcher, and he felt eternally grateful for it. Although he doubted Jehosea Cahmael in many ways, he couldn't get it out of his head that Cahmael had saved her life. Now he was more than willing to do his bidding.

The remainder of the interview consisted of a long discussion of the Trinity of Man and the concept of *Willing the Good* at every moment.

CHAPTER 67

The first thing Shires Lampton did when he arrived back in San Francisco was call Mike Arzetti on a public phone. It had been early morning when his plane arrived at SFO. He knew Mike would be at the precinct getting ready to go on patrol. He figured Mike could tell him if it might be possible to see Jordan. Mike had never admitted to being in the underground, but Shires knew he was connected in some way to it.

Definitely not! had been the emphatic answer. The hopelessness that flowed from that statement depressed Shires.

"No way at all?" he asked.

Join the underground. Only then could it be a possibility, and even then I wouldn't say that it was likely to happen.

Shires didn't want to hear that. He had to see Jordan. He had promised her he would. It had been already two months. Shires was sure she would be an unhappy camper about now…no she would be angry. He felt badly and consoled himself with the thought that at least she was safe. He had to do something, and do it quickly.

"Okay, how do I go about joining?" He heard himself asking the question although not believing he would actually go through with it.

How serious are you? You'll have to get your chip removed if you have one. You can't go wandering around underground locations with a traceable chip. I guess you probably know all this. I can set up a meet between you and a certain other person if that's what you really want.

"Can I still meet with him even if I'm not sure?"

Desperation is usually the deciding factor. Tell you what. Go to Gordy's Bar and Grill over on Commerce Street where all the cops go. Be there at 1:00 this afternoon. I'll arrange a meet.

"How will I know him?"

You won't. He'll know you. Go there and wait.

The line went dead. Shires stared at it for a moment then hung up his phone. Butterflies cavorted in his stomach at the thought of the step he was contemplating for that afternoon. He had thought of this moment from the day he rushed Jordan to the underground nearly two months ago, but then it was always in the abstract— in the future and unreal to him. He held out the hope that there might be a way to temporarily remove the chip so he could visit Jordan and not give up his normal life.

CHAPTER 68

Matthew Stoneham was frustrated. He had failed to find the missing chip jumpers. They had eluded his search for almost two months now. He couldn't believe it. His cutting edge technology had lost them. He had tried every possibility he could think of, but to no avail.

He knew he hadn't given it his best effort. His time had been divided between them and Jordan Smith. He had been told to make Smith a priority. He had failed to find her as well. Someone who knew the inadequacies of his equipment was thwarting his efforts.

After two months of searching it was an inadvertent observation that finally set him on the right path. He had noticed the black SUV at the BART station and had followed it for awhile, but didn't have time to look too far as he had orders to move on and search for Jordan Smith.

It looked to him like Shires Lampton had dropped her in a parking lot in Napa, California; however the drop point had been under a sidewalk awning extending the length of the block. He hadn't known what section to watch for a likely pickup; and that was when he saw the SUV. He must have missed it before, but the familiarity of the SUV was too coincidental. It had picked up a passenger from under that awning and driven away. A similar SUV had picked up a passenger at the Bart station. A quick check back confirmed his observation.

He followed the vehicle to a trailer house just outside the mountain community of Anglin and watched it disgorge a passenger. From straight above it was difficult to tell, but when he zoomed in he would have bet it was a woman. *"Hello Jordan Smith,"* he muttered under his breath.

He quickly sent the email notifying headquarters of the whereabouts of Ms. Smith and then moved his observations back to the Bart station to watch the comings and goings of a certain SUV. It was almost a certainty that the others had been dropped in the Napa area. They couldn't get away now. He had the identity of the vehicle and soon he'd have their hiding places.

His earlier assumption of success had been a tad premature, but this time there would be success. All the chip jumpers would be rounded up and sent back to jail. The fools, they just had to comply with Cahmael. Now they were headed back to jail and possible execution.

Nine hours later he had followed the SUV through the ins and outs of picking up all eight of the BART participants. He was able to fax five addresses from the information he gleaned. He sent another email informing central of his success. He sent another to Melissa Hardin's crew thanking them for their help. It had taken him two months to unravel the mystery of the disappearance of Jordan Smith and the chip jumpers, but perseverance paid off.

CHAPTER 69

Melissa Hardin stared hard at the email from Matthew Stoneham while jubilation swirled around her. This was their first success and it felt good, but the feeling wasn't so great for Melissa. Homeland Security would soon recapture Mike's dad. She felt a strong urge to call Mike; actually fought with herself about it.

For Mike's sake she couldn't let him get caught. She couldn't live with herself. Mike would hate her if he ever discovered that she knew ahead of time and didn't tell him. But if she told him she could lose her job. She loved this job. Besides, if she told Mike where would it end? But it was his dad's life; she had to warn him immediately; there was no other choice.

She usually didn't call Mike at work, he would call her, but this was special. She pushed caution aside and punched in his code on her cell.

Hey! Sweetheart, he answered cheerily.

"Can we have lunch together today?"

Is it important?

"Extremely."

There was a pause. She heard Mike say something to George. She heard George say *Yes* then Mike was speaking again. *Okay Honey. I won't have much time so how about Tubby's down the street from you at one.*

She agreed, told him she loved him and folded the cell. Relief swept over her. She was taking an awful chance with her future, but she couldn't bear the thought of Mike's father being caught and executed, and then have Mike find out later that she knew ahead of time.

George dropped Mike at the Diner. He would pick him up in an hour—sooner if a call came for them. Mike frowned when he saw Melissa's worried expression.

"What's wrong?" he whispered in her ear as they hugged.

"They know where your dad and his friends are. They're going to arrest them today," she blurted back in a strained whisper.

The news hit him like a bolt of lightning, but he wasn't one to panic easily. "Let's go in and order," he said calmly.

At lunch time Tubby's Hotdog Stand was always busy. They lined up to place their order. Mike's mind raced through his options. He had to warn his dad immediately. He had to keep him from being arrested and thrown back in jail…maybe executed. That thought sent an arrow of panic slicing through his mind.

Mike stood behind Melissa with his arms around her. He kissed the back of her neck inhaling the sweetness of her body, attempting to distract himself from the urgency of the moment tugging at his brain.

He had to call Nathan Conrad. He looked around for a public phone and saw it on the back wall of the dining area. After they placed their orders and sat down he excused himself and went to the phone. His cell phone was useless in emergencies involving the underground. Cell phones could be traced and monitored as he was sure his was. The underground used messengers and landlines—never anything high tech.

The message phone rang once. He hung up and waited. His phone rang twice. It was a signal for him to call another number, which he did.

Yes, Nathan Conrad said.

"Mike Arzetti here, they're going to arrest my dad and his friends this afternoon."

And you know this how?

"My girlfriend works for Homeland Security."

You're being played. I told you about that. I don't believe it. They are checking you out my friend.

Mike didn't want to argue with the man. He felt the urgency in Melissa's voice when she told him. "Please humor me and move them right now. It's better to be safe than sorry," Mike pleaded.

Nathan Conrad never took chances with the lives of others, and placed the call to move Tony Arzetti and the others immediately.

Melissa never asked Mike about the call and he didn't tell her, in fact he neither thanked her nor gave her any indication that he might have called about his dad although they both knew he had.

CHAPTER 70

Matthew Stoneham kept a close eye on the locations of the escapees. He was determined they would not get away this time. At three that afternoon he saw the arrival of the agents at each location, five locations in all, and then he saw his great failure as no escapees were found. He was deeply perplexed and embarrassed. He had sounded the alarm so sure had he been that he had the right addresses. He had seen no one come and go. They had to have been there.

He knew he had the right addresses. Someone had warned them. That was the only plausible answer—but who and how? He had made the discovery only this morning, and the decision to move to arrest was put into place just a little before noon: not much time for a warning, unless it had been an inside job, but that still didn't answer how they escaped without being seen. He had been watching for it.

Maybe they weren't there. That was a possibility. Maybe he had caught them while they were out. He might agree that some of them had been out, but not all—not at the same time. They had to have been warned.

Who would have something to gain by warning them? He could think of no one inside the company. The phone rang interrupting him.

"Stoneham," he answered.

Matt this is Harry Cole. I wanted to tell you that the report on the residences you gave us said that those particular houses had been empty for a considerable amount of time. None of them had signs of recent habitation.

Matt explained that his information was two months old, but he thought it might still be current and went with it. He didn't know how the underground operated, but he learned one thing that day. Residents of the underground do not stay long in one place. He apologized to his Director, stating he would try in the future to share more recent information.

Don't worry about it Matt we'll make a lot of mistakes. We can chalk all of them up to experience. We'll lose some and we'll win some. Keep up your good work and better luck next time.

Even with Harry's words of support and encouragement, Matt still felt the sting of failure. Now he knew for sure there had been no inside leak. He was thankful for that.

He sent an email to Melissa Hardin apprising her of the situation. It read: *Melissa our arrest gambit was fruitless. The culprits weren't there. I thought they had been warned. Turns out they hadn't been there for a long time. My information was too old. Sorry about getting you excited about nothing.*

Melissa read the email and thought: *Matt you don't know the half of it.*

CHAPTER 71

Shires Lampton arrived at Gordy's Bar and Grill about a quarter to 1 and sat at a table in the back from where he could see the front door at all times. He told himself he wasn't paranoid just cautious. Besides, as far as he knew he had nothing to fear. He was going to attempt to pick out the man who was coming to see him.

He was hungry and ordered a burger, beer and fries. It was the special of the day for half price. Not a bad deal. The TV was blaring a basketball game between the Warriors and the Utah Jazz.

"Hey," a voice burst over the blare of the TV, "aren't you that TV reporter Shires Lampton?" The young man approached him from the bar carrying a beer in one hand and a hot dog in the other. Shires was not in the mood for talk, and braced himself for the worst.

"Can I get your autograph?" he asked tossing a piece of paper on the table. Shires took out his pen to sign and noticed the paper contained a note. GO SIT IN THE FIRST STALL OF THE BATHROOM; THE FIRST STALL NO OTHER. Shires signed the paper and handed it back. "Thank you Sir," the kid said and walked away.

Oh the fun of it all. Playing hide and seek with an unknown person. Shires had thought they would meet and talk face to face. Not so said the fixer of all things dubious. You can just keep guessing.

Shires followed instructions only to find the first stall inhabited. He waited until it cleared and entered the smelly haven. Lord God it stunk. Jordan had better appreciate this he joked to himself. He was going to tell her once he saw her again. She'd get a good laugh out of it.

He waited, and waited, and waited. Just about the time he was ready to give up a voice from the next stall asked, "Why do you want to join the underground?"

"My fiancée is there and I need to go see her."

"So you think this is Disneyland and you can buy an excursion on the tour bus?"

"No! No! I'm sure she's lonely and I have to join her."

"You don't sound desperate to me. When we admitted Jordan she was running for her life. That's desperation. You don't sound desperate to me. You just want to visit. Isn't that right?"

Shires thought for a moment. The man was right. He wasn't ready to give up his life and join the underground. It was a stupid idea anyway. He was ready to chuck the idea and leave, but he thought again of Jordan. He couldn't get her out of his mind. For him not to go to her was like abandonment. His conscience wouldn't let him do it.

"So what are you going to do?"

There was a long pause as Shires weighed his options. "Look! Make up your…" the voice stopped as a stranger entered the restroom.

Neither man spoke as they waited for the stranger to finish with the urinal. Another factor that colored Shires' decision was his new found popularity after the Cahmael interview. The interview had been the talk of every newscast and talk show. He was proud of it. In less than twenty-four hours his name had been renewed in the news world. He truly believed one of the larger networks might offer him his own show or at least an anchor position.

The urinal flushed then the sound of the man washing his hands was followed by the door opening and closing. They were alone again.

"I need an answer," the voice was impatient now.

Shires knew one thing. All the fame and fortune that he might make would be like nothing without Jordan. He knew this was his moment. He may not get another anytime soon. He wanted love in his life. He wanted Jordan.

"Okay! I'll do it," he heard the words come out of his mouth as if they floated from somewhere else in the room. He was going to leave his fame and fortune behind. He knew any rational mind would tell him "No! No," and scream from the mountain tops of the world. "You fool! Look what you've done."

"Okay then. After you've eaten go outside and get in the white van. They'll be waiting. Follow their instructions exactly."

"That's all there is?"

He received no answer. All he heard was the stall door next to him closing and the main door opening and closing. He opened his stall door, went to the sink and washed his hands for no apparent reason. He guessed for appearance sake, but there was no one with him in the room. Oh well it satisfied him to do it.

He walked back to his table where the food awaited and took a long swig of the beer. The coolness felt good sliding down his throat. He ate the burger and fries slowly as if staving off that last final act that would seal the deal. His commitment to a completely new life would be finalized when he climbed into the van.

He had one thought that helped his morale at the moment. If he didn't like the underground he'd just take Jordan and leave. Actually this alternative had been in the back of his mind all along. He didn't know whether he'd act on it or not. Time would tell.

CHAPTER 72

Nathan Conrad was relieved when Homeland Security failed to arrest the Arzetti group. They had gone to old addresses. He figured their information was two months old yet they acted on it like it was current. He was mystified. After rushing to move them away from their current residences nobody showed. He heard later that they had gone to the old places. Homeland Security really didn't know their whereabouts. Nathan had breathed a sigh of relief for that—this after kicking himself for messing up. He couldn't figure out how they knew. Turns out they didn't.

His friends nicknamed him Paranoid Pete. He laughed about it, but it was true. Staying one step ahead of the authorities was difficult. Paranoia worked most of the time—that and a lot of prayer.

He held Bible studies every Tuesday and Wednesday night at different locations to promote a sense of togetherness and a unity of purpose, but mainly just to study and discuss Cahmael's latest tactics— which of late seemed to be a waiting game; waiting for the Temple to be built in Jerusalem.

What surprised Nathan was that there were no trials and condemnations by Cahmael. Nathan figured that was because Cahmael was still playing the good guy since it was still within the first forty two months of his reign. The prediction was that he would be in power for seven years. Forty two months of it would be good and forty two would be bad. During the last forty two months the truth would be known about him. Although some said he hadn't come to power as yet. Nathan figured the first forty-two month period would come to an end just about the time of the Temple dedication. After that he figured all hell would break loose.

This was the message he brought to the people of the underground—nothing sugar-coated, only the pure unvarnished truth as he saw it. During this last period people would be executed for refusing to take the Cahmael Chip. No more Mr. Nice Guy would be Cahmael's mantra. It was a scary scenario. One that Nathan wished weren't true.

The fact that Nathan was still alive, he believed, was a testimony to his faith in God, the two large angels who seemed to follow him everywhere, and a small bit of paranoia. He didn't know if the men were angels. They had never introduced themselves to him. They were always there on the fringes watching. The only way he knew they were there for him was the day at a rally when a man came rushing at him. They stepped out and jostled the man to the ground. Evidently they scared him enough for he ran away. They never said a word to Nathan. He tried to thank them but they didn't allow him to come near. After that, he never tried and just accepted it for the protection it was. He spoke of the angels only in regards to having guardian angels looking over him, but he never tried to make anyone believe they were there. He could see them. He knew they were, and that's all that mattered.

Nathan drew his message and his inspiration directly from Pastor Tom Horn and Father Vince Nalone. They had died for what they believed. He figured he could do no less. And that was why Nathan Conrad devoted all of his time to the underground.

People came to the underground for various reasons. Not everybody was there for religion. Call it his paranoia, but Nathan also believed there were spies in the underground. He tried to screen everybody personally, but the task was too daunting, even in his one little area of San Francisco.

He was sure a few had slipped by, and in the last forty two months of Cahmael's reign, they would turn on the underground. That would be their main purpose for being there. He knew he had to find those people before then and eliminate them, but he didn't know how or even who they were, although he had his suspicions,

Mike Arzetti was his screener at present. At least as much as possible Nathan liked for Mike to have vetted the candidates before he talked to them.

Above all Nathan liked secrecy both for himself and for the underground. He never let his face be seen whenever he interviewed prospective members. If a future member didn't have the personal recommendation of Mike Arzetti he wouldn't bother interviewing them at all. He trusted Mike implicitly.

When Mike asked him to interview Shires Lampton because of a special circumstance he agreed to do it. Mike explained that Shires wanted to come for a visit.

Nathan had laughed. "You're kidding…right?" he asked.

"No, I'm not," Mike answered, "He wants to visit Jordan Smith. That's why you need to talk to him; tell him the facts according to the underground."

Nathan had interviewed Shires Lampton and accepted him in to the underground with reservations. He didn't think Lampton would want to be a permanent member no matter how much he said he did. He'd bet anything that Lampton would take his girlfriend and leave the underground after a few weeks. Nathan was sure that Shires Lampton was giving up more than he might want to and would realize that. His reason for being in the underground was not desperate enough for him—for his girlfriend it was, but not for him.

It would be up to Nathan to convince Shires to stay. Security would be breached in the worst way if he were to leave. It is life or death living in the underground. Lives would be in jeopardy if any one person were allowed to leave, Nathan would have to singe that fact into the brain of Shires Lampton. It was life or death from Nathan's point of view and it would have to be so for Shires Lampton. Nathan could not allow anyone to go back to their regular life.

This is why Nathan Conrad feared the second forty-two months of the Cahmael reign. People would be selling out the underground to gain privileges for themselves. It would be a scary time. This had to be prepared for long before it arrived. Everyone in the underground had to understand the severity of the times ahead. The situation would be dire—much more so than at the present time.

Therefore the penalty for leaving the underground is death. There was just too much to lose to allow anyone to leave. This is what Shires Lampton must learn. The underground in this day and time is not a game. It is real and it has a reality more grim than can be imagined, and all who are in it must understand that. Your presence here cannot be taken lightly by you or by your friends, he would tell them over and over again. Your life is at stake.

CHAPTER 73

Mike Arzetti had heard Nathan Conrad's spiel about the forty two month periods, and how bad the second forty-two would be, but he never took it seriously. He didn't believe the part about Cahmael being the Antichrist so everything after that was moot as far as he was concerned.

His sister Ann brought up the subject one night when they happened to have some time together during her quarter break from school. It was early March. Since neither of them had been brought up attending church, they were never instructed about anything Biblical; however Ann's friend Jamie knew all about it, and had talked to Ann.

"Mike, do you know what an Antichrist is?" Ann asked.

"Yeah," Mike answered looking up from the sports page. "He's an evil doer like the devil who comes and pretends that he's Christ…something like that."

"Jamie says Jehosea Cahmael is the Antichrist."

"A lot of people say that Sis. It's all just a bunch of baloney."

"Are you sure?"

"As far as I'm concerned it is, Sis. First of all the man has done nothing but good. Doesn't sound like any evil doer I know of."

"She says there's this Nathan Conrad who goes around talking about all this stuff. She says I should go hear him. I guess he's very persuasive."

Mike knew Nathan moved around quite a bit, and spoke to many people, but he didn't know he went to college campuses.

"Nathan sounds like a busy man,", he said. He didn't mention to Ann that Nathan also ran the local underground. No wonder he kept his identity secret. Mike didn't know who screened new members before him, but that was the first thing Nathan asked him to do after he joined.

He had guessed that his dad had a great influence over Nathan. It had been sort of a natural thing for Tony Arzetti's son to be included in the underground—even more natural for him to be helping in some way. Mike had never put much thought into it until this talk with Ann. Ann knew nothing about him being a member of the underground.

"Jamie says there's a rumor that Nathan Conrad is connected to the underground for his religious beliefs. Do you think that's possible?"

"Sis, just about anything is possible in this day and age."

"What would you say if I told you I was going to join the underground?"

"I don't know. Are you?"

"Jamie thinks it might be exciting to try it for a little while to see what it's like."

"I think being in the underground would be like jail. You would be totally restricted to where you could go and what you could do. I don't think it would be any fun at all. Why would anyone want to join if they didn't have to? But I don't think it's possible to join for a short time."

"Jamie thinks it is; especially if you don't tell them the truth when you go in."

"The truth being what?"

"That you aren't planning to stay."

"I wouldn't suggest you do that. I don't think you can get out after you get in," Mike said trying to be as persuasive as possible without divulging the complete truth. The truth being they would shoot you if you tried to leave because of the security concerns. He didn't want his sister to know how closely he was connected to Nathan Conrad or that he belonged to the underground.

"Jamie and I thought we'd try after the quarter is finished in June. Maybe go in for a month or two."

Mike was ready to tell her the exact truth, but decided to wait until later in the school year like in May sometime. There was plenty of time. He knew he might have to tell her at some point.

"Ann, do me a favor and forget about going underground. You have the Cahmael Chip right?

"Yes. It was required at registration in December."

"That will stop you from getting in the underground. That thing is traceable." He didn't bother to mention that it could be removed. She would wonder how he knew all that and then he'd have to explain—and on it would go until he had told her everything. He just didn't want her to know until it came time for him to save her and send her to the underground; if such a thing ever happened. He supposed later would be better than sooner. It was probably something he would never have to do. Such events did not figure into his scheme of things.

Only from Nathan's point of view was it going to get worse. Nathan pictured a long line of people waiting to be judged by Cahmael. If they refused to bow to him their heads were lopped off then and there. People would be crying out in anguish and fear. Bodies would be stacked high from the slaughter as families were ripped apart and murdered for their beliefs. To save his family under this scheme he'd also have to save his mom and brother Will, but he didn't want to tip his hand too soon if that were the case.

There are others who are doing the same thing as Mike, sort of a half-in and half-out deal, taking the chip injection, joining the underground, but not disappearing; however they were like Mike and couldn't attend meetings.

Nathan Conrad knew who they were locally, but they were not known to each other. These were the troops who helped him with the logistics of keeping track of everybody in the underground system and moving them around from place to place at different times. There were many like Mike. George Wildes was another who helped although he knew of Mike Arzetti and Mike knew of him—there were few such cases.

Ann had been quiet for some time.

"Has Jamie told you how this Nathan pictures the… what did you say…the last forty-two months?" Mike asked her, pretending ignorance of the subject.

"She has never said. Just wants me to come and listen to him. I think I'll go."

"Good idea. Then come back and tell me about it and we'll discuss it. What do you say?"

Ann agreed to that and their conversation ended for the night. She went back to her studies and Mike called Melissa Hardin who was working overtime. He would pick her up later.

CHAPTER 74

Pope Linus the Third was irritated with Lord Cahmael. Here he had all but given control of the Vatican over to him and he had done nothing with it that glorified the Lord God in heaven, which he thought would be a glorious thing with Lord Cahmael leading it.

Cahmael had asked Linus not to call him Lord on any number of occasions. The Pope had trouble with that. What else do you call someone who resurrected you from the dead? Christ was the only other doer of such a deed and he was the Lord. Linus had heard the accusation made against Cahmael that his resurrection was a sham perpetrated to fool the world into thinking Cahmael was Christ. Linus knew in his heart of hearts that was a false accusation. Although he never felt dead he had been unconscious for some time and then he was awake. The other stuff was what he saw on videos of the actual event.

He saw the men firing the shots and the bullets hitting his body. It fell, actually collapsed or crumpled, beside Cahmael. It looked real to him, but it didn't feel real. He had no memory of it. Yet he knew it was real. His faith told him so. He'd had faith his whole life and it always worked for him. He would trust it in this instance as well.

The world situation troubled Linus though. It seemed to him that for all the good that had been done, some bad things were creeping back. He couldn't quite put his finger on what bothered him. Maybe it was the upcoming dedication of the Temple and all the security that Cahmael thought it needed. Peace had settled over the world. There were no more wars or rumors of them. The pain of war had passed into history. Hopefully it would stay there forever. He remembered the scripture from Matthew the 24th chapter where Christ was describing the last days. In verse 7 he said: For nation shall rise against nation and kingdom against kingdom; and there shall be famines, and pestilence, and earthquakes in divers places. And in verse 8 he described it: All these are the beginning of sorrows.

Linus figured if those things were gone, except for an earthquake here and there then we must be truly living in the era of the end of sorrows. Cahmael had ushered it in and refused to take credit for it.

CHAPTER 75

The Mediterranean Sea extends from the Straits of Gibraltar on the west to Asia on the east. The name Mediterranean means *in the middle of the land*. It is surrounded by land on the north by Europe, on the south by Africa and on the east by Asia. It covers an approximate area of 965,000 square miles. It is connected to the Atlantic Ocean on the west, by the Straits of Gibraltar. The straits are only 9 miles wide.

Given its size there is plenty of space to fit in two Carrier Groups quite nicely. They had been ordered to the Eastern side just off the coast of Israel. Overkill as far as President Richard Butcher was concerned, but only in his private thoughts since he had ordered the two groups to be there at Cahmael's request. It was good security from Jehosea Cahmael's point of view. Stupidity claimed the Joint Chiefs of Staff.

Admiral William Franklin Scott in command of Carrier Group designated Alpha for this exercise was aboard the carrier Jimmy Doolittle and his counterpart the Commander of Carrier Group designated Delta, Admiral Harry Nelson Winthrop, aboard the carrier Douglas MacArthur agreed with the Joint Chiefs. This close proximity put both groups in jeopardy, but the Commander-in-Chief had ordered it for the duration of the Temple dedication in Israel in the month of May. The duration was a three month period, two months prior to the dedication, meaning they were to be on station from the beginning of March through the month of May. Such close proximity was a serious breach of all security protocols. President Butcher could not be swayed from his insistence on it.

Admirals Scott and Winthrop held a secret face-to-face on a destroyer near the island of Corsica to discuss the matter. They were old friends from the same graduating class at Annapolis and held the meeting under the guise of a conversation between old friends.

Scott had called for it, but they met on one of Winthrop's ships, a destroyer code named Catfish. Winthrop was waiting. The men shook hands and pounded each other on the back. Both men were alone, leaving their XO's in charge while they attended a meeting that officially never happened.

No minutes were taken. There would be no record of any kind—only a friendly get-together between old friends.

"So Winthrop, do you know why I called for this?" Scott asked, watching Winthrop pour their coffee. Winthrop had excused the steward who usually did the honors.

"I could sum it up in one word, 'concern' for our mutual upcoming exercise," he answered seating himself and offering cream and sugar to his guest.

"You hit it right on the head," Scott answered declining the condiments, "and I don't like it one bit. We'll be offering the enemy just too big a target to resist. All it would take is one nuclear warhead, not so well-placed even, and we'd lose almost half the naval forces of the United States. We can't allow that to happen. It seems there is no will among the Joint Chiefs to stop it, so you and I are the only ones who can. What do you think?"

"You mean by disobeying an order?"

"Not exactly, I have a plan. Are you willing to listen?"

"You've got the cannon old buddy, so fire away," Winthrop said.

"The whole plan hinges on our making others believe we're somewhere we aren't. In SATCOM we have a concept for this called 'shadow images'. Have you heard of it?"

"Yes I have, but not in the concept of making a whole group of ships disappear. Who are we trying to fool them or us?"

"Therein lays the catch. We can't fool our enemy since they aren't high tech. We're trying to fool ourselves, well, ultimately, the bosses in Washington D.C.; those in the 'war room.'"

"Don't let anyone tell you to aim high my friend," Winthrop said jokingly. "We are inviting the wrath of God if this were to fail. How do you plan to pull it off?"

"It never hurts to have friends in high places who work in the 'war room'; Major Percival J. Tuck—no relative to the good Friar—United States Marine Corps and an Annapolis grad some ten years ago to be exact."

"How do we know he'll go along with it?" Winthrop asked.

"He's the one that suggested it. I happened to be in Washington around Christmas. I heard scuttlebutt about this deployment. I asked him if he'd heard anything. He said he had and wanted to meet me at a local Pub later that day. We met and he laid out the upcoming deployment and this scheme of his to keep a bad thing from happening. I told him I hoped we'd never have to resort to such a thing." Scott paused there and took a long swig of coffee. "This is some good coffee. Is this the usual Navy issue?" he asked.

"Actually, it's from my own stash. I bring it every time we ship out—been doing it for years. It's much better than regular issue."

"I will agree to that," Scott said.

There was a long pause in the conversation. Both men sipped the coffee and thought about their predicament. Winthrop broke the silence.

"I guess we both understand how high the stakes are. So what do you have to do to start the ball rollin'?" he asked.

"Make a phone call to Tuck. He's the one who sets it in motion. Until you hear from me you will follow your orders exactly. I will tell you when to deviate. That's about all there is to it."

"Sounds simple enough, in fact it sounds too easy for such a dire undertaking."

"Hopefully we will have done it all for naught and there will be no death and destruction. Then the worst that can happen to us is early retirement if we are discovered. If not than nothing happens and we go on as usual."

"Is that what you really expect, Scotty?"

"No, Win, I don't think it will go easy. Nothing ever does. Murphy's Law you know."

Winthrop nodded that he understood. The two men spent the next thirty minutes reminiscing about college and their families. Scott had a wife and four kids. Winthrop had married, but never had children. His wife suffered a disease that prevented her from getting pregnant. They had learned to live without children, ultimately replacing them with dogs—not a great trade off, but a satisfying one.

This would be the last time Scott and Winthrop would see each other until after the upcoming deployment—a deployment wherein they hoped to avoid a terrible disaster. They were putting their careers on the line to prevent it. They shook hands and then Scott climbed into the chopper for the hundred mile ride back to his ship.

CHAPTER 76

Jordan Smith had considered leaving the underground more than once. She vacillated between loneliness and anger. Happiness was a distant memory. Boredom clung to her like stink on skunk. She was ready to go back to the East Coast and die. Whoever wanted to kill her could go ahead. Anything would be better than this.

Two and a half months ago, give or take a week or so, Shires had promised not to abandon her. "Don't worry Honey, you'll see a lot of me," he had said. Right now she could wring his lying neck.

She tried to remember what she had worked on that might have been so secret, so threatening to National Security, that she had to die. She knew it had to be a National Security issue, but she had never worked on any project directly related to it that she knew of. Of course all projects at DARPA were ultimately related to National Security in some way since it was run by the Department of Defense.

Over and over she played it in her mind; never a satisfactory answer rose from the musings. There were many situations that could be the culprit, but she couldn't pick one. Everything she thought of always carried with it a tinge of anger at Shires for dumping her in the underground.

And then Shires arrived completely out of the blue. No one told her was coming. He just appeared at the doorstep. Her heart jumped for joy. All her anger drained away as she leaped into his arms crying and showering him with kisses.

"Boo, I love you," is all the anger that came out of her mouth that morning. Her joy was complete. They made love slowly, enjoying the touching, savoring each moment as a lifetime; sometime later they languished on the bed. Her head lay on his chest. They were quiet. She could hear his heartbeat—only then did she show her anger. "I was so pissed at you I could've killed you," she lamented, tapping him lightly on the chest with the flat of her fist.

"I know sweetheart. I'm so sorry I didn't get here sooner. You have every right to be upset with me. I'm here with you now though, and I don't plan to leave you ever again."

"I'll understand if you have to leave for short periods of time, just don't be gone so long. Three months of loneliness almost drove me crazy," she said in a conciliatory manner to smooth some of her earlier sharpness.

"Look sweetheart," he said running his fingers through her shining black hair, "I got lonely for you so bad I swore I'd never leave you again and I mean it. I swear I've never felt like that before. So rest assured you have me for the duration now.

They made love again before they ate the lunch delivered to the door. A note on the sack said they would be picked up and taken to a meeting that evening

"Is this how all the meals are?" Shires asked.

"Mostly, yes; cold and impersonal, but you get used to it. It keeps you alive. That's what counts I guess."

"When is the last time you had a really good meal?" Shires felt a little guilty. He hoped she wouldn't say three months ago.

"Three months ago when I was with you, unless you consider Kentucky Fried. We get that now and then."

The ham and cheese sandwiches were good, but Shires didn't say that, not to Jordan, not at this time. She was eating slowly. He couldn't tell whether she liked the food or not. She didn't say she did so he didn't push it.

"So, where do we go for meetings?"

"It's never the same place twice. Your guess would be as good as mine. What happened to your chip? You're not still wearing it are you?"

"Oh God, no! I'd never have gotten here with it. They wouldn't allow that. They removed it, but they're keeping it active so I won't be missed for awhile."

"They can do that?"

"I guess so. I have the idea of coming in and bringing you out with me, so I asked them not to smash it."

"Can you do that?"

"Sure, why not."

"Because from what I've heard since I've been here no one can leave because of security."

"Oh I'm sure if I want to leave here bad enough they'll let me go."

"I'm not sure about that, Boo."

They discussed the pros and cons of that and other things on into the afternoon. About 5 in the evening a horn honked summoning them, to ride to the meeting. They did so and were taken to a rather large home located somewhere in the Napa Valley. Shires wasn't sure where, but he thought it might have been Sonoma.

To their pleasant surprise a meal awaited them. Shires counted eighteen people present. They all would share a potluck meal of spaghetti and meatballs, garlic bread and salad. He noticed Kinzi Tern among those gathered and nodded to her.

."Shires," she exclaimed, "How are you?"

"I'm fine Kinzi," he said extending his hand. "This is my fiancée Jordan Smith." The women shook hands.

Kinzi turned to the man standing at her side. "This is my fiancée Anthony Arzetti."

Jordan shook his hand first and said hello. Shires did the same and said "You must be the father of the famous Mike Arzetti with whom I've had the privilege of working on a number of occasions. And Kinzi you must have noticed I wasn't much help in getting you released."

"I think we have Cahmael to thank for that, even if I don't understand his reasoning behind it," Anthony Arzetti said.

"Free will," Nathan Conrad said as he walked over to them. "He wants everybody to have a free choice. Same as God wants. Cahmael is the Antichrist and he wants you to choose him freely. Come on everybody sit down and enjoy the food," he called out loudly, ending the conversation.

Shires figured everybody was in the same boat and that would be *hungry for good food* and the spaghetti was delicious. For the most part silence prevailed during the meal. Once in a while a laugh here and there, but mostly it was silent.

Nathan Conrad finished first. He stood and walked to the front of the group then spoke.

"I have you all here this evening for a very specific reason. Our time is running short and it is imperative that you hear what I'm going to say tonight.

"As I'm sure most of you are aware I believe that Jehosea Cahmael is the Antichrist and I won't mince any words in saying that. I'm sure there are some of you here tonight who would argue with me about that. That's okay, but I'm not here to argue ideologies with you. So you'll just have to listen to my side tonight. We can do all the arguing later. I feel that what I have to say is too important to delay. So tonight I get the floor since you're all here because of the underground, and it exists because many of us believe that Cahmael is the Antichrist. So you are my captive audience for this evening.

"Now according to the Bible the Antichrist gets to reign for seven years. Three and a half will be good years and three and a half will be bad. The Bible uses 42 months to describe the three and a half year segments.

"There is a definite end to the first—the first being a period of time where good times roll. The world is fed and clothed and there is peace upon it just like now. Remember we are willing the good. That is Cahmael's motto.

"I figure this first period of his reign will end with the dedication of the Temple in Jerusalem. There are those who argue that he isn't reigning right now. Believe me folks he is. It may not seem like it, but he is. I guarantee that. He has his finger on all the buttons around the world and he pushes them as needed.

"As good as the first half is, the second half will be as bad in fact it will be horribly unimaginable. Piles of dead, headless bodies will line the streets—so many there'll be no time to bury them. The stench will foul the air for miles around. It will be hell on earth. If you think you've had hard times these are not the usual. You can't imagine what is coming—not the slightest idea."

Shires wanted to stop the man and take issue with him. Somebody should. What he was saying was completely absurd bordering on paranoia and out-of-whack with factual reality. But he didn't. This was Nathan Conrad's party and he could talk if he wanted to. It was his gig, and like he said, he had supplied the food.

"I hope the picture scares you. It should. It does me. Now there are those who argue that the chip is not the mark of the beast. Okay then what is it? Without it you can't buy or sell. You can do nothing without it.

"Granted it's not a mark like what you might expect a mark to be, but it certainly marks you. You can't get away from it unless you have it removed, but then you have to go underground as some of you know."

A knowing chuckle spread around the room as many agreed with the statement. Shires knew that Arzetti and Tern had done it, as had he, but for a different reason. He guessed a few others had as well. He nudged Arzetti and said, "Didn't you guys have a couple of friends?"

"Yeah Greg Littlejack and John Monroe; They're at an undisclosed location that has something to do with guns and other lethal instruments."

"Any specific reason for that?" Shires asked.

"Not that I know of," Arzetti answered.

"Might be a good question to ask Nathan. After all we're in it. We have a right to know."

"So what does going underground mean?" Nathan asked. There was silence.

"If you are alone it means extreme loneliness," Jordan said over the silence. There was a murmur of agreement.

"Yes it does," Nathan agreed, "and that is because you have lost your identity. You no longer have a mortgage or rent to pay. You buy or sell nothing. You have no bills because you have no address. You are homeless. You are living off the grid. You have no friends. You have nothing, and as Jordan said, if you are alone you are extremely lonely.

"I'll not paint a rosy picture because living in the underground is not rosy at all. So you better have a good reason for being here or you won't be able to stay, and therein lies the rub because you can't leave. We can't let you leave; rather we won't let you leave. The stakes are too high. We will shoot you to keep you from leaving. I'm sorry, but that's just the way it is."

"You can't do that," Shires protested.

"I know it sounds harsh," Nathan said, "but we can't take a chance on someone telling the authorities about a certain area where they might find certain members of the underground hiding. Maybe right now in this first 42 months of the reign of the Antichrist these measures might seem severe.

"But we have to live with it now because in the second 42 months it won't seem extreme. Believe me folks you don't want to be caught by the authorities during that period of time because then you'll either take the mark or die. Your head will be lopped off and your body tossed on the pile with the rest of the dead. Your stink will join the others in a harmony of stench. The horror will be unimaginable.

"I know you don't want an argument, but there are those of us who don't believe that Antichrist stuff. It doesn't matter how you describe it, nothing like that is going to happen. You're using scare tactics like the old hellfire and brimstone preachers of the past. So you'll have to excuse me if I go down as a nonbeliever," Shires said.

"You are free to believe what you want; however the underground was established to hide believers and the rules were set up accordingly. So whether or not you believe Cahmael is the Antichrist you are bound by the same rules. If you take advantage of our service you will abide by those rules. Does everybody understand that?"

Shires was angry, but he shut up. His idea about leaving didn't sound so good now, especially with the threat of being shot hanging in the air; he disagreed with that policy altogether. In the back of his mind he didn't believe they would do that, but it was a good threat.

"Now, there is pie and ice cream in the kitchen. We want you to enjoy that before we send you on your way. I'm sorry I sounded so threatening with that warning. I'm not usually that way. It's imperative that all of you understand that being in the underground is not a game. It is real serious business. I'd like you all to remember that."

Shires was sure he would.

CHAPTER 77

Matthew Stoneham heard through the grapevine—one of Melissa's co-workers—that she was dating Mike Arzetti; the son of one of the escapees. That interested him. With the embarrassment of two failures eating him alive (he failed to find Jordan Smith for the Director and he gave the agency wrong addresses on the safe houses). He grasped the tidbit of information and ran with it.

He pulled up the chip tracking records and followed Melissa's the day he discovered the underground safe houses. She was at work and then she left for lunch. She met Mike Arzetti at the hotdog place.

She was with Mike that day, but that doesn't prove anything except they were together. But he wondered if she would warn Mike of his father's impending arrest. She would, he was sure of it. He could prove nothing, but he would be aware of that in the future.

That was when he began tracking Melissa's past. He went back three months and tracked her to the present, and counted the number of times she had met with Mike, where they were and how long they were together. He wrote it down. Then he composed an email, which he would send to Melissa Hardin at his leisure.

He smiled inwardly. She would take it as a threat. That's what he meant it to be in an innocuous way—half joke, half serious. He was sure that her meeting him so quickly after the discovery of the whereabouts of his dad was coincidental, but you don't know. If it were anything else she has been forewarned.

So again he began the tedious task of relooking at everything from start to finish—from the BART station forward to the present. With so many cameras and so many places around the world to watch, he hated to be focused only on one area, but, if anything, Matt Stoneham was tenacious. He would never give up until he solved the problem. If that took until Hell froze over so be it. For Matt it wasn't so much catching the bad guys as it was making the technology work.

His phone light blinked. He had an incoming call. He hated to be interrupted, but it was his personal line so he took it.

Matt, Tuck here, the voice said.

"Admiral, ole buddy how ya doin'?

If the rank is that high it has to be General, I'm a Marine remember?

"Navy…Marines…if you toss it in the air it comes down the same. I never understood those ranks anyway. Percy, what are you doing in my part of the world?"

Need to go fishing. Thought I'd talk to you about a good ole fishin' hole you might know about out there. I'm flying to San Francisco tomorrow. I'd like to have dinner with you. Talk about fishing and do a little reminiscing about our time together at MIT that summer when we worked with shadow imaging. What do you think, can you swing the time?

"Of course, you buying?"

Tuck chuckled over the phone. *You haven't changed one damn bit; still as stingy as ever. What you going to do with all your money?*

"Leave it to my grandkids."

You don't even have any kids and you're not married. Your money will end up in the pocket of the government.

"Maybe I'll leave it to charity."

Okay, I'm good for the tab. You be sure to be there…our usual place. I don't want to travel all that way for nothing.

"You got it see you then." Matt folded the cell and placed it back on the flasher.

"That was one cryptic conversation to tell him they were going through with some operation. He didn't know the details, but he knew it would be a challenge for his technological knowhow and that was fascinating. The words shadow images raced through his mind. Oh yes this would be interesting.

Now back to the BART station and chasing bad guys.

CHAPTER 78

The threatening email shocked Melissa Hardin. She would never have suspected such treatment from Matthew Stoneham. It wasn't like him at all. The man had been spying on her personal life. She felt wronged and violated. Wherever she and Mike had spent more than three hours he had written HAD SEX HERE in bold type.

That was the morning Melissa Hardin realized the awesome power of the technology she had at her disposal. It could save lives or destroy them. The destruction of innocent lives concerned her the most, especially after her treatment by Matthew Stoneham. Suddenly it was no longer just chasing *bad guys*, which is the focus it had always been for her; now you could frame a *good guy* if you felt like it.

Matt Stoneham had shown her how easily it could be done. He had turned the technology into a weapon of evil by changing innocent situations into criminal activity. You could build a case against anybody and claim they were terrorists. It would be circumstantial evidence, but it would be a strong body of such evidence, and difficult to defend against or explain away—and therein lay the scary part. Not all men, or women, have motives as pure as the driven snow. There will always be those who will do the evil if they can find a means, and believe they'll get away with it. It's human nature.

Melissa knew she was naïve, but the depth of it shocked her. She'd never thought about it before. Now it overwhelmed her. It was a fast moving train on a one-way track and she was caught in the middle, playing smash mouth with a train—not a clever thing to do even if you're wearing a helmet.

She answered Matt's email. He deserved nasty, but she was above that—naïve maybe, but not vindictive. For now she would take the high road; the one less travelled by the bulk of humanity, and be the better person for it. She would not allow him to know that she had perceived his threat, and it scared her.

Dear Matt: Thank you for sharing my life with me. It is flattering that you have spent so much of your precious time researching my every move. I know how busy you are catching criminals these days (she couldn't resist putting in that little dig about his recent failure) *Did you do it on your own time or during company hours? It gives one the feeling of family to know that someone cares in such a special way.*

It is comforting to know that you are watching after me. I feel secure in that knowledge. Thank you so much.

Melissa Hardin

She patted herself on the back. She did it without rancor or a hint of vindictiveness…well maybe a little with the dig, but it was a good first effort.

Mike would need to know, and he was going to be upset. She considered not telling him, but decided against it. He should know there was someone spying on him. Of course in this day and age it was expected. She was sure Mike was aware of that. Maybe not as aware as she was, but he would know.

CHAPTER 79

Mike Arzetti knew of the spy in the sky from the chip—probably more than most because of his position with the underground. He knew he was being watched all the time in a random manner. So he tried never to make any moves that were out of the ordinary; however getting the news about Matthew Stoneham building up a three month background of their comings and goings was disturbing. Even if it just included Melissa and him, it still made Mike uncomfortable.

He knew there was always a possibility of someone reading more into a situation than might be there; that was always the chance. In the future it might become necessary to go completely underground, fall off the grid, and become invisible. He would put that day off as long as possible.

She brought him a copy of the email that evening. He read it slowly looking for any clue as to how much Stoneham might know, but he found nothing. He firmly believed the guy was just checking it out. He must have thought he had a leak when the fugitives were all gone. Mike wouldn't blame him. That must have been a shock.

The underground evidently hadn't used those safe houses in a while, good thing for it saved Melissa and his butts, but the underground lost 5 safe houses. Melissa didn't tell him, but he knew that each one of those residences would be under surveillance 24 hours a day. Anyone arriving there would be arrested immediately. All people in the underground had been labeled terrorists by law enforcement. This label makes it easy to detain them for inordinate amounts of time.

Mike had often wondered about Nathan Conrad and how he escaped detection by Homeland Security. According to Ann, he came right on Campus and talked. As far as Mike knew the man had never been arrested. If the claim that Cahmael was killing everybody who spoke out against him were true, how has Nathan escaped the fate?

In fact Mike had heard of no one who had died under suspicious circumstances, accidental or not, while speaking out against Cahmael. He knew fear had driven many to the underground, but reality did not uphold the claim. There had never been any proof of misdeeds by Cahmael—all he had ever done was good things.

In every aspect Cahmael was the victim of bad publicity. He fit the description from the Bible therefore he must be the evil one. It's just a case of mistaken identity. He's getting a bad rap for being a good person.

Mike worried that Melissa would get spooked by the threat and want to discontinue their relationship. She assured him that would never happen, but he knew the real pressure hadn't been applied. She loved her job; she had said so many times, so he wondered how she would do if that were a threat.

"Mike, I love you. I would never put my job before you. I couldn't stand to lose you. Trust me baby I'll always be here."

"I feel like a needy little kid, and I'm embarrassing myself asking for all these assurances from you. You make my life complete. I'd hate to lose that completeness I feel when I'm with you," he said sheepishly.

Melissa hoped above all hope that she could live up to her promises, but she didn't think it would ever come to such a test. All this scary stuff about Cahmael was somebody's fear tactics. The underground was filled with religious nuts who thought the devil was everywhere. Homeland Security existed to protect the Continental United States from terrorists foreign and domestic.

Mike's dad was considered a terrorist. Even if Mike said he wasn't, that didn't change the fact that he was arrested with a bunch of people who were considered to be terrorists at the time. That classification had never been changed. And now Mike's dad was hiding in the underground. She also knew that somehow Mike had a connection to his father or to the underground. Matthew Stoneham didn't realize he had stumbled onto something that could be a problem for her and Mike in the future. That part scared her.

And then again, Matthew Stoneham might not be as dumb as she wanted him to be. He might have done an excellent guessing job and already suspected a connection. Melissa would have to be careful in the future not to awaken Matthew's curiosity any more than it had been.

She had been so idealistic when *she first arrived at the job, but that was slowly dissipating as the line between the good guys and the bad ones became fuzzy and difficult to see. When you're spying on everybody it's difficult to decide who is good and who is bad.*

CHAPTER 80

Ghirardelli Square was the only place that Matthew Stoneham remembered meeting Percival Tuck when he visited Frisco 5 years earlier. That had to be the 'usual' meeting place he was talking about, so Matt waited for him there on a bench by the chocolate factory.

"I see you remembered," said a voice from his right side. Percival Tuck walked into view.

"Civilian clothes, I didn't expect that," Matt said.

"Special circumstances my friend," he said as they shook hands. "Let's get some coffee," he suggested, pointing to the outdoor café.

The two were almost equal in size with Stoneham being slightly taller at three inches over six-foot. Their appearances were polar opposites. Stoneham with waist length blackish gray hair, a black beard, wearing a bright Hawaiian shirt, cut-off jeans, and tennis shoes was the exact replica of a mid 20th century hippie. Tuck was ever the Marine with butch cut hair sporting white sidewalls over his ears, wearing a blue dress shirt with tan dress slacks, and spit-shined oxfords. He was neat as a pin in every respect even in civilian clothes.

"I've always wondered, do Marines starch their skivvies too?" Matt asked.

Tuck guffawed. "It's only myth my friend; just urban legend," he said, defending all squared-away Marines everywhere.

They ordered coffee and waited for their names to be called.

"So Percy, what brings you to my part of the country?"

"I'm on a mission for one who must remain nameless."

"The President?" Matt asked somewhat aghast at the insinuation.

"I can't confirm or deny that. Suffice it to say, it's someone very high."

Their names were called to pick up coffee. The conversation stopped until they were seated again.

"Remember the discussion we had about shadow images that summer at MIT?" Tuck asked.

"Yes, it was a theoretical concept," Stoneham answered.

"They want you to make it a reality."

"How so?"

Tuck looked around quickly, almost furtively, looking for something, anything, out of the ordinary. Satisfied at what he saw, or didn't see, he spoke. "There are some ships that will be in the Mediterranean that must appear to be somewhere else. This status must be maintained for a period of three months, beginning almost right away, well, at least by the middle of March."

Matt Stoneham took a sip of coffee and leaned forward. "Explain this to me very slowly. Tell me exactly what you want, and I'll tell you if it's possible," he said.

Tuck spent the next few minutes explaining the problem that faced the Navy. "The Middle East is bristling with nuclear weapons; although it is believed that Israel is the only country to have a nuclear bomb, the fact isn't set in concrete. The intelligence is lacking poorly on such a vital question.

"The U.S. Navy is being asked to place two Carrier Groups in close proximity to each other and to the shore near Israel, which places them close to our enemies. Such a large target may be the opportunity of a lifetime for a country with a bomb. We could lose almost half our naval forces in one blast.

"The plan is for both groups to take up stations, but the second group will only stay long enough for you to do whatever it is you have to do, and then it will move to an undisclosed location under the cover of darkness. It must seem to onlookers in the war room that the ships are still there. We observe this by satellite and the shadow images on our big board.

"Do you think you can pull off such a feat?"

"If I had a year, definitely, but you're asking for the impossible in a little less than two weeks. I would have to hack your satellite systems to feed in the false picture data plus hack your war room systems to feed in the false shadow images. That is going to take some time. Are the ships on station yet?"

"Yes, both groups are exactly where they're supposed to be."

"Good, then I'll already be getting the pictures I need. That's quite an assignment you brought me. I'll need you to call me in a couple days and I'll tell you exactly what I need from you. I do hope you don't come up with any new catches, or with something you've forgotten."

Tuck chuckled and assured him there were no other catches. Then he reached in his pocket for a slip of paper, "One last thing that might make your assignment a little easier," he said handing Matt the paper, "The passwords to get into the systems I asked you to hack; might make your job a little easier."

Matt smiled and nodded. The two men spent the rest of the evening discussing their lives and careers to the present. Tuck bought them dinner as he promised at a nearby restaurant and broke off about nine so he could catch a midnight flight back to Washington DC.

CHAPTER 81

Richard Butcher had stared hard at the position map on the table of the war room. It had shown two carrier groups on station near the Israeli/Lebanon coastline. He was pleased that his orders were being followed.

He had heard the concerns of the Joint Chiefs regarding a nuclear strike by terrorists, or by countries not friendly to Israel even with a treaty in place. Cahmael had assured him that nothing of the sort would take place. He felt confident about it. When Cahmael said something he was usually right—plus he had an uncanny knack of predicting things.

The buzzer on the hotline went off jarring him from his thoughts of his trip to the Pentagon that morning. The hotline had been the most difficult thing to adjust to. Every world leader had the number so he never knew who might be calling unless it had been prearranged.

Mr. President it's Jehosea Cahmael for you, Sir.

"Thank you Cynthia, put him on…This is President Richard Butcher," he said when he heard the open line.

My dear friend, said the familiar voice of Jehosea Cahmael, *I hope I've found you in good spirits. I certainly am after hearing that your Carriers are where I requested them to be. Thank you very much my friend. I'll sleep much better knowing they are there.*

"Your wish is my command," he said, knowing that statement wasn't completely true. He sometimes wondered if Cahmael knew the truth. He was the blackmailer in the relationship. What he got he got by coercion, nothing more. At least that's how Richard Butcher rationalized away his behavior whenever he gave in to a Cahmael request.

This is an election year for you, is it not?

"Yes it is."

You are going to run I presume?

"Definitely!"

That would be your second term?

"Yes Sir!"

Have you thought of a third term?

"That's not possible."

Everything is possible.

"No, you don't understand. Under our system of government there is a two term limit."

Given the right circumstances that could change. What do you think of the idea?

The suggestion caught the President by surprise. The limit was put in place to fend off a one party rule or, worse yet, a dictatorship. It would be a highly partisan debate with the party out of power resisting it completely.

"There would be so much negative reaction against it the debate would never get off the ground. It could never happen," Dick answered matter-of-factly.

There need not be a debate given the right circumstances. I guess I'm saying, or rather asking, would you be willing to continue governing if the right set of circumstances were to give you a third term?

They were talking in the realm of possibilities about a scenario five years away. He hadn't won his second term yet, and here was another of Cahmael's famous insinuations, bordering on a prediction. The prediction that he would win a second term and be in position to serve a third—quite a heady assumption for a sitting President to digest. Dick Butcher didn't ask what kind of circumstances, he wasn't sure he wanted to know.

"Although I can't think of any circumstance that might lead to such a thing, I would definitely be ready to serve a third term if the opportunity arose."

Excellent! I knew I could count on you, Sir. Now remember I need you to keep your battle groups in the Mediterranean for the full three months.

The President assured Cahmael that he would do so. They exchanged their parting farewells and hung up, leaving Dick Butcher to contemplate the exchange.

First of all, he knew he was being played by a master of deception—

if not deception at the very least manipulation. The more he thought about it he realized that everything about the man could be a veil of deception—a sham even down to the resurrection of the Pope. But how do you separate the real from the unreal?

CHAPTER 82

It took Matthew Stoneham exactly one week and three days to hack the systems and have operation Catfish ready to roll. Catfish was the code name that Tuck had given him the day he called for further directions. It had been two days after their meeting.

There are two battle groups by the Israeli coast. You are to cover for the one farthest at sea. It will move away when you give the word. This little shift is called Operation Catfish, and good luck, Tuck had said.

Those were the only other instructions Matt had been given. The rest was up to him. The battle group designated Alpha commanded by Admiral William Franklin Scott aboard the carrier Jimmy Doolittle moved away from its position by the Israeli coast in the dead of night with all deck lights out. They were there one day and gone the next.

Carrier Group Alpha had been on station for twelve days before it moved. That gave Matt plenty of information to feed into the loop that would repeat every twelve days. The span of time was such that Matt figured anyone watching would have to watch a long time and pay really close attention before he realized it was a loop. The only way the truth could be known was by on site observation—a difficult task for a terrorist with a small boat.

Only the pilots of task force Delta were aware of the change of position by task force Alpha. Admirals Scott and Winthrop were loath to tell anybody, but the pilots would have to know since they would be flying over the area on a daily basis. They were told it was a countermeasure and to treat it as top secret. That was the extent of the information they would get on the subject.

The planes from Alpha group still came every day to fly the joint missions as if nothing had changed. The exact location of Alpha group was unknown even to its own commanders who didn't know they didn't know—just as Scott and Winthrop had planned it.

The military presence in the Mediterranean was meant to be a show of force, nothing more. In a world at peace for the first time in centuries it was the 10 ton elephant in the living room.

To Hassan Enau it was an answer to prayer. Allah had sent the Americans to him. He had been observing them for the past week with the binoculars given to him by his late grandfather whose lands had been taken away by the Jews. They claimed it was their land given to them by Allah.

The Jews were money grubbing pigs and they needed to die along with the Americans who supported them. Hassan had dedicated his life to making that happen. He had helped dig the tunnels from Egypt into the Gaza Strip—all the while burning with the fire of revenge.

And now, along with the Americans, Allah had sent the bomb, and he had been chosen as one of the few who would deliver it right to the gut of the American Armada floating in the Mediterranean.

He smiled to himself when he thought of the great task that lay before him What a great revenge for his grandfather. He was blessed to have been given the opportunity to serve such a noble cause.

Nobody said where the bomb came from. Hassan didn't care. It was there and he had been chosen to use it—that's all that mattered. They called it a big word, thermonuclear device. They said it would bring the light and heat of the sun down on earth in one glorious moment. The fireball would incinerate anything within a mile radius of the explosion; nothing would be left. It had been brought in from Russia through Iranian supply sources. It had to be exploded away from the mainland or they took the risk of wiping themselves off the face of the earth. The fifty miles out to the American ships was far enough away to keep any damage to a minimum, but it would kill the entire fleet. What a blow to the Americans and to the Jew pigs that spawned them. What a glorious revenge in the name of his grandfather Enau.

Hassan took one last look through the binoculars and then rose from the sand and returned to their hastily built camp. The camp was nothing more than a low canopy for shade and a few tan colored blankets for warmth at night. Tins of food were buried in the sand nearby along with their supply of bottled water.

Their presence here had to remain unnoticed. The American planes flew over the area on a regular basis—so there was never a fire. Food was eaten cold. It was meager but it only had to last until May 14th. They would be resupplied regularly every month. The supplies would come under the cover of darkness. Everything happened at night. They had come here in the middle of the night from a small boat anchored just offshore.

This was a windswept part of the beach and in March the cold chilled Hassan to the bone. He didn't care. He would suffer the pains of hell for this mission.

Hassan thought about his mother and the tears she shed for him when he left; some were sadness and some were joy that he was going to do a great thing for the Palestinian People. Although nobody knew at that time what it might be, they had been promised it would be unforgettable; as unforgettable as that great plane strike in New York. The one the Americans called 9/11. And that was all that mattered to him.

There were others involved with this, not just the six of them. The others would bring the stolen Israeli fishing boat with the bomb attached on the night of their departure. Three hours, maybe just a little more, should get them to the Americans. They wanted to be near the center of the ships if that were possible, but it didn't matter; close proximity would be enough.

Time was endless. He passed the time reading from his Koran. The wisdom of Allah was special to him as it is to all Muslims. He kept his mind active by memorizing verses that seemed special. His five friends did the same when they weren't talking among themselves. All six had known each other since childhood. They had been born and raised in the Gaza Strip. None of them knew life without Israeli domination. Hatred of the Jews was a daily aspect of their young lives. Hatred and revenge is what they were fed with their baby milk.

Cahmael had made peace between the Israelis and the Palestinians. The People of Palestine could never accept peace with the Jews, and only agreed so they would have time to prepare for another attack.

Hatred and revenge were the nourishment of the Palestinians from the womb to the grave. They lived and died for them. For Hassan and his five friends to go among the American ships and explode a thermonuclear bomb was as natural as going to bed at night—something to do on the way to the grave.

CHAPTER 83

It was in March when Michael Arzetti discovered that somebody was checking up on him. George Wilde, his partner, was the one who noticed it and asked him if he knew anybody in Personnel.

"The clerk, Amy, at the front desk, why?"

"Some guy said he was from Homeland Security wanted to know how long you had worked here. It sounded like they were doing a background check on you. He was asking all kinds of personal questions."

"How do you know this?"

"When I heard your name mentioned I eavesdropped."

"Did she answer the questions for him?"

"I couldn't tell for sure. You might want to contact Amy and ask her if she knows what it's about."

That afternoon after shift, Mike went to Personnel and confronted Amy. She wasn't a friend more like an acquaintance. He had met her in passing, but they were never close.

"A man came in here the other day asking questions about me. Want did you tell him?" he asked tersely.

He could tell she was shaken by his question, and somewhat taken aback by his abruptness. "Mike we aren't allowed to give out information to anybody unless it's a court order."

"According to my source you did though. I want to know what they were asking."

Her shoulders drooped visibly and a resigned expression covered her face. He knew he had her, and for a moment he felt sorry about that. "Look I'm not going any farther with this. I just want to know. I'll never hold it against you."

"They wanted to know if you had ever belonged to any subversive organization. That question made me laugh; Mike Arzetti, old straight arrow himself, belonging to an organization like that is like mixing oil and water. I told them 'no' in no uncertain terms."

"What else?"

""They said they had information that you belonged to the underground. I told them their information was probably a whole lot better than mine because I knew nothing about that."

"Anything else?"

"Yeah! They asked me about your girlfriend. I couldn't believe they asked me that. I said, 'Hey, we're the Personnel Department for the Police Department not a social club'. I don't even know who his girlfriend is. Believe me Mike, that's all I told them."

"Well, if that's the case there's no harm done. Thank you Amy," Mike said, and walked away far enough to be out of Amy's sight. He watched her make a hurried phone call, and wondered who she called. It certainly looked more ominous then his conversation with her had indicated.

CHAPTER 84

Henry Bishop the head of the CIA brought the news to President Butcher at his daily intelligence briefing. They had good information that a thermonuclear bomb has left Russia into Iran and from there the trail is gone.

Dick was stunned by the news. "Thermonuclear? They said thermonuclear? What exactly does that mean?"

"It means, Sir that it is a really bad bomb—a Hydrogen bomb. The United States built one in the 1950's but never tested it above ground always below and with a very small explosion. It could be a thousand times more powerful than the one dropped on Hiroshima, Japan. So I'm emphasizing bad here in the worst sense of the word," Bishop said.

"In other words it's a dirty bomb?"

"It's more than just dirty— maybe enough destructive power to crack the earth. It's unimaginable," Bishop said loosening his tie as if the words were too much to say with it tied.

"Did we develop it?"

"No! It had to have been Russia during the cold war."

"Why in God's name would anybody want a bomb that powerful?"

"There are factions in Iran, especially among those in power, that think they have to cause as much destruction as possible to bring about the Messiah. So, we think it's headed straight for the carrier groups. That seems the only plausible answer. We're working that hypothesis anyway. It could be blackmail too, but there is nothing to gain by that. If it is blackmail we'll hear about it."

"How would such a bomb be delivered?"

"That's where we might be ahead in the game. They, whoever they are, have no delivery system except to hand carry it. It would have to be done by suicide bombers."

"Can we stop it?"

"We have a good chance, yes sir."

"No! No! That's not the answer I want to hear," Dick said, raising his voice an octave or two, "I want to hear 'yes we can definitely stop this nuclear threat'. That's what I want to hear."

"We'll work on getting that answer, Sir."

"Is there any good news?"

"No Sir, sorry, it's all bad this morning."

Dick Butcher stewed on the intelligence session all morning. Cahmael had better have some reassurances to give him. Those ships were in harm's way, and the threat was eminent, not theoretical.

At noon he picked up the hotline. "Cynthia, would you get me the Vatican please. I need to speak to Jehosea Cahmael," he said.

Certainly, Mr. President, one moment please, Cynthia Underwood cooed in her usual sweet voice.

He heard the dial tone and the buzzing. That stopped and a highly accented male voice answered in English. **Good evening this is the Vatican. How may I help you?**

The President of the United States is calling to speak to Mr. Cahmael, Cynthia said.

One moment please.

A minute later, **"My dear friend to what do I owe this wonderful surprise? I trust you are okay and Lydia too,"** Cahmael said. Then he paused for a moment and stated, *There's something troubling you.*

"A thermonuclear bomb on the loose and headed for my ships in the Mediterranean; that's what's bothering me," he said tersely.

Dick could tell that the news had caught Cahmael by surprise, and that was difficult to do.

A thermonuclear bomb?

"That's correct, Sir. It came from Russia, and it's headed for my ships. I have a lot of ships there. You gave me your assurance that nothing would happen to them. Are you sure you can still deliver on that promise?" Dick hated to question the man, but this was serious.

You can always trust my word. I can understand how such news could

give you pause, but you are not to worry about it for it will be taken care of in due course. Trust me my friend. I won't let you down.

Somehow Cahmael's words did soothe his fears; although he didn't trust the man enough to let go of his worry. That would continue until the weapon had been found and disposed of—only then would he stop worrying. His credibility was on the line because he went against the recommendations of his commanders and put two battle groups in close proximity to each other. The nuclear strike the commanders had feared was about to come upon them.

"I'm going to take you at your word and try to stop worrying. I have my security forces searching as we speak. Maybe, between us we'll be able to stop it."

No maybes my friend; remember that.

Richard Butcher hoped the man was right. This was a thermonuclear bomb threat they had been talking about—not a walk in the park on a sunny day. He thought seriously about withdrawing both carrier groups, but that would anger Cahmael, and he didn't want to do that; besides Cahmael was so positive. The President decided he could wait a little longer.

CHAPTER 85

The light was flashing on Matt Stoneham's phone. He didn't want to be interrupted, but answered anyway.

Matt this is Tuck. We have a problem, the voice said.

"What?"

Terrorist with a nuke.

"Are you kiddin' me?"

No! It's a serious threat. It's a thermonuclear nuke, and that makes it a bad dude. We've got to do something. So what can you do for me?

"I can do a lot of observing, and if I'm lucky maybe I'll find him for you; however don't get your hopes up, I haven't done well with finding people. Do you have any idea where I should start looking?"

Don't know for sure. I might suggest along the coast over there. Maybe look for anything odd that might be going on—anything that seems out of place. Otherwise I don't know what to tell you.

"Okay, I'll give it a try. Wish me luck. I'm gonna need it."

Matt knew the cameras by heart after working with them to create the loop. Now he would have to search all around the loop while being careful not to disturb it. His fingers worked the keyboard rapidly to bring him a view of the Israeli coastline. He picked a segment and zoomed in to a viewable position, meaning he would be able to see any activity that presented itself.

Of course there was none. He would have to go back at least a month and come forward, sweeping the whole coastline as he did. This would probably garner him nothing either, but it was a place to start.

He knew time was of the essence, so he had to hurry yet be extremely careful not to identify the wrong target. Eight hours later his eyes were burning from the strain of looking at aerial photos of the coastline. A drop of Visine helped to allay the stinging. He leaned back in his chair to relax.

It seemed to him that he had done an enormous amount of work for the DOD recently. He knew the dedication of the Temple in Israel was a great occasion not only for Israel, but for the United States as well. It was certainly drawing the attention of all the scumbags. An idiot with a nuclear bomb is one scary thing—especially if you don't know where he might be hiding, but they knew the target; or did they? Maybe it wouldn't be the ships at all. He wondered if anybody had thought of that.

At least they wouldn't have to worry about it being detonated in Israel. A thermonuclear bomb would completely destroy Israel; even the craziest of terrorists wouldn't want to destroy their own homes. A blast like that would make the whole area a wasteland much like Chernobyl in Russia—uninhabitable for a few hundred years.

So where would a good terrorist want to detonate the bomb? Matthew figured it would be away from Israel and away from the Middle East altogether. They weren't going to blow up the ships either; that was still too close. Whoever planned this was using the ships as a distraction. He called Major Percival Tuck back, and woke him at home out of a sound sleep.

"Admiral, they're not going to blow up the ships. They're too close to home for that."

You waited until three in the morning to call and tell me that? asked the sleepy voice.

"Sorry about that…forgot the time. After giving this a lot of thought, it seems to me that the location of the ships is awful close to home for them. It is my humble opinion that the bomb is meant for a large target much farther from there. I however have no idea what that target could be."

We have worked different scenarios on the problem for exactly the same reasons you have suggested, but the problem we have is that we may be giving these guys too much credit. We gotta remember they're fanatics. They may not care. There are factions in Iran who want to create carnage to usher in the next Messiah, and that's a whole other discussion. Therefore we have you searching. We want you to keep it up until you can say for certain there is nothing strange going on around there. Okay?

"Sounds like you're way ahead of me. I'm sorry I bothered you."

No! No! Don't be. I should have discussed it more with you. It's all right you're forgiven for interrupting my sleep. You had best be getting some yourself.

Sleep wouldn't come for Matt Stoneham—not that night. The sobering conversation with Tuck had finally brought home to him the terrible realization that there were people out there who wanted to destroy the world by any means possible. He wasn't sure how he had felt before, but he suddenly felt the urgency of it, and that made sleeping impossible that night.

CHAPTER 86

Mike Arzetti was more than a little upset with his sister Ann. She had gone to listen to Nathan Conrad and sometime during the presentation she joined the ranks of the religious nuts who believed Cahmael to be the Antichrist; but that wasn't how she described what she had done.

She said, "I gave my heart to the Lord. I asked Christ to forgive me of my sins and to come into my heart, and be the Lord of my life. I feel so good Michael. I can't describe it. Jamie did it too. Oh Mike, it's so wonderful! You've got to do it."

He didn't want to dampen his sister's enthusiasm, but she had to realize what she had done. "Sis, stop and think about it. You and Jamie already have the chip implanted and you've sworn to follow Cahmael. The only way you can take that back is by having the chip removed, and, if you do that you'll have to go into the underground."

"We don't think it has to be an either/or situation."

"Have you talked this over with anybody? Did you talk to Nathan about it?"

"Michael, don't get so upset. I just gave my heart to the Lord. That's all. It's a good thing."

Mike didn't know why it bothered him so much. He figured his sister could keep the chip and still worship the Lord. There were people doing just that in a lot of churches, but they didn't believe Cahmael to be the Antichrist. Nathan did, and therein lay the difference. Mike was sure Ann would finally come to that conclusion too if she listened to Nathan long enough. "If you hold that belief, Sis, you will end up in the underground at some point in time. I guarantee it," Mike told her.

Mike didn't believe any of it and only used his membership in the underground as a backup system to help buy and sell things in the event of a calamity like his father said could happen. The calamity being that Cahmael really was the Antichrist, and all those terrible things came about.

"Look Sis, don't get into that stuff too deep. I don't want you to be looked at as one of those nutcases that think Cahmael is the Antichrist."

"They're not nutcases Mike. They're people who believe a certain way, that's all."

"What do they talk about? Do they talk about giving in to Cahmael's wishes and continuing to live? No they don't talk about life, they talk about dying. They talk about dying for Christ, which is what Pastor Horn and Father Nalone did. That's crazy, Sis. Only a nut would think that way."

"Michael, it's called faith."

"All the same Sis, I don't want a front row seat at your beheading. So please, don't get too involved in that stuff."

Ann was stubborn and strong minded, like her dad, his mom always said. Mike knew arguing with her was useless. "Okay Sis," he said, "I'm going to get in the shower. I have a date with Melissa."

"Aren't you getting in kind of deep with that woman," she said good-naturedly, imitating his warnings to her. His warnings didn't go unheeded though. She heard them loud and clear. The beheading remark sent chills up her spine.

CHAPTER 87

Shires Lampton and Jordan Smith had become friends with Tony Arzetti and Kinzi Tern; although such friendships were discouraged by the underground for various reasons. The number one most important reason was the possibility of capture. The more you knew the more you could tell. It was better to stay anonymous and unnoticed.

Especially now with Homeland Security becoming more aggressive in chasing them. Now they had to move every few days to keep ahead of the law. They managed to stay together during that time by trading places with others.

Then the day came when they were all gathered up with the others and taken to a new safe house for a parley. This time it wasn't to hear Nathan talk about Cahmael. This time they were issued guns.

"Wait a minute! What is this?" Shires protested. "We're not supposed to do any fighting. That's why we're hiding in the underground."

Nathan Conrad walked through the door just as Shires was speaking. He raised his hands, palms open, and motioned for everybody to be quiet.

"Sorry I was late," he said, "there is an explanation for this. There are death squads seeking us out. When they find us they kill us on the spot. No judge no jury, nothing but death. You have to be able to protect yourselves. This is a prevalent thing in the East and the Midwest."

"Who are these people?" Tony Arzetti asked.

"We don't know, but six of our folks here on the West coast have been murdered. Two were from this area. We think they might be vigilantes, but we're not sure. So you've got to do what we tell you. The first thing is to be wary of strangers. Watch out for them. Look for people sitting in cars on your street. Any vans parked nearby. They will be trying to look ordinary, like they're supposed to be there."

"Why death squads?" Jordan asked.

"We don't know, but they've been wreaking havoc on the underground back east. We believe it's a more directed attack. Cahmael has substituted this for the random accidents he arranged for people in the past."

"What about you? I would think you'd definitely be on their hit list. Don't you think so?" Shires asked.

"I have very good security around me at all times. I think that's what has kept them at bay."

"Yeah but you are all over in unsecured places. It would seem to me that you offer them all kinds of opportunity. So if these death squads do exist I would think you should really be scared," Shires wouldn't let it go.

"I am scared, but I just turn it over to the Lord. I'm doing his work here, so I guess I'll live until God says 'that's enough'."

"So you're saying God himself protects you?" Shires was being a journalist, a probing journalist.

"I'm saying that I have angels protecting me. You've heard of guardian angels I'm sure."

"Well yes we've all heard of them. I'm just astounded that you put all that faith in them."

"I do appreciate the concern, but I guarantee you that I'm well taken care of. That's all I'll say about the subject. Do not worry about me. Worry about yourselves. In the past we have discouraged friendships, but now we are asking you to partner up with a couple more people. There is safety in numbers, and four sets of eyes are better than two—three sets better than one, and so forth."

"You are being given 45 caliber pistols and three fully loaded ammo clips; 10 shells to a clip. You will each receive one box of ammo containing 50 shells. All total you will have 80 rounds of ammunition. The 45 caliber bullet packs quite a wallop when it hits somebody. It also creates quite a hole; not so much on entry, but on exit. We were able to buy these at a good price since the 45 isn't as popular as other guns.

"We don't have time or space to give shooting lessons, so here's what you must do if you have to use the weapon. It's called point and shoot. Point it at the widest part of the person coming at you and pull the trigger. Oh yes, and make sure the safety is off before you try to shoot. The safety on the weapon is the half cocked position. You can pull the hammer back and feel it click. Stop pulling it there as that is the safety. We want you to practice putting it on safety for awhile without ammo in the gun—we don't want any accidents." There was a murmur of laughter around the room.

"Now this is the serious part folks. They'll come at you fast that's why you keep these weapons with you at all times. They'll come fast and they'll be shooting. You won't know when or where and that's why you must be vigilant—wary and watchful are the operant words here. Know where you are and what's going on around you. Discuss it among yourselves and practice it every day. I can't emphasize that too much; practice and practice and practice.

"Now before we leave here tonight I want everybody to have at least three in your group; four would be better. I don't want anybody to be alone. I want you to get familiar with the term paranoia, and get very paranoid."

CHAPTER 88

Melissa Hardin was upset with Ron Hartwell's discreet investigation of Mike Arzetti. The word discreet could never be applied to that botched up mess.

She should never have gone along with the idea, but it would have looked like Mike had something to hide if she hadn't.

Mike had been angry about it last evening. "What's with those people over there where you work? Are they so concerned about their employees that they check up on their boyfriends? There was a guy from Homeland Security in Personnel today asking questions about me. George overheard them talking and told me. I went to see Amy this afternoon. She said they were even asking questions about you."

"It all has to do with dumb email that Matt sent—the one I showed you. Somebody must have seen it other than me and jumped to the wrong conclusion," she lied.

"Look, I know your job has a lot to do with National Security issues. I just didn't know how involved it seems to be with the rest of your world. What do you do over there? I get the feeling you do a lot of spying on people with or without their consent. Is that what you do?"

Melissa thought about what she was about to say as compared to what needed to be said, and what she could say. She loved Mike and didn't want to lose him. "First you must understand that I have a secret security clearance to do the work that I do. I can't share anything with you that might violate that trust; however I can tell you that we spend a lot of time watching people, not only on cameras, but on the chip tracking system as well." She paused and looked at Mike for some time until he finally said, "Yes what?"

"Okay! What I'm going to tell you now I shouldn't. You saw the email from Matt. He got all that information from our chips—yours and mine. There is no hiding when you have the chip implanted. You know what's even scarier; he could have supplied us with photos of our trail as well. It's the technology. You can't get away from it; nobody can.

"I never thought about it before, but we can make a case of guilt against innocent people. When I took the job I was excited about catching criminals, like you do. I've been there nine months now, and I've discovered we don't catch criminals, we watch everybody. That bothers me."

"So you've been watching me, or at least, Matt has. Is that what you're saying?"

"Well it isn't watching so much since the trail is always there. All Matt had to do was type in your name and the system will account for you all the way back to the time of your chip implant. He would know your every move. He could even pull it up on visual. I'm telling you Mike it's astounding what we can do,"

"So big brother is with us."

"Yes and I've told you more than I should have; now I'll have to shoot you."

"Don't worry your secret is safe with me. Since we're exchanging secrets, and to show good faith, I'll give you something to hold over my head."

"No Michael don't! This has already gone too far. I don't want to know a secret about you," she protested, covering her ears.

They were sitting on the couch in Mike's living room. He put his arm around her, mussed her hair and wrestled her down, laughing all the time. They made love right there in the living room. All the while Melissa worried that Ann would come home. Mike told her later that Ann was spending the night with Jamie. She punched him on the arm.

All in all it had been a wonderful night, but she was still upset with Ron for his friend's bungling attempt to investigate Mike. In the future she would be more careful. Working for Homeland Security was a privilege she didn't want to squander.

CHAPTER 89

Early in the morning of March 10th Admiral Harry Nelson Winthrop commanding Carrier Group Delta in the Mediterranean 50 miles off the coast of Israel received the coded message regarding the runaway thermonuclear bomb.

He immediately called Admiral William Franklin Scott the Commander of Carrier Group Alpha located two hundred miles away, also in the Mediterranean. Scott had received the same message.

Both men agreed to be proactive. They would initiate an immediate search of the coastline and nearby environs. This would be done on rotating shifts twenty-four hours a day seven days a week until either the terrorists were captured or killed or the bomb was found, or both.

The navy jets equipped with heat seeking equipment could find a gun emplacement or the body of a man hidden in the sand. This was used during the first Iraq war in the latter part of the 20th century, the early 90's, to find Saddam Hussein's tanks embedded in the desert.

Saddam's army would dig a hole, back the tank into it, and cover everything with sand. The tank could not be seen by the naked eye. The heat seeking sights had no problem at all. The heat from the tank's motors gave them away. They never knew what hit them.

The search area was extensive, and had to be divided into grids with each battle group taking different overlapping grids thereby putting fresh sets of eyes over the same areas in the hopes of missing nothing.

High above the navy jets were the ever watchful eyes of Matthew Stoneham. Through his satellite cameras he too divided the area into grids, and carefully scanned back and forth for anything unusual. It was as if the eyes of God were staring down at this little slice of land.

Below the hubbub in the sky on a windswept beach at the edge of the desert that was Egypt lay six young men from Gaza poised to do battle with the great devil from America. They waited impatiently for the night that would send them among the ships to destroy the Americans with one almighty blast. The will of Allah would be done that grand and glorious night. The pig Jews would quiver at the blast that took away the Americans.

The search had gone on for days, but when it happened it seemed to Matt Stoneham that the discovery was simultaneous. At the exact moment he found the six bodies by the sea, the pilot of one of the jets radioed "Mother we have six bogies in the sand. What is your pleasure?"

"Stay on site. A Seal team is on the way. Let's see what we've got," was the reply.

Hassan Enau felt warm for the first time that afternoon. He was under the tarp behind a small berm they had built as a windbreak. He stretched luxuriously as he thought of the great sacrifice he was going to make. He thanked Allah for such a great privilege.

At first the commands, "Stand up! Put your hands over your head! Stand up! All of you stand up!" didn't make sense. He understood English, but it was out of context here. Shots rang out yanking them to their feet.

"Don't move! Place your hands on top of your head!" All the commands were repeated in Hebrew. Hassan and his friends understood both languages. Confused as they were, they did just as they had been trained and spoke to no one, not even to each other.

Heavy belts were placed around their waists and their arms were shackled to the belt at their sides. Their feet were shackled at the ankles with short chains that made them shuffle when they walked.

Hassan heard the helicopters coming; two of them landed nearby. The six captives were led to the crafts, and loaded in—three on one and three on the other. They were chained to the seats, and then the black clad, hooded men stepped in; guns still leveled at their heads.

Hassan knew Allah must be testing them, but for the life of him he couldn't figure out why.

CHAPTER 90

Shires Lampton had never before in his life carried a gun. It felt like a ton of bricks shoved into his belt under the shirt that he wore untucked to conceal it. Jordan carried hers in her handbag as did Kinzi Tern. Tony Arzetti was the only one among them who had carried a gun before, but it had been a while for him too. His was tucked in his belt under his shirt as well.

They had been allowed to go to the beach near the ferry boat landing in Vallejo on an outing. Eight people had been brought, but four others were dropped at a different location so as not to attract undue attention. It had been what they called a supervised outing with sandwiches and coffee for lunch. It was a welcome chance to escape the confines of their small trailer, and the endless card games they all enjoyed however tedious they might become. They placed their picnic blanket in an area protected from the breeze and went for a walk.

Tony noticed it first. "We're being followed," he said to no one in particular.

"I was just thinking about saying something," Shires said, "that guy over there by the shore keeps appearing and disappearing."

"To me it's that woman to his left. Maybe they're working together," Tony conjectured. "Let's circle the wagons," Tony suggested. It was a plan that he had conceived for an emergency such as any perceived danger real or not. The four stood with their backs to each other; each facing a different direction so they had eyes all around them. They would only draw their guns if they had to.

Jordan Smith wasn't comfortable playing cops and robbers, or whatever this crazy game was called. Playing with real guns was even crazier. She had practiced all the moves with Shires and their two friends, but she still felt awkward. She had done everything but fire the gun, and she dreaded that time if it ever arrived. She hoped today wasn't going to be the day. Maybe these people were just joggers like they appeared to be. She hoped so. They didn't look suspicious to her.

"Anything look suspicious to anybody?" Tony Arzetti asked.

"Not so far," Kinzi Tern observed, "that couple you talked about; they just kissed and walked out toward the water."

"Watch'em close," Shires said, "they may be up to no good."

Everybody laughed at the warning.

"Paranoia is a good thing though," Tony said, "we may have been wrong this time, but maybe not the next. You never know. It's better to be safe than sorry."

"You mean the kind of paranoia I have right now?" Jordan asked.

"What's that?" Shires asked.

"That couple we watched as they walked toward the water."

"Yeah."

"So where did they go so fast?"

Her observation was true, they had disappeared. "Let's go sit on our blanket and have our sandwiches. We can observe better from there," Tony said.

"Yeah," Shires said jokingly, "we may have talked ourselves into a giant case of paranoia. Now everybody we see is going to look like an assassin."

"Even the ones we can't see," Jordan added.

It was not a warm day in March especially across the bay from San Francisco. The ham and cheese sandwiches were good, and the hot coffee washed them down well. They were watching the ferry while it loaded passengers when they saw the couple again. They were walking quickly toward them.

It was Tony who reacted first. "They are assassins get your guns!" he yelled, flopping to his stomach and pointing his pistol in the direction of the approaching couple. "Don't shoot until you see the guns!" Tony directed.

Shires aimed over the barrel of his pistol at the approaching assassins, and wondered how this would turn out. He could picture the headline.

A GREAT CASE OF PARANOIA TAKES THE LIVES OF TWO INNOCENT JOGGERS: it read.

The couple wore sweat clothes and hooded sweatshirts, and was jogging up the beach toward them. The words of Nathan Conrad raced through Kinzi Tern's mind. "They'll come at you fast. You won't know until the last moment!"

At that exact time she realized she'd forgotten the safety. It was still on. She pulled the hammer back. It slipped off her thumb and fell forward on the firing pin with a loud click, but no explosion from a shell. She hadn't loaded the magazine into the weapon. She didn't even have a magazine with her. She had dropped the gun into her purse that morning sans magazine—no magazine no ammunition.

The offending couple jogged on past them before everybody broke down laughing at the stunned look on Kinzi's face. It was a welcome relief from the tension during the approach of the assassins.

CHAPTER 91

Hassan Enau was not afraid even when they dumped him alone in an isolation cell, and left him in darkness for a long time. He prayed to Allah to keep him strong.

They blindfolded him later and dragged him somewhere, and sat him on a chair. Nobody said anything. They left him there for a long time. He wet himself, but he said nothing.

He heard screaming somewhere in the distance—then another; this one closer. He heard steps behind him. He was forced from the chair to his knees. The blindfold was viciously yanked from his eyes. A hand grasped his hair on the back of his head. His head was pushed down. He saw the tub of water at the last moment—not in time to take a breath.

He choked on the water that rushed into his lungs. Still they held his head under. His hands were shackled at his sides. He couldn't pull his head out. He knew he was drowning. He soiled himself. The struggling did no good so he stopped. His head was yanked quickly from the water. He coughed and choked. Loud rasping noises emanated from his mouth as he gasped for breath, and then, just as quickly, his head was shoved back under the water where he again choked. He wet himself. He had lost control of that part of his body, and he didn't care anymore. His head was yanked out of the water again.

"Where's the bomb?" a voice screamed at him over the rasping noise that was his breathing. The smell of feces that permeated the room was all he could think about, and he wondered why?

Again the voice screamed, "Where's the bomb?"

He was choking again. A fist slammed into his solar plexus. He passed out. He awoke some time later amid the smell of urine and feces; his own he was sure of that.

He heard voices, muffled at first, coming closer, and closer. Two men grabbed his arms and lifted him onto the chair.

"We know about the boat. Where is it?" asked one of the men. He wasn't screaming. His voice was quiet, almost a whisper. "Where is the boat?" the voice was louder.

When Hassan heard the word 'boat' he knew that someone had talked. It struck fear in his heart. He wondered how much they knew.

"Where's the boat?" the voice was screaming again.

"He was forced to his knees again beside the tub of water. He knew what was coming, but he didn't wait for them; instead he forced his own head under the water and inhaled the water. He choked, but kept his head under. His hair was grasped roughly and his head was jerked out of the water. He coughed and choked—again his breathing was a rasping growl.

"No you don't! You don't get away that easy. You can die when we tell you to, not before. Now where is the boat?" The voice yelled.

Hassan said nothing and stared at the floor still in the throes of coughing and choking.

"Oh well, you want to die, so be it," screamed the voice, and shoved Hassan's head under the water again.

Hassan was choking, and then the blessed darkness engulfed him.

CHAPTER 92

Major Percival Tuck was back on the phone with Matt Stoneham.

We're pretty sure the bomb is on a boat, he said, *but what boat and where we don't know. These guys we got were waiting for a bomb attached to a boat, but that's all they knew.*

"Were they telling the truth?" Matt asked.

We got two out of the six to talk. They said pretty much the same thing. So we think that was their mission; however this could just be a distraction from the real location of the bomb. That's what I'm afraid of. These guys were just too obvious, especially being out there so far ahead of time. Someone planned for them to get caught and interrogated—thus the story of the boat. It's all too convenient.

"What do you want from me?"

Use your cameras this time to go back in time. See when they arrived on the beach and how they got there, and where they came from. All the good stuff like that.

"What about Cahmael chips? Do they have those?"

I'll have to check that. I don't know.

"It would really help if they did. I could pinpoint their movements for the time they've had them. It may lead us to the bomb, or at least to the people responsible for it."

I'll have to get back to you on that.

"Or you could just give me their names. I can check it myself."

Or I could just give you their names. I'll email those over to you.

"If you can give me one off the top of your head I'll get started."

Let me think. There was one hard case. He never spoke during the whole interrogation.

"Was that an accomplishment?"

According to the interrogator I talked to it was…yes

"Whoa! What did they do to them?"

I don't really know, and I didn't ask, but I don't think it was pretty. It seems to me his name was Hassan…I'm not sure about the last name… something like Anau or Enau or Enow; not sure which. They believe they were from Gaza. That's about all I know. I'll get more information to you if I can find it.

"Are they dead? You talk about them in the past tense."

I'm not sure about that, but I don't think they are; just a slip on my part."

"Okay, I'll get back to you if I find anything and you get the other names to me. I'll talk to you later," Matt said.

They hung up and Matt immediately switched his computer over to the chip program and typed in the name of Hassan Enow; nothing came up. No matter the spelling he used for the last name there was no Hassan Enau in the chip program. Matt knew this was a dead end. He would wait until Tuck sent him the other names, and went back to working the cameras, searching back in time a month and then coming forward to the present. There had to be something there.

After four hours of scanning he had found nothing. The six must have moved onto the beach at night, so he switched to the night vision lens and searched the nights. He usually didn't use the lens since most of his targets were non-specific and could be found in the daylight hours.

He found a large fishing boat without running lights moving down the coast from Tel Aviv. It had started the journey on the 11th of February, stopping once off the coast of Southern Israel to pick up eight passengers, and then moving down to the coast of Egypt before it stopped again.

A group of ten men disgorged from the boat and made their way to the beach, and to the area where the six terrorists had been found. It looked like they were digging and burying something. When they finished four men returned to the boat leaving the other six behind.

Matt stayed with the boat as it made its way back up the coast of Israel until it docked in a small inlet. Matt was on the phone immediately to Tuck giving him the location.

Don't you ever sleep? It's four in the morning, were the first words out of Major Percival Tuck's mouth

"Sorry," Matt said, hardly able to contain his excitement, "This couldn't wait until morning. I think I may have found the boat the terrorist were waiting for." Matt was ecstatic. The terrorists had been waiting for a boat carrying a bomb. Matt may have found it. Tuck was more subdued. He would wait and see, and wrote down the coordinates.

I'll get back to you as soon as I can, he said and hung up, leaving Matt to his own celebration.

CHAPTER 93

Admiral Harry Nelson Winthrop Commander of Carrier Group Delta aboard the carrier Douglas MacArthur fifty miles off the coast of Israel received the information regarding the location of the boat late on the night of March 21st. He immediately dispatched a Seal team to the location.

He warned them before they left that the intelligence said they were dealing with a thermonuclear bomb; a hydrogen bomb that could be one thousand times more powerful than the bomb that dropped on Hiroshima. If they found the bomb handle it carefully.

It was a grim faced Seal team that went out that early morning. None of the usual banter was evident. A bomb a thousand times more powerful than the ones on Japan was a sobering thought. It was difficult to imagine an explosion with almost unlimited power, but that was what the Skipper had said. So this bomb was an unknown quantity. The bomb could be as powerful as the builder wanted to make it.

The team of six would be dropped five miles out and taken underwater by three submersibles to within a mile of the cove; from there they would swim.

Lieutenant Seth Wyatt leader of the team checked his watch; 3AM. They should be on site at dawn. They would catch the bogies while they slept or groggy from it.

He had been on many missions, but never one of this magnitude. Why would anybody in their right mind want such a powerful bomb? He figured fear was the motive. You could be the biggest guy on the block with a bigger bomb. But this bomb apparently wasn't for blackmail— somebody would have heard by now. No its purpose in this case is to kill people; pure and simple. A bomb that powerful could easily wipe out their battle group. That would be a lot of men and ships; fifteen thousand as near as he could figure. There was supposed to be another carrier group nearby so you could double that and then add any civilians unlucky enough to be near the shoreline. It was a scary scenario.

Five minutes to drop point, the voice in his earphones said.

"Gear up," he yelled and pulled the small submersible to him. He would drop it when the command to disembark came. It would be followed by the two others and then all six men would follow the tiny crafts into the water. The helicopter would hover for less than a minute while they unloaded, and then it would be gone.

An hour later they reached the submersible drop point. From here on it would be swimming for the last mile. They anchored the submersibles below the surface of the water a short distance from shore, and began the mile long swim. They surfaced just long enough to get their bearings and to judge the darkness; a moonless night. Billions of stars blazed across the cloudless sky giving a dim glow to the darkness. It was a breathtaking sight, but they had no time to enjoy it.

They were gathered in a circle, but they never spoke. Seth checked the compass on his wrist making sure of his direction. He nodded. They all submerged, heading for the target.

They swam slowly, carefully at a depth of thirty feet. The water was black. They had small glow lights (the team called them running lights) attached to the hood on their forehead; more for seeing each other than for guidance in the murky blackness. Each man carried a larger flashlight attached to his belt. Every so often Seth would glance at his glowing compass to check their course.

They surfaced quietly about two hundred yards from the target. Dawn glowed slightly to the east. They paused for a break and to synchronize their watches; from here on through the operation everything would be done at specific times and intervals.

One minute after arrival weapons would be removed from their water proof bags for the boarding members. They would all move a minute later. Josh and Frank would go under the boat looking for the bomb. Seth and Greg would go over the port side; one on the bow and one astern. Will and Otter would do the same on the starboard. All would be seeking bogies, hoping to capture one for interrogation; operant slogan, shoot to kill first, ask later.

Seth climbed over the side to meet one face-to-face. He reacted quickly, shooting the sleepy man in the forehead. The flash suppressor and the silencer did their work. The only evidence a shot had been fired was the dead man lying on the deck at Seth's feet.

He moved quickly and stealthily to the ladder leading to the bridge just as a figure ran to it from the upper deck. The runner turned and descended right into Seth's waiting arms. Seth clubbed him in the head just as his feet reached the lower deck. He fell heavily and didn't move. Otter's head appeared over the rail. Seth waved him off then bent to gag the man and secure him in shackles.

Five minutes later they cleared the boat. Josh and Frank returned to report no bomb underneath. Seth broke out his radio.

"Mother this is baby chicks," he said, "need pick up for three live ones and three dead, plus six team members. There is a landing site nearby. We'll pop yellow smoke when we hear you."

Roger that. Did you see a bomb?

"Negative! Not at first glance will check more."

Roger! See you in a few.

CHAPTER 94

Melissa Hardin read the email with some trepidation. It said Homeland Security had reclassified all persons in the underground as domestic terrorists. The Agency would begin an immediate crack down on all people suspected of belonging to or having connections with the underground. Here was the scary part. A reward of 10,000 dollars would be given for every name turned in if Homeland made a successful arrest.

This is the email in its entirety: *To all departments and department heads. Effective April 1st: It is the purpose of this Agency to protect the Homeland against all terrorists foreign and domestic. We are reclassifying all persons who are members of the underground or have any connection with the underground as domestic terrorists. As such they will be arrested on sight and detained as long as deemed necessary for the safety of the country under the authority of the Patriot Act of 2001.*

House Appropriations Bill 890 has given this agency the funds to offer a 10,000 dollar reward to anyone turning in a member of the underground if that information brings about a successful arrest.

This announcement will be forthcoming by our Director at a 3pm news conference this afternoon. It will also be announced on all news channels at 6 this evening. I think we may see a great uptick in our arrests. Be prepared. Good luck and good hunting.

Melisa knew from past experience she couldn't hurry to tell Mike. Matthew Stoneham would be watching for any such behavior on her part.

Her best course of action was no action at all. She would tell Mike that evening. She suspected he might have a connection with the underground, but she wasn't sure. She hoped he didn't.

So what would she do? She and Mike had become a couple. They were together every night. What if Mike had connections and was turned in to Homeland and arrested. Could she let that happen? Would she let that happen? What would happen to her?

These thoughts were going to drive her crazy. She wanted to leave for lunch early, but didn't dare. Matthew Stoneham was watching. Or as Mike would say "Big Brother is watching".

She had heard of the reference to Big Brother from the George Orwell book 1984, but she never thought she would know him personally. And now he was about to have an enormous impact on her life. Go figure.

She hoped it would never come down to the point where she would have to choose between Mike and work. She had spent so much time preparing for the job, and to get such a well-paying, highly classified one was no mean feat. She was really good at what she did. She couldn't throw it all away on a whim.

"It's not a whim you fool," Carmen Roadend said at lunch time.

"That's right," agreed Terri Glen, "this job is temporary; Mike is forever."

"How do you know that Mike is forever?" she asked Terri.

"You love him don't you?" Terri asked.

"Yes! Yes I do," she answered.

"Well then it's simple. Love is forever. You have to choose Mike. You have no choice. You will always regret it if you don't."

"Do you think Mike is connected to the underground?" Carmen asked.

"I don't know. Sometimes I think so, then other times I don't. He never talks about it."

"Neither does George. In fact he never mentions it to me. We talk about a lot of things. He truly loves Mike as his partner. Says he's fearless and he'd follow him anywhere."

"That's what Mike says about George," Melissa said.

"So, let's sum up this conversation," Terri said, "You girls have two guys that are cops, each other's partner, who think great things about each other. They love you and you love them. But you are having doubts about your feelings. Have you girls lost your marbles? Two great guys are in your lives. If I were in that situation, I would go for the love every time. It's not going to get any better. It could get worse, but not for you if you hang on to these guys—when the going gets rough hang on to your man. That's all I got to say about the whole thing."

Melissa and Carmen stared at their friend. "Girl we gotta get you a boyfriend," Carmen Roadend said. And all three friends laughed together.

CHAPTER 95

Nathan Conrad spoke as if his life depended on it, and from his viewpoint it did. He had done all he could to protect the members of the underground. They seemed to be learning their lessons well; although he didn't think many of them really understood what was coming—most didn't even believe him. He could tell them about the two large protectors who followed him around, but they couldn't see them, so they still wouldn't believe. He prayed about it constantly.

A portion of his prayers for Mike Arzetti had been answered. His sister Ann and her friend Jamie had given their hearts to the Lord. He was thankful for that. He hoped Mike and George might come around to it, but they remained skeptics. He also knew at some point in time guns would not be enough to protect the folks in the underground; believers or not they would be subjected to the same judgment as everybody else. The thought weighed heavy on his heart.

The second forty-two months of the Cahmael reign was not that far away—it would begin in May sometime after the dedication of the Temple, and it would be hell on earth. Those who were so quick to welcome the end times would change their tunes once they discovered they too had to live through it.

What a surprise it would be to the millions of people around the world who believed in the goodness of Cahmael—to be suddenly awakened by the ugly truth.

Cahmael wasn't after their bodies he wanted their souls for eternity. It was the spiritual part that nobody understood. They couldn't see it so therefore it wasn't real. How can Cahmael be the devil? There is no such being as the devil.

Nathan Conrad stood in the living room of the large home in the Napa Valley staring at the few who waited for him to speak; most of the time he didn't know what to say. He had to trust the Lord that what he would say would reach someone.

"When I was a kid," he said, "I hated doomsday preachers most especially the evangelists who visited us from time to time. They scared me to death with all the fear they preached. I was a little kid. I didn't understand that the death and destruction was of a spiritual nature. There is a spiritual war going on for the souls of men. It is between God and Cahmael. Cahmael is the devil. There is no other way to say it, that's who he is.

"Now I'm going to tell you about doomsday the subject I hated most in my childhood. I want to warn you that doomsday is fast approaching. I'm not talking about the doomsday that ends the world. I'm talking about the second forty-two months of the reign of Jehosea Cahmael. That second period will begin on or around May 14th the very day of the dedication of the Temple in Jerusalem.

"The Bible says there will be weeping, wailing, and the gnashing of teeth when people realize what they've done. There will be crying in the streets. Picture in your mind people running down the street crying, looking for solace, and there will be none—begging God to forgive them, but it will be too late.

"What can you or I say to them? Nothing then; we can only say it now before it's too late. We can tell them to give their life to the Lord. It's imperative that they ask him for forgiveness, and invite Him to come in to their heart and become Lord of their lives.

"They will have to remove the Cahmael chip, and that will be a problem. They'll have to go into the underground immediately afterwards."

A lady to the back of the room asked, "Why can't you continue with the Cahmael chip?"

"It will be more difficult if not impossible to get away from the judgment of Cahmael if you still have the chip. You are traceable with the chip. He will call you, and he will ask you where you stand, for or against him. Now you must remember you will be choosing between Cahmael and Christ; that's the choice. If you choose Christ you will be beheaded. If you choose Cahmael you will lose your eternal soul. If you don't have the chip you will be able to evade him for a time—we hope for a long time; especially if you're in the underground. Now does that clarify for you why you can't have it both ways?"

"Yes Brother Nathan it does," she said.

"Why? Were you thinking about getting the chip?"

"I have a friend who thinks it's alright to have a chip and believe in the Lord."

"It is alright Sister, but it won't be okay after the second forty-two month period begins. Of course if Cahmael isn't the Antichrist then we don't have to worry, but I honestly believe he is. If you come before him to be judged you will have to accept him or die. That's the danger of having the chip and being traceable. Your friend needs to know that. Everybody needs to know it. This is not the time to be fooling around. It could cost you your life or your eternal soul.

"Now that I've said all that I have one more terrible thing to talk about. You might have heard the announcement on television last night about the 10,000 dollar reward for turning in a member of the underground. Now we not only have to worry about death squads, but our friends and neighbors; hopefully not our friends, but certainly our neighbors turning us in to law enforcement as terrorists. That's our classification now; terrorist.

"This is what you must do to protect yourself from this new threat. First thing to remember is act normal. Wherever you are, you belong there just as much as anybody else. Second: Stay away from any unnecessary interaction with your neighbors. Third: stick to your cover story. Fourth: say nothing that makes you memorable such as outlandish opinions, conspiracy theories, and things of that sort. Fifth: try to be ordinary in every way. Sixth: Do nothing to arouse suspicions—in other words try not to act as paranoid as you may feel." A rumble of laughter interrupted him.

"Seventh: Above all be friendly," he continued, ignoring the mirth he had caused. Then he looked around the room sternly. "I'm sorry I made you laugh. I didn't mean to. Please don't take this warning lightly. Ignoring it could cost you your life."

Silence descended on the room.

CHAPTER 96

Hassan Enau was shocked to see his friends from the boat being led into the compound, but his captors never saw the look on his face. He made sure of that. They would never know the contempt he felt for them until the day of the bomb—then they would know.

He had awakened after his near drowning lying on a foul smelling mattress filled with mildew and human feces. His feces he knew that and his urine too.

They forced him to strip, and then they washed him with a water hose that stung when it hit his flesh—especially his private parts, which they seemed to aim for with glee. Laughter rang out when they hit him. He doubled over in pain, trying to shield himself he turned his back and they hit him from the rear—to another loud screech of laughter. The pain was excruciating. He fell to his knees. They shot the water in his face nearly blinding him. His right eye stung so intensely he couldn't open it.

Finally he lay in a fetal position with only the top of his head and his knees facing his captors. They stopped the water and left him there. Sometime later he found the clothes they had left for him. The clothes were wet but clean. He shivered through the night; finally warming up with sunrise and a warm day. They fed him a slice of bread and some thick porridge. He didn't recognize the taste, but it had been the same food every meal since then.

He had been there three days before his friends from the boat arrived. He wondered how they found them. He knew they would be going through what he had gone through. Men would be screaming and yelling at them "Where's the bomb?" while dunking their heads in the water. He didn't envy them, and prayed to Allah to keep them strong.

He wondered himself where the bomb might be. Nobody had told them anything other than the bomb would be along when the time came. He supposed it would be and didn't worry about it.

The bomb would not be affected by their capture. He knew that. It would explode with or without their help, but he wanted to be one of those who exploded it. He was sure Allah had chosen him for the task so he would never give up hope.

All five of his friends had wanted to be the one. They had agreed to share the honor among them. They would explode it together. Each would be touching some part of the bomb when it exploded. If they all could touch the trigger then that's where their hands would be.

He heard a scream, but he didn't flinch. They would be watching for any reaction. It was as if the Israeli Mossad had been turned loose on them for the screaming went on for a very long time. The Mossad had many ways of extracting screams.—mostly by inflicting terrible pain.

He listened to the screams and felt the sweat under his arms. He wanted to get up and leave where he was sitting, but fear restrained him. They would notice his reaction and drag him into interrogation. Allah would have to make him very strong to withstand such pain.

Perhaps it was two hours later, maybe only one, that the screaming subsided. Hassan didn't watch the time he just endured the screams of his friends—all the time asking Allah to make them strong.

CHAPTER 97

President Richard Butcher followed the search for the bomb as much as possible. They kept him updated with every new development as it happened. He was excited when they found the boat. He was sure the bomb would be there, but the Seal teams search had found nothing. They literally tore the boat apart. In fact they had spent one whole day doing nothing but ripping at it. Walls, cabinets, drawers, even the engine compartment, nothing was spared, but to no avail. There was no bomb aboard.

They found one piece of evidence that might be something. It was a reference to a trucking company in Haifa. Israeli police immediately jumped on the information. Dick was waiting to hear back from them.

Cynthia's voice on the intercom interrupted his meditation. *Mr. President I have Mr. Cahmael on the red phone to talk to you. Are you available?*

"I am Cynthia, put him on."

Dick punched the speaker phone button. "Yes Sir," he said, "how can I help you?"

My dear friend Dick, how are you and your lovely wife today?

"I am happy to report that we are just fine Sir, how are you?" Dick said, sounding a little cheerier than he really felt.

I'm just fine Mr. President. I have a few loose ends I would like to clear up with you, if you have a moment or two.

"For you I have all the time you need as long as you can still tell me not to worry about the bomb."

Cahmael chuckled. *Your team seems to be doing a very good job from all the reports I've received.*

"Well, we're chasing it, Sir. I'll say that much, but so far nothing," Dick said and walked to the window to watch the yardman cut the grass. It was a windy spring day in the Capitol. The kind Dick really loved. He considered springtime the greatest season of all; everything was so fresh and new.

I'm sure they will solve the puzzle of the missing bomb. You must have faith my friend.

Dick half turned, looking back toward the direction of the phone on his desk to answer. "I have all the faith in the world in my men. They're out there giving their lives for the rest of us. I don't want their sacrifice to be for nothing as I'm sure you don't. So tell me what loose ends you needed to clear up with me?"

That's what I like a direct approach. I suppose it's more in the line of a favor or two. May 14th is such an important date for the United States I would like for you to celebrate it, partly anyway, by beginning the trials for the Armageddon Group.

"But what does that group have to do with anything?" was Dick's question. He knew Cahmael favored public executions for them, but they certainly had nothing to do with May 14th.

That's a red-letter day for your country, my friend. They were the first to recognize Israel as a nation in the United Nations. In your country's never-ending battle against terrorism, the Armageddon group was the first large terrorism group to be captured. I just thought it would be a nice meld of two firsts on the same day.

For the life of him Richard Butcher couldn't see how the two really tied together at all, but since Cahmael was so set on it he figured he could work it out with the Justice Department. He knew they had been working on the case since the great debacle in January. It hadn't been that long ago, but they should be able to put a case together by May. "Well Sir, I certainly don't see how that could be a problem. I'll get the ball rolling right away. Is there anything else you would like?"

Yes. Could you check the location of the one Carrier Group? It seems to me that it's not in the proper place.

"How do you mean?"

I mean, my friend, that one group is two hundred miles away from the other. I mean they're not in close proximity like I asked. I want a show of force that will be so overwhelming no one would dare attack it.

Dick Butcher was dumbfounded. That's what he had out there. That was what he had gone against his commanders about. Now he was being told that wasn't true. He had been to the war room and had seen it with his own eyes. He didn't know what to say. He didn't want to call the man a liar, but he knew what he was saying was simply not true. "Where did you get this information, Sir?" he asked.

Sources close to you my friend, he said cryptically.

The news had taken Dick by surprise. He decided not to say anything and to investigate before he opened his mouth to defend his position.

"This is all news to me. I'll check it out and get back to you right away. I'll also talk to Justice about your request. Is there anything else?"

No Sir, my friend that will do. If you can get those fixed for me I'll be a happy man. I'll wait for your call, Cahmael said. His phone line went into dial tone.

Dick buzzed Cynthia. "Get Frank Hubbel over at Justice for me," he said.

Right away, Mr. President.

Dick waited. He heard Cynthia say to the receptionist. **The President is calling for Mr. Frank Hubbel.**

One moment please," was the reply, and a moment later Hubbel answered.

Yes Mr. President, this is Frank Hubbel.

"Frank, how are you?"

I'm fine Mr. President.

"Frank, I called because I was wondering how the prosecutions are progressing on the Camp Armageddon members?"

There are a lot of people there to prosecute. It may take some time to put it all together, he said.

"Is there anything we can do to expedite it, and maybe start the hearings on May 14th?"

Well I'm not sure. Joe Flanagan is the Prosecutor in charge of the case. I'll let you talk to him. I'm sure there might be something he can do. I'll have my secretary get him on the phone, hang on, Sir.

Dick waited again. Perhaps two minutes went by before Joe Flanagan said, *Yes Mr. President this is Joe Flanagan.*

"Joe, thank you for taking time out of your busy schedule to talk to me," Dick said.

Anytime Mr. President.

"Joe, I understand that you're handling the Armageddon folks."

That's correct, Sir.

"I was wondering if there would be any way you might be able to open the case in court on May 14ᵗʰ?"

I'm sure if we could get a court date for that day we could.

"You could have your case ready to present by then?"

Yes Sir. I'm trying them all together as a group and not by individual cases. Individually it would have taken the next five years to try everybody. The title of the case is The United States versus Panguitch Hewey et al. I will have it ready by the 14ᵗʰ for sure. I'll just have to get the court date out in San Francisco. That's where the case will be tried. I'm sure Sir, with your name on the request the Judge will be more than happy to oblige.

"Thank you Joe, just let me know when you need the request, and I'll sign it for you."

Yes Sir, I'll have my boss call you.

"Okay thank you Joe. You have a good day now."

I will Sir and you too.

Dick cradled the phone and stood up to leave. He was headed straight for the war room. Either he would get to the bottom of the missing Carrier Group fiasco or some heads would roll—maybe both.

CHAPTER 98

The message from Major Percival Tuck to Admiral William Scott commanding Carrier Group Alpha aboard the Carrier Jimmy Doolittle in the Mediterranean Sea was marked urgent. It read: ***Move back to original position. IMMEDIATELY!! Explanation later.***

Scott didn't waste time wondering what had gone wrong; something had, he knew that. He quickly gave the order to weigh anchor.

When he was well under way he called Admiral Winthrop over a secure line, which meant their conversation was scrambled and sent out in short bursts.

"Win, I've been notified to move back to my original position. I think something has gone wrong. You heard anything?"

No I haven't. I don't like it though. Think we can get back to where we were?

"I don't know. Tuck promised to explain later. I'll find out then. I'll put twenty-five miles between us and stop there. That will be exactly our original position. I'll get back to you as soon as I hear anything."

Their conversation ended there, but Scott knew it wasn't over, and he was right. He received another message a few minutes later. The message from Admiral Lemuel C. Perkins read: *You are ordered to return to Washington DC for immediate reassignment. Leave your XO in charge.*

It was quick and to the point. Although he didn't believe Admiral Perkins felt any different than he did. Perkins hands were tied. He was doing the bidding of the President, and whether he agreed with it or not he had to do it. Scott knew that. He and Winthrop had taken a gamble, and it hadn't worked.

Winthrop called on the secure line. *I got a message from Perk. Did you get yours?* he asked.

"Yes, I'll bring a chopper by and pick you up. I guess we'll go to Haifa and catch El Al home," Scott said.

It sounds good to me. So what do you think?

"I think we're in deep cow pucky. It will all depend on how Perkins feels about it. That's what I think."

I hope you're right. See you in a few, Winthrop said as he discontinued the conversation.

A few meant a few hours. It was ten hours later that Scott's helicopter set down on the deck of Winthrop's carrier and picked him up for their flight to Haifa and an El Al flight to Washington DC.

Neither man spoke much during the flight home. Scott thought it just as well since they didn't know exactly what they were facing, and speculation did no good. He hadn't heard back from Tuck and that concerned him. It wasn't like Tuck not to explain.

Scott felt sorry for the men he had left out there. They had no idea of the terrible fate that could befall them. He knew he had to do something to stop it. He hoped he could find a way.

CHAPTER 99

When Melissa Hardin heard of the death of Matthew Stoneham she didn't know why the news struck her as odd. He was killed in a head-on collision on a side road leading up to his apartment building—Matt Stoneham dead at the age of forty. The words didn't fit together. It had been a head-on with a truck. Witnesses said the truck was out of control. The driver of the truck wasn't hurt. These were all just sentences she had heard from the local reporter on the scene of the accident sometime after it happened.

Actually the reporter never said Matt's name. She had shown a picture of the smashed vehicle and Melissa thought it looked like Matt's Volkswagen Van with the peace signs painted all over it. Later she received a call from her boss, Harry Cole, telling her about Matt's death.. Everything just seemed to run together after that. She was having difficulty getting her mind around Matt dying. People she knew didn't die—not contemporaries anyway; certainly not Matthew Stoneham.

"You've got to replace him," Harry said. She misunderstood his statement and wondered why he wanted her to do the hiring it was his job after all. She asked him why. There was a long pause. She could have kicked herself for asking the question, and then suddenly a loud burst of laughter in her ear.

I'm sorry I know it's not funny, he said, *I meant I want you to take over his job starting immediately. Leave your desk in the good hands of Carmen Roadend. You report in to Matt's job first thing tomorrow morning. I need you up to speed on it as soon as possible. Good luck,* he said and abruptly terminated the conversation, not waiting to hear any kind of protest from her.

Melissa knew she wasn't ready to do Matt's job. She only had a Master's in Computer Science. Matt had a Doctorate from MIT and was a technical whiz. There was no way she could ever get up to speed on Matt's job. What did Harry expect of her; miracles or what?

Harry was desperately grasping for straws, losing Matt Stoneham was a shock for him. He didn't have the slightest idea of how to replace him. Melissa figured he thought she was probably a bright person so he would send a bright person to fill the gaping hole, hoping it would work; besides she had the security clearance for it. Matt had once told Melissa that he had asked Harry for help, but Harry was dragging his feet about hiring another person.

Mike cooked spaghetti for his sister Ann and Melissa that evening. It was one of those rare nights when they were all together. Martina and his mom, Peggy Woodhill, had come over. Her husband, Bob, was out of town, so they made it a family thing since Mike liked to see his mom at least once a week anyway. George Wildes called, and Mike invited him and Carmen to join them. So the evening that started out as a threesome ended up being what Mike called a sevensome.

"Don't worry folks I've made plenty of spaghetti. Mom taught me how. You'll love it. It's the Peggy Woodhill special."

"So Mike when you gonna give up being a cop and open a restaurant?" George asked jokingly.

"He could never do that," Martina said, "Mom said he was born to be a cop. It's in his genes; like my dad."

"I'm afraid so," Peggy Woodhill agreed with her daughter.

"Mike did Melissa tell you about her new job?" Carmen asked.

"Okay everybody grab a plate. The food is on the stove. We'll do this buffet style. I'm too lazy to serve. No she didn't tell me. Honey what kind of job?" he asked, adding the question to his earlier statement.

"I'm sorry Melissa. Maybe I shouldn't have mentioned it, but I think it's exciting."

"No! No! That's okay," Melissa said, picking up a plate. "Mike do you remember the guy that sent that email about you and me being together at different times and all? His name was Matt Stoneham."

"Was? Why did you say it like that?"

"Because he got killed in a car accident early this morning. I think on his way to work."

"And you're getting his job?"

"She sure is, and it's a big old raise in pay," Carmen said enthusiastically.

"Well I don't know about the pay we never discussed it. I'm a sort of stop gap measure until they can get a real replacement. There's no way I can handle his job. I think my boss stuck me in there because he didn't know what else to do and panicked. He has to have somebody manning the cameras and things. I think he thinks I'm smart and can figure it all out. That's what I think. But there's one catch. I don't think I'm that smart."

"Well, you are sweetheart. Believe me you are," Mike said.

They were all seated around the dining room table when Mike suddenly blurted "Garlic bread! That's what's missing. It's still in the oven. I put it there to keep it warm. Forgot all about it," he said, retrieving the pan of bread from the oven and giving a piece to everyone.

"I thought I smelled garlic bread," George said, "Then I thought maybe he's just prepared for vampires," he added.

Everyone laughed. They ate in silence for awhile.

Mike wanted to ask Melissa why she killed Matt Stoneham just as a joke to lighten the moment, but he refrained. He detected a note of sadness in Melissa's voice. She was truly sad about the guy's death. As far as Mike was concerned it was a great evening, but the death of Matt Stoneham had cast a long shadow on it. And he, like Melissa, wished Matt had never been killed. It felt strange to him too. The guy had been trying to link him to the underground and now here he was dead; almost as strange as Roy Cassidy's death. Roy had been trying to do the same thing. Mike knew the underground was responsible for Roy's death, but who was responsible for Matt? Was it really just an accident? In the comings and goings of everyday life he had almost forgotten Roy's unsolved murder to which he was inextricably linked

CHAPTER 100

Melissa Hardin reported to Matt Stoneham's office for work that next day. It wasn't an office just an old brick warehouse bristling with antennas all over its roof. A feature that could not be seen from the ground, but one Melissa knew about because Matt had told her one time when he was attempting to describe where he worked. His description failed in the light of reality. A security guard awaited her arrival and handed over the key to the building.

She let herself in the door and was confronted with a rickety old stairway. The old building was a throwback to the mid-twentieth century. Even the handrail didn't look like it could be trusted. It moved a little when she touched it, but it was secure enough. She was struck by the total lack of security for a building housing such high tech equipment— equipment that required someone with a high security clearance to operate.

A door at the top of the stairs opened into a world of doodads and gadgets. It was Matthew Stoneham World. Everything here had his name written all over it. This was his domain for sure. Television screens were everywhere. She found a panel of switches and turned them to the 'on' position. Everything came to life. Pictures of the earth from different positions popped onto the screens.

One screen puzzled her. It had a sticky not stuck to it. On the note was written the word LOOP. That was all and the picture was of a bunch of ships somewhere. They weren't moving, just setting there. That was curious.

She found his computer setting atop an old roll top desk. Where in the world did he find this stuff? She set her own laptop on the desk beside his, placed her purse on the floor, and sat down. Now came the fun part, figuring out his password. She knew she could never do that. Not in a million years, but she was going to have to try. Problem was she didn't know where to start. She knew nothing about the man; not even his birthday.

She leaned back in the chair and looked around the room. This was heaven for Matt Stoneham. Everything he loved was here. He must have lived at work most of the time. The wastebasket was full of empty sandwich bags. It looked like he made his own sandwiches. She saw a refrigerator in the corner went to it and opened the door. Sandwich meat, bread, and milk—everything was fresh. He had just replenished his supply. He must have made sandwiches ahead of time and put them in bags, then ate them when he got hungry. There were cans of soup on a shelf against the wall. Soup and sandwiches chased down by milk. At least she knew his diet. For being so bright he certainly was a simple man. She would bet anything his password, whenever she figured it out, would be simple too.

And it was. After two days of searching with her own software and being unsuccessful she just stopped, threw her hands in the air, and said that's enough. She thought about Matthew whom she had found liked to write definitions for everything. She supposed it was a quirk or maybe a tic. A foot for instance wasn't just twelve inches it was an appendage with five toes or the base of a foundation. It seemed like that's how he thought. She extrapolated from that the definition for password might be asimpleword or maybe 1simpleword or maybe simply1word. When she typed in the last definition simply1word his computer said "Hello Matthew where have you been? You are three days late." She jumped in the air yelling "I did it! I did it!" to nobody in particular, and then she called Carmen to gloat.

"It took you two days woman. As bright as you are you should have had it in a couple of hours."

"Yeah right! Okay I'll talk to you later. Wish me luck on all the other stuff."

"Luck to you. See you later," Carmen said as she hung up.

Melissa began looking for the controls of the different cameras. She supposed they would be in his computer somewhere. She called up his programs. He had a lot of weird ones. She found one titled Alien—

subtitle Aerial Lens Insect Eye Nomenclature. That had to be the cameras. She clicked on it and a bank of computer monitors lit up with pictures of the earth from different angles and locations. It was a sight to behold; like she was seeing earth from everywhere all at once. You could feel like God from such an exalted position.

She wished Matt had left a set of directions; like how to manipulate the different cameras etc.

"What is your name?" a voice asked her.

She realized it was the computer. It had already said hello Matthew and where you been? She hadn't expected it to talk to her. She answered. "My name is Melissa Hardin I'm here taking Matt's place."

"Did Matthew die?"

The question surprised her. "Yes! Yes he did."

"That's why he built me. I'm his back-up system if anything were to happen to him. My name is Hal. Matthew named me after a computer he saw in a movie."

"Well, Hal you even have the same voice as the other Hal. Can you tell me how to run all this equipment?"

"That's my function—exactly why I was built."

Harry Cole must have known about this. That's why he sent her. The most difficult thing would have been figuring out the password. He must have known a long time ago. Maybe that's why he never hired anybody to help Matt. He didn't want too many people privy to the goings on here. Melissa knew Matt was brilliant, but she never realized just how brilliant he really was; not until now.

She felt like an intruder, but Matthew planned for his own death and that was just more of his brilliance. He wanted his work to continue. A computer that talked was almost as good as him being here; not quite but close. Matt had made it easy for her to intrude. He had even made it comfortable to work in this strange place.

It was strange in another way too—the phone never rang. It rang only once her first day here.

"Matt Stoneham's office," she answered not knowing what else to call it.

There was a long silence before the voice said very formally, *Hello, this is Major Percival Tuck of the United States Marine Corps calling to talk to Matthew Stoneham.*

She was at a loss for what to say. The man evidently didn't know about Matt's death. She was going to have to tell him. How was he connected with Matt? "Sir," she said, "I'm sorry to be the one to inform you of this, but Matthew Stoneham was killed in a car accident yesterday morning on his way to work."

This time the silence from the other end was almost deafening. The Major was clearly shocked by the news. She could almost feel it.

He's dead? he asked. A tone of disbelief tinged his voice.

"Yes Sir, yesterday in a car accident."

And you are?

"His replacement, Melissa Hardin," she said.

I'm sorry for your loss, he said.

"Thank you," she answered.

I know this is a bad time, but how much do you know about his different projects?

"Absolutely nothing, I walked in here for the very first time this morning. I'm still trying to figure out his password."

Have you by chance found anything with the title of loop?

She remembered the sticky note and went to it. "A sticky note here on one monitor says 'LOOP' in large letters and just below in lower case are the letters 'd.i.s.c'. Now that could mean it's on a computer disc or it could mean discontinue or it could mean discontinued. I am learning to think like Matthew."

So you can't tell me if the program has been stopped or not?

"Not definitively, no."

When do you think you could have an answer for me?

"I'm just not sure, Sir. It could take me months to figure it out. Matt was a brilliant man and I'm no match for him. I may never figure out anything if you want to know the truth. But, I am working on it."

Would it be okay with you if I were to call back every few days to check on your progress?

"That would all depend on how high your security clearance extends."

Would 'top secret' be enough for you?

"Yes Sir, it would if you can prove it?"

Well then, to show you how much faith I have in your ability, and you must have a lot of it if they sent you in to replace Matt, I'll send you my rap

284

sheet in Matt's email. Then you'll know who you're working with. Is that a deal?

"That sounds good to me," she said. They discontinued the conversation then.

That had been two days ago. It had left her wondering just who the Marine really was and what did he have to do with Matt and this LOOP business. That was the very first question she asked of her new friend Hal.

CHAPTER 101

Things had not gone well for Admirals Scott and Winthrop. When asked who ordered them to move the ships they had said they did it of their own volition. Rear Admiral Lemuel Perkins claimed he had no one named volition on staff. He wasn't saying it to be funny—he was angry that two such high ranking officers had done such a thing.

He knew why they had done it. Had he been one of them he might have done it too. Having two carrier groups in such close proximity was sheer stupidity. He had told the President so when he ordered it. The President told him he could quit if he disagreed, but it would be done by the first of March whether or not he liked it.

It bothered Perkins that the President had been so adamant. It wasn't like him to get involved in things military. He had never before done such a thing. It had surprised Admiral Perkins at the time. He knew that the President had just come through a bad time with his wife being shot by his best friend. That hadn't been the official story, but Perkins had heard the truth from a friend in the Secret Service.

The President's best friend Earl Price, his economic advisor no less, had shot the President's wife, Lydia, and then shot himself. Perkins wondered about that. Price just wasn't his best friend he had been his lifetime friend. Now what would make a man like that go off and shoot the woman, and then himself? It made no sense unless the guy was gay, which seemed highly unlikely. What triggered him to do this terrible act?

It may have been the same thing that drove the President to get involved with military things. He was bent on having the two carrier groups close together off the shores of Israel. It was an open invitation to the nearest terrorist. Now they were chasing a bomb—a thermonuclear bomb no less. That made what they had done a good thing even if they had disobeyed their orders.

Then three days ago into the war room stormed President Butcher frothing at the mouth, demanding to know who had ordered the ships to be moved? The question had caught him by surprise. This was the first that he ever heard of any ships being moved anywhere. That was the way Scott and Winthrop had planned it. Evidently somebody else had found out and informed the President who was now demanding some heads on a platter. Rear Admiral Perkins knew that in order to keep his own job he had to please the man. Scott and Winthrop would pay the price as much as he hated to do it.

"Mr. President," he had said, "in light of the fact that we are chasing a bomb don't you think it might be better to leave the ship groups apart?"

"That's true it might, but finding the bomb doesn't worry me. I know we'll do that. I want whomever it was that disobeyed my orders to be dealt with immediately and harshly. We have some delicate diplomatic matters pending on this deployment and I don't want them to be jeopardized by someone acting on their own. I want to send a firm message that I will not tolerate disobedience."

Perkins fired Scott and Winthrop. He didn't fire them dishonorably however, he admired their courage to do the right thing in the face of such great odds at whatever cost to themselves. They deserved an award not a firing so he allowed them to retire with full pay. He was sorely afraid they might be proven right in the end, but he hoped not.

CHAPTER 102

Nathan Conrad was incensed that Michael Arzetti accused the underground of killing Matthew Stoneham. Mike had mentioned Matthew's accusatory email to Nathan and suddenly Matthew Stoneham was dead. It was just a little too convenient to have been coincidental as far as Mike was concerned.

"We don't run around killing people for the fun of it, Mike. We are Christians after all."

"But you rationalize too easily. Not all of your enemies deserve death."

"I know that Mike, and we did not kill Matthew Stoneham I can assure you of that. I will swear on the Bible."

Mike knew he was telling the truth especially if he were willing to do that. He was not a man who took his faith lightly. Mike wanted to let the death go as just another accident, but his gut feeling wouldn't let him. So who killed Matt Stoneham and why?

When he mentioned it to Melissa she didn't react favorably to the idea at all. She didn't even want to discuss it. "I'll be looking for evil doers in every nook and cranny of his office, and believe me, there are a lot of those."

"Please sweetheart, just watch for anything funny. I don't mean the ha-ha funny either."

She laughed at his attempt at humor, knowing full well he knew he had planted the seed in her mind and it would grow there. Now it would be difficult for her not to look for out-of-the-ordinary things. Most things in Matthew's workplace weren't ordinary anyway, so it wouldn't be a difficult assignment.

CHAPTER 103

Major Percival Tuck was saddened by Matt Stoneham's death. It was difficult to believe. He had accepted it as just that—a terrible accident. Foul play never entered his mind. Major Tuck escaped the wrath of the President and Admiral Perkins. Admiral Scott had never said a word about his involvement in Catfish or that there ever was an Operation Catfish. It had been unofficially official; meaning it was never sanctioned by anybody.

Tuck had taken the assignment to Stoneham. Stoneham had been the one to pull it off; no one else could have done it. But, somebody knew about the operation; did they know about Matt and kill him? Did they know about him? Scott was the only one who knew, he hoped, but he wasn't sure.

He had contacted Melissa Hardin a second time and she had been able to tell him that Matt had stopped the loop. There was no evidence that a loop ever existed as far as she could tell. Why he had left the sticky note was beyond her comprehension unless he just forgot to take it off the monitor. That's what she thought had happened.

Tuck had never asked Melissa if she knew about the bomb. That was high priority intelligence, but he needed to know what she might know. Maybe Matt had left something that might help them find the bomb. If Melissa had been asked to do Matt's job she must have the clearance. He had to call her. He made a note to do that right away.

Time to find the bomb was getting short. Here they were in early April and no bomb as yet. They needed to do something positive right away or time was going to get away from them, and May 14th would be here.

He found Admiral Perkins in his office. "I'd like to see the Admiral for a moment if it's possible," he said to the receptionist.

"The female Lieutenant Junior Grade. spoke in her mouthpiece to the Admiral, looked up at him and said, "Go right in, Sir."

With his cap tucked under his left arm, Major Tuck smartly saluted the Admiral with his right. The Admiral returned his salute.

"Have a seat Major Tuck."

"Thank you, Sir," he said and sat down.

"What is on your mind?"

"The bomb, Sir, and how to recover it."

"You have some ideas?"

"I have one, Sir. I thought I would run it by you."

"Let's hear it."

"It has to do with using the Seal teams. There are two teams out there now, we might need one more. My plan is simply to inject chips into our prisoners and allow them to escape. Let them lead us to the bomb. We have the chip monitoring hardware at our disposal and a person to run it, so why not use it?"

"And the Seal teams would do what?"

"They would be at our beck and call somewhere near the terrorist's location or locations; whether it would be one or two or maybe three. We would have all options covered. We would be on top of them at all times. In other words we would be near when the time came."

"Do you think they would go for it and escape if they had a chance?"

"I do, Sir. They would take it in a heartbeat and not look back."

"Could I depend on you to run the operation?"

"Definitely, Sir I will be on site at all times."

"Okay then I'll cut orders for three Seal teams and for you to meet on site at the Camp where they're being held. You have your tracking system up to speed in two days and we'll make that the start date."

Tuck was ecstatic. The Admiral had bought the plan. It was a good one and definitely proactive.

He punched in Admiral Scott's cell number.

"The plan is a go," he said when Scott answered. "Now, I need for you to get to San Francisco if you want to help with the operation. I'll meet you at the airport there and take you to meet Melissa Hardin; she'll be running the tracking system only she doesn't know it yet. You can assist her because we'll need twenty-four hour surveillance."

CHAPTER 104

Melissa Hardin's head was spinning. Never had she had so many people interested in what she was doing. Well, if you consider three a lot. There was Major Tuck, and Michael, and her boss, Harry Cole. They all wanted to know what Matthew was doing just before he died. She didn't know. Hal didn't know since to Hal, Matthew was always doing something.

It appeared to her that the very last thing he did, as far as she could tell, was discontinue the loop—whatever that was. Hal said it was pictures of ships somewhere in the Mediterranean. With Hal directing her she guided a camera to zero in on the flotilla and found the two carrier groups within twenty-five miles of each other. She would have to remember to tell Tuck the next time he called.

Hal mentioned something about terrorists and explained how she could recall the pictures from that search.

"What was that search about, Hal?"

"A thermonuclear bomb," he said simply as if that were a common thing. Melissa nearly fainted.

"A what?" she
asked disbelieving the words she heard.

"A thermonuclear bomb," he repeated.

"A terrorist and a nuclear bomb?" she asked.

"A thermonuclear bomb," Hal corrected.

"What's the difference?"

"Thermonuclear is a hydrogen bomb. It could be a thousand times more powerful than the Hiroshima bomb."

"Hal, please tell me about the Hiroshima bomb."

She spent the next hour reading about the bomb and looking at pictures of it exploding as well as pictures of the Hiroshima and Nagasaki aftermath—the devastation was horrific.

Her phone rang. It was Major Tuck.

I'm coming to see you, he said.

"Why and when?" she asked a little irritated by the interruption.

It's about National Security and I'll be there about 3 this afternoon, he said and just as quickly as he had called he broke the connection. She wasn't stupid; she knew it would be about the bomb. That was a very big threat to National Security.

She had five hours to wait.

"Hal show me everything that Matthew had done while looking for the bomb," she said to the computer. She still felt weird talking to it.

Hal showed her all the sweeps of the coastal area that Matt had made. She found the one that discovered the six men in the sand and the ones showing the boat at night running down the coast, stopping to pick up passengers and then dropping them later.

She had begun eating her lunches Matthew style. Bologna sandwiches, chips and milk were very good. She had discovered the first day that it was too far to drive to the nearest diner so making lunches was more a necessity than choice. She didn't get to see Mike as often, but he understood. She hadn't told him about the bomb; of course it had only been a couple of days. She knew she would at some point—National Security or not.

The alarm went off signifying someone had arrived at the door. Matt had alarms everywhere; almost to the point of paranoia she thought. She pressed the button and buzzed Major Tuck through the door.

Two men walked in. For a fleeting moment she thought of security and how lax it was. Anybody could walk in. She was only expecting one visitor whom she had never met and now she had two. One seemed a little older than the other, but she didn't know which one might be Major Tuck. The younger man was taller, over six feet she was sure, and the older one looked to be less than six feet. That and age were about their only differences. They both wore short cropped, military style haircuts, and both men were to the muscular side of slender; both wore civilian clothes. She stood as they approached.

"No need to stand for us," said the younger man, "You must be

Melissa Hardin. I'm Major Percival Tuck this is Retired Admiral Bill Scott," he finished and extended his hand. She shook both their hands.

"Here, over here is a lunch table. We can talk here," she said speaking back over her shoulder as she walked to the small table and four chairs next to the wall by the refrigerator. There was no such thing as an office desk anywhere in the building.

"Sorry it's so informal. Matt Stoneham wasn't interested in formality," she apologized as they all sat down.

"That's okay. I like it better this way," Admiral Scott said.

"Me too, Tuck agreed, and continued, "Do you have any idea why we might be here today?"

"Well this morning you told me National Security and, according to Hal, the very last thing Matt was doing was looking for a thermonuclear bomb. It has to be the bomb."

Both men looked around the room.

"Who is Hal?" Tuck asked.

"I'm sorry. Hal is the computer. It's another Matt Stoneham thing," she explained.

"2001 A Space Odyssey that's the title of the movie that featured Hal the computer," said the Admiral.

"If it hadn't been for Hal I would never have been able to run this place. Thanks to Matt's wisdom and foresight I was able to step right in and run everything. Hal is like having Matt here. It's very easy to get up to speed as my boss says. Hal did it all. Anybody could follow his directions. He practically does everything for you."

"Let me tell you why we are here, Melissa," Tuck said and then continued, "We have a plan that will actively seek the bomb. It will require your assistance twenty-four hours a day seven days a week. That's why Admiral Scott is here. He is going to help you.

"Our plan is pretty simple. We are going to implant the chip in each of our terrorists without them knowing it. Then we will allow them to escape, and then using the tracking system we will follow wherever they lead. Hopefully they will take us to the bomb. You and Bill here will keep us apprised of their movements at all times. We'll have three Seal teams standing by to swoop down and grab them when they lead us to the bomb.

"We are positive these guys are the ones designated to deliver the bomb. We just need to be there when they connect with it. It's imperative that you not lose a one of them.

"I'm going out there to run the operation. We'll be in contact with you at all times. Melissa you and Bill are our eyes and ears for this. Can you do it?"

"I haven't as yet delved into the area of chip reading, but with Hal's help it won't take long to get in the swing of it. Yes I think we can handle it for you if Bill is willing to stay here and work nights. We can take twelve hour shifts. One of us will sleep while the other monitors then we'll work together when it's necessary."

That was how Melissa began to do the work that felt good to her. No longer was she monitoring everybody. Now she was chasing bad guys for real, like she wanted to from the beginning.

There was a cot in the back. Evidently Matt stayed over some nights. Admiral Scott bought a sleeping bag and took up residence on it. Melissa was able to keep her regular schedule without disrupting her life too much. She had asked the Admiral if he thought it might be alright for him to meet Michael. He nixed the idea until they were able to find the bomb.

Maybe she couldn't introduce Michael, but she was definitely going to tell him about her guest. That was a secret she wasn't willing to keep from him. He wouldn't like it if she didn't tell him—he probably wouldn't like it when she did, but at least he would live with it that way. That's all she wanted because doing this job for the country was the most important job of her life. It would be one she would never forget.

CHAPTER 105

Shires Lampton was itching to get back to work, but he couldn't leave the underground; if he did they would shoot him. No amount of reasoning with Nathan Conrad could shake the man from the one-point view. Conrad had told him two months ago, when he joined, there was no leaving. Now with Homeland Security cracking down, the threat of death squads, and the threat of being turned in for a reward the triple threat was becoming a difficult burden to bear for many residents of the underground—Shires included. It restricted their movements even more than before, making it nearly impossible to get out and do things.

They hadn't had any other scares like the one by the Bay. Shires didn't want another. They had severely restricted their own movements after that. Nobody had to tell them anything. But, this was not the way to live; not in a free world.

Shires still couldn't explain why anybody would want to kill Jordan and her friend Olivia Melton. The only possible thing they had witnessed together was the evaporation of the bodies of Tom Horn and Vince Nalone. But, he had witnessed it as well. It didn't seem they were trying to kill him. Maybe that's where he had misjudged the intent. Maybe they were trying to kill him and Jordan simultaneously. When he thought about it, the bomb in the parking lot at the restaurant might have gotten both of them if it had not exploded prematurely. When he thought about it he realized there was more truth in that assumption then he wanted to admit. Maybe it was a good thing they had both taken to the underground.

He knew if he could he would return to his old job in a New York minute. He also knew that may not be a good idea now that he thought about it. He would like to talk to his producer, Maria Sanger, but that would be taking a desperate chance. He knew that Nathan Conrad had a copy of the tape and showed it at different times. He was still alive. He was still alive through all the threats. Shires wondered what his secret might be. In fact Nathan never appeared to worry about his life.

"Did you ever notice that?" he asked absentmindedly of Jordan who was dozing in the settee next to him.

"Notice what?" she asked drowsily.

"That Conrad never seems to be afraid of getting killed."

"He has two big angels watching out for him," she said matter-of-factly.

Shires burst into laughter. "That's another of your jokes, right?"

"I didn't mean for it to be. That's what Kinzi told me. He told them that nobody can see the angels except him, but they are there to take care of him. He told them about a time when a man ran toward him. These two big angels stepped in the man's way knocking him down and scaring him so badly he got up and ran away."

"Do you believe that story?"

"I guess if Nathan believes it that's all that really counts. I don't believe it, but Nathan sure does. But then, he can see the angels. It would be easy to believe if you could actually see them. He claims we all have these guardians."

"If that were the case then why did he issue guns to us?"

"Boo, why are you grilling me? I'm not the one who claims to see angels. I was just trying to sleep."

"I'm sorry sweetheart. I was just thinking out loud when I asked those questions." He kissed her neck and the top of her head. "I'll leave you alone now."

He stood and walked outside, then over to the trailer house next door, and knocked. Kinzi Tern answered the knock.

"Shires come on in. Tony, Shires is here," she called over her shoulder.

Tony Arzetti put the paper he was reading on the table and pointed to a chair. "Have a seat. Take a load off," he said.

"Thanks. How are you guys anyway?"

"We're fine Shires. We haven't changed much since last night," Tony said and they all laughed. "But Shires you look like a man with something on his mind. What is it?"

"Do you guys want some coffee?" Kinzi asked.

"Yes, I'll take some coffee, Kinzi, and boredom is the answer to your question, Tony."

"That's a boring subject, Shires. We were expecting something lively and stimulating," Tony joked.

Kinzi set their cups on the table and filled them. "Neither of you like cream or sugar so my job is done," she said.

Both men thanked her. Shires took a sip, set the cup down, and looked at Tony.

"All these threats we have confronting us worry me, mainly Cahmael death squads, and reward money. Jordan and I were talking and she told me about the angels that Nathan claims protect him."

"They're not just angels they are big angels. He claims he can see them and that's why he never worries."

"We should all be so lucky," Shires said.

"That's what I say," Kinzi agreed.

"Do you believe him?" Shires asked.

"It doesn't matter if we do as long as he does," Tony said.

"Yeah, that's what Jordan says. So if that were the case, that we might have guardian angels, why do you think he issued us weapons?"

"I'm not sure he ever said we all had guardian angels. I guess if we had them and he could see them he probably wouldn't have given us guns. The way I look at it is simple. He did it to make us feel safer. That's about the only thing I can think of."

"I guess you're probably right. That does seem to be the logical answer."

Suddenly a loud banging on the door interrupted them. It was Jordan. "We've got to get out of here. They're on their way to arrest us. Somebody turned us in," she yelled through the door.

Just then the phone rang. Tony answered. It was Nathan telling them to get out of there someone had turned them in. And just like that, in the snap of a finger, their pleasant afternoon turned into hell.

CHAPTER 106

Nathan Conrad couldn't believe it; didn't want to believe it; a traitor in the underground. In one afternoon this unknown person had turned in thirty names with accurate locations. Seventeen people had been arrested as terrorists. He had saved a few, but very few; thirteen out of thirty.

Somebody was 170,000 dollars richer. He had just issued weapons to everybody so that would make the charges worse; enemy combatants no doubt.

He racked his brain trying to think of who it could be, but no name came out of it. Most everybody was a Christian, and he couldn't believe a Christian would do it. It had to have been somebody in the underground. Every location was correct—names and all.

His contacts at Homeland Security and at the police department, not including Mike Arzetti, had never let him down. Homeland had given him the warning quickly enough, but he hadn't been able to reach the seventeen in time. His one contact worked right in the office that received the reward calls; so there was plenty of warning. But cell phone users are sometimes unaware they have forgotten to turn it on; or they have misplaced it. He made a mental note to reiterate the importance of the phone at the next meeting.

The problem with cell phones is that they are traceable. As soon as a phone is used for underground business it had to be destroyed. Well, the common practice is to remove the memory chip and then destroy it. That's why he only used the cell phones in cases of emergency such as this—it's always a landline for regular calls. He was sure he needed to go over the complete phone protocol again, losing that many people was unacceptable even with a traitor among them.

His contact at Homeland said the caller had been a woman. That surprised him even more and narrowed his search or widened it; he wasn't sure which, but it gave him another direction to follow.

The contact had gone on to say there had been nothing distinctive about the voice; however the wonders of technology had won the day; somewhat anyway since there had been a recording made of the call. His contact, whose identity he would never reveal, made a copy and brought it to him.

He trusted Tony Arzetti and Shires Lampton with his secret, and played the recording for them in the basement living quarters of the safe house in Calistoga where they had been secreted since their narrow escape. Jordan Smith and Kinzi Tern sat in on the listening session. Tony said it sounded a lot like Beverly Goodin the lady from Napa Valley who, along with her husband, opened their home as a safe house for large meetings.

"I would never believe that of Bev, she's a wonderful Christian woman," Nathan said.

"I'm sure if there had been Christians back in the day, Judas would have been described as a very good Christian. Don't you think?" Kinzi asked.

A long silence followed.

Nathan was shaking his head. "I could never believe that of her," he said.

"Well, don't believe it. I only said it sounds like her. I didn't say it was definitely her. I don't even think anybody else agreed with me," Tony observed.

"I would have thought they would disguise the voice over the hotline to keep people from identifying the caller," Jordan surmised.

"I don't know. Is that what they do?" Shires asked.

"Think about it. She would be telling on herself if she did that wouldn't she?" Kinzi asked.

"Bev was one of those Christians who believed that Cahmael wasn't the Antichrist, but she believed in the underground and what it was trying to do."

"Yeah, but she didn't have the chip implant. How would she spend all that money?" Tony asked.

"Yes, she had the chip. She's like your son. He has the implant and helps us."

Silence again.

Nathan removed a cell phone from his pocket and punched in Bev's number. The ensuing recording said it all.

I'm sorry! The number you have reached is no longer in service.

CHAPTER 107

President Richard Butcher was disturbed that the Mossad—the Israeli equivalent to the CIA—had taken so long to get back to him. They were usually quick with their assessments in situations where intelligtence matters were cncerned They had promised him some news regarding the possible location of the bomb, and he had heard nothing from them or the Israeli police. He wanted to hear some good news about the bomb. So far they had none to give him of any consequence.

The moving company had shipped a basketball sized package to a location in Haifa. That location turned out to be an empty warehouse. However a storage facility nearby had records showing a similar package had been stored there until three days earlier when it had been retrieved by the owner. Contact with the package was lost after that.

The report was so neutral; so unemotional and lacking in what Dick called humanness, which was difficult for even him to define. He didn't like the report for a number of reasons; the main one being it told him exactly nothing. He wanted progress. A thermonuclear bomb was not something you could forget. He had a lot riding on the outcome here.

Mr. President, Cynthia's voice interrupted his thoughts, *I have Admiral Perkins on the line for you*, she said.

"Fine Cynthia, put him through." He waited until his phone buzzed then he picked it up.

"Hello Admiral Perkins, How are you?"

I'm fine Mr. President, and you?

"My health is good, but my spirits could be better," Dick said.

Well, Sir I might be able to do something about your spirits at least that's why I called.

"You've found the bomb," Dick exclaimed more hopefully than he had wanted to sound.

I'm sorry I can't tell you that, but I can tell you about the new plan we are embarking on to find it. I think it has a very good chance of accomplishing that goal.

Dick spent the next few minutes listening to the new plan devised by Major Percival Tuck. It would commence the next day with the inoculation and transfer of the captives to less secure facilities.

"So what makes you think these men, who have so far been undeterred by any of our tactics, will go for the bait?"

I don't know if they will, but it's the hand we've been dealt. In fact, it's all we have to work with, so we'll go with it and find out. Believe me Sir, I think there is a very good chance it will work.

Dick thanked the Admiral for the update and hung up. It was a flimsy plan as far as he was concerned. They were relying too much on the behavior of the terrorists who had not given up a thing to this point.

Dick was skeptical that such a plan would ever work. These terrorists would see right through it; unless they were egotistical enough to do it anyway, thinking they could still outsmart the Seal teams. He was not going to get his hopes up, not yet.

CHAPTER 108

Pope Linus cast a questioning glance toward his newly hired secretary, Father Jeremy, and asked, "What do you mean?" Then he sat down in the chair next to the younger man's desk in the reception area of the Vatican.

The young Priest leaned back in his chair to explain himself. "Nothing bad, Your Holiness, but it seems as if there is a lot of business being conducted from the Vatican with which you have nothing to do or say."

"What do you think, Father Jeremy, is that a good thing or a bad one?"

Silence settled over the room while the Father thought about it. "I think that if you think it's a good thing then it's a good thing. If you think it's a bad thing then it's a bad thing."

"Father Jeremy you're going to have to stop expressing your opinion so blatantly and learn to be diplomatic about what you say," the Pope joked with the younger man.

"Your Holiness, I just mean everything hinges on your opinion except, it seems, when it comes to actually running Europe, which, I think is supposed to be the plan under the new Cahmael Regime. That's how it seems to me anyway."

"Are you troubled by it?" The Pope asked, clasping his hands together and leaning forward to place his elbows on the desk. The position gave him the appearance of a willingness to listen intently to the Priest.

"I don't think troubled is the word, Sir. It's more of a wondering about what's going on. There is this tremendous build up of the military in the Middle East, for instance. That can't be good, not with the dedication of the Temple in Jerusalem coming up on May 14th."

"Cardinal Mencini has told me that the buildup is crucial to security at the dedication, and that's why Lord Cahmael has ordered it,"

"That's kinda what bothers me. Is it really necessary? All the countries in the region now have peace treaties with each other. The military buildup looks a lot like getting ready for war. Even the United States is there with a large force; an enormous amount of ships. What's with that?"

Pope Linus had no explanation to give his young secretary. For himself all the military goings on didn't bother him. He left those things up to Lord Cahmael and didn't worry about it. "What seems to bother you the most?" he asked of the young priest.

"Your Holiness it doesn't bother me so much as it scares me."

"Scares you?"

"Yes. It's like we're getting ready for Armageddon."

CHAPTER 109

Lieutenant Seth Wyatt stared at his team sitting before him on the deck of the carrier Douglas MacArthur. It was about noon, almost time for lunch, but he wanted to tell them of their upcoming assignment. One about which he was very excited.

"Gentlemen we've been given a new assignment. We will still be chasing the bomb, but in a different way. They are going to let our captives lead us to it. We will be giving them inoculations and taking them to a less secure camp on the premise that we no longer believe they have anything to do with the bomb.

"They will be allowed to escape and then they will be tracked by the computer chip that was implanted under the guise of an inoculation. Don't ask me how these guys escaped the chip implant the first time, but they did—probably from living off the grid somewhere in the Middle East. Nobody knows.

"There will be three Seal teams, two besides us; we'll all be deployed close to where our friends have regrouped after their escape. We'll wait there until we're sure they have the bomb, whereupon we'll be dispatched to gather the eggs…so to speak. Anybody have any questions?"

"What size of bomb are we talking about?" Otter Tousley asked.

"This is the only size description I know of. Our Intel says there was a basketball size package delivered to a company in Haifa. When the Mossad got there they found an empty warehouse. I hope the size description is at least close to that size when we find it."

"Are you sure we'll find it?" Frank Barnes asked.

"You gotta be careful what you wish for, but I think we will."

"And then what?" Josh Hinkle asked.

"And then I hope Otter is close by to disarm it. That's all I ask. Anyway, we'll be leaving the Carrier around midnight to take up our new positions close to the new POW camp. So get your gear in order and be ready to go. Any questions?"

There were none and Seth supposed it was just as well. He had no answers anyway. They all knew it was a serious mission; probably more so than any other they had ever undertaken.

CHAPTER 110

Hassan Enau couldn't understand why they were being inoculated. Their captors hated them. Why would they turn suddenly and do something good. He expressed his doubts to their leader who quickly shushed him.

"Let the Americans do what they will now," he said, "we are being moved to a different compound, one that has much less security. I overheard the Americans talking about it. They believe we have nothing to do with the bomb, and don't want to waste any more time with us. We are being inoculated because of the International Red Cross inspection tomorrow just before we are moved. We have to remember to say only good things about our captors.

"We want them to want to move us, the more cooperative we are now the better it will be. Let them look good for the Red Cross. Tell its representative you were treated well if they ask. Our goal is to destroy the Americans. We must get to the bomb."

"Do we know where the bomb is?" Hassan asked.

"We have friends who do. Allah will provide. Do not worry. It is as it is. Allah be praised."

"Allah be praised," Hassan repeated.

CHAPTER 111

Melissa Hardin was excited. The day of the great escape was upon them. Four days ago the prisoners had been inoculated and moved to less secure facilities. The prisoners have had all that time to check out the lax security at the facility. A total of nine terrorists had been transferred. Each had been given a number that would identify him on the computer tracking system.

Hassan Enau was number 9. Melissa made a note of it since he had been the one who never complained or flinched from his treatment according to his captors. They considered him a hard case and the one most likely to carry the bomb to its final destination.

Admiral Bill Scott had settled in rather well with his sleeping bag and cot. He had even gone grocery shopping, equipping them with enough groceries to feed an army.

"I didn't want you or me to go hungry," he said, laughing at himself and his extravagance. One thing you didn't have though, coffee grounds. Evidently neither Matt nor you drink it, but there was an old coffee maker in the back."

"I drink it, but I haven't been here long enough to delve into what the necessities might be."

Hal had been a wonderful teacher. They learned the manipulations of chip tracking with all its nuances. They weren't experts for sure, but they would get the job done.

Mike understood the circumstances of Admiral Scott being there to help her with a project about which she could tell him nothing other than it was of the utmost importance to our National Security. He agreed to wait to meet the man when their project was complete.

Melissa utilized two computer monitors so they each had one and could work independently of the other. If the subjects spread out more they would utilize other monitors as well; a bank of ten monitors would ensure the observation of all subjects at all times on both chips and cameras.

The time zone difference was ten hours. The Middle East was ten hours ahead of San Francisco. They expected the subjects to escape at night so their more intense watching was scheduled to start around 8 in the morning. Melissa watched during the day and the Admiral watched during the night; although the Admiral never left before noon to sleep in the back room. He would get up around 8 in the evening when Melissa went home. She had altered her schedule somewhat but Michael didn't mind. They could have dinner together about 9 at night and breakfast together about 6 in the morning before Mike went to work, and that was alright with him. Melissa and Mike had never actually moved in together, but she spent most nights at his house anyway.

The captives did nothing; not on the fourth or fifth or the sixth night. They continued to huddle together in the huts.

Melissa and the Admiral were getting concerned that the plan wasn't going to work. But, they had no one other than each other to express it to except now and again to Major Tuck during one of his "What are they doing now?" calls from aboard the Carrier Douglas MacArthur.

The days dragged into weeks of watching—2 weeks to be exact, and all for naught. Concern rose among the participants; had they misjudged the terrorists?

Major Tuck counseled patience. He was positive the terrorist would act when it was time for them to go for the bomb. He felt the target date would be May 14th. They wouldn't do anything until that date was close.

He was also positive one of them knew the location of the bomb, but he would wait until the very last moment to get it. Everything then would happen fast. They had to stay alert. There was pressure from the present commanders of the carrier groups to look somewhere else, but Tuck was able to talk them into staying the course.

There had been a strong argument against it. The main focus of that argument held that this was all a ruse perpetrated to draw their attention away from something else.

Tuck felt this was a well financed operation that had to have been backed by a country that might be interested in injuring the United States and Israel; maybe even dealing a death blow to Israel.

CHAPTER 112

They had hidden out for almost a month now. Their escape from Homeland Security had been narrow to say the least. It was like they had gone out the back door as the authorities came in the front. Any harmony they had gained in their lives to that point in the underground had been completely destroyed. They had the clothes on their backs and the weapons Nathan had given them. Jordan had lost her weapon when she ran out the door to warn them. She had stopped for nothing.

They were living in the basement of a house in Calistoga and their only visitor in that month had been Nathan Conrad who came to let them listen to a recording of the person who turned them in. It had been Beverly Goodin from Napa Valley; "A good Christian woman," according to Nathan Conrad.

Shires could tell that Nathan had been surprised and disappointed. A Christian woman was the last person he would suspect. But, she had done it, collected her money, and moved away; all within the same week of the deed. The feat had taken some planning, and that had to have been even more disappointing to Nathan.

Trust was a golden commodity in Nathan's business. It had to be, and to have that trust thrown down and trampled underfoot was devastating.

Nathan had decided to have the next meeting in the basement where they were hiding. It wasn't too large but it would suffice since the numbers had dwindled drastically.

"I'm starting this evening with a heavy heart. Our Sister Beverly Goodin and her husband betrayed us. I have asked God to forgive them, and I'm sure he will; however, I've had to ask God to forgive me for not forgiving them. I have tried and tried. So I'll ask for your prayers in this matter, if you're a praying person that is.

"We lost those other folks because they weren't paying attention to their cell phones. Either their phone was shut off, misplaced or the battery was dead. I couldn't get them to answer when I called. Seventeen of them are in jail due to inattention. "It's like I'm preaching to the choir talking to you folks about it. You're the ones who answered. Tonight before I leave I'll collect all your old phones and give you new ones. You know the drill, remove the information card from your old phone and place it in the new one before giving it to me. I'll dispose of the old ones.

"I know you know, but I'll say it again. This phone is only for emergency use, meaning if you get a call on this phone it will usually be me telling you to run. That's the emergency. It means that I've heard from my contact inside Homeland or the San Francisco Police Department that they're coming to arrest us.

"There is one other thing, and I want you to remember this; do not shut off your cell phone for anything. I must be able to get in touch with you. What I'm counting on is your groups. If I can reach one of you in the group I should be able to save all of you. When you leave here tonight remember to be paranoid."

CHAPTER 113

May 1st came and went; still no movement by the terrorists. They appeared content hanging out in their shelters in the camp as if nothing at all depended on their being somewhere else. Melissa and the Admiral had given up watching their every move. The excitement of three weeks ago slowly dissipated into the humdrum activity of everyday living.

Suddenly, on May 8th that all changed; it was 9 in the evening Middle East time, just after sunset—12 noon in San Francisco. Admiral Scott radioed Seth Wyatt that the subjects were moving North on his ten o'clock. To Seth that meant they were moving away from him on his right side. His team, along with the other two, moved immediately.

Melissa operated the chip tracking while Admiral Scott focused in with the infrared cameras. It appeared Tuck's patience had paid off.

Tuck hoped so anyway, and breathed a slight sigh of relief, but he didn't want to overreact as it might be nothing at all. He wished he could feel as confident as he knew he had sounded to others.

They're heading for the coast, Wyatt's voice blared in Tuck's ears.

I have four boats coming fast down the coast, Scott's voice cracked in Tuck's ears immediately following Wyatt's voice.

Egg gatherers this is mother hen there are four boats coming fast down the coast be aware, Tuck spoke in his microphone.

"They're still all together," Melissa said to Scott who immediately radioed the information to Major Tuck. The Major knew that wouldn't last long after their rendezvous with the boats. These guys were going to spread out all over the Mediterranean.

Egg gatherers this is Mother Hen. Be advised I am sending four helicopters to pick you up. Team one; you guys have to split up, three in each chopper. Sorry about that, but I need eyes on all the boats. The choppers will be at your twenty in fifteen.

Seth's team was designated *team one* so they would be split. Otter Tousley, his second in command, would lead the other half. Otter was also the explosive expert so he hoped Otter would be close by if they tangled with the bomb. Each team had an explosive expert, but he trusted Otter with his life, and this was one huge bomb; after the explosion, not before.

Melissa stared in fascination at the monitor and the drama unfolding right before her eyes, "Why don't they stop the boats right now; capture and search them?" Melissa asked.

"They won't have the bomb as yet. That will be picked up by one of the boats after they've dispersed. They're going to disguise who has it. They'll make it as difficult as they can, and impossible if the circumstances are right to make that possible. That's what they're hoping for I would think.

"Hal, do you have any way to recognize a bomb?" Melissa asked.

"No the cameras don't have the capability to distinguish those things," it answered.

"Hal is there anything we could do to enhance your capability?" Scott asked.

"Hal has searched the programs and found no algorithm that would accommodate such an enhancement," the computer said.

"They've reached the boats," Melissa announced.

Admiral Scott relayed the update to Major Tuck; who relayed it on to the Seal teams.

"Chicken Coop those boats are going to go every which way. Keep a close eye on them. Major Tuck said.

"We're on it Mother Hen." Scott radioed back

Melissa laughed at the names—mother hen; chicken coop; egg gatherers; oh the wonders of technology.

Mother hen the choppers are here. Where are the eggs? Seth radioed to Tuck.

In the basket to your twelve at thirty minutes, all egg gatherers maintain 10 minute separation. I will advise, Tuck answered.

CHAPTER 114

Mike Arzetti's life had taken a hit from two fronts. Melissa had to spend more time at her job regarding National Security concerns and then a member of the underground had turned in other members for the reward. What scared him about that was the fact that Bev Goodin also knew him and George as being members of the underground—that's another 20,000. Why hadn't she turned them in? It was like waiting for the other shoe to fall.

He tried to remember the woman as being something other than positive, but he couldn't. She had been a happy person any of the times he had talked to her.

He discussed it with his partner, George Wilde. They made a pact between them. What happens to one happens to the other. They knew of no one else in the department who belonged to the underground, and neither Melissa nor Carmen knew about their involvement. If worse came to worse, and to protect the girls, they would leave them and disappear. It was a difficult decision for they were both in love; but, because of that love, they were willing to make the sacrifice. They would have to give up everything, and live off the grid. Jail was an unacceptable alternative.

The phone rang just as he walked in the apartment. Ann was gone so he answered, thinking it would be for her.

Sweetheart, this is Melissa, the voice said.

"Hey Baby, to what do I owe this nice surprise?" he asked.

National Security I would say. Look sweetie I'm going to be stuck here all night. All hell is breaking loose. Admiral Scott told me to tell you to come on down. He figures you're a cop so you can keep a secret. Plus we could use your eyes to help us with these monitors.

"Are you serious?"

As a nuclear bomb.

"I'll be right there," he answered quickly, picking up on the innuendo.

Ring the buzzer we'll buzz you in; then just come up the stairs. I love you. See you soon.

"Back at you, Babe," he said, practically running out the door.

CHAPTER 115

President Richard Butcher was ready to tear his hair out. Here it was the 8th of May; less than a week before the dedication of the Temple and still no word about the bomb or any progress with finding it.

He had placed a call to Cahmael but the man hadn't been available at the moment. Cahmael had promised him the bomb would be found—told him not to worry about it.

He received the call from Admiral Perkins at 5 in the evening.

Mr. President, he said, *I thought you would want to be informed that we are in pursuit of the terrorists that are retrieving the bomb as I speak. They are in boats on the Israeli coast fleeing north and south—four boats; two North and two South.*

"What is our position?"

Ten minutes behind the fleeing boats.

"Is that good?"

That's very good. We also have eyes in the sky.

"Eyes from where?"

From the ALIEN program. Remember the Aerial Lens Insect Eye Nomenclature program you were briefed on about a year ago.

"Now that you mention it, just vaguely, but tell me about that at a later date. Right now I want to know about the bomb."

Well, Sir we are purposefully maintaining a ten minute interval between us and them. They can't hear us at that distance and we can close on them quickly if anything develops.

"Who is chasing them?"

Three of the best Seal teams in the service today, Sir.

"So we are in excellent shape on this one?"

Yes Sir we are. I'll keep you updated through the night. This will go on for quite a while. The moment I hear something I will let you know…good or bad.

The words 'good' or 'bad' tacked on at the end weren't comforting, but Dick relaxed somewhat after that conversation. He tried Cahmael again without success. He wanted more of his assurance.

CHAPTER 116

Hassan Enau thanked Allah for the stupidity of the egotistical Americans. Now they would pick up the bomb, which had been buried by their camp about ten centimeters away from the food. The Americans had found the food, not realizing that not so far away a bomb lay in waiting.

Their leader, Ashram, had told them of the location as they hurried to the beach to catch the boats. He said it was necessary for all of them to know. If one person were stopped it was up to the next to get the bomb and deliver it. Hassan was headed south in a boat with Ashram. They would pick up the bomb. Hassan could hardly contain his exuberance.

There was a time at the torture camp when he thought it was all over, but Allah would not allow the Palestinian People to be denied their revenge. All Praise to Allah!

He looked around at the beautiful night; the moon shining out of the West and stars everywhere. It wouldn't be long before the night would again belong to the Palestinian People. They could smile and laugh again like his father remembered his own father laughing. Hassan couldn't remember his grandfather's laugh. He didn't remember ever hearing him laugh. The joy had left the Palestinian People many years ago. Hassan would bring it back.

They had gone along with Jehosea Cahmael and made peace with the Jews. He couldn't understand it. His father counseled patience. "You wait. Allah has a great purpose in this; a purpose we cannot understand. In time we will know, and rejoice in it."

Hassan could see that prediction coming true, and he was rejoicing in it. His father had been right. Allah knew what he was doing. All things work together for the will of Allah. Jehosea Cahmael was just one more useful tool. All praise to Allah!

CHAPTER 117

Mike Arzetti arrived at the old warehouse and rang the buzzer. The place didn't look like it might contain secret high tech equipment. It looked like no government building he had ever seen. Maybe that was the genius of it.

The buzzer rang. He yanked the door open and ran up the steps into the upper floor. Melissa was walking toward him accompanied by an older man. He kissed her.

"Sweetheart this is Admiral Bill Scott. Admiral Scott this is Mike Arzetti."

They greeted each other and shook hands.

"Mike I'll let Melissa tell you what we're doing. I cleared it for you to come aboard because we need help and we need it fast. Welcome aboard."

"Thank you, Sir I'll do all I can," he answered.

Melissa sat Mike down by a monitor and keyboard. She explained everything to him. They were chasing terrorists and looking for a missing nuclear bomb; a thermonuclear bomb, which he knew nothing about until she explained it to him.

"Holy cow, I thought you said your job was boring," he joked, and then realized it wasn't a joking matter. Neither Melissa nor the Admiral laughed. They weren't listening to him. Their eyes were glued to the monitors. Sorry about that," he added to no one in particular.

"It looks like they're stopping at they're old camp site," the Admiral burst out then radioed the information to Tuck. *Mother Hen this is chicken coop two eggs have gone to the original nest.*

Mike listened in amazement when Tuck answered back, *Hen this is chicken coop two eggs have gone to the original nest.*

"**Roger that Chicken Coop.**"

"Where's he talking from?" he asked.

"From the Mediterranean Ocean off the coast of Israel," Melissa explained.

Mike just shook his head. "That's a lot of miles to sound so close," he said.

"It's called satellite communication," Melissa said.

In Seth Wyatt's headset he heard Tuck tell the pilot to hold his present position as the quarry had stopped. He had heard the earlier message from Scott saying they were going back to their original campsite. Scott had said nest, but they were the same. Why? Why are they going there? That's when the thought hit him. *That's where the bomb is.* Either it was there all the time or was placed there later. That's where it is right now. He'd bet on it, and radioed Tuck to tell him.

Mother Hen this is Egg Gatherer One. Possible big target just ahead, he said.

That's affirmative One. Wait for confirmation from Chicken Coop.

Tuck had guessed it too.

Mother Hen this is Chicken Coop be advised all four subjects have disembarked and are moving toward the original nest. I Will keep you posted, Scott said in the microphone.

Roger that Chicken Coop.

CHAPTER 118

Ashram had stopped running and halted the others. He stood quite still as if frozen in his tracks. He shook his head. "Something is not right," he said suspiciously."

"What? What is it?" Hassan pleaded.

"I do not know. Did you hear that noise a moment ago?"

"I heard no noise," Hassan said.

"Neither did I," said the boat driver, Amrahn.

"I tell you there was a noise floating on the wind," Ashram insisted.

"A noise like what?" Hassan asked.

"Like a helicopter; only for a moment, but it was there."

"What would a helicopter be doing out here?" Hassan asked.

"That's what I asked myself. I didn't like the answer I got."

"What answer did you get?" Amrahn inquired.

"Following us. It's following us. The Americans lied to us."

A long silence followed. They stood digesting what Ashram had told them. Hassan was severely disappointed.

"Why would the Americans lie to us?" Hassan asked not wanting to believe that they did.

"They want the bomb and they still think we have it. They want us to lead them to it," Ashram answered.

"What will we do?" asked Amrahn.

"Maybe I'm wrong. We shall go back to the boat and wait for the Americans to come. If they fail to come we will get the bomb and complete our mission."

Hassan was disappointed but proud that Allah had sent them a message on the wind. All praise to Allah!

CHAPTER 119

"They've stopped moving. They're going back toward the boat," Melissa called out.

Mother Hen check out the other boats! The one going south to the old nest was a decoy, Scott said into his microphone.

"One boat going north has stopped in a cove on the coast," Melissa called out.

Scott repeated it to Major Tuck who relayed it to the Seal teams.

Team Two chopper this is Mother Hen hold your position, I say hold position your boat has stopped" Tuck radioed.

"What are they doing? Can you see anything, Mike?" Scott asked.

Mike strained to see the images on the screen. Melissa quickly typed an order and moved the zoom on the camera lens for a closer look.

"Whoa! Now I can see really well; looks like they're getting out. They're carrying something—they're carrying shovels," Mike said.

Mother Hen this is Chicken Coop we may have something here; they're out with shovels. We'll get back to you. Tell the team to be ready to go,

Team one come back up the coast to the Team two position. Team two be ready to go they're out and digging.

Chicken Coop where is Team one A? Tuck asked.

"They've gone down the coast toward Egypt," Melissa answered, and Scott radioed it to Tuck.

"Team Three is up the coast north of Team Two," Melissa said to Scott who relayed it as well.

Roger Chicken Coop and thank you.

"I can't really tell with this infrared, but it looks like they've dug up a small container." Mike said.

"Does it look basketball size?" Scott asked.

"Yes," he answered.

Mother Hen tell 'em to go they have the bomb. I repeat they have the bomb. Go! Go! Scott radioed.

Seth heard the go order. He pressed the intercom button on his helmet and spoke, *How far we out from their location?*

Fifteen minutes, Lieutenant give or take, the pilot replied.

Okay! Make it less if you can, Seth answered. Seth knew these guys were not going to give up the bomb easily. Team Two had a hell of a fight ahead of them. He had Hinkle and Barnes with him. The three of them would be there to help in a few minutes.

CHAPTER 120

Mike, Melissa and Admiral Scott were transfixed by the tableau taking place on the monitors. The night vision lens showed six little green figures running from the helicopter toward a group of four men. Suddenly the runners dropped and rolled.

"They're being shot at," Scott explained.

The group of four men had fallen to a prone position pointing toward the Seal team. One of the four jumped up to run; fell quickly, and lay still.

"They got one of them," Melissa yelled.

Seth Wyatt's helicopter landed in the background. Three men jumped out and ran toward the gunfight.

Seth moved his team to flank the terrorists, and sent Josh Hinkle to get to their rear. Then they poured gunfire into their position. The exchange went on for some minutes before the firing from the terrorists ceased. There was one last burst, and then all was quiet,

Lieutenant Wyatt rolled over on his back to look at the stars so bight in the sky. The moon was low in the west. He blew out a sigh of relief that the bomb hadn't exploded.

"Hey! This isn't a bomb," he heard somebody yell.

CHAPTER 121

Mother Hen this is Egg Gatherer two we have no bomb. I repeat we have no bomb.

Chicken Coop this is Mother Hen Egg Gatherer reports no bomb. Are there other suspects?

"What?" Melissa was shocked by the news.

Mike immediately looked back at the original boat they had been following, Melissa beat him to it. "It's the first boat. They're running across the beach carrying a package," she said.

Mother Hen the bomb is moving with the original target of Team One. They're carrying a package, and it looks like they're heading for the open ocean, Scott radioed loudly.

Egg Gatherers one and two this is Mother Hen your quarry is heading for the open Ocean one hour south and west of your position. Get on your horses it's going to be a race. I will guide you, Tuck said. He realized they had been duped out of their boots by people using low tech or no tech at all. And then to Scott he said, *Chicken Coop you must keep us apprised of their position.*

Roger Mother Hen we're on it.

Melissa checked the chip monitor. Number one and nine were aboard with the driver and passenger. Somehow she had known Hassan Enau would be in the mix with the bomb. She had figured that earlier because the interrogators had said it would be him if anybody. She should have stuck with her original hunch, but then she was new at this bomb chasing business, and allowed herself to be distracted. But, she didn't feel completely foolish the others had been distracted as well.

"They're making pretty good time. Where are the choppers?" Mike asked.

"About forty-five minutes behind, but coming on fast," Melissa said.

"There's no way they can get to the ships before the choppers catch them, but it depends on the size of the bomb. They may not have to reach the ships at all—just the vicinity is fine. They'll try to get as close as they can you can bet on that," Scott explained.

"Why can't they just shoot the boat out of the water?" Melissa asked.

"It's called a dead man's switch. The bomb will be rigged with one. The moment the bomber dies his grip on the switch is loosened and the bomb explodes. Our men have to go in and take the bomb away from them if they can," Scott said.

"You don't think they'll explode the bomb first?" Mike asked.

"I'm afraid they will, but hoping they won't. I think they'll wait until the very last second before they do that. They'll want to be as close to the ships as possible; that's only my supposition. I may be wrong. I hope not for the sake of those men doing the chasing."

Silence settled over the room as the three watched the monitor and the deadly chase unfolding on it.

"They're thirty minutes away," Melissa said.

Mother Hen the Egg Gatherers are on course to intercept in thirty minutes. Will keep you posted, Scott radioed.

Roger Chicken Coop. Egg Gatherers one and two this is Mother Hen you are on course to intercept in thirty; I say three zero.

Lieutenant Wyatt glanced at his watch. It was coming up on midnight; three in the afternoon in Seattle where his folks live. They would be going on about their everyday things. His brother Clay would be just finishing a class at Gonzaga, and now that the Basketball season was over—Gonzaga had gone to the Elite Eight—he would probably be going off to study or on a date with a chick. Clay never let his studies interfere with his women.

Seth smiled thinking about his brother. They were close and shared their thoughts quite regularly in their emails. Seth was shorter than Clay, and although Clay was the youngest, he endearingly called Seth 'little brother'.

It had been that way since High School where Clay's six foot four frame excelled at basketball and Seth's six foot frame swam well. Clay's basketball prowess was good enough to earn him a basketball scholarship to Gonzaga when he graduated High School two years after Seth.

Seth had received no scholarship. Four years later he graduated from Boise State, and joined the Navy as an officer candidate. His goal always was to be a SEAL. It took awhile. There was boot camp, officer candidate school, frogman training, and jump school before he finally realized his dream as a young Lieutenant Junior Grade. Now he was a First Lieutenant in charge of his own team. He had wanted to be where the action would be, and tonight was the epitome of that dream. It was the big one; the mother of all action.

Egg Gatherers one and two you are ten minutes out and closing. Good luck guys, Tuck's voice spoke in his ear, interrupting his thoughts.

CHAPTER 122

"Allah be praised! Allah be praised," Hassan Enau repeated over and over again under his breath. He stood at the bow of the boat as it skipped lightly over the water on its way to the American ships. The moon was gone now making the stars even brighter. All of Palestine could see that sky; that beautiful sky, and soon it would bear witness to the revenge of all Palestinians.

He tightened his grip on the trigger of the bomb. He knew that next when he let it go there would be a smile in all of Palestine.

A light flashed over his head, splashing the deck in brightness. He looked up. The light was momentarily blinding; long enough for him to miss the figure descending on the rope from above. A hand gripped his trigger hand. He tried to let go; he couldn't. He felt something cold against his arm and then he heard a shot and felt the pain in his arm. Still he couldn't pull his arm away. Another shot; more pain in the same arm, and then another shot. He realized through the pain that now clouded his brain that the man was shooting off his arm, detaching him from the bomb. He grabbed the figure with his right arm and jumped overboard, bringing the figure with him. Another shot and he felt his arm tear away. The agony was great, but he smiled.

He felt the life blood draining from him, but he laughed at the stupid American who held his fingers on the exploding trigger. The American couldn't let go. Hassan's whole purpose was to let go and allow the bomb to do its work. Now the American had the bomb, but it would still explode. Hassan had delivered it as Allah had directed him. The Palestinian people would have their revenge. The joy would come back to Palestine. Hassan had brought it back. These were his thoughts as the darkness of death engulfed him.

Seth struck the automatic inflation device on his waist. His life vest inflated and helped him back to the surface with the bomb and the bombers hand tightly gripped in his. The boat had sped away from his location, but it had stopped about two hundred yards away; too far for him to call. His pistol was still in his free hand so he shot it in the air, trying to attract their attention. He heard yelling. It sounded like "shoot again" so he did.

The searchlight from a helicopter illuminated the water around him; he stopped shooting. He heard yelling again, "We see you! We're coming!"

In that moment he marveled most at the silence of the helicopter. No wonder the terrorists never heard them coming. He supposed there was a military name for it, but he thought of it as the silent mode. He could hear them yelling at him over the sound of it; the wonders of science. He knew he had heard the silent mode before, but never had he appreciated it so much.

The boat pulled alongside him.

"Need a little help?" a voice called out.

"That and one very good explosive ordinance disposal man, and radio Mother Hen that we have the bomb," he answered.

One and a half SEAL teams—eight men squeezed aboard the small boat with the ninth in the water beside it—all yelled "Who Yah!" at the top of their lung capacity.

"I'm the EOD, names Jim Lightfeather of the Sioux Indian Nation my brother. Let me help you out of the water and I'll get the tool kit," he said as calmly as if he had just toweled himself at the beach.

"Okay, Jim let me tell you what I have. I have my hand gripping the terrorist's hand that is still gripping the dead man switch. I suspect I'll have to stay like that until you finish disarming it. I would like to climb into the boat if I can."

"I'm sorry my brother I can't let you do that. Your job is to hold on to that switch like your life depended on it because it does;" he chuckled; "now we'll move the bomb inside the boat and I'll get to work."

Seth heard three splashes in the water then six more. Otter Tousley and the other two members of Seth's team swam to his side; as did all six members of SEAL team three.

"Need any help in there?' Otter asked.

"Otter is that you?"

"Hey Jim fancy meeting you here. Yes it is I Otter Tousley," he said in a choked up tongue-in-cheek English voice.

"Tousley your English ancestors would turn over in their graves if they heard your accent."

"How about your tribe back there in South Dakota when they hear your war party consisted of two black men, one Chicano and fourteen white men. That's gotta be a disgrace in any Indian village," Otter joked back.

It was an eerie scene that Melissa, Mike and Admiral Scott watched on the monitor. Four helicopters hovering around a boat full of men; the one directly above illuminated the boat while the searchlights from the other three did the same for the immediate area.

"What are they doing?" Melissa asked.

"Disarming the bomb by disconnecting the triggering device," Scott answered.

"Oh my God," Melissa exclaimed."They're all huddled around it."

"They can't run from it. The best place to be is where it gets you instantaneously. You'll never know it exploded; that and they're giving moral support to the guy who has to disarm it. He's got a lonely job even with seventeen friends and eight helicopter pilots surrounding him."

"I've seen some brave cops and firemen, but these guys win my award for bravery," Mike stated.

"I know some of them," Scott said, "they're in it for the action. That's what they thrive on. They know that every mission they undertake could cost them their lives, but they go because that part is a given. It wouldn't be excitement otherwise."

No one spoke while Jim Lightfeather worked on the bomb. His nickname was Chief, and he was proud to be a Native American serving his country.

The flashlight in his hand moved from side to side on the bomb as he searched for the proper opening to access the inner core; a touchy procedure. The wires leading to the dead man trigger were incased within molding that was wed to the bomb; no way to go in there. He searched that area closely and found a tiny slit beside a small octagonal shaped panel about the size of a baseball.

He searched slowly, patiently; this was not the time to rush. The first rule of EOD was patience; impatience can get you killed. He searched the remainder of the exterior looking for any other slits like it and found none; that must be the one.

He turned his attention back to the panel and carefully inserted the tip of a tiny screwdriver into the slit, and wiggled the tip. The panel moved slightly to the side. He pushed more; it slid open exposing the wiring.

He identified the trigger wiring, but this is where he had to be careful. If one wire was still attached and they touched each other the bomb would explode as that would close the circuit. He would have to loosen one wire then tape the bare end; thus insulating it. It wasn't rocket science, but it had to be done with the fingers of a surgeon.

Seth's hand was getting tired, but he had to hang on. He had the tiger by the tail and couldn't let go. He had finally been able to return his pistol to its shoulder holster so now he could hold on to the side of the boat rather than tread water, which he felt he had to do even with the life vest inflated; that helped some.

"Anything I can do?" Otter asked.

Otter was right next to him. "No, but thanks anyway," he answered.

"I'm here if you need me."

"Gotcha," Seth said.

Lightfeather's small screwdriver had a clip at the end of it. When he had loosened the small screw enough he could slip the clips under it to secure it to the screwdriver, preventing the screw from falling into the inner workings, and somehow exploding the bomb anyway.

He fetched a plastic cover and a roll of electrical tape from his bag before he started the unscrewing procedure. When he finished with the little screw he lifted it delicately out of the inner cavity of the bomb and placed it on the deck, picked up a red plastic cover and slipped it over the end of the wire, then tore off a piece of tape and wrapped the plastic cover completely with tape then affixed it securely to the wire. He bent that wire aside and commenced to unscrew the other side. It seemed to be going well, but he wouldn't allow himself that thought. He would repeat the same procedure on the second side just as carefully and slowly as he did the first. Ten long minutes later he taped the two wrapped ends together to get them out of the way.

"Okay Lieutenant Wyatt you may let go of the trigger and that piece of arm. We have not only disarmed the terrorist we have disarmed the bomb," Lightfeather said.

A great cheer rose out of the Mediterranean on that dawn of a new day. It had taken all night there in the Ocean, but they had accomplished their mission.

Mother Hen this is Egg Gatherer One; we have the egg; it is disarmed; we are heading home, Seth said.

Melissa, Mike, and Admiral Scott were celebrating themselves. Scott broke out a bottle of wine and glasses and they drank a toast to the SEALS and to themselves for successfully supporting such a dangerous undertaking. And then they decided that soup and sandwiches would be the order of the evening. None of them had eaten in over ten hours.

CHAPTER 123

Mother Hen this is Egg Gatherer One; we have the egg; it is disarmed; we are heading home.

"That's the last communication we had with the Seal teams about 8 this evening, Sir," Admiral Perkins said as he handed the note to the President.

Richard Butcher read it and a big smile crossed his face. "They did it. By God they did it," was all he could say, but the relief was great. "Thank you Admiral. I appreciate your bringing this to me. What time was it over there?"

"Six in the morning, Sir. It's a seven hour difference. They are seven hours ahead of us here on the East coast."

"Thank you, Admiral. You have a nice evening," Dick said.

"I will Sir," the Admiral said and stood to go.

"Admiral, one last thing before you leave. Tell those men involved that their deed will not be forgotten by their country. And effective immediately I want you to transfer them and the helicopter pilots to Hawaii for a two week R and R. After which they will be brought here to Washington."

"If you mean all the men; that's twenty-six men, Sir."

"That's what I mean all twenty-six."

"Aye; Aye, Sir," he said. He did a perfect heel-to-toe about face and exited the Oval Office.

Dick stared at the door long after the Admiral had gone. He was going to get the names of those men and bestow upon them the medals that would depict their level of bravery.

He pressed the buzzer but Cynthia didn't answer. He forgot it was midnight. He definitely wanted to call Jehosea Cahmael, but he wasn't sure whether he wanted to gloat or to thank him. He knew he couldn't believe what he was thinking. Maybe it was better he couldn't call him.

CHAPTER 124

Nathan Conrad was worried. Someone had asked him how much damage Bev Goodin had done. He told them he had lost seventeen people. Then he began thinking about the question of damage, and realized he didn't know what she had told the police.

He wracked his brain to remember the safe houses she might have known; that was an exercise in futility. He could never be sure.

Mike Arzetti had called said he needed to talk to him right away so he would run some of this past Mike and get his ideas about any safe houses he would have in mind.

It was four that afternoon when he met with Mike at Gordy's Bar and Grill. Mike looked like he had been up all night. That was Nathan's greeting. Mike ordered a hamburger and a beer. Nathan ordered a hamburger and fries with a coke.

"You look like H E double L my friend," Nathan said when they were settled with their food.

"I feel just as bad as I look. I was up all night thinking about the implications of what I saw yesterday afternoon and evening/"

"And that was?"

"Well I can't tell you. I can only ask questions that I've derived from it. Is that okay with you?"

"Sure go right ahead," Nathan said.

"What does the date May 14th mean to you?"

"Well, today is the 10th so it's 4 days away. It is the date that Cahmael will begin his second forty-two month reign. I know that. Is there a right or wrong answer to this question, Mike?"

"I don't know. You'll have to tell me."

"Let me think. Let's see. Oh yes, It's the birthday of the land of Israel. May 14th 1948 was the date, and, by the way, they have rebuilt the Holy Temple of Solomon and it will be dedicated on that day this year. It's a big shindig they've got going. Is that the right answer?"

"I don't know. Would the Antichrist have anything to do with that dedication?"

"Oh no I don't think he'd have any reason to go near the place, well, wait a minute," Nathan paused, "It says in the Bible that the Antichrist will defile the most Holy of Holies, which is there in the Temple. Only very special priests are ever allowed to enter. If he were going there it might be to do that so that the world will know who he is. That would begin his last forty-two month reign. That certainly coincides with the start of the final forty-two months like I've been saying. Yes there is a very good reason for him to be going there this year. What brought all this up?"

"I can't tell you, but it was something I saw that reminded me a little bit about what Armageddon might look like."

"Are you serious? That must have been one heck of a movie," Nathan surmised.

"It wasn't a movie it was real life. There's something going on Nathan. There's definitely something going on. I wish I could tell you, but I can't; not right now."

"Well, are you saying Cahmael will not be at the dedication?"

"No, I'm not saying that either. It's really nothing about Cahmael, but it is about the Middle East."

"Have I helped you at all; answered your questions. Whatever it was that you wanted of me?" Nathan asked.

"I guess so."

"Well, I need to ask you a question then," Nathan said.

"Okay, go ahead."

"I'm at a point where I don't know what to do about safe houses. I'm not sure what Bev has told the authorities so I'm afraid to hold meetings at any of the old places. Can you think of any place she might not have known about?"

Mike thought for a moment, took a bite of his sandwich, and a sip of beer. "About the only place I can't remember seeing Bev was at the old warehouse down by where I live. You were using it when I first joined.

The one where we had a secret sign-in; remember? It was down by where that Policeman, Roy Cassidy, was murdered by the sniper last fall," Mike said that as an indifferent third person who had nothing to do with it might say it. And Nathan who had ordered the shooting listened in the same manner. Two innocent men speaking of an incident about which the other supposedly knew nothing.

"That's why we stopped using that place. I think we'll have to start again. I have no other place to meet. I don't think the police have it under surveillance, but you might check that for me."

Mike agreed to do it and the two men ate in silence for a while. "I was worried that Bev might have told them about me," Mike said breaking the silence.

"That was my concern about myself," Nathan said, "but it appears she didn't."

"They haven't arrested us yet, anyway, but it doesn't mean she didn't tell them. I have given serious thought to this, and the more I think about it the more I believe she did tell them. The money is just too good to turn down. She's already shown us that she's a greedy, traitorous, wretched woman, so why wouldn't she. I think we need to start acting like she did. What do you think?"

"That kind of thinking has a lot of implications for your life, Mike. Are you sure you want to come to grips with it?"

'I have to at some point. It might as well be sooner rather than later; besides isn't the 14th coming up here. Now might be a good time to make that decision."

"What about Melissa?"

"I don't know. I haven't broached the subject with her. George and I have discussed it. We're together on the decision to lose ourselves and our families in the underground when the time comes."

"You believe that time is now?"

"Yes I do," Mike said firmly.

"Well then we better get started this evening," Nathan said just as firmly.

CHAPTER 125

Melissa Hardin was crying. Mike had just told her he was a member of the underground and there was a strong possibility he could be arrested in the next few days. He was going to take his family and disappear into the underground, and did she want to come with him?

"I don't want to live without you Mike, but I don't want to give up everything I've worked so hard to get. You were there last night. You saw what I was doing. I love that job," there was a long pause after she said that and then she said, "but I love you more. I don't want to but I will go with you to the underground. Without you nothing would be fun anyway."

"Oh thank God," Mike said and hugged her. "I couldn't have lived without you. Now I'm going to cook hamburgers. Mom and Bob are on their way over with Martina. Ann and Jamie will be here soon as will George and Carmen."

"Everybody is coming?"

"Well, not everybody. We don't have any of your family or Carmen and George's families."

"My family would never go into the underground anyway. They don't believe in that stuff."

"Actually it's not the religious part. I have to go to keep from being arrested and kept in jail for an indefinite period of time as a terrorist. Then I'd never get to see you. They might even arrest you. You never know. So we have to go right away. You'll hear all this again when everybody gets here though," Mike explained.

Mike grilled hamburgers while they waited for the others. Melissa sliced onions and tomatoes and covered the dish with cellophane. George and Carmen arrived. Melissa let them in when they knocked.

"Did Mike tell you what's going on?" Carmen asked.

Melissa nodded sadly. Her reddened eyes told Carmen that Melissa wasn't taking it well. Carmen hugged Melissa consolingly.

"If it will make you feel any better I'll be with you too," Carmen whispered in her ear.

"How did you know I would agree to go?" Melissa asked pushing her friend back to arms distance to see her face.

"You would never give up Mike so when George asked me and said Mike was going to ask you I agreed because I know you."

They were still talking when Ann arrived home with Jamie in tow a few moments later.

"What's going on and why is Michael grilling at such a late hour? It's nearly 8," Ann asked.

"You'll have to ask him. It's a long story, which you will hear about once your Mom and step-dad arrive," Melissa answered.

Ann noticed Melissa's red eyes and took her puzzled look out to ask Mike what was going on.

"Hey Sis," Mike called to her as she came through the sliding glass door onto the patio.

She walked around the barbeque to look him directly in the face. "What are you doing?" she asked. Her voice was as puzzled as the look on her face.

"Grilling our dinner," he answered.

"Why has Melissa been crying?"

"I'll tell all about it when Mom and Bob get here."

"She's pregnant isn't she? I'm going to be an aunt. That's it isn't it. Come on Michael tell me the truth," she insisted.

"I'm going to tell the truth when Mom gets here, but none of that is the truth," he said, flipping the hamburger meat as he talked.

"Oh, I'm not going to be an aunt?" she asked with exaggerated disappointment in her voice.

"No, Sis, not this time, but some day I promise you it will come to pass," he joked.

They heard their mother's voice asking, "Why is Michael grilling so late?"

"I'm so like Mom," Ann observed, "that was my first question when I walked in." They both laughed at the observation

I'm out here, Mom," Mike called.

"Is Melissa pregnant?" Peggy Longwell asked as she came through the sliding door. Ann and Mike burst out laughing.

"Didn't I tell you I was so like, Mom," Ann said.

"Hey, Bob how's it going?" Mike asked of his stepfather, removing his grilling glove as he spoke to shake hands with the tall, bald fifty year old man.

"It's going well, Michael," he spoke as they shook hands, "Our business is doing well, keeping us in house and home; haven't seen you in a while. How's the cop business?"

"They promised us a new product line, but it hasn't happened yet," Mike joked, and then said, "Annie, you want to get the paper plates out of the cupboard, and put them on the table for me. This meat is ready to be eaten."

"I think Melissa and Carmen already have that done," Ann said.

"Michael, why has Melissa been crying? Is she pregnant?" Martina asked as she came through the door.

Mike and Ann lost themselves in laughter.

"What? What did I say?" Martina asked.

"I swear the women in this family have a one track mind," Mike said.

"Why? What do you mean?" Martina asked getting a little defensive.

"No, don't get upset Marty," Ann said, "he was just observing that the three of us Mom, you and me all jumped to the same conclusion when we saw Melissa's red eyes. We all thought she was pregnant."

"Yeah," Mike agreed, "and how do you get from red eyes to pregnant? Yet, you all made the same jump. It's amazing."

"The plates are on the table. Where's the food?" Melissa called from the door.

"On its way," Mike called back. "Come on Bob and Mom let's all go eat. I have something I need to talk to you about."

"So that's why this late dinner invitation," Bob surmised.

"Sorry about that. This has just come up and it needs my attention immediately."

Mike allowed everybody to get their food and settle down to eat before he began his explanation,

"I called you all here tonight because something has come up. It just popped its head out a little while ago so that's why everything is so late.

"I was actually going to invite you all tomorrow night so I've rushed it some. This can't wait so here it is. I've been a member of the underground for almost a year now. I joined at Dad's suggestion. He thought it might be important to have the access in case of emergency. I joined and began helping Nathan Conrad evaluate people who asked to join."

Mike paused, took a big bite out of his hamburger, chewed, took a sip of the coke Melissa had brought him and spoke again.

"I could have continued doing that a long time, but Homeland Security offered a ten thousand dollar reward for turning in members of the underground, and one of our own members turned in thirty names, not her own of course, and seventeen out of the thirty were arrested as terrorists. I wasn't, and that's the big question; Why?"

"Because you are handsome, good looking and not a terrorist," Martina interjected and everybody laughed.

Mike ignored his sister's comment, "We're not sure why. She was aware of my membership and George's and Nathan's of course since he coordinated everything, but none of us were arrested. With Nathan I think she was afraid of the two big angels he claims watch over him." There were chuckles around the room. Mike didn't go into telling them that Nathan truly believed he saw two big angels protecting him.

"Nathan thinks, and I have come to agree with him, that she did turn in our names; why not, that's more money. Now the police are waiting for something else to happen then they will arrest us, well more George and I than him—and that may not be true at all. So here we are hanging between maybe or maybe not getting Guantanamo Bayed for the rest of our lives."

"What would they be waiting for?" Bob Longwell asked.

"Nathan thinks it could be the 14th of this month. It's the big dedication of the Temple in Israel. Everything seems to be pointing toward that. It is important that I make myself scarce before then, So Melissa was crying because we have to disappear off the grid. She doesn't have to but she wants to go with me, and I'm so happy she's willing. George and Carmen are going as well.

"There's another thing that Nathan believes." He paused here and started again. "I sound like all the things I do hinge on what Nathan might believe or think and that usually isn't the case; however in this instance there is too much of my life riding on the outcome. I'm not religious like others in the underground, but it exists for others besides the religious.

"Now, if what I'm going to tell you here comes to pass it may be that you will want to join us in the underground, and. if it does begin, that would be the wise thing to do.

Okay, Nathan believes that May 14th will begin the second forty-two month period of Cahmael's reign as the Antichrist. He will change into this evil person, the Devil if you will, and persecution the likes of which we have never seen will begin."

"That's true. That's exactly what he says," Ann agreed. Mike needed no confirmation, but she gave it anyway.

"For sure," Jamie echoed.

"It might be possible to escape that slaughter in the underground. That's what Nathan says. I tend to believe the slaughter will never happen. I do believe I could get arrested and thrown in jail for a long time for being a domestic terrorist though, and I don't want that," Mike said.

Silence followed as his audience ate their food, and digested what he had just said. The plates were paper and the forks were plastic so there was no clinking of silverware to glass; they were eating hamburgers anyway.

CHAPTER 126

In the early morning of Friday, May 11th Mike Arzetti and Melissa Hardin were joined by George Wildes, Carmen Roadend and Mike's sister Ann on their flight into the unknown of the underground. Nathan Conrad met them after they bid Mike's family and Ann's friend Jamie farewell and sneaked out of the apartment about midnight, carrying only backpacks.

They opted for stealth and crept out of the apartment building in the middle of the night on the premise that the building might be staked out by police; although they could not see a stake-out vehicle anywhere in the street. They left one at a time and met two blocks away behind an old house that set to the back of a vacant lot. From there it was a short walk to a small garage in an inconspicuous alleyway where Nathan awaited their arrival.

They loaded into the black SUV for the ride off the grid. There was no conversation. Ann had decided to come at the last minute. Jamie didn't want to leave without talking to her parents, but had agreed to meet them later. Mike wasn't sure about that and said he would talk to Nathan about picking her up at a later date.

Mike wanted his mom and sister to come with him, but his step-dad couldn't get away at the moment.

"Michael this isn't something you can do at a moment's notice," Peg Longwell said to her son.

"I know Mom. I know, but you and Bob need to be thinking about it. What if an emergency arises?"

"We'll do what we always do; take care of it."

"I know you will Mom. I know you will, but if anything happens like what Nathan describes you may not have a whole lot of time to get away."

"What is Nathan describing?"

"It is horrible stuff, Mom; bloody horrible slaughter; unimaginable things."

Even with the description Mike couldn't jar his mother from her decision to wait. For Mike everything was immediacy. Whether or not he believed Nathan, he wasn't taking any chances with his or Melissa's lives.

"I thought we were going to try the old warehouse," Mike said to Nathan.

"Changed my mind; didn't like the idea of not knowing police thinking on the site. My contact didn't know either."

"So where are we going?"

"To join your Dad."

"Really! Now that will be different. What location?" Mike asked.

"It's a location that only I know about; nobody else, and I'm going to keep it that way."

"Dad's already there?"

"Yes he is and twelve other people with him."

Nathan turned up a long driveway leading to a vacant construction site.

"This is it?" Mike asked.

"Nope! Gotta make one stop first," Nathan explained.

Nathan stopped the SUV behind the construction that would someday be a house. Also parked there was a darkened trailer house that appeared to be the office.

"Follow me," Nathan said, stepping out of the vehicle.

His five passengers followed him to the steps leading up to the door. He knocked twice, stopped than twice more. The door opened slowly to expose a well lighted interior. The windows had been blackened to hide the light.

They crowded inside and Nathan introduced them to Doctor Grant Holden and nurse, Elma Watson. They were going to remove the chip implants. This time however Nathan said the two would continue the trip with them since they had to go into hiding as well. Nathan didn't know whether or not the police had any information about them, but he was taking no chances. Everybody he could contact would go underground.

Removing the implant was a simple procedure. The doctor used a small chip detector; nothing more than a small radio receiver with a bulb that dimmed whenever the receiver crossed a chip. The nurse marked the spot with a dark marking pen and injected the site with Novocain, then cleaned the area with alcohol.

The doctor's scalpel was quick and incisive and he plucked out the chip with tweezers, placing one stitch over the cut. Each chip was removed within seven minutes; start to finish.

All the chips were placed in a little glass jar for disposal at a later date in a safer, untraceable location.

They drove on North after that. The SUV was filled with the seven passengers and the driver, but they were comfortable. Later they found a truck stop and sent the little jar of chips back South on the bed of a truck headed that way. Nathan purchased gas here and told them to buy some munchies because there would be little else to eat for awhile, but nobody was hungry.

Three hours later, near dawn, they pulled off the main road into a wooded area and drove back into the hills for about three miles into the mouth of a canyon with large pillars on either side to what appeared to be an enormous old lodge—three stories of it. In the early morning light Melissa thought it looked scary. Ann said creepy.

"Shades of 'The Shining' and we're not in the mountains," Carmen announced.

"But it's completely unknown to anyone in the underground except for me. That's the good thing," Nathan said, climbing from the vehicle into the early dawn.

The seven others joined him and stood in the crisp morning air. A glow through the trees to the East announced the sunrise. The smell of new leaves filled the air. It was spring announcing itself.

Nathan reached back into the SUV and honked the horn twice. The porch light came on and then a light from a window and then another. The scary old mansion sprang to life.

Mike noticed his dad first, yelled, "Dad," and ran to him laughing. He leaped up the porch steps in one bound, grabbed his dad and hugged him. They laughed together.

Melissa, not to be outdone, ran to the porch cleared all but one of the steps yelling Dad as she ran. The three of them ended up in one bunch of hugging laughing arms. Everybody laughed at Melissa's antics.

"Dad this is Melissa," Mike yelled over the laughter.

With the seven new additions their numbers swelled to a grand total of twenty not counting Nathan whose tendency it was to exclude himself from all counts.

Shires introduced Jordan to Mike, Melissa, George, Carmen and Ann. All of whom, except for Mike, he was meeting for the first time himself.

"It's a grand homecoming," Tony Arzetti said of the proceedings.

Mike agreed with him and it certainly was for the two of them after so many years apart.

Later, inside the Lodge, the travelers learned that breakfast had been prepared for them; bacon, eggs, and pancakes were the order of the day, and everybody was famished.

While they ate Nathan filled them in about the place.

"This is Pillars of Angels Lodge. It's my place. I inherited it from my grandfather who used it as a hunting lodge back in the old days; way, way back.

"I have never used it for the underground before, but desperate times call for desperate measures. I promise you we are entering desperate times. I wish I didn't have to say that, but it's necessary.

"We are dropping into the second 42 months of the Cahmael reign and times will become difficult and challenging. Now I know you don't believe this, but I have told you before that I have two guardian angels who watch over me at all times. I can see them. I know they're there. I'm not asking you to believe me, but I want you to trust me on this.

"The guardians will protect us here. Remember, as long as we're here we're safe. If you're not here you need to get here. As long as you are within the two pillars you're okay.

"I brought you all here because I didn't know what houses were safe anymore. I was afraid Bev had given away all the locations past and present. This was always to have been my last resort; no pun intended.

"We're going to hunker down here for the next few days or weeks to see what might be going to transpire, and to hide from the police, just in case they're looking for us.

"I don't know when it'll happen, but I believe it will in the not-so-distant future. We won't be there waiting to be arrested.

"Does anybody have any questions?"

Shires raised his hand.

"Yes Shires," Nathan acknowledged him.

"It's the obvious one, of course. How did you come by the Angels?"

A few chuckles spread through the listeners.

"I inherited them from my grandfather," Nathan said, staying eith the humor. This brought a resounding laugh from the group.

"I'd like to have a great story surrounding them, but I don't. I don't know how I got them other than one day they were there. I think I've told you the story about how I noticed them.

"One day a man rushed toward me and these two big guys stepped in front of him, knocking him down. It scared him. He jumped up and ran away. I'll never forget the look of fear on his face. I don't think he saw them. I don't know, but something about the encounter frightened him.

"I went over to thank them; to ask what happened. I couldn't get close. When I moved toward them they moved away from me. It was like we were magnets with our polarity switched.

"I can't talk to them. They are always there. I have come to accept their presence as a good omen. So, over the years, I have accepted them as my guardian angels."

"Why would you think they were angels and not demons or something?" Mike asked.

"In the book of Enoch, which is not in the King James Version of the Bible, it tells of the angels who lusted after the daughters of man and chose to fall from grace to procreate with them. These angels were large and the children of these unions were known as giants.

"I assumed they were angels from the description of their size; not the giants, the angels.

"It's going to be a spiritual war when Cahmael comes at us this time. Angels are better at fighting those kinds of wars. We will fight the physical battles and they will protect us from physical harm while we're here in camp.

"I have no agreement with them about that, but it seems to be the way it works. When this all gets started we will rescue as many as we can and get them back here. This will be our base of operations and our protection. The TWO PILLARS PROTECTION AGENCY if you will.

"Every rescue operation will require we race back here to safety. This will become a known factor over time; then the authorities will try to block us. We must prevent the knowledge of our whereabouts to become known. We will neither leave en masse from here, nor return en masse. Two Pillars must never become common knowledge.

"I think I have spoken enough for one day. I am going to give it a rest. There will be plenty of time to go over this again. That is something we do have; a lot of time."

CHAPTER 127

Cynthia Underwood finally reached Jehosea Cahmael at the Vatican on Friday morning the 11th. He was upbeat and in an almost euphoric mood, or so it seemed to Dick Butcher.

"My friend I am looking forward to your speech on Monday, but I do wish you could have been there in person.

"Thank you Sir, but Lydia is still undergoing physical therapy, and I wouldn't want to come without her, but I did want to thank you for any help you might have provided to the men who finally reached the bomb," Dick said.

"Oh ye of little faith my friend; you must learn to have more trust in your men. Now, thanks to their bravery, the bomb is safely tucked away in the belly of a whale, or in this case the belly of an aircraft carrier. What more could you ask of them?"

"Nothing more for awhile I'm sure. That's why I sent them to Hawaii for a little rest and relaxation. They deserve so much more than that. I'm going to give it to them too. I'll bring them here the end of May and bestow the Medal of Honor on them. They all deserve that."

"I agree with that my friend."

Cahmael always agreed with Dick in most ways. He couldn't remember a time when they'd had a serious disagreement. Cahmael usually gave everything to him as well. Like he could have anything he wanted. Yet, it seemed to Dick that Cahmael knew exactly what he was doing and that the man was always in charge; in charge of everything. Something about him led one to believe there was much to be known about this tall man from Tel Aviv; it wasn't a sinister aspect, but it was deeply disturbing to Richard Butcher. He had watched Cahmael get ready for this dedication as if he were completely disinterested; now he acted euphoric almost to the point of giddiness.

Dick's only explanation for the change was heightened expectations. The Seal teams had definitely saved the day not only for himself, but for Cahmael as well. Maybe Cahmael didn't want something he had orchestrated so well to have a bad ending. This was simply relief registering in his voice and mood. The thought pleased Dick. He was happy to have been of help; after all the man had done so much for him. But there was one last question on his mind about the man. How did he know where the bomb was stored? Dick didn't even know that.

CHAPTER 128

Monday May 14th arrived like any other day would start on planet earth. As always the day would dawn in thirty-seven different time zones before it quit and became another day.

A seven in the morning dawn in Jerusalem would happen at midnight in New York City, at 9 pm on Sunday evening May 13th in San Francisco, and at 6 pm Sunday evening May 13th in Honolulu.

Time is only relevant from the perspective of the observer where it is at once immediate and fluid; happening and moving on at the same time. There is something to be said for every moment documented or not.

Dignitaries from all over the world had descended on Israel, wanting to witness the single most historical event in the history of the Jews since the inception of their nation.

Pope Linus III was there accompanied by the ever-present Jehosea Cahmael.

For all intents and purposes Admiral Bill Scott had inherited Matthew Stoneham's bailiwick, but he didn't know it yet. He waited for Melissa to arrive at 10 pm Sunday evening so they could cover the dedication the following day. They would do the coverage from the wide angles of space. He was looking forward to it. She didn't show.

It would rain in Russia, and England, and Chile, and Argentina and in the central plains of the United States. All this will be recorded and documented as the happenings of May 14th; no more or no less.

The following is actually what happened as near as it is possible to tell, beginning with the dawn in Jerusalem.

Pope Linus III had only great expectations for May 14th. He and

Cahmael had arrived in Jerusalem the day before amidst a flurry of activity. The Press Corps wanted words with them.

Interviews were requested, but none were granted. Everybody wanted to know the Pope's feelings about the great event; the fulfillment of prophecy no less.

Catholicism could trace its roots to the Holy Temple. Linus was pleased to be so connected to the event. He was excited, but not like Lord Cahmael who seemed positively ecstatic. Never had Linus seen the man so happy; so giddy for lack of a better word.

That was the part that troubled him most about the day. Cahmael had begun to act differently about a week earlier. Linus would find him off by himself in a vile mood, staring at nothing in particular. The moodiness increased to the point that Linus no longer enjoyed their conversations.

That changed about three days ago. Suddenly he was himself again with the ecstatic giddiness included. There had been a transformation.

Cahmael maintained equanimity most of the day and that pleased Linus, but he still seemed hyper and somewhat unsettled. The speeches by every conceivable dignitary in the Middle East were difficult even for Linus. The speech by President Butcher seemed to calm Cahmael and he sat quietly through it.

A small nuclear bomb exploded aboard the Aircraft Carrier Douglas MacArthur. The ship and its six thousand man crew disappeared from the face of the earth, along with many of the ships nearby. It sent a fifty foot tidal wave racing toward shore where it spent itself a few miles inland.

The explosion was coincidental with the ending of the speech given on closed circuit television by the US President, Richard Butcher. It was 7 in the evening Jerusalem time.

At exactly the same time Jehosea Cahmael opened the door to the Holy of Holies, and, over the protestations of the priests and security guards, stepped inside, walked to the altar, turned to face the empty room, and proclaimed in a loud voice, "Hark unto the hand of God! I am the Alpha and the Omega. I am that I am. I am the Lord God Almighty. I come to save the world not destroy it."

At the same moment the Armageddon Group went on trial in Federal Court in San Francisco. It was 9 am Pacific Daylight Savings Time. The Federal Court building was too small to hold the three hundred defendants who had to be accommodated. They didn't have to be in the courtroom, but they had to be able to see the proceedings. This was accomplished from another building through closed circuit TV.

In cities and towns throughout the countryside in the United States the agency known as Homeland Security exercised its arrest warrants on tens of thousands of its citizens hiding in the underground; names bought and paid for by the program known as the Great Reward Fair—10,000 dollars a name. It was the single most sweeping arrest in American History to that time.

High above the commotion the cameras of the late Matthew Stoneham operated by retired Admiral William Scott recorded the events—just another day on planet earth.

ACKNOWLEDGEMENTS:

I wish to thank Holly Rose for being my editor-in-chief. She is always the final word.

Thanks to all my writing friends for their encouragement and support through all my writing endeavors. Elizabeth Huber whom we lovingly call "E," Carol Kumpu, and Jack and Stephanie Troy. Thanks guys for everything.